The 13th Disciple

Tony Carangi

The 13th Disciple

Copyright © 2024

All Rights Reserved

ISBN:

Synopsis

And then Jesus said, "God has no fists," so with that simple truth, he gently corrected the Holy Bible, a book steeped in sin, guilt, conditional love, and fear.

Based on the astonishing principles of A Course in Miracles, The 13th Disciple follows two people who meet at the time of Christ and are reincarnated lifetime after lifetime on their way to enlightenment. It is the story of a promise, a promise made, and a promise kept; the promise was kept even before it was made; it was made when one of them was a disciple of Christ.

Dedication

Roberta, this is for you;

I lovingly pray that you made it this time.

The 13th Disciple

Acknowledgment

To my twin spiritual fathers from different teachers, Dr. Ken Wapnick and Dr. Bob Schenk.

The 13th Disciple

Contents

- Synopsis
- Dedication
- Acknowledgment
- Author's Note
- Book I The Gladiator and Jesus
- Book II Lost
- Book lll The Last Pope

About The Author

I was turned to fiction writing as a child by a babysitter, but as an adult, I pursued studies in math and statistics, obtaining a bachelor's degree first and an MSPH second. I enjoy traveling and have lived in Rome, Italy for 3 years. I currently live aboard a sailboat in Miami.

Author's Note

It said that you should only write about what you know—there, I said it—that being said, I wrote The Gladiator in spite of the fact that I knew literally nothing of A Course in Miracles at the time. I knew only that, it was a thought system which holds that the entire universe is an illusion—so sensible that it should have been obvious—and I read the visually sensual dream of Dr. Helen Shuckmen in the cave by the sea when she opened the scroll and the voice said if you look left, you will see the past, if you look to the right, you can view the future, but if you look straight ahead you can see now. She answered, "I don't want to look to the left or the right, only straight ahead at now". The voice was reassuring when it answered, "Congratulations, you made that time." The Gladiator was written that very instant by someone who had never read it and still hasn't; there, I am the unqualified, non-qualified Course teacher. I make no pretense at being such. I have done my best to understand core Course concepts and relay them by entertainment through fiction, but my goal is to entertain.

"Nothing real can be threatened.

Nothing unreal exists.

Herein lies the peace of God."

A Course in Miracles

The 13th Disciple

Book I
The Gladiator and Jesus

The Gladiator surveyed his world dispassionately through the spotted shade of his face shield and overheard the cacophony of disparate and discordant paroxysm from the frenzied hordes by dint of eardrums muffled with sweat in their water-clogged canals. The diminished senses coalesced into a dream-like state in which he regarded his body from above the battlefield, the burning sands of the arena.

Sweat formed in huge droplets across his forehead and poured in stinging his eyes, which were already pinched hard against the slanting Roman sun. Out there, somewhere in the space of the arena, a retiarius, swift and agile, moved rapidly in and out, striking deftly, taking a little, then taking a little more of his body's precious lifeblood with each cut. That blood flowed more copiously now, from gashes across and stabs to his body, bloody sweat spilled around and over his brows, as with everything else in his increasingly exhausted body, they by degrees provided less and less protection to his stinging eyes.

Around his right ankle, he felt the ripping of the fisherman's net. It failed to fell him this time. Earlier, he had been in control of the fight against a smaller, more agile opponent, but now, exhausted, he was striking like a wounded buffalo at the pecking hyena. He was always turning a second too late, responding to the prior attack just after the current one. He was wearing inexorably down but was still able to bring his shield up to parry the triad as though he were reaching for an apple from a bowl of fruit.

Though the body was depleted, it remained disciplined, and he did not panic. The Guiltless Mind, as Christ had taught cannot suffer. He neither feared death nor preferred it. His next block was in time as well, but he had had to bend his knees to achieve it, feeling it absorbed into his forearm, then glancing off of his shield. Instantly, he countered with the gladius in his right hand, bringing it down and across at a 45 degree angle, lurching forward with his right foot after the swing. Too late—the retiarius was far removed.

He circled around to Pompilli's left side,

feigned another thrust, stepped back, then thrust the triad at his face with lightning speed. Pompilli was scarcely able to avoid it with a combination of a rising block with his shield and bending his knees while ducking his head under it. Close! There was no counter this time; he was too entirely spent. The two combatants circled each other warily in the sand that burned their feet under the scorching Roma sun.

Pompilli, sweating profusely, was losing the battle of attrition; he was the heavier and more powerful of the two—but was less agile, less resilient. Now cramps were setting into his legs. He was well accustomed to suffering the wounds of combat under the intense heat of Roma's sun. He had been well trained; discipline and indifference wove a sturdy pattern in the gladiator's psyche, but training also taught that the body had its limits and Pompilli realized that his was fast approaching its own.

Sweat stung his eyes, and he could no longer ignore the screaming cramps in his legs, making them even heavier by the second. The retiarius feigned to his head, which brought his shield high again, but the effort was enormous—his left shoulder burned. When he hoisted the shield too low, a point of the triad found its mark again piercing the forehead, making it bloodier, and making it even more difficult to see the swiftly retreating Retiarius. It was only his view from above the battlefield that allowed him to perceive the retiarius at all.

Locked in a downward spiral toward a slow death of a thousand cuts, the gladiator would make a life-or-death decision on his feet, with blood burning his eyes and cramps setting in. He would likely regret either action, but he had to decide, and training took over again. His left arm needed rest. So, he dropped the shield, and it fell soundlessly against the deafening roaring of the arena, pushing into the sand like a stone into water, coming to rest curved side up in the center of the arena.

Without his shield, Pompilli's left arm immediately relaxed, and he had it free to strike and grab, but he was exposed to the trident. Now the retiarius swung the net at his head, forcing him to duck his head, but this allowed a precious opening as the retiarius's follow-through exposed his rib cage. This time, Pompilli did not hesitate as he jabbed his gladius at the open ribs like it was a piece of meat. The opponent twisted his body and mitigated the impact. It sliced rather than pierced, blood pouring, and Pompilli hoped he had broken a rib, but he had only bruised it.

Feeling as though he had been hit by a charging rhinoceros, the retiarius brought both elbows in to protect the recently assaulted ribcage; they had been cut but not seriously broken. The reaction was involuntarily leaving him momentarily rooted, exposed to Pompilli's sword, but this time the follow-up was lacking. Instead, he moved around to his right, keeping a safe distance while desperately trying to take control of his breathing. It was something he would not regain until one of them was dead.

The retiarius, however, seemed already to have endured the worst of it as he was able to swiftly cast his net over Pompilli's head and moved closer with the trident while the net was continuing its slow-motion descent through the acrid air. Pompilli hacked at the open net, deflecting it harmlessly to the ground and in one move parried the trident at the last second. The retiarius deftly spun back, reached his net on the ground, and returned to face him squarely. The near misses were getting closer.

Pompilli moved back, circling to his right trying to buy time, but the retiarius had very different intentions; he pressed the attack. Stepping backward, Pompilli felt the net wrapping around his left ankle. Calmly, he lifted his leg, stepped in, and thrust his sword, but the retiarius moved back out of range and efficiently countered with his three-pronged spear. Pompilli, having dropped his shield, could block it only by jamming the point of his sword in between two of the three prongs. It was close, and he could feel the clinging of the three-pronged spear against the iron anklet of his left leg.

Pompilli clenched his free left fist and delivered a crushing blow to the retiarius jaw. The retiarius staggered back and dropped his spear. The instinct was now for Pompilli to plunge his gladius deep into his opponent's chest, but fatigue from an hour of combat in the scorching Roman heat made him hesitate. It was fatigue that forced him to drop his shield, and it now intensified, allowing the swiffer retiarius to roll on the ground toward his trident and come up with it standing. Pompilli was not as disheartened as he was astonished. He decided that now was the time to retrieve his shield.

Facing his opponent squarely, in a left forward stance with his sword firmly in his right hand, he shifted to his left, the retiarius would not so easily allow him to. This time, when the fishermen threw his net around his left ankle it latched on, and he pulled it straight. The gladiator staggered but caught himself. But the fishermen buried the center prong of his trident into his straightened left knee. The excruciating pain jolted him as though he had been struck by lightning, but it lasted only long enough to intensify his pain. Pompilli saw the blood gushing from his leg that was bent backwards and fell hard between his shoulder blades.

Supine, positioned as a man being crucified, about to be run completely thru by the trident, yet He was at peace, *the Guiltless Mind did not suffer,* Christ had taught. The retiarius moved deftly to his left, imposing himself critically between Pompilli and his shield. He moved in cautiously for the kill, making sure that Pompilli was too injured and fatigued to counter him. Satisfied, he began his approach.

But when he moved in, Pompilli saw something that made him forget to make his appeal, forget all about the retiarius entirely. It made him ignore the pain and forget his body altogether. It made him doubt all that he had till this moment come to believe and know of Jesus. It made him lift his head, and through distraction and fatigue, his training held sway—the gladius was still in his hand.

As the sky behind the Retiarius began to drop out of existence in black boulder-sized chunks Pompilli had to make, with no basis for comparison, a split second decision: was death the greater disaster or was it life? When a black lightning bolt sliced across the late afternoon sky, it seemed that death was more welcome, but a second after when more black chunks of the sky were ripped away showing only starless, dark empty space behind, it seemed that the edge of the world had come up to Roma, to the arena, to his very body, as the sea rolls to the shore. It was as if the world had been broken into two, right down the center of the arena, and he was going to be swept away into the inexplicable, unimaginable vastness, void of all light whatsoever.

Pompilli became too uncertain to act; it was the body that knew what to do. From his back, Pompilli's body brought the gladius across, and the retiarius lost his left leg above the knee. Then, on the backstroke, it was the right leg that ripped away, just below the kneecap. Pompilli never saw that which he had accomplished in less than a second, focused as he was on the sky falling away in chunky slabs, as though the earth were a room in the sky, whose walls came down like papaya in a storm to reveal a darkness so total that all light was taken in there and from there none returned.

Then, as the advancing darkness opened its ugly mouth and drew nearer, nearer, so near that he could feel the sand into which he clenched with all that remained of him screaming into the abyss. So, near that, he was certain to be washed away with the sand which ran through his fingers and into the thick blackness. The darkness whispering death and deception, and the urgent denial of Christ, the impossible. So, he put his head back down and was still clenching the sand. He did not feel the light sprinkle of blood that dappled down upon his body nor any other sensation of the world. Instead, he turned away and shut his eyes tight, hoping for the darkness inside his lids to protect him from the darkness on the other side of them.

Lucilla's doe-like eyes remained clenched so tightly that spots cluttered her field of vision when, at long last, she released them to ever so pensively allow the world in, fully expecting that when she did so, the retiarius would have impaled her husband to death. She would have let them remain forever closed, save for the faint cries of her husband's name—Pompilli, Pompilli, Pompilli—rising from the throng. She could not believe that he had won again; she was even less than they were.

Slowly, cautiously, not to be deceived, she opened, then focused. Her jaw shuddered as she strained in the distance to see the unthinkable—her husband—alive. She was in no condition for rational thought as tears streamed down her face and drool unabashedly dribbled from the corner of her mouth. Her love for her husband, matched only by her pure joy to see him alive, brushed back tears only to confirm the vision. Then, as he lay there prostrate on the ground, about the length of her tiny, smallest finger, writhing in agony, her joy became enmeshed with his pain. His pain was an altogether new experience for her, and for him, for that matter. The joy was catastrophically overwhelmed by his pain becoming hers. She could see her husband's body in all of its paroxysms, but she could not see the darkness he had just seen and could not know that for him everything had changed, much more than if the retiarius had just run him straight through.

She was on her feet, moving down to where they were taking her husband. Her only thought was to rush to her husband, to tend to his wounds. She needed to comfort and take care of him, though even that was as much for herself as for his needs.

But for now, the Romans and iron gates still separated her from him. Yet Lucilla blamed Jesus not the Romans for her husband's slavery, her separation from him, and the horrendous tortures he endured, suffering which she could not even think about, along the brutal bloody trail which led him from intellectual discussions on spiritual enlightenment in Judea to a bloody gladiator pit in Roma.

Now, angry, grieving, and terrified for the life of her husband, she was pleased that he had been crucified; now she felt he was deserving of it, making it less painful to her. Even in death, it was Jesus, not the Romans, who separated her from her husband.

But just one more victory, and that would be no more; Vettius had sworn it personally and contracted it legally. Just one more victory, and her husband was again a free man to be with her forever. That sweet thing, she and her husband together again forever; it was so close that it was almost real, she could almost touch it.

But with tears still streaming and her body wracked at once by both agony and rapture, knowing as she did that right now her husband, in agony, probably screaming, badly injured, was being carried again away from her, she knew that for now one more victory and forever was a thing very far removed.

Moving down, she kept her eyes only on the stones beneath her feet. She bumped shoulders and slipped in between one faceless person, then another. Moving in and out of the light as she descended, men stared at her as she passed, unaware. Someone else moved her body through the maze of debauched fanatics intoxicated by the wine and blood of the games; as a boat on the ocean, she was merely a passenger in it.

She was completely in the shade now, though the air was still hot from seething in the sun all day. A fight broke out between two men gambling, but it sounded vicious and guttural, like the lions that had been fighting in the arena earlier. She looked up just in time to see one man's face ripped open by the club seemingly brought down from the heavens. Blood splashed like a rock thrown into a still pond. Then others gathered around as the violence spread. She fell back against a wall, scarcely able to stand, and stared hypnotically at the conflict before her, unable to comprehend it, unable to peel her eyes from it.

There had been violence that day too, that day in Judea when they first saw Jesus in the Temple where the money changers plied their trade. There was always a foul air about them she thought, a cloud of discontent which they breathed out as they took advantage of one group or another. On this day, they exploited the Jews who had to buy their silver coins to pay the temple tax.

The Temple tax gave the money changers a monopoly which they used to bleed the market for all that it would bear. Eventually, the poorest Jews became desperate and then angry, and they raised their voices when they had to give over all of their possessions to the money changers, for which to pay the temple tax.

She remembered how suddenly, her own husband, Sanyi (defender of man), took action, turning over their tables and letting their coins spread around. Then, he made a whip out of cords and drove all from the temple area, both sheep and cattle; he scattered the coins of the money changers and overturned their tables. To those who sold doves, he said, "Get these out of here! How dare you turn this temple into a market?"

The 13th Disciple

Sanyi was a giant who towered over all men there in the market, in all of Judea. She felt proud and righteous watching her strong, good husband doing the right thing. And it was the right thing, what could be more right, what else could the right thing be? That was when everything that she thought she knew about right and wrong changed—that was when Jesus came.

Absorbed in the actions of her husband, she didn't notice another man of slight build who was also watching until that man had walked over to where her husband was scattering the coins and driving both the sheep and the cattle from the temple. She could see him then, but she could not hear him. But whatever he said to her husband, it stopped him there like a stone statue. Then, in what seemed like the longest second later for reasons, Lucilla couldn't understand Sanyi let the money changer's coin box slip out of his large grasp and fall with a clunk to the temple's stone floor, the coins bouncing and rolling away. That was the first that she had laid eyes upon Jesus, the only time she had seen her husband do violence. But that violence was wholly unlike this, nothing that she had ever known was

The 13th Disciple

anything like this.

Yet, she descended down, down to pit level where a cacophony of the anguished banged and reverberated across her brain, suffocating the one unmistakable sound she sought so desperately, but it would escape her. The clanging of slaves in their shackles, the roars of wild animals in cages, grunting gladiators clashing, and from down the long corridor beneath the seats, she could hear the anguished screams of men in pain. In her heart, there arose the sickening certainty that somewhere down there, her husband writhed in unimaginable agony, the agony she was helpless to ameliorate. She wrapped her slender fingers around the bars which ran the long corridor separating her from her husband. She struggled to peer into the darkness and around the corner to glimpse a piece of Sanyi or isolate a fragment of his agonizing cries from the ensemble, the vain attempt making her heartbreak even more bitter. She remained there, hopeful and heartbroken, until there were no more slaves clanging in the shackles, until the sounds of men suffering subsided, until the day waned and she finally realized her husband was no longer down there; there was no one else down there. She was alone.

Confused and exhausted, she left the arena and wandered pensively along the vast and dark cobblestone street. There, all of Rome seemed to be out, still intoxicated by wine and blood of the games that ended hours ago. There were more faceless people to not look at and more lusting men to not see. She paid less attention to the outside world than she did to even her own body, which, now that she was vaguely aware, was starving for not having eaten in more than a day. Nothing else registered until the street opened into a large courtyard, on the far side of which was a wedding. She remembered instantly her own wedding to Sanyi.

Sanyi was Lucilla's true love at first sight. Her mother told her that when she loved a man at first sight, it meant that she had loved him before in previous lifetimes. That may be true, she thought, but it was not easy to gain his love in this lifetime. So, it was that on her wedding night she savored her prize—the greatest prize in all of Judea—the handsome and wealthy Sanyi. He was a prize worth fighting for and she had won him.

The 13th Disciple

Oddly, though there was no competition, she had come to wonder. Indeed, there was a moment, a very short time where she actually thought the impossible was real, and that he cared not for her. Their early courtship was a series of prearranged accidental meetings at the market or in the temple. And even after he noticed her and courted her, it seemed too long before, at long last, he married her.

But then it did seem to have been worth it, especially when he came toward her on their wedding night. All of her fears and doubts washed away by the delicious mingling of wine and the mixed juices of their lovemaking which lasted until the morning. And as the sun rose that day, it rose on a new, deeper level of her love for him than even she could fathom. Before Jesus, in spite of herself, Sanyi made her deliriously joyful.

And while she never doubted his love for her, and despite her joyful delirium, she did doubt her place with him. She sensed that she would always be second—but second to what for whom? It was a subtle, subconscious doubt that she was not wholly aware of. It gnawed at her, unseen. Sanyi was a man in search of something other than her, in search of what he knew not, it was not another woman. But when she saw Jesus standing there with him, she knew that Sanyi had found exactly that which he was unaware that he sought.

The time with him before their wedding was as labor before childbirth, horrible but would be instantly forgotten as soon as a new child is brought into the world. The time after Jesus was like a mother whose child is snatched up suddenly by death. Now consumed in the agony of missing him, it was as though it was Jesus who made her life unbearable. And yet, she would have to bear it until gentle Sanyi could win one more terrible match—if he could win just one more match.

She looked away from the wedding and made her sorrowful way down the narrow street alone and got lost. She had taken the wrong road by which to leave the courtyard and didn't notice the prodigious darkness of the tunnel-like cobblestone street, didn't notice it until the Romans nearly ran her down. Immersed in her sorrows, she couldn't hear the two horses galloping down the narrow macadamized passageway. So, as she entered into the crossway, they appeared as if instantaneously. She leaped back but not in time to avoid a violent encounter with the hairy front shoulder of the onrushing beast.

It spun her around in midair and threw her hard to the cobblestone, landing on her hands and knees. The second rider cursed at her as he rushed past. She crawled away as best as she could, but it was slow; it was the most physical pain she'd ever experienced in her life. Her knees were black and blue, and her palms were bleeding. She leaned back against the wall, curled her legs up like a child, and cried. She cried not the deep sobs of anguish, but the gentle ones of despair.

Sitting there, knowing not what to do she shut her eyes tightly as if trying to awaken from a nightmare. As though she would open them and be safe in bed beside her big gentle husband. Instead, she opened them in the cold and dark to see what by her sense of pain she already knew, namely that she was bleeding.

She waited there, waited for the bleeding to stop, waited for the pain to subside. But just like waiting for the return of Sanyi, it was hopeless. When the rain began falling she got up to find her way home.

Long before Lucilla entered the apartment that Vettius had provisioned for her, she was drenched in cold and fatigue. Roma was the center of the world, the hub to which all roads lead, but here in her dark apartment on the top floor corner of a stone building Roma disappeared, and the anguish of her broken heart was all she had to fill the emptiness.

She walked past the fireplace, which she had never seen burn to light a candle on the bedside. She hesitated at the edge of the bed, staring as if not sure what to do, as one would test the temperature before entering a bath. Gradually, ineptly, she curled her tiny body into its center and stared blankly at the flickering shadows in the room.

The last time she could remember curled up in bed this way was with her husband's big, safe body behind her. She remembered gently caressing the hairs on his arm about her waist and feeling as comforted by his presence as she was frustrated by Jesus' message. "I try, I try" she explained, "but try as I might, I can't get it, I can't understand. Jesus is the tiny mad idea," she screamed in a whisper.

Then, her husband, as though he were moving a pillow, effortlessly turned her to her back, brushing the hair away from her cheek. "You will, you will," he said in a tone that was as gentle and powerful as any she had ever heard. And then she looked up, catching his eyes, then confirming the certainty, and the seriousness that his voice carried. That view of Sanyi she'd had a thousand times, had it burned into memory. His dark eyes were white, with tapered brows riding a finely sculptured ridge that balanced a nose of the gentlest Hebrew variety. He was the one who understood Jesus better than anyone. And then they made tender love.

She didn't care one bit about Jesus, but oh God, how she needed Sanyi now. But on this night she wasn't reassured, nor did she make love to her husband. She lay as she had for so many nights in Roma, alone, in a cold, empty room. She, who had endured such pain for so long, was certain that her deliverance must be soon at hand. **But** beautiful, privileged and protected, young Lucilla could have never dreamed that she was just

The 13th Disciple

beginning to hurt.

Jesus

As in the creation of the world, there was not a witness to it. Beginning as just a tiny eddy scarcely able to stir the dust in the desert outside of Cairo, it became a vortex that carried the burning sand to the sea. There it turned to clay and then to stone; and finally, with the most coarse crash of lightning, the stone to living bone, the Mind making the body seem real. Before that body was first seen by John, who was baptizing on the east bank of the Jordan River, it had walked thousands of miles under a parching sun and freezing night without water or warmth or the need for either. When John looked up and saw Jesus standing on the bank, he knew instantly that the light for which he had so long sought had found him instead.

John, a self-righteous man, had heard many confessions and done many baptisms by then, saying, "Confess your sins and God will forgive them." Until that moment, John the Baptist believed in sin, and so he condemned it. Having no idea what true Forgiveness really was, or that sin was not at all, he watched as Jesus stepped into the water and came toward him.

"Lord, I cannot hear your confession as you have none to make," John said. "Nor do any of us," answered Jesus. Then, Jesus took John's hands and put them on his head and went under the water. When he came up again, John understood that he did not understand. Jesus smiled and watched as John walked out of the river and up the bank, then out of sight, leaving John with the perfect peace of God which he had never experienced before. But it was the last time that John the Baptist walked out of the river Jordan, nor did he ever baptize again.

Jesus went on to Nazareth to find Mary and Joseph who had lost their only son during the slaughter of King Herod more than 30 years before. They had remained childless since, unable to have children, living still in the insufferable sadness of that which could have been, and the crushing guilt for not preventing that which could not have been.

When word reached her of King Herod's mass execution order, she took up her son and fled into the sparse woods outside of Nazareth. There, she hid for two days. Through heat and cold, she ignored the raging thirst in her own mouth, but she could not bear the suffering of her only child. She had to get him water, or he would soon die.

So, she put the child in a basket, covered with clean linen, and carried it boldly back into the city, to the water well. There were two Romans on horseback in the street, and as the child lay silently in the basket, she began to draw the water. Then, a horrible realization came over her—she had brought no jar to carry the water away with. So, she had to expose the child to the light in order to let him drink. It was a horrible mistake.

The two Roman soldiers with their swords and cloaks already bloodied from multiple prior hours of cruel infanticide closed in swiftly. She clutched the child desperately to her breast, but one of the soldiers violently straightened her arms and the child fell from them. Miraculously, she caught him in the air and fell back hitting her head hard against the bleak stone of the well, with the child in her lap.

The soldier, as though he were stabbing at a leaf on the ground in order to pick it up, thrust his sword at her child still in her lap. The blade skewered her left arm and went through the child's heart and didn't stop until it had cut her through. The last thing that Mary remembered before she fell to the dirt was the faint sound of a limp child splashing into the water far below.

She should have died there, but instead, she lived forever with the guilty memory and the deep gouge through her womb which had left her barren. Since she'd never seen the child actuget him water, or he would soon die.ally be killed, it was easy to pretend that some miracle had occurred. That she had not heard a dead infant splash into the water. Over the years, she told herself this till she almost believed it was true. But she never drew another drop from that well.

Joseph suffered from a similarly pernicious form of self-attack. He blamed himself for not having been there when the Romans attacked his wife and son. But it was Joseph who drew the Romans away in the first place. It was he who hid a bundle under his arms and ran off in the other direction to draw the soldiers. It worked. When the soldiers discovered that it was nothing but a log that he concealed from them, they beat him within a camel's hair of his life, and that beating gave his wife and child time to get away. But the world, this world of illusions, gives only to take, and too soon it takes everything, *a dry and dusty place where starved and thirsty creatures come to die.* Jesus felt their deep pain and was moved as he was by all dreamers, understanding that they believed their dreams to be real. He was still in Galilee when he told Mary that she would soon see him. She, in turn, told her husband, Joseph, that "our son is coming home." She did not have to explain it to him. They decided to prepare a feast.

Jesus was followed there by Simon (who is called Peter) and his brother Andrew; James son of Zebedee, and his brother John; Philip and Bartholomew; Thomas and Matthew the tax collector; James son of Alphaeus, and Thaddaeus; Simon the Zealot and Judas Iscariot, who they say, but Jesus did not, betrayed Him." These then were 12 disciples.

When Mary and Joseph saw Jesus for the first time, they did recognize him instantly as their son. it was not a mistake; it was simply as Jesus wanted it. For them, it was as though he had simply left for a while and was now returning.

Jesus had many ways of easing people's anguish. For Joseph and Mary, he used the simplest, letting them no longer think about what had happened, not by way of controversion, rather as seeing in another way. Jesus would often teach that, "Nothing in the past or the future could harm you here in the present, for the past and future do not exist at all."

Jesus did not remove the memory of what had happened. He simply removed the parent's habit of thinking about it at all, thinking instead of only that which has no beginning nor end nor extent, yet which always is, the thing which is called now.

So, Jesus bequeathed to Mary and Joseph a gift which others, for the remainder of time, would have to by discipline practice acquire. To them, nothing of the past was forgotten nor the future is hidden, but for the remainder of their days, the once grieving parents lived fully in the joy of the only instant that really existed. Later, Christ would instruct that even the seemingly undeniable present is false. For Jesus who was remembering a body, remembered too the myriad of methods the human mind had to attack itself.

Overjoyed at the return of their only son, Mary and Joseph held a feast on vast tables of long planks on either side of a row of figs and palms. The tables were so long that one could not speak to another at opposite ends. They were bursting with mountains of meat and cheese in the center with piles of bread toward the outside, all spaced at regular intervals by clay candle holders. They passed red and brown clay jars and poured wine into clay cups of the same. The clay making itself heard in thumps against the wooden planks as they drank from those cups and replaced them down again and again through laughter and music and joy. They poured that way until they noticed that the wine had run out, then one of Jesus's disciples said to him, "The wine has run out." "What am I to do about this?" Jesus asked. Then, a smiling Jesus rose.

The Jews have strict rules about ritual washing. So, there were six large stone water jars there, each one large enough to hold between 20 and 30 gallons. "Fill these jars with water," Jesus said to his disciples, and they did it. When they were done, Jesus paused for a second and then said, "Draw out the water and give it to the people." They did, and to their astonishment, the water had turned to wine. The other guests did not see this but remarked it was the most delicious wine they had ever tasted, saying to Mary and Joseph, "Everyone else serves the best wine first, and after all the guests have drunk a lot, they serve the ordinary wine. But now, you have served your best wine." Not only the disciples but a beautiful young girl named Mary Magdalene had seen this, and they were all amazed, especially Mary Magdalene.

Jesus and Sanyi

In those days, there was great hatred toward the money changers as they controlled all monopoly on a coin of the half-shekel required to pay the Temple tax. They controlled the wealth from Judea all the way to Capernaum. It was the money changers who told Caiaphas to turn the Temple into a marketplace, and he made it so. And a few days later, in time for the Passover, Jesus and his disciples and Mary Magdalene traveled to Jerusalem. There, they witnessed the weary and worn-out way the working people lived, moving as though chains were about their arms and legs as they labored under the oppressive weight of Roman taxes. The Romans took all they could, and when this caused people to produce less, Roma raised their taxes in a deranged form of retribution.

Jesus said that Roma produces nothing while taking all in all it can from those around it. Therefore, Roma would forever extend its forces outward at ever greater cost retaining even less wealth in return. Soon would be a time when Roma was no more. But as they entered the Temple, there was a raucous and great commotion. When they moved close enough to the noise, Jesus could see a huge man—the biggest man he had ever seen—who had made a whip of cords and was chasing the animals away. Also, he had overturned the tables of the money changers and scattered their coins on the temple floor. His disciples tried to persuade him out of it, but Jesus walked over to the big man, saying, "My brother, trust not your good intentions, for they are not enough."

Mighty Sanyi was so disarmed by the tiny Jesus that he stopped in a place like a statue, going at once from fearsome to comical. But he stammered and stopped there for what seemed like many long seconds, asking himself, "Is this the young Rabbi I have heard about?

Then, staring into the eyes of Jesus, he remembered something that all, save for Jesus, had forgotten. For only a holy instant Sanyi, forgot about all symbols, words, his body, and symbols of symbols, but remembered the perfect peace of God instead. It was remembering a peace we all can have but few choose to take, a peace remembered more than discovered.

The 13th Disciple

Once remembered, it was known almost in full—a peace that, for Sanyi, took only and nothing less than the sight of the slight Jesus. So, despite the awkward outward appearances, Sanyi was at that moment far more aware than confused. Jesus knew that Sanyi believed himself to be a righteous man acting in a correct manner, but just as John the Baptist, he was confused about what righteousness was or whether there was any such thing. Jesus was aware of the man's wife scrutinizing him as well as he was aware that there was much more to the big man than his mere size.

Then, the Jewish authorities appeared and wanted to seize Sanyi, who had said, "This is a temple, but you have turned it into a den of thieves." The Jewish authorities demanded that Sanyi perform a miracle to prove that he had the right to do such a thing. But it was Jesus who answered them by reciting the Scripture, which said, "My devotion to your house, O God, burns in me like a fire." The Jewish authorities looked at Jesus for a long time, and they said amongst themselves, "Who is this man who recites our Scripture?" Then, they looked at Sanyi but walked away without laying a hand upon him. Sanyi relaxed and stood, looking at them until Jesus put his hand on his shoulder. Then, Sanyi turned to see Jesus smiling up at him, and he smiled back.

"How do you know my name?" Sanyi asked Jesus. "I have not known you before, nor have you known me."

Jesus squeezed Sanyi's shoulder and answered him saying, "Ah, Sanyi, you are a good man who wanted to be a physician, but for his father's sake became a merchant instead. You who wanted to heal, now give away your wealth and fight iniquity wherever you think you see it."

Jesus walked away from Sanyi toward the steps the money changers had just fled. Then, he turned and came back toward Sanyi saying loud enough for everyone to hear, "You now heal the world, finding that which was wrong and putting it to right."

When Jesus drew near to Sanyi again, he said so that only he could hear, "Great Sanyi, don't you know that despite all your righteous might, you can save not

The 13th Disciple

even one lonely lamb?"

Sanyi was amazed. Who was this man, he wondered to himself, who knows my deepest secrets?

Jesus said these words to Sanyi because he knew that Sanyi was the only child of a wealthy merchant who wanted for his only son to be like him. Sanyi did not know what this stranger meant by his words. "What does he mean by 'you cannot save even a single sheep'? Does he say that it was my fault?" he wondered to himself.

But as the man drew closer to Sanyi, he could see great compassion in his eyes. Later, Sanyi would say that he had never seen such compassion in a man's eyes, never before nor since.

Then, he heard him say, "You were just a small boy, who could never have stood up to the wild dogs. You can no more bring back the sheep than could you have saved it. Can you not forgive yourself for it? And I tell you the truth, that you can no more save the world now, the large powerful man that you are than you could have that lonely sheep when you were just a

The 13th Disciple

small boy."

Then, Sanyi's large hands dropped to his sides, and he remembered. He remembered that he was a small boy who would rise before the sun to attend his father's flock. His father had a hired man who came to attend them after the sun was up. The hired man was paid, but Sanyi's only reward was to be with the flock. He loved them since the first time he'd seen one of them born. First, there was one sheep, then there were two. How? From where comes the baby lambs, from where comes life, what magic is it that the world exists at all?

These questions Sanyi asked himself as a child and a man, with no answer. To young Sanyi, it was just magic, the magic of life, and he wanted to be in that magic for the rest of his life. So, he stayed with the sheep all that he could. The flock knew the hired man, but out on the rocky slopes of his father's pasture, they came to him, to the sound of his young voice, for they trusted it alone. And it was out there where only stubby grass grew on the rocky terrain where it happened.

A pack of hungry wild dogs attacked the flock

and separated one of the sheep from the rest of them. The hired man was able to take the flock back to the pen. But he was a hired man, and he would not try to save the one that was lost. Sanyi left the hired man and went after the pack. He could not see them for they were hidden behind a small hill over which his tiny body could not see. But he could hear the vicious snarling and the frenzied pack feeding upon the rock. The little lamb was no more, only shredded remnants remained.

Armed with only a branch of dead olive trees, when his tiny legs had finally carried him to that bloody spot, the dogs turned on him. Sanyi did the only thing he could; he struck out with his stick. It was a vain attempt, and the dogs swarmed in from all directions. He tripped, and all the dogs mauled him. As he lay on his stomach, his hands behind his head, he could hear the animals growling, feel the hot air and blood on their breath until he fainted.

Many hours later, Sanyi woke up. Somehow, he knew to crawl to the edge of the cliff. When he looked over, he saw the bloodstained rock below where the dogs had murdered his lamb. The image was seared into his mind from that moment on. This was what Sanyi remembered as he stared at the curious stranger coming closer to him, wondering, "How does this man know everything I have ever done?" When Jesus got close, he put his hand on Sanyi's shoulder and said, "Sanyi, my brother, forgive yourself, at least in the way of the world, or you will try to save that same sheep for the rest of your days. Forgive yourself in the way of the Holy Spirit and be free of all things." This was only what Sanyi could hear.

Sanyi did not know what Jesus meant by "Forgive yourself in the way of the Holy Spirit" anymore than his father understood how a small boy could receive such serious injuries by the dogs and live—but watching Jesus teach, he felt something that, until this moment, he had never imagined. He felt that with Jesus, for now at least, all things were possible.

The ever-growing crowd around them was filled with much agitation and discussion. "Who is this man who says of the money changers that they have done no one harm?" they demanded of one another. But no answer was to be provided there, so they asked Jesus, "Who are you?" Then, one of them said, "Sanyi was chasing the money changers from the Temple, but you said to him let them be." And they accused Jesus of defending the money changers.

"I tell you what I told him—judge them not, for they have harmed no one," Jesus answered.

Angered, the crowd drew near to Jesus, and the disciples and Mary gathered around. Lucilla also came near to Sanyi. The crowd was loud and accusatory, but they quieted down and demanded that Jesus explain himself. So, Jesus did. As Jesus was waiting to speak, Lucilla was just commencing her multifaceted lifelong scrutiny of Jesus.

"But they—the money changers—are stealing from the poorest Jews. On their holiest ground, no less," they replied.

"They are evil," others persisted. And now the fury was directed at the slender stranger. But Jesus gently corrected, stating that no one is good or evil and that nobody could possibly be victimizing anybody,

The 13th Disciple

saying:

"I tell you the truth that everyone acts in service of their own perceived needs. Everyone acts selfishly. The money changers, attempting to maximize their profit on every single coin, as were the poorest Jews attempting to pay as little as possible for each coin. To each his motives are moral, but each acted so that his needs would be met first, each acted equally selfishly in service of those needs. And as we each act equally selfishly, we each act completely selfish in the service of our perceived needs. Even the martyr is totally selfish; for what else can he be?" So, said he who would in the days seemingly perform the most extreme act of martyrdom for the ages.

The point of view of Jesus was unexpected and unacceptable to all, save for Sanyi who recognized so early on the correctness of Jesus point of view and noticed too that his hatred for the money changers caused him no personal distress, but his judgment of them had cost him his peace of mind.

Lucilla was especially judgemental of Jesus because she could not understand that he had not acted in defense of the despicable money changers. Rather, he simply had not judged them. But even amongst the disciples themselves and Mary Magdalene, it was Lucilla who would struggle most to understand that good and bad were only what we called it.

Sanyi had more shocks in store for his wife, inviting Jesus and his disciples, and Mary to stay with them. "Please, you and your friends come and stay with me at my house, for I am a wealthy man, and I have room enough for all of you." Upon hearing this, Lucilla jumped quietly out of her skin. But Sanyi had not consulted her, so Jesus, the disciples, and Mary went and stayed there awhile.

The very thought of spending the night with these strangers and Jesus sickened her. If asked, she could not have said why indeed she never pondered the question. But she had judged Jesus as a defender of the money changers and for something else which she knew not, nor did she know that any loss of peace that she felt was directly resultant of that judgment and of her own doing entirely.

That was exactly what Jesus was going to tell

her, though she would not hear it. But Lucilla only thought that she was repulsed by the thought of Jesus and his disciples spending the night under her roof. She had no idea that she was truly threatened by Jesus; threatened because Sanyi's attention to him detracted from his attention toward her.

Sanyi felt the gentle breeze wrap around his legs and watched it ruffle the cloth on the table while Jesus was drinking wine. He had learned by now that Jesus had turned the water into wine in Cana in Galilee. Sanyi was not surprised that Jesus could perform miracles, for the slender stranger had told him everything that he had ever done. But he had provided a dinner in which the wine would not run out, for he knew that Jesus had not come here to perform miracles or magic, not in the ordinary sense at least. Nothing about Jesus was ordinary. Jesus had come to teach.

In time, he would teach Sanyi what a Miracle really was and remove all barriers to the awareness of Love's presence. Yet, to see and hear Jesus with the eyes and ears of the body could only be misleading, he thought. Sanyi realized early on that if you could understand Jesus at all, then it must be with something more. Yet, what was it?

For Jesus was the answer to every question; to receive one, all that was required was to ask. Jesus was constantly trying to get through; one simply had to allow him. Just now, Sanyi was attempting to do precisely that. Oddly, he felt unable to think of a thought about which to ask the question. He was slightly distracted by children who had been playing at a distance but were now drawing closer to the adults.

Yet, as he struggled for the question which eluded him, it was a small child who provided the question to the answer. It was, in fact, the answer from which all other answers sprang, the only question that needed to be asked, the only answer there really was. From a child, Lucilla's young niece came to the question about the world and all of creation.

She had been lying on the ground, looking up at the stars. Now. pointing up at them, she asked, "Jesus, where do they come from?" As Jesus began to answer, Sanyi could never have believed how profoundly changed he would be when Jesus was done. Had he known then of the depraved death and eons of despair and destruction it would bring to himself and Lucilla, he still could not resist the lesson of Christ, for it was a required lesson, indeed a lesson long since completed. Sanyi was familiar with the law as given by Moses and interpreted by the chief priests and the Pharisees. But until now, he had never heard anyone speak with such gentle authority on that question. Before now, no one had ever said where the world comes from, and more importantly, why. For Jesus said, "Little girl, they come from you."

The Tiny Mad Idea

The law says, "In the beginning," but there is no beginning or end. I tell you the truth: there is only this very instant. Now is forever, and God is everything; God is all there is. But my words make no sense to a little girl or to an old man because you think you are of this world. Very well then, *I shall meet you where you think you are.*

A very long time ago, but it never really happened at all, the Son of Man was in Heaven, in a state of eternal bliss and in perfect oneness with the Father. That is all that can be said of Heaven: it is perfect, undifferentiated oneness, a oneness such that no place is different from another. So perfect that there is nowhere we begin or that He ends, so complete that you can have no thought that is not a thought of God, you cannot imagine anything that is not God because there is none.

There is no difference, save one: the Father is the first cause. He created the Son; the Son did not beget Him. Yet, in the Holy Trinity, it is said that God is first, but there is no second, neither is there a thought of separation; you were one with God who created you. We are not separate from God, we are not part of God, and each and every one of us is God. There the totality and ubiquitousness of God is such that God is all there is and we simply say, *God is and then we cease to speak.*

Then, into the Mind of the Son, there crept a sick, insane thought—*A Tiny Mad Idea.* The idea was mad because it was not of God, but at the Tiny Mad Idea, the Son of Man remembered not to laugh, the forgetting being the beginning of nothingness. Later, Sanyi would understand that it was the failure to laugh away the Tiny Mad Idea that was the root of the nightmare. The idea was: what would it be like to be apart from God? The Son waited for God to answer, but He didn't. It was a tiny mad idea because there is no such thing as separate from God. So, God, not willing to make that which was unreal appear real did not answer. The non-answer from God to the non-question, The Son mistook it as a rebuke. It was a great mistake, the greatest mistake, one whose impact is matched only by the magnitude of its incorrectness. In forgetting to laugh away the tiny mad idea the Son now mistakenly believes that God is angry with Him, angry for His thought of separation.

So, this Tiny Mad Idea is your imagined original sin. For his imagined sin, The Son imagines real, annihilating retribution."

The first fire went low, and as the hired man of Sanyi's started another, everyone moved closer to Jesus, not simply to see or even hear him, but to be closer. There, they saw his face as he looked at and into theirs. In the dimming, orange-red dying light, they saw his face illuminated, showing his infinite compassion for them, for all of their kind, but they could not yet understand it. Continuing, Christ said, "Believing in this original sin, the entire Sonship feels deep, unknowing, abiding guilt and expects severe and merciless retribution for a crime that never was. the Son of Man, with sin in his past, guilt in his present, and fear of retribution in the future that will never come, flees from the angry Father. *An angry Father pursues his guilty son—kill or be killed.* So, in terror, we flee the only home we have ever known: Heaven. But where then do we hide from God? This is where the io, or I self comes to our seeming aid and says, "I'll help you, I'll give you a body in which to hide, for God will never find you there; furthermore, I will give you a world in which to hide the body, all the bodies. Then, if God does find you, point to thy brother and say: there God, there is the guilty one. Cast your judgment there. The io is not a demon or a devil, it is no more real than the body, rather is just trick, or devise of the panicked mind, of the guilt-ridden Son. The io is the part of your mind that makes up and protects the illusion of separation from God. It is what makes the illusion seem real, so very real. Every person, every beast, every rock, and every tree and even the io itself is part of the illusion, and there is the cruelest hoax, that the io protects most viciously the illusion of itself.

This is how the world came into being. How silly—could the Son really offend God? But burdened by original sin and mistaken guilt, the Son of Man sold his soul to the io to deny the undeniable reality that God is. To protect the mad dream, the io must preoccupy the

The 13th Disciple

Son of Man with ever more and more grandeur illusions. So, the false world that we fill with cruelty, inhumanity and bloody wars, with friends and enemies, with money changers, heroes and villains, and Romans—all of them—all aught but distraction, for so terrified is the Son of the Father that he runs to the devil to hide.

So, all the world, all that you think you see with the eyes of the body comes from but a Mind turned inside out and spilled onto a world outside of itself. A world outside of God is one outside of everything that's real. Remember, God is, and we cease to speak. This world that you believe you see is but a turbulent nightmare caused by a tiny mad idea. the Son of Man is asleep, and Heaven dreaming the dreams of exile. Each lifetime you think you live in this world is but a nightmare to a dreamer in heaven. To awaken from the dreams, the Son must learn Forgiveness. Not the kind of Forgiveness that the world knows, but true Forgiveness of the Holy Spirit which knows that the world is not. But it takes many dreams of many lifetimes to train the Mind to ignore the io and listen to only the Holy Spirit. And in the myriad of dreams and lifetimes in the multitudinal forums of joy and horror they bring, at one time or another, we each play the other's part. We are each master and slave, we are each predator and prey, we are each everything there are to be many multitudes of times over. The Father has sent me to gently wake the Son from his dream, to ease his burden, to reduce the number of his nightmares, to free the master from the slave, and I tell you the truth—I have already accomplished it. I have already undone that which was never done. But follow or ignore the Word, it makes no difference, everyone awakens, everyone makes it out, everyone already has. Nor am I above you. *Therefore, you shall see me as an older Brother who has traveled the path before you, and now is reaching out to help you along. I am not entitled to your awe, that is reserved properly only to the Father. I am entitled to your devotion because I am devoted to you. I deserve your obedience as an older more knowledgeable brother, I can lead, but you must choose to follow.*

When he was finished the little girl understood,

and so did Sanyi. Jesus had given to all of those gathered there what had never been given before: the meaning of existence, it's served purpose, as well as nature of guilt of the son-ship, one and all, saying, "Any man who so ever it is that he shall be who expects punishment, will also unknowingly demand it, so then shall that same man receive it."

When asked about Love, Jesus answered, saying, *"I come not to teach Love's meaning for that is beyond what can be taught. I am here to remove all barriers to the awareness of Love's presence, which is your natural inheritance "*.

Awaken to escape the dream. As Sanyi seized on those words and symbol they represented, he acquired an accompanying, burgeoning sense of purpose. He wondered openly if he could wake to make it out of his dream, and make it out this time. What Sanyi could not know at that time was that purpose was a two-edged sword.

Sanyi was going to follow Jesus, making no mention of it to Jesus, but Lucilla was stunned when he told her. Her 19-year-old world being torn apart, she fell and had to catch herself on the table, and Sanyi had to help her into the chair. Such a little girl, he thought as she sat legs together, hands twisting and writhing on her knees as she gently sobbed. "It's not as though you never see me again," he said, taking her tiny hands gently into his huge ones. He was as miffed by her severe reaction as she was by his desire to leave her. She tried to be angry with him, but when she looked up, she could do aught but put her slender arms around his thick neck. He picked her up from there and carried her gently into bed.

Sanyi was patient with Lucilla as she protested with all her slight strength. But there was no way to stop him. Sanyi was leaving with Jesus no matter what the costs or consequences. And even had he known then just how ruinous, bloody, and cataclysmic those consequences would be for all involved over the eons of destruction and despair, still, Sanyi would have followed Jesus; he already had.

The following morning Nicodemus came to visit Jesus. Nicodemus was a money changer. He had not fled when Sanyi came through the market and heard

Jesus speak. He came inside where Jesus was resting from the heat of the day and spoke alone to him.

"Jesus, we know that you are a spiritual man and speak the truth," Nicodemus began. "We want to help you spread the truth all across Judea," he continued. But Jesus perceived his treachery and interrupted him by saying, "Nicodemus, I do not judge usury, nor do I sanction it."

Then, Jesus stood up and put both of his arms on Nicodemus' shoulders and asked him, "Nicodemus, what good does it do a man to gain the world and yet remain of it. Profit and loss are simply opposite sides of the scarcity coin, designed to keep the attention of the Son of Man on worldly things instead of the infinite treasures in Heaven where no one has any need, nor there be scarcity or want."

Jesus was aware that the money changer realized the truth in the words he had just spoken, yet Nicodemus persisted, saying, "Jesus, we have not just wealth, but influence, influence with the Jewish authorities and the Roman ones. We can do all manner of things to get our desired way."

Then, Jesus stepped back from Nicodemus, looked him directly in the eyes, and said, "I am aware of all that you think you can do to me. You may do all manner of things to my body, but you cannot touch the guiltless Son of Man. You can cause me no pain for the *guiltless mind cannot suffer*. You already realize this, yet must you try, yet must it be done."

Nicodemus had caused much suffering in his life yet never felt remorse once. But, just now, even he did feel pity for Jesus, and for what he would do to Jesus.

Sanyi watched Nicodemus leaving his house. He walked in anxiously and found Jesus. He knew what Nicodemus wanted, but Jesus, opening wide his arms and palms as if to hug the entire world, said with a light heart, "Worry not big man for all this has never really happened."

The following morning, Jesus, his disciples, Mary Magdalene, and Sanyi left Jerusalem. Jesus had been asked to return to Cana in Galilee, where he had turned the water into wine. The people there remembered how he had turned the water into wine and wondered if he would try to heal a sick young girl possessed by demons.

"Jesus," protested Thomas. "It will take too long. By the time we get to Galilee, the girl will be dead."

But Jesus, smiling, replied, "Have faith, Thomas, and she will be healed in this very moment." And just as Jesus said, the young girl's demons left her. And there was great joy among them as well for they believed and knew that she had been saved.

Later, along the way, a Roman centurion with his men coming from Jerusalem approached them rapidly on horseback. He was already aware of Jesus's miraculous ability to cure, and he had a sick son, yet he was there to seize Jesus at the behest of Nicodemus and the money changers.

Sanyi counted twenty mounted soldiers as they circled Jesus and his followers threateningly. The disciples and Mary were frightened and moved toward Jesus to protect him, but as Sanyi anticipated Jesus brushed them to the side. Sanyi was more calm; he had already seen Jesus perform miracles, and he already knew that nothing could happen lest Jesus let it happen. But, still, a little peace was lost.

And so it was that when two soldiers put their hands on Jesus, they stopped just before touching him. The horses stopped, the dust stopped, everything, even the air, came to a dead stop. And Jesus, looking up at the captain, said to him. "You are Captain Aurelius Dalmaticus Marcellus, and you act in service of the money changers, but you distrust them. So, why then do you do their work?" With that, the soldiers stepped back from Jesus. And the captain was amazed, but when Jesus told him, "Your young son is afflicted with the fever." The captain was astonished again. "Go home and attend to your son and leave the work of the money changers to the money changers."

With that, the man dismounted and came toward Jesus. When he got close, Jesus put his arm around the man's shoulder, looked him seriously in the eye, and the man said, "I must attend to the money changers. I have no choice for I have my orders, and disobedience on my behalf would be severely punished."

The 13th Disciple

Then, Jesus answered, saying, "We each have our orders, Captain, but we still have a choice. You have simply made yours. Without delay, the man said, "Command me, and I shall do it." Then, Jesus looked at the man, smiling, and said, "By your faith at this very moment, your son is saved."

The captain wept at Jesus's feet, but Jesus lifted him up and told him to go. In time, Sanyi would understand just what Jesus meant when he said, "By your faith, it is done." (referring only to worldly miracles)

Later that day, they entered a town, and Jesus, tired out by the trip, sat on a wall, while the disciples went ahead of him. Sanyi, who walked slower than them because of his huge size, came up to Jesus and sat next to him. Jesus rested his hands on the top of the wall while his feet dangled off the ground, but Sanyi, more leaning over than sitting, was too tall to get his feet off the ground.

Sanyi, looking at the dirt, turned to Jesus and was about to speak when Jesus asked, "Did you walk these past miles frightened by the threats of the money changers?"

Sanyi smiled, not surprised that Jesus could perceive his thoughts. Then, Sanyi said, "My father was a wealthy and powerful man. He was unafraid of the Pharisees or the chief priests. But my father always feared the money changers."

Jesus put his hand on Sanyi's big shoulder and, with a squeeze, said, "Sanyi, you who wanted to be a doctor, a healer. You are so close, Sanyi. You may just wake this time, but you still have an important lesson to learn, that you cannot save the world, not even yourself."

Then, Jesus came down off the wall and went toward his disciples. They were led by Mary Magdalene with a bucket of water coming toward Jesus. They reunited as though they had been separated from him for a year rather than just a few minutes. Jesus stroked the side of Mary's face and then hugged her before he drank.

Then, he touched all the disciples as they gathered around, on the arm or the shoulder or even the top of the head. Sanyi noticed that Jesus had done it to him too. It was Jesus's way of saying, "I acknowledge you even though I am not looking at or speaking directly to you right now." Sanyi was not trying to fit into this group, but slowly, stealthily, they were growing effortlessly on him. They were becoming part of what Jesus would call each other's special relationships, a subtle and especially treacherous trap.

Then, they left that town, and as the evening drew on, they found themselves at last in the cool dark aloneness of the desert. Sanyi was tired, his big legs had carried his large body far, and it felt good to rest them as he leaned back against a stone. He fell asleep briefly, and when he had awakened, Jesus had just returned with his arms full of logs. He dropped them into a pile, then knelt on the ground and started putting them one at a time onto the fire.

Sanyi didn't exactly notice when it got completely dark or when Jesus was the totality of his vision. He didn't notice when Jesus went from idle talk to teaching about healing. He didn't even notice that he didn't notice the achiness of his legs and weariness in his large body any longer. All he noticed was what they all notice: how Jesus became so much bigger when he was teaching, how they were completely absorbed in the moment with Jesus, and each felt that he was speaking only to them. Sanyi was sure of it.

"When you are healing," Jesus began, "remember this. The acceptance of sickness as a decision of the Mind, for any purpose for which it would use the body, is the basis of healing. And this is so for healing in all forms."

Notice that before I heal them, I ask, 'do you have faith that I can do this?' Then, after I heal them, I say 'by your faith I have cured thee.' Who then is the physician?"

"Jesus," said Mary Magdalena, "I heard that the young girl whom you cast the demons out of in Cana was levitating and speaking Egyptian, which she had never heard before. Are such things possible?"

Jesus stirred the fire, and in the distance, a cock cooed. Jesus' white robes were bathed in the firelight, but it was now so cold his breath showed as he spoke.

"All these things are possible," he said. "And all these things are not possible too." Then, he held the stick that he had just used to stir the fire above it for a long moment. Jesus then opened his hand and let the stick drop into the fire. It fell, being engulfed by the licking flames, and there was a sharp sudden report.

"Why did it fall down, rather than up to the heavens?," He paused, and all looked at each other, searching for exactly what each thought Jesus was searching for.

"It is the way things work," Mary said shyly, "things fall down."

Peter and Paul shrugged, saying, "We cannot know such things.

But Jesus answered, saying, "Because we, the entire Son of Man decided in our tiny mad idea to make just such a world. And if someone truly believes that it would fall to the sky, then so would it be."

Then, Jesus held a large stone the size of an orange over the fire and released it. There, it hovered a moment, rolling over in the air before them all, then raised slowly and gently into the dark sky, its underbelly glowing red, getting smaller, smaller, then disappearing altogether just as the mist from Jesus' mouth, and again the cock cooed. "Remember that we made this world, the sky, and the seas, and all the laws which seemingly govern them, and remember why. In our mind, we believe that we took perfect oneness and split from it, thus killing it, for that which is one can never be two. As I have said, this was our sin against God, and I have said that this gives birth to the io, whom we believe when he says God will punish you."

The wind blew cold from all directions, and Sanyi wondered if it was Jesus or if it was themselves, their guilt made manifest. Jesus continued, "The io says, 'Think not that He has forgotten.' Stay in Heaven and face the angry, merciless Father pursuing His guilty Son—murder in the heart of one, blood on the hands of the other—kill or be killed. At war with God in Heaven, this is the Son's dilemma. The io councils, 'You cannot possibly defeat God in Heaven, but choose me, and I'll give you a world to hide in—a world too big even for almighty God to find you. One with a sky, mountains, seas, and sprawling deserts.' Then, the io gives you the body—the one you think you are."

Jesus touched his arms with his hands. "And more importantly, the Son provides the laws by which all made up things behave, for to make the illusion seem real. To make it seem real, there is the condemnation of God, the loneliness of infinite separation, the terror of an angry Father in pursuit of the guilty Son."

The cock cooed a third time. No one said a thing, nor even did they blink an eye despite another bone cracking pop of a log in cold dry night air. Then, still illuminated by the orange glow of the firelight, Jesus said, *"Peace on this,"* the cold vapor streaming from his breath in white clouds, "peace to thoughts of loneliness and separation and sin, peace to the misperceptions called guilt and judgment and pain, peace on all of the terror of retribution and reprisal forever yet to come and of an angry Father pursuing His guilty Son, peace to it all at last for none of it really happened. The Son is asleep at home dreaming a dream of exile."

The 13th Disciple

Another ember burst in the diminishing firelight, and Jesus' voice reverberated from stone to stone and through all their bodies, through Sanyi's body, and there in his big body it remained. Then, Jesus paused, Sanyi knew not whether it was for an eternity or an instant, but when Jesus spoke again, it was softly from the blanketing darkness, saying, "Next time, I say only that the next time the io beckons you to judge a brother, at that time please my brother, please choose again."

Peace on it—what a beautiful thought, Sanyi reflected. Peace on it and choose again, and Sanyi did choose again, and having done so put the perfect peace of Jesus to himself. He stretched on his back with one hand under his head. For a long time, he just looked without thoughts into the dark sky, then in the cold night air, and he found peace.

On the following day, they arrived at Joseph and Mary's house. They were the agonized parents whom Jesus healed by returning them to their natural state, their true state of bliss. It was there that Jesus performed his first miracle of turning the water into wine to celebrate his becoming their son. This time, he would create a feast to celebrate his marriage to Mary Magdalene.

Jesus did not wed Mary Magdalene in a way which the world understood. The ceremony took place when she anointed his feet with oil. Sanyi dipped his massive body and slightly twisted his shoulders in an act made naturally by a lifetime of practice of passing through doorways and entering houses. Inside his nose, he caught the sweetest scent of perfume oil he had ever smelled. It wafted gently around the cubicle, soaking every chair, table, drape, and even Jesus' feet. Once inside, Sanyi saw Mary Magdalene caressing Jesus's feet with her tender hands. Then, she put the end of her long, beautiful hair into the oil and anointed his feet. Not everyone there realized that from that moment on, Jesus and Mary Magdalene were married, or so Jesus proclaimed it. This made Joseph and Mary extremely joyous, but not Judas Iscariot. Judas Iscariot was a thief whom Jesus had put in charge of the money purse, and he helped himself to it. Everyone there wondered why Christ tolerated Iscariot so, save for Sanyi, who never even questioned the matter.

Jesus did not judge Iscariot, so he drew no personal discomfort from the man's transgressions or presence; only those who practiced true Forgiveness could accomplish such a feat. Judas, Jesus realized, was simply learning his life's necessary lessons.

When Mary Magdalene had finished anointing his feet with the oil as if perceiving all their judgment, Jesus spoke more about the matter.

"Judgment is what the Mind makes to separate us one from another, a brother from brother, and to create a different experience for each, one which is not true but seems to be." Jesus continued, saying, "Judgment, coming from the Mind, also turns within and attacks us, creating self-hate and unworthiness. Instead of judging ourselves for having sick thoughts, realize it is just sickness, and turn to love in faith to show Him your sick thoughts. Most of all, do not judge yourself."

Then, Jesus finished, saying, "Remember always that God is neither temporary nor mercurial;

therefore, neither are any of his creations. Nothing which is not perfect oneness is of God. Nothing real can be threatened. Nothing unreal exists. Herein lies the peace of God."

The 13th Disciple

Jesus and Sanyi on the open sea

After the wedding, Jesus stayed in Cana for three days. Then, he, his new bride, the disciples, and Sanyi left Cana and went to Haifa. There, they boarded a large boat to Sidon, for there was a great feud in that land, and Jesus was implored to go there to try to end it, and so he went.

When they left to land it in the middle of the day, the single sail filled up fast in the afternoon heat. The mood was lighthearted. They were all happy to be done walking and alone together on their little island in the sea. Jesus and Mary danced on the foredeck while Thomas and Peter fished with nets off the rear deck. Everyone laughed when Thomas caught one.

As he showed it to them flapping around in his hands, they said, "Don't you see we have the greatest fishermen in the world right here and pointed to Jesus? Don't you remember how he turned four fish into 4000? So, Thomas threw the fish back into the sea, laughing.

Sanyi relished in and shared mutual joy of the

moment, even as they teased him mercilessly for his ungainly bulk which could find no comfortable place to rest. The boat seemed much too small for him. Also, after about an hour had passed, he was becoming visibly sick. This was the reason, rather than his size, that Sanyi stayed out of boats most of the time. Some of the disciples remarked that if Jesus wanted to perform a real miracle, then he should cure Sanyi of his seasickness. But Sanyi, focusing his site back on the land, said, "There is no need to annoy Jesus with little things. I will cure myself." They all laughed again.

Jesus sat down and leaned back against some barrels offered to help Sanyi. But Sanyi, waving his hand, said, "I am fine." With that, Mary Magdalene sat down in front of Jesus, and he put his arms around her as she leaned back into him. Sanyi lay down on his side, propping himself up with his right elbow, at the rear of the boat.

From there, he was both a watcher and a participant of the goings-on on the little island in the sea. Now, what he wanted to do was to observe his thoughts in the same way. He saw Mary Magdalene curl up and lean sideways into Jesus as he stretched out completely on the deck. He fell asleep to the rocking of the sea and the raucous sound emanating from the pure joy of being with one another, of being with Jesus.

Sanyi woke under a canopy of cacophonous colors that reached down, completely down, in all their gaudy boldness to the granite water in every conceivable direction. The gently rolling waves upon the sea were reflected therein strips of clouds across the sky, bathed in orange and purple, and it was possible to believe that a man so large as Sanyi could walk across that sea without so much as getting his big feet wet.

And as the sun settled down somewhere in the west, a blood red attendant moon rose with cantilevering perfection into the burgeoning night, rising, filling that ever blossoming evening, eastern sky with the blood red and gold of the dying day's diminishing brilliance. Sanyi watched transfixed as the dance of light took place overhead—a dance he had seen many times on dry land: the banishing of one light engulfed orb under the rim of the world to be simultaneously replaced, by another rising high above it, only to be followed by another displacement that very day. But never before on such a stage as this. He could seemingly reach into the sky and touch the dazzling, dancing colors with his own mighty hand; he almost tried to. Jesus, seeing all of this, presently prepared to gently correct mighty Sanyi.

Jesus, Peter, and Mary Magdalene were cooking fish on the foredeck, the scent wafted back and deliciously tickled Sanyi's senses. Everyone woke and ate. The dinner was delicious.

When he was finished, Sanyi went to just behind the mast. It was dark by then, but the moon illuminated a huge swath of the sea, and it seemed that their boat was flying on it as if it were a cloud in the sky. Sanyi looked to the east and was astounded. Where was the land? For all his worldliness, Sanyi had never been on the open sea far removed from the land. It was amazing. The immense expanse of emptiness defeated his imagination.

Lost in its awesomeness, he was unaware of the goings-on in the boat; it took him a while to notice Jesus standing beside him.

Smiling, Jesus looked up, saying, "You have never seen anything so grand, have you, Sanyi? Ha ha, drink it all in the entire experience, Sanyi, for the next time you see this, it shall not be half so grand. Nor half as much again the time after that."

Now, it was Jesus that Sanyi studied intently, wondering what he could mean by such words. Jesus perceived his confusion and answered, saying, "The grand new vista or experience is an example where the Mind has no prior experience with which to compare. The mad mind searches the past frantically for reference with which it can explain the present experience, which it cannot. The awestruck mind is speechless. You think that you are awestruck by something outside of you, yet it comes from aught but within you, and splashes on to the outside world like dye into the water. Just as the sunset at which you marveled earlier, it is real only in the Mind for it can be experienced only there.

At these times, the io is speechless, and its unreality may be briefly perceived, so that the Holy Spirit can come in. But the io is quick; it must have you believe that the world is real. So, the next time you have the experience, just beneath the surface of your cognizance, the io lurks and replaces the second experience with memories of the first. This could keep real what is unreal and the Holy Spirit out."

Sanyi looked back up at the sky, then out to the sea, and finally back at Jesus, trying to take it all in. But before he could even get started, Jesus gave him even more, saying, "And even the next time is an illusion just like tomorrow and yesterday, Sanyi. When the Mind thinks about yesterday or tomorrow, it thinks about that which does not exist. And when the Mind thinks about what it thinks is now, it considers that which has no beginning and no end yet is eternal. Therefore, it does not think. Indeed, the greatest illusion the Mind is under is that it thinks that it thinks at all, the equally greatest deception that the io is under is that it thinks that it is at all."

Then, Sanyi thought that Jesus must have been alone with him for quite some time now, and the rest of the disciples and Mary Magdalene would soon be coming to him. But when Sanyi looked toward the bow of the boat, he noticed that nothing had changed since Jesus had come to him. Neither had the moon climbed any bit higher in the night sky nor had even the sail made a ruffle. The whole world, save for him and Jesus, seemed still as a statue.

Then, Jesus said in a whisper which, nonetheless, carried unfettered through the night air across the deck, "Sanyi, I'm just trying to show you how what is now for them is not now for us." Then, Jesus turned and went to his disciples at the bow. Sanyi hugged his one knee and let the other straight out and looked up at the stars in quiet contemplation.

In Sidon

There was no one on the shore when they landed in Sidon just south of the Saida Citadel. Jesus led his disciples, Mary Magdalene, and Sanyi inland for a day to the place in the mountains where the tribes were at war. As the evening drew near and dark, Peter, Paul, and Judas Iscariot prepared a fire and cooked meat of fish which they had carried from the sea. The general sense of goodwill from the boat still prevailed, only that they were hungry and tired now and ate mostly in silence. The fire was down to a low glow when Jesus spoke gently on Forgiveness, so gently that Sanyi could not even see the spot from which Jesus spoke, whether he was standing or sitting.

"This war between these tribes is not like a war of armies," Jesus began. "Armies fight until one is losing and retreats, or even until the last man is dead. These tribes have come into each other's villages and killed each other's wives and children, destroyed each other's crops and animals. They threatened not just each other's lives, but the very things each other held even dearer than life," he continued.

The 13th Disciple

Then, Simon Peter's urgent voice came through amber darkness saying, "Then, that is the reason you have brought us here. You who heal the injured and bring the dead back to life. For if not you, who will stop the slaughter of innocents?"

Jesus was not disappointed anymore than he had been with Judas Iscariot, or any of them. Rather, he gently corrected, saying to Simon Peter even as he had Sanyi before. "You cannot save that which is not, Simon Peter."

Then, Jesus continued, saying, "This, all of this, is aught but a distraction. It is the purpose of the io to keep the Holy Spirit out. It is not by good deeds that you get to Heaven but by the judgment of any deed that keeps you out. No deed done in a false world can be real but by your judgment you make it seem so. This is what you must all learn, not how to save the world but rather how to forgive it, and to do so with the Holy Spirit rather than the io. The Holy Spirit does not forgive as the world does. The world recognizes that one has done wrong to the other, that the wronged and the wrongdoer are separate and unequal. The wrongdoer acknowledges his guilt, and then the wronged will grant a pardon to the guilty one by setting all that was wrong to right. But the Holy Spirit recognizes that no one is wronged, no one is guilty, and that no one can do anything to anyone. Our bodies may do all manner of terrible things to other bodies, but none of us is a body. Only when this truth is realized can true Forgiveness begin. Only when all Forgiveness has been given can we awaken from the dream and return to our home we have never left, which is in Heaven."

Sanyi watched the disciples as they looked questioningly amongst themselves. It was difficult for them to deny the seeming realness of the world. A world dressed up as a puppet in all of its splendors and horrors to seize our attention, to seize us for all time. The io can paint the world, but only we can judge it to make it seem real. This is what Jesus was teaching. But because Jesus realized that his disciples still believed their dreams to be real, he took them, Mary Magdalene, and Sanyi down to the village, for their own sake rather than for that of the villagers.

The 13th Disciple

When they were in the village, fighting was done, but the chaos remained. Screams were the first thing they noticed—the screams of children for their dead parents tore at Sanyi as if the dogs were tearing into his own boyhood flesh. The fact that the screams of children anguished him the most informed Sanyi about himself. But there was no time for judgment of oneself; there were too many dying to attend to, and Sanyi was still a physician.

Sanyi noticed that there were no fires. Indeed, there was nothing to burn; no structure, no crops—nothing of permanence prevailed. For years, they had repelled one vicious attack, only to launch another themselves. Even the uninjured were hungry. In a short time, lacking a substantial peace, these two tribes would be no more.

The disciples had spread themselves among the afflicted and desperately urged Jesus to aid the ones who they presently attended. Judas Iscariot and Simon Peter were covered in blood of a mother clutching the limp bodies of her two dead sons. Judas Iscariot and Peter, believing that the children might yet be saved, attempted to do so. Their desperate calls to Jesus could not even be heard by those making them over the vociferous paroxysms of anguished dying bodies. But Jesus was just now entering the village, walking calmly down the road, his sandals making slight round imprints in the blood-soaked mud. Then, staring out upon the manifest violence as if in a dream, Jesus said, "Instead of this, I can see peace."

Jesus placed his hand on the stomach of a young man dying from a sword wound. The young man grabbed Jesus by his wrist as he did so, but when Jesus pulled his hand away from the man's side, he was healed. A few of the people who saw this were amazed, and they told others about it.

Then, Jesus walked to the dead body of one of the others who had been killed by them. The limp body lay face first in the dirt, the club that had been used to kill him still buried in his skull. Jesus knelt, placed his hands on the man's head and, in a moment, the man got up and knew everything that had happened to him.

The man tried to leave, but those in the village wanted to seize him for he was one of the others. But

Jesus knew their word and told them in their own language to let the man go, allowing him to return with his own leader so that they might make peace. Jesus pointed to the top of the hill between the two villages and told them, "After the sun rises again, we shall meet there."

Then, Jesus bade the man to go. And even as the man was leaving, Jesus was healing the injured and raising the dead.

Because he had saved so many of them, Jesus now had great authority in that place. But one of their elders admonished Jesus for letting the enemy go. But Jesus said to him in his own words, "Where were your men to protect the village?" Jesus did not wait for an answer but responded, "They were away attacking that village. See not the spec in your brother's eye until you remove the plank from thine own." This admonition was on the level of the world, but Jesus would soon address them all at the level of the Mind.

When the sun had risen on the next day, everyone from both villages climbed to the spot Jesus had pointed to. Each remained on the same side as their own village as Jesus, the disciples, Mary Magdalene, and Sanyi met the elders on the ridgeline between the two.

Sanyi and the disciples studied Jesus and the goings-on but understood it not. Jesus could speak all languages; they could not. But they all sensed great hatred between the tribes each for the other. If it were not that Jesus held great authority in that place, then surely he would be dead, and the tribes locked in bloody conflict even at this moment.

They were all frustrated and fascinated over the several hours that Jesus worked a miracle seemingly greater than bringing the dead back to life. He was bringing peace to a region that had known none for the lifetimes of anyone there on the hill. But then, all the elders threw down their swords in a pile and embraced one another in rigid, formal hugs, indicating deep distrust, but war was past. Sanyi didn't have to understand the intricacies of the language or the doctrine to realize that something amazing had happened. But Jesus said it was as natural as the sunrise.

The 13th Disciple

On the hilly return to the coast, the disciples and Sanyi could not contain their curiosity. They implored Jesus to tell them how he had done what he had done. Jesus teased them, saying, "I don't know how I did what I have done." And he tapped Simon Peter on the forehead as he said it. Everyone laughed. They walked, and when it was dark, they made fire in a hilly crevice and ate. Sanyi could see the firelight in Jesus's face and the shadow of his head cast on the rock behind him. As always, when Jesus began to talk, nothing else seemed to matter.

"When you try to make peace, always remember this. You deal with the world of dreams, and you deal with God. On the level of the world of dreams, everybody's acts are motivated from a sense of scarcity. It's just as with the money changers and the poor Jews in the Temple. Everyone is trying to satisfy their perceived needs to fill a void. But in reality, there is only one need, and that is the loneliness the Son of Man feels because he thinks that he did the impossible and separated from God. It is the same sick insane idea of something that could never really be."

The 13th Disciple

Jesus looked back and forth at them as an ember cracked and popped in the fire. "I spoke mostly with the chiefs and elders. I chose the chief form of one tribe and asked him, 'What do you want from them?'" Jesus said it as though he were pointing at someone reenacting the event. "He answered me, saying, 'That man is a murderer. He murdered my son.' I already knew that this was so, but I asked so that you might learn from his answer."

Then, the disciples and Mary Magdalene looked around and questioned among themselves, "What can he mean by this?" But Sanyi kept his eyes fixed directly on Jesus. "Notice that I asked, 'What do you want?' and received instead judgment and condemnation. So, I asked him again, 'What do you want from this man?' But he could not answer me. So, I asked him, saying, 'Do these men threaten you when they attack? Do you need more security?' You see, this was his perceived need. You must go past judgment to perceived needs that are being threatened. I say perceived needs, for the Son has not a single real need. He is like me; we each have everything. The difference between us now is that

The 13th Disciple

I have nothing else.

Then I asked the other chief the same question, 'What do you want of this man?'" Jesus pointed to his other side still reenacting it. "'They are dogs,' he told me. But what do you want from them? He could not answer me either. Nor would he be able to answer me yet, for he was different from the first chief. His needs were different from the other chief." They all looked at each other and at Jesus, but Jesus, looking at the ground, shook his head and said, "You see, this chief wanted nothing from the other chief. His needs could not be satisfied by the other tribe because he had no needs from them." His need stemmed from this false sense of worthiness to be chief. He was too young and too inexperienced in battle. His father, a great warrior, had died, and he had become chief.

In his own mind, he alone perceives his unworthiness. But he casts that unworthiness like paint upon a canvas onto his own tribe, misperceiving it in them. He then attacks the other tribe again and again for what it does not have, what it cannot give, that he alone can give himself through a simple shift in perspective.

But now, he sees himself through the eyes of the Holy Spirit, seeing himself as he truly is, as we all truly are, the guiltless Son of Man.

All was still, even the flickering of the fire seemed still. "Again, when you mediate conflict, pay no attention to the judgment of one side for another. Search instead for perceived lack and fill it. But even doing so, realizing it too is an illusion, for all lack is as a result of a belief in the separation from God that could never have occurred."

On the worldly level, it seemed to be an isolated insignificant peace treaty, but on that level, at least Sanyi thought the protracted, disparaging war of attrition between the tribes had come at long last to an end.

They came the following day to rest in the shade of a large rock, where they decided to eat. Sanyi could smell the sea air, hidden by the hill to their west, the other side of which sloped gently to the sea. As they sat there, Jesus said to them, "We return now to Jerusalem for the religious festival. There, I will be taken up by the Romans at the behest of the money changers and the

Jewish authorities. And they will seemingly do all manner of things to me."

Sanyi felt his stomach coming up through his throat, and amongst the astonished disciples, there was a much-agitated discussion. Mary Magdalene remained serene standing to Jesus' side. Then, Simon Peter, who counted on Jesus the most, rushed toward his master saying, "No, no, Jesus, don't go to the festival in Jerusalem. Stay away from that place." Then, Jesus put his hand on Simon Peter's head and said gently, "Peace on this, Peter."

Jesus turned to them all to say without judgment, "You yet lack the discipline, so I remind you that this is all a dream." Jesus tugged at his arm as he said this. "It is important that you see this and that you forgive this as I have, which is through the eyes of the Holy Spirit. I forgive it, realizing that it never happened. Though their bodies may crucify my body in the dream, in truth no one has done harm to anyone because no one is a body. This realization is the essence of true Forgiveness. Therefore, the world will say that I was torn and shredded and made to suffer mightily, but know that I do not share this opinion with them. Therefore, peace to this silliness, peace to you all."

Sanyi observed Jesus putting the perfect peace of God to the disciples and observed too how they did shun it, even as he had in the boat on the return voyage from Sidon. But not now, not this time. They had been gone for exactly 30 days and nothing of the world had changed—only their information about it. They each suffered now for separation that was about to come as though it had already happened, the anticipation making it seem real. Jesus though did take pity on them, just as he had the childless parents, Mary and Joseph. He took pity on them as he did all dreamers because they believed their dreams to be true. So, he gently reminded them that when the Mind thinks about the future, it thinks about that which is not and therefore nothing in the future could harm any of them now. But Sanyi did not feel better. The same boat which had floated them merrily here seemed now to be a death ship as a deep melancholy set in as a cloud over them.

They had set sail in the late afternoon and Simon Peter sailed the boat directly east until they could see land no more before turning south toward Jerusalem. It became dark around then, but Sanyi did not notice the full moon until it was almost straight up in the sky. He did not notice it until the clouds came in to obscure it. Then, he remembered what Jesus had told him that it would not seem half so grand the next time.

The storm moved in rapidly, the wind picking up and growing cold. Jesus slept like the rest of them, took down the sail, and threw up the tarps in the slanting rain. As Sanyi pulled a blanket around himself, he thought about the dreaded future against all of Jesus' past teaching and his own current knowledge. 'The mind cannot think about that which isn't; therefore, it thinks about neither the future nor the past. So, there is only now and it is forever'. This was what Jesus had preached so fervently, so often, but suddenly even forever seemed to be so very fleeting. Jesus could so easily save himself. With his hand, he could waive the Romans and the money changers into the sea. Why didn't he do it? Sanyi wanted to wake Jesus and beg him to do so just as Peter had, but to what end? And it wasn't odd that it was he who had everything, and

The 13th Disciple

nothing else was the only one unafraid.

But as Sanyi deeply lamented over Jesus' future, in the cold, as the rain dropped heavily into the hard canvas, a tiny idea of a different sort crept into his mind. It was an awareness of what Jesus wanted for them when he rebuked Simon Peter. It was something more important than the body of Christ, more important than all bodies altogether. Something more important than even happiness here in this world; it was that Jesus wanted us to use this to practice our own Forgiveness to deliver us from this world. Jesus was as indifferent to our happiness in this world as he was dedicated to our salvation, for Jesus, it was only our salvation which was of significance.

Sanyi realized this as daylight came, yet it did not aid to ameliorate his sadness. The sun did rise but did not show through the clouds for a storm had formed. *A cloud does not put out the sun* Sanyi recalled, but the remembering did not help him to feel better. Then, he laid his big body down on a bed of fishnet but did not sleep.

He was awakened by Thaddeus when they

disembarked at Yafo. Sanyi looked around himself as he staggered out of the boat. Towards the sea, the clouds hung oppressively low to the gray horizon. To the east lies Jerusalem and somewhere between here and there, Jesus would be taken up by the Romans at the behest of the money changers. Sanyi felt his mind say, heard its voices. They told him, "You are going to lose him and all that you love." But Sanyi neither obeyed nor resisted, nor did he listen to them. He did not notice when he could not hear them any longer; they would be many miles away. But the gray and melancholy that had seemed so oppressive just moments ago seemed now a slight, cool comfort as he walked. It wasn't a shift in perspective, a miracle, but it was a single crucial baby step.

On the way to Jerusalem, there came a man to them, saying, "Are you the Christ whom we seek, or shall I ask another?" Jesus stopped walking but did not answer him. Then, the man said, "I have a sister who is possessed, and only the Christ can save her." But Jesus perceived his treachery and answered him, saying, "Return to Nicodemus and tell him that you have found me." So, the man turned toward Jerusalem and ran there. To all of the disciples, Mary Magdalene, and Sanyi, there came a grave fear. But Sanyi, as he had the night on the boat with, neither accepted nor denied his fear; he simply observed it.

When they came to Jerusalem, it was on the day before the Passover festival. A man came to him and said, "You are Jesus the Christ. I saw you in the Temple which the money changers had turned into a market. Come—you and your friends—to my home, and we shall feast and drink wine." So, Jesus, the disciples, Mary Magdalene, and Sanyi went with the man to supper.

The Last Supper

Sanyi once again took up his self-appointed position as participant and observer as Jesus, his disciples, and Mary Magdalene had supper. Because of his great size, Sanyi took up a place on the floor in front of Christ much as he had been on the boat. As he listened to the mingling subdued sounds of the supper, the long table with Jesus at its center and everybody leaning as trees in the wind toward Him. Save for Jesus, no one spoke, and Sanyi pondered his own significance here. Unlike the other 12, Jesus had not chosen him, rather he had chosen to follow Jesus uninvited. But Jesus, so inclusive, so uniting, would have declined no one. Why was he the only one to choose Jesus? He couldn't understand his own question. He was not separate from the group, but more like the means by which the group could observe itself. He was like the third eye which one sees in totality what the other two eyes cannot. Then, Sanyi smiled to himself as the understanding unannounced suddenly appeared.

Rather than a loving Father punishing His Son for all the sins of the world yet to come, Jesus, he realized, was orchestrating all of these events, up to his own crucifixion, insisting upon it. Why else would he who could deliver himself immediately not do so? "Even the martyr is selfish," Jesus himself had said so.

Then, a peace came to him, not the final peace that was near at hand, but yet to come, but a broad and gentle peace. So, he was calm as Jesus rose to say these words: "Love one another, not as the world knows love which is to gain love in return, but as the Holy Spirit does, which is simply to love, as I have loved you, so you love the world. The world will not love you in return, but you do not need its love.

You need only to forgive the world as it is, as it is not there, this is the path out of the dream, the way out of the nightmare. All of you, all of your sad suffering brothers and sisters will make it, it has already been accomplished. Some of you this time, some of you will make it another time, but the Son of Man will make it, there is aught else he can do, for by the Grace of the Father it is already done.

Even so, the dream seems to live on, and will until the Son of Man remembers this time to laugh at his own tiny mad idea. Until then forgive the world and its trespasses. Remember, we are each of us figments of a guilt-ridden dream. We share many dreams and many lifetimes.

We are both man and woman, predator and prey, teacher and student, and master and slave. But I am telling you the truth that the time will come, and it is already here that the predator no longer hungers for the prey, and the master is free from his slaves. *Nothing real can be threatened, nothing unreal exists—herein lies the peace of God.*"

And then Jesus said, "God has no fists. Love is not a weapon, nor is salvation a bargain for obedience, that which is irrevocably granted can only be refused, but never rescinded."

This was what Sanyi learned from Jesus, 'That what is real is real, not that which is perceived to be real. A cloud does not put out the sun.'

But when Jesus told them that his time had come, despite all his teachings that the world was a meaningless dream, a pall was cast across the entire room and into the soul of each and every one of them. Judas Iscariot openly wept. Jesus went to him, slowly knelt across the table from him, and put his hand on his head. Then, he told Judas to take the money bag and return with some wine, some supplies for the festival, then to go and get a prostitute to ease his pain. So, Judas took the money bag and left.

After Judas left, much sadness remained in the room. So, Jesus took the rest of them and went to the other side of Kidron Brook. There was a garden in that place, and Jesus, the disciples, and Mary Magdalene went in. Meanwhile, Judas found the wine and the supplies for the festival and returned with them to where they had the Last Supper. When he found no one there, he became very sad. But instead of finding a prostitute as he had thought to do, now he thought to find Jesus and be with him. He knew that Jesus would likely be at the garden by Kidron Brook because the disciples had met there with him many times. But what Judas did not know is that the man whom they had passed on the road to Jerusalem was following him. The man whose treachery Jesus had perceived sent someone to fetch Nicodemus and the Romans and they followed Judas to where Jesus was.

The Romans came upon Jesus, the disciples, Mary Magdalene, and Sanyi in the garden of Gethsemane. Pointing to Jesus, Nicodemus said, "That is him there. Seize him." Whereupon the soldiers moved toward Jesus who was walking toward them saying, "I am Jesus Christ. If you are looking for him, then you have found me."

Before Sanyi even saw him Peter took up his sword and cut off the ear of one of the arresting soldiers. Sanyi understood at once that even now, in Peter's perception, Jesus needed physical protection from a physical world. But Jesus had always taught that there is no world. So, Jesus said to Peter, "Peter, put back your sword, for as I have taught, no man can attack his brother for any reason without guilt, and any man who experiences guilt shall expect punishment, and as I have also taught, of any man expecting punishment, so then shall that same man receive it."

Then, Jesus stepped forward and touched the soldier Peter had wounded on his bloody ear and healed him. Then, Sanyi upon seeing the example of Forgiveness set by Jesus, in a world of illusion, found the perfect peace of God as he stepped at last fully into his right mind.

Jesus paused and then, turning to the others, said, "Let these others go." But Nicodemus remembered what Sanyi had done to his money changers in the market, and he said to the Romans, "Let them go, all of them except that one there, the big one." And then Sanyi, as did Jesus, allowed himself to be seized and taken away by the Romans. Sanyi watched the Romans as they led Jesus away.

Jesus disappeared down the road, and Sanyi never saw Jesus again, ever. The last thing he heard was Judas wailing aloud again and again into the night. They were taking Jesus to be crucified, but they had many different plans for Sanyi. And as his ever-deepening sadness of missing Jesus mingled with the lamentation of the agony, he knew that he would endure. Sanyi still would have lamented just as much over his own, if he could've had any idea what it was. For where the money changers and Jewish authorities take prisoners, Romans take slaves.

They took Jesus firstly to Caiaphas, the high priest that year. Caiaphas questioned Jesus about his teachings. Jesus said about those teachings:

"That nothing, in this world, save for God in Heaven, is real. God is, the rest is not. Everything that you see, feel, and know is an illusion. All the world is but a dream within a dream a million times over. Jesus had never been sent to the world to suffer and pay for the sins of mankind. For mankind had no sins for which to pay. He had been sent instead to teach Forgiveness and shorten the journey that we had each of us completed before it was begun.

Caiaphas laughed, but he found no quarrel with Jesus' teachings for Jesus never said that he was Lord or a king. But Caiaphas and the Temple were also under the domain of the money changers for that is why he had turned the Temple into a market. So, Caiaphas sent Jesus, still bound up, to Pontius Pilate.

It was early in the morning when Jesus arrived at the palace of Pontius Pilate. The Jews themselves could not enter the palace of Pontius Pilate for they wanted to keep themselves ritually pure so that they might eat the Passover meal that day. So, Pontius Pilate went out to them and asked, "What do you accuse this man of?" The Jewish authorities answered, "We would not have brought him to you if his crimes were not serious."

Pontius Pilate too could find no wrong in Jesus. But Pilate was a politician and wished to appease the money changers and the high priest. Just as Jesus had taught Pontius Pilate, seeking to satisfy his own short-term perceived needs gave Jesus to the Jews. When Pilate asked the Jews what he should do with Jesus, the response was loud and immediate; they said, "Crucify him."

Then, Pontius Pilate took Jesus and had him whipped. The soldiers made a crown of thorny branches and put it on his head. And they found a purple rope and put it on him. Then, they dragged Jesus back out before the crowd and the crowd said, "Crucify him."

When the servants told Lucilla that there was someone at the door, she had been expecting Sanyi, but the man standing there instead was Judas. He was weeping and he was drunk and he dropped to his knees on the floor before her. "Where is my husband," was all she could think to ask? Through tears that he could hold back for only seconds, Judas told her that they had both been taken up by the Romans. Then Judas found his feet and left, walking into the night. What he didn't tell Lucilla, because he was unaware of it, was that after they took Jesus away the Roman spy stood up and paid Judas 30 pieces of silver that he never wanted for doing what he'd never known that he had done. When he learned that the spy had followed him to where Jesus and Sanyi were, he went to find a piece of rope and hanged himself.

Lucilla heard Judas say that Jesus and Sanyi were taken up by the Romans, but she thought he said they were taken up together. So, she went off in panic to find them. So terrified had she been of losing Sanyi to Jesus, she never thought that he could be taken by the Romans instead. One thing that she could have never foreseen was that before Jesus could be nailed to a blood soaked cross in Jerusalem, Sanyi would be shackled in the hold of the slave ship set sail for Roma, and joy was what she would never know again.

When Lucilla arrived at Pontius Pilate's palace looking for Sanyi, she did not know that they were already separated by years and thousands of miles. She could only hear the throngs screaming about Jesus, "Crucify him!"

It was not unlike the masses she would later hear in the gladiatorial arena. She moved eagerly to the front, but when she saw the bloody disarray that had become of Jesus standing next to Pontius Pilate, she fainted. It was only the sharp impact of her knee caps on the ground which woke her. She looked back up at Jesus whose blood-soaked face she could barely recognize. "How could this happen?" she asked herself. Grief for Jesus set in deep and instantly. "Who would do such a thing to him—to anyone?" But as she would see, the Romans were just beginning to torment the Christ.

Lucilla somehow managed to capture Pontius Pilate's attention. Being beautiful had some advantages, yet it was impossible to change the course of some events once set in motion. She beseeched him to stay his hand, but he was just beginning to wash them. He looked directly into her eyes as he dipped them into the bowl.

"You can wash the blood, not the deeds from your palms!" she screamed, though he didn't hear her through the vociferous din of the mob. Then, she looked at Jesus, blood was thick and pouring around his eyebrows, also oozing from the top of his head and down beside his face.

Though his lips never moved, it sounded like he said to her, "I know." She looked at her own palms, then buried her face in them and dropped to her knees unable to believe her eyes.

The guards pushed Jesus down the stone steps. She heard him groan and fall off each level to the next one with a sickening bloody thud. Jesus was thrown to the stones in the center of the Villa with a deep thump, and the people dispersed around him. Spread out on his stomach, he was whipped, but not so much as to completely incapacitate him. He still had a cross to bear.

The 13th Disciple

Then, the guards cleared a way to the fountain and took Jesus by the feet and dragged him to it. They set him upright and pushed him back against it. His head hung down, and the guards grabbed it and reset the crown of thorns upon it, digging it, twisting it deeper. Blood poured from newly opened wounds as they did this.

Next, they threw him on his hands and knees and brought the cross. They put it across his back and wrapped and tied his hands around it. They commanded Jesus to carry it, but Jesus was weak. His right leg quivered, and he put it down again.

Lucilla heard a whip whistle through the wind and ripped more flesh from Jesus's side and back. Jesus felt the pain, but his body was too weakened to react. Slowly, unsteadily, Jesus rose to his feet and slowly began to drag his cross behind him.

This, Lucilla thought, can't be possible. She was on her knees when she opened her eyes. She could not believe that so much blood had come from one man. Even the water in the fountain had turned to a blood red hue.

The 13th Disciple

She pulled back her hair and put it behind her head, and then with her skirt tried to soak up blood as though to recover and restore it to him at a later time. She could hear the sounds of the tormenting crowd following Jesus up the hill to where he would be crucified. She wanted to hide, she wanted to die, and she wanted to have never existed. Instead, she came to her feet and staggered off in pursuit of them. She walked through the streets in much the same manner as she would later leave the arena. But it was the first time she had ever known such a feeling, such a feeling as what, as despair, misery was as strange to her as it was indescribable.

She had not, in her short, sheltered life, experienced anything like it, nor wildly imagined such a thing possible. But the time would come, and was already that it would become more than familiar, it would be her entire world.

She arrived at the place where they would crucify Jesus as he was being nailed to his cross. She thought he was already dead, but when the Roman drove the spike through his palms, Jesus' galvanized body jumped again and again so that only his hands touched blood-stained timber, screaming. She had never heard a man scream before, and this was anything but human, but what else then is crucifixion?

Lucilla could feel the painful friction of every inch of the nail in her own body. The anguish didn't stop with one hand; a guard rammed another spike through the other. Standing at Jesus's feet, Lucilia thought that his suffering was so great that it encompassed the pain of all of mankind. Now, she wanted so desperately to save the same man she had thought that she hated. But what could she do?

She went toward him, but the guard pushed her back. Jesus lifted his head to look at her to speak. Then, the soldier becoming indifferent to both of them, let her through to Jesus. She put her ear to his bloody lips so that she could hear his bloody, wet voice against her ear.

His voice was a raspy whisper that said, "I can see peace instead of this." But Lucilla did not hear this for the voice was too low and weak, she understood only that the man suffered mightily and failed completely to change the world.

What she did not understand was that Jesus had said, "I come not to change the world, rather to change your Mind about the world," and lacking that understanding Jesus presently achieved a level of peace she could not hope to accomplish.

Then, the guard pushed her away again, and she hit the ground on her hands and knees, mixed with blood and sand. Unknowingly, she missed an important lesson: the thing about Jesus which she least understood and to her utmost detriment, that even while being crucified Jesus could always see aught but peace.

The soldier crossed Jesus's feet and drove the spike through them both. Initially, his body tensed, but then Jesus forgave the pain, and his body relaxed. "*The Guiltless Mind cannot suffer.*" And so it was that Jesus's mind did not suffer even when they drove the final huge silver spike through his side.

Jesus remained calm—so calm that Lucilla thought he was dead. But when they hoisted the crucifix upright, the wind blew cold from across the gorge behind it. Jesus looked up, but the sun was still in his eyes. Lucilla could not now see the pain in him.

Looking up at him, her only hope was that he would soon give up the ghost. Behind her, she saw Mary, the mother of Jesus, and Mary Magdalene were weeping.

It was a different wind, a bitter one which blew hard as it lifted Mary's dress and pushed her back. Lucilla didn't see the thunderbolt of lightning but rather sensed it raze her skin, lifting every follicle straight, then the deafening, instantaneous, sudden crash of thunder.

Other than she and Mary and the Romans there was almost no one else. For all of the multitudes whom he had saved from suffering, there was no one else to witness his. Only the jeers of the onlookers saying, "He who rescued others cannot rescue himself." Then, they threw stones at him. But Jesus understood their attack for what it truly was, a desperate *call to Love* and said, "Forgive them, Father, they know not what they do. "

She looked back up at Jesus, and the sky behind

the crucifix was black. The rain came, sudden and hard. Another thunderbolt of lightning struck diagonally across the sky, and the thunder shuttered the ground.

Jesus looked up and screamed something which she could not hear, and then he gave up the ghost. His body hung on his arms as limp as string. The rain slammed deafening against the ground and tore into their bodies, the growling shriek drowned for the time of all other things.

A guard stabbed Jesus with the spear. His body did not move but blood gushed from his side and ran down to the base of the crucifix in a torrent. It will never run dry, Lucilla thought, holding herself up against the wind as best as she could. When she looked up the entire sky was raining blood red. What she heard next was louder than even that of Christ screams, louder than anything she ever had or would ever hear again.

A thick powerful bolt of lightning electrified the air instantly before striking the crucifix. Electricity covered her skin, the wet hair on her arms rising, then she covered her head with her arms while dropping to her elbows and knees before the cross bearing the dead and crucified body of Christ.

The rain had ripped most of the clothing from her skin and from her elbows. She looked back up at the crucifix as another lightning strike lit the night, and in the electric light, all she could see for all of her efforts was a silver spike on a bloody cross. The body of Christ was gone, had completely vanished.

For a near-second, there was a dark dead calm. Then, the rain came down horizontally and ripped at her olive skin. She paid no attention to it. From her knees, she cleared the stringy strands of hair from her dark and tear shot eyes. She looked to her left at Jesus' mother, Mary, and Mary Magdalena, clutching each other in a tearful embrace. They clearly saw the body of Christ. To her right were strangers, some throwing stones at the dead body of Christ. She tried to look back up at the cross, but terror overtook her, the terror that she would not perceive the body of Christ there. She didn't leave that place until it became impossible to stay. The wind seemed to push her back down the hill, and so she went, but she never looked back upon that cross nor did she ever again witness the visage of the brutally crucified body of Christ.

Lucilla at length returned to her home soaked to the bone and shivering from the cold, informed by the servants that Judas had hanged himself. She was too enervated to manifest a single subtle reaction. Sanyi, she thought, wanting nothing, save to be in his warm touch.

So, she went to where she knew he could be. There, she found Peter, Paul, Mary Magdalene, and others. From their manner, she could tell that something was dreadfully wrong. After all that had occurred on this day, Lucilla thought that she was emotionally broke, and she could feel pain no more. But for beautiful, protected and privileged Lucilla, life, as she had known it to be, was no more; it remained for her to discover how terribly and permanently she could truly hurt.

A Slave

As Lucilla was looking up at an empty bloody cross, Sanyi awoke, gagging and coughing, as the salt water went through his nose and down his throat. He had been rendered unconscious three days prior, but the water woke his body instantly to acute panic. Blind in the darkness with lungs already burning with their own acrid expulsions, the thought that his brain excreted was, "I need to breathe."

But then Sanyi gently remembered: "I don't need anything. My body needs to breathe, yet I have all that I need and nothing else." Then at peace, he saw—with the Mind—his body from above the battlefield. By that vantage point, his body was shackled to the bulkhead of a slave ship, which was sinking. The burning in his lungs intensified as did the anguished screams of men afraid to die. But Sanyi was not afraid of anything, realizing that he was not going to die, but rather he had never been born at all.

It was then that Jesus came to him, saying, "Sanyi, this is A Course in Miracles. Please take down all that I give you."

"Jesus," Sanyi asked, "how did you get here?"

Jesus replied in a light tone, "Don't you already know? I walked."

His head dipped under the water, and he went to sleep again.

Unconscious, his head rose up and bobbled in the water against the bulkhead. The storm still raged and waves continued to break over the deck, but somehow the sailors managed to keep the ship afloat until it subsided. It took three more days for the ship to make Roma. They were three horrific days of starvation, disease, and constant threat of sinking again.

But Sanyi knew of none of it until he awoke at the coast of Ostia east of Roma. From there, he and the other slaves were taken to work at a rock quarry to the East of Roma. For most of Roma's male slaves taken near and far, there are only two possibilities: swift and certain death by attempted escape or a slow death by slave labor in the rock quarries. But for gentle Sanyi there was a third, yet unknown way.

The Quarry

To the workers concentrated there, the quarries were a place of desperation, a hopeless pit from which none could emerge. The old and feeble were fortunate and broke soon; the young and mighty took longer, providing more labor for the Romans. But starved and worked to death, no one left the quarries; sooner or later, all of their bodies broke.

For eleven months, Sanyi had watched his body withering away. When he was arrested with Jesus, he was powerful and stocky; now, he was tall, still bulky, but starving. Sanyi knew that the end for his body lay at hand deep in the bottom of this pit, and he knew it would be soon. But Sanyi also knew that he was not a body; this awareness made the apparent destruction acceptable. He thought he understood why the Christ was so joyful. It was to the degree that he was needless.

Understanding the falseness of the world means understanding the falseness of need and want and scarcity. Even now, fully expecting that he would soon awake in Heaven from which he never left, Sanyi was not distressed. He could not see through the dream or manipulate it directly as could the Christ, but by his faith. He was already free. His body was what was exhausted, and that mightily so.

Sanyi put his head down, nearly naked and cold, wondering, "How many more months? Two or maybe three?"

He knew that he would be dead soon even though they had doubled the rations the past few days, and he casually wondered why, and on this very morning, all was to be revealed, for there was already a great excitement in the camp.

Today, a Lanista would visit in search of gladiatorial talent. To some men it meant a way out, most simply meant a better way out, to all many things better than this. To all, save Sanyi. His body, though far from frail, had been greatly emaciated. He doubted that any Lanista would choose him or any of the men there for that matter.

When the Lanista did arrive, all the men stood eagerly in line, while those with the strength, hoped. But the Lanista went up the line in front, and down the line behind, selecting no one. It was like he wasn't really even lookin; no one caught his eye. But there was a man who intended to make the Lanista look.

Sanyi was watching the Lanista leave. Shockingly, he felt his head snapped back so far that all he could see was blue sky as a charging bull slammed into him from behind. When he hit the ground, his face was in the sand, but he had no idea what was happening. He was able to get his arms up underneath him, and with dirt dripping off his face, he was rolled over to see Vibius raining down punches on his face. This was odd indeed. Vibius was the only man in camp nearly as large as he; they had never spoken, and every man in camp was too overworked to engage in extraneous violence, until now.

Sanyi bucked his hips, wildly throwing Vibius forward, forcing his hands on the ground to keep himself righted. That allowed him to wiggle free, and get to his feet. Vibius stood and charged instantly, clenched tight fists at the end of wildly spinning arms that seemingly made Vibius as dangerous to himself as anyone else.

The 13th Disciple

Sanyi was able to duck under the first salvo, but he did so with his eyes closed. He could not react to Vibius' second attack. Initially standing on his feet seemed to be the correct strategy, but when Vibius granite fists dug into his ribs, Sanyi rethought the ground strategy. So, Sanyi wrapped his still powerful arms around Vibius body, arms, and gave a mighty hug. It broke Vibius like a huge oak, and as he grunted, they both crashed to the ground.

And here they were again, but this time Sanyi was on top. He had an intuitive sense that it was the superior position, but he had no idea how to take advantage of it; Vibius was wiggling free.

Reflexively, Sanyi pinned the other man's alarms under his knees, and then with his left hand, he turned the other man's head so that the right side of his face was pressed hard into the sand. This was well and good but control was tenuous. So, with a sense of urgency, Sanyi drew back his huge left fist and prepared to drive it home, but someone pulled him from the elbow from behind. It was the Lanista; he had decided to take a look after all.

The 13th Disciple

The two slaves were taken from the quarry via a single ox-drawn cart large enough to hold eight or nine average size men, just enough space to afford them a modicum of comfort.

The quarry itself was located near and already providing material for what would be, in fewer than 50 years, the most recognizable arena the world would ever know—a slaughterhouse for the ages, centered in the grand expanse of Roma. Nearly 70 years before, a slave army led by a gladiator named Spartacus had swept the length and breath of the peninsula of Italy before being finally contained by Marcus Crassus and his 50 legions. But that gladiator, seeing no way to replace the old order with aught but the new old order, never approached Roma. And here was Sanyi, at the spectacular center of the world.

For now, the cart was forced to move slowly along the roughly placed cobblestones in the broad and tempestuous via Nomentana as it thronged in the commerce of Roma. If all roads lead to Roma, then Sanyi thought they all lead first to the Nomentana.

There were votive offerings from sellers and

desperate pleas from buyers as they exchanged fruits and vegetables for animals, large and small, they traded art and artifacts, sigilla, clay figurines. They bought and sold everything imaginable. They bought and sold animals and slaves.

Perishable items were sold and immediately eaten. Prepared foods included hot sausages and pastries and chickpeas were all eaten on the run.

The Nomentana, for a length, paralleled the equally mighty Tiber. Then, it crossed and continued north through the spillage of humanity across its thresholds and onto its hard, irregular cobblestones.

All about, there were the statues and buildings, intricate monuments, fountains, and the awe-inspiring aqueducts which passed overhead on arched passageways in the sky. Sanyi looked up as he passed through the shade of one of its broad filigree archways. From its shade, he could see the sunlight flowing, cascading as the water around a dam.

When he was thrust back into the naked rays of the sun again, he found himself flowing again through the sea of humanity. And it seemed that if one more cart or mule or man or woman stepped out onto it then surely it would sink, but it held afloat and they were drawn its length flowing and mixing on the wild and winding, broad and turbulent Via Nomentana.

Vibius was obviously affected, lifted even by the perceived energy, that of the gladiator for the crowd. But Sanyi remained calm about all of this, for he remembered what Jesus had said to them in the boat on the way to Sidon. The mind seeks to make much of, especially those things which it had no experience.

Yet, it was aught but a distraction. But Sanyi would not be distracted by a world which did not exist anymore than by guilt which put it there. Knowing that nothing here was real, only that it seemed to be, he smiled, observing these thoughts as he would puppets on a stage. He could see and hear them, but not go onstage with nor become one of them. Thus, he was in the world, but not of the world.

Sanyi watched his mind thinking about its thoughts. Eventually, just as the mountain gave way to foothills and they in turn to the flat plains, so too the wide Via Nomentana finally waned into a thin strip of dirt worn into the grass. It was many hours after that the cart turned west and headed to the sea and the port city of Roma, Ostia.

Sanyi rode in the rear of the cart with his hands hugging his knees. Vibius, who had attacked him, sat front diagonally across, with his legs outstretched, suffering from cramps. The two men were not allowed to speak, so Vibius glanced askance at Sanyi for any clues, but Sanyi was deep in consideration of what had happened between them.

He had, of course, perceived Vibius's motives, but what he contemplated now were his own. The attack was a complete surprise. His body had defended itself reflexively and instinctually, the suddenness and ferocity of the attack left him no time to do otherwise. His body had taken over.

But Sanyi remembered what Jesus had said, that *"Forgiveness is still and quietly does nothing, for in a world which is nothing, nothing need be done."* So, through it all, he had been at peace. He judged neither the attack nor the attacker. In fact, he had forgiven it without judgment. At this moment, holding his knees and bumping along in the back of an ox-drawn cart with the man he had just fought, he was as indifferent to everything in the past as he was to what could be in the future.

He was even indifferent to gentle Lucilla, who would by now surely be constipated with grief, not of cruelty, rather because there was simply nothing to be done about it. So, he did nothing, remaining as indifferent to the fight as he was toward gaining his freedom in the gladiatorial arena, or dying in the rock quarry. God's will will be done. Sanyi did what Jesus had done, the only true thing there was to do: forgive as would the Holy Spirit, and so was at peace.

The two weren't permitted to speak until they stopped at a riverside, and Sanyi assured him that all was well. Both men were too parched to urinate, but Vibius' condition improved soon after he drank. Sanyi was not thirsty. He was aware, however, that his body was so. Therefore, he drank until he thought that it had enough.

When the cart finally stopped, they were almost

to the sea at Ostia, where the Tiber River split, and the water which went one way from there would not meet up again with the water that went the other way until the Tyrrhenian Sea. It was in this place that the men's new lives began.

The Ludus

When the two men arrived at the ludus, they immediately swore their oath of loyalty to their new owner of that land, a stingy little nobleman named Vettius. In their recital, the new initiates swore to be burned, beaten, kill, and die on the sands for their new owner or Dominus. They were entering the nightmarish kill or be killed world of the gladiator, deliverance from which rested firmly and solely on the Knowledge that even as Jesus had known upon the cross that he was not a body.

The ludus of Vettius was a two-story rectangular building with its longer side facing east and west. To the west beyond the walls lay the Mediterranean Sea. The main training area consisted of the sandy pit in the middle. Spaced evenly between the broad rectangular columns were the men's quarters, a hospital, baths, beds, and the kitchen which cooked up a steady diet of bland beans and barley.

Every gladiator was intensely muscled, but that muscle and, importantly, the vessels carrying blood to them were well protected by a layer of fat. Absent was much of the baroque opulence of traditional Roman architecture that was spared for the more ostentatious offices and upper floor living space of Vettius.

There was space enough up there for a large family, but Vettius lived alone. On that higher level were fountains on each of the longer sides and attendant leafy green plants, filigree art, and ornaments so filled the walls that there remained not a square inch of bare wall on the inside all going unappreciated and unnoticed by the imperious Vettius.

Outside the sand leaning against the west wall sloped gently to the sea intermingling with the mercurial coastline, rising and falling there, shaped by its daily battle with the Mediterranean sea, but that sea would never rise so high as some men hoped as to threaten the imprisoning structure itself. On the western side of the ludus, higher up, nearer to the ludus itself lay about 20 graves in a graveyard, the only way by which some of Vettius's more unfortunate investments to purchase their freedom.

The length of the western wall was relieved by

an iron gated door the breadth of 20 horses. Just above the arch on the outside wall was a large V in gold. As with all of his ostentatious wealth, Vettius paid no attention to it whenever he passed under, attended by his servants and soldiers.

Between the main gate and the graves and several feet higher than the rest of the red sand was a wide flat patio space where Vettius and guests could enjoy the sunsets and sea. But Vettius rarely had guests, reserving it instead as reward for satisfactory training effort during the day if his "Doctore" or gladiator trainer, so granted. Then, the men were permitted to gather there and discuss the day's events. During the cool of twilight, escape was unthinkable.

Romans were extremely equitable in who they selected as slaves, coming from all quarters and four corners of the Empire. There were slaves and criminals from the mines and quarries, mixed with former freemen who sold themselves to noblemen such as Vettius, to gain coin or forgive debt.

To Sanyi, the contrast could not have been starker. For men like Vibius, the baths and rubdowns were luxurious. Former freemen interpreted the same experience at the same time as imprisonment, and a loss of everything they held dear.

One group of men was ecstatic, the other dismayed. It had nothing to do with the men's pasts, and everything to do with what Jesus said: "Some will make a heaven of hell, others a hell of heaven."

Both Sanyi and Vibius were still exhausted from the rock quarry, but their training began promptly the following morning. Practicing with Vibius made one thing very clear to Sanyi, which was that, with a sword in his hand, Vibius was much better. Vibius, rather than being a political or religious prisoner, had been captured during battle by the Romans. He was a seasoned warrior, and it showed. Vibius liked Sanyi, and they trained often. Within weeks, Vibius was showing him very treacherous little tricks that only a seasoned warrior could know. Sanyi never thought of using them, yet, but he genuinely appreciated the gesture.

All of the training took place under the stern eye of the "Doctore". No one knew his name; they just called him Doctore. He was a fierce, mean Gaul who had won a wooden sword of freedom with an astonishing 23 victories in the arena, a feat not to be accomplished again.

It was said in the ludus that to be as good as Doctore was to gain one's freedom, for then surely no one could defeat you in the arena, but no one was yet as good. Under Doctore's training was intense, but not cruel. To avoid the staggering heat, training took place in two shifts of three hours each. The first was at sunrise, the second began at three hours after midday. The gladiators were a highly valued investment, and Doctore meant to maximize Vettius's returns.

Doctore was immediately impressed with Vibius, but he could not understand Sanyi. The big man was not a trained fighter, neither was he fierce, nor aggressive. But he trained with more intensity than any man he had ever seen, trained himself to exhaustion each session and was soon the best fighter for his experience that he had ever seen. Eleven months of labor in the quarries could not account for it. Such labor destroyed men rather than fortifying them.

The 13th Disciple

Once, as punishment for poor performance, Doctore trained the entire ludus to the last man standing—it was Sanyi. He was impervious to pain and would absolutely not complain. Doctore concluded he must have been a spiritual leader because his mind was stronger than any man he'd ever known. What Doctore could not know was that it was the Guiltless Mind of Sanyi from which his body drew its strength.

Still, Doctore was concerned that Sanyi might never become a gladiator. For all of his other attributes, he was clumsy, and his bulk which was an advantage in unarmed combat was a disadvantage to a smaller man swiftly wielding a sharp gladius. Vibius was exceptional; hopefully, his added tutorship might make the difference. Hopefully.

Doctore was not the only warrior to notice something about Sanyi. Vibius had himself noticed these traits. And more, Vibius had talked with and taught Sanyi, over many hours, more than any other man in the ludus.

During the cool of the dusk, some men would sit on the patio and watch the sky turning hues as the

The 13th Disciple

Roman summer sun set in the west. For all the initiates, it was a natural custom, including the former nobleman from Hispania, Asinius. Each evening the men would join, recline, and view the splendor in ardour, some wishing even to become the sky to escape the captivity of the ludus.

On one such evening, just as the sun began its ritualistic decline in the west, it's rays changed from direct to indirect as it began to sink slowly in the Mediterranean Sea. Just as the eye could look at it directly, the attendant canyons of black clouds wrapped themselves as a blanket about the flames of red and gold, then orange and violet and gold. Just before the gold was extinguished beneath the breakers to the West, Asinius spoke in awe of such beauty to Vibius and Sanyi.

But Sanyi, remembering his night with Jesus on the sea, quietly explained that such judgments were unnecessary. "The sky," he said, "is not out there. The sky is in your Mind and you do put it out there. Then, you do marvel at it, as being out there, distracting you from your Godliness within."

Vibius and Asinius stared at each other, astonished, then at Sanyi, and smiled because they understood him less than Lucilla, and yet were accepting of him the same. And Vibius became aware as Lucilla had that events in the outside world did not change Sanyi. With slavery and violence and viciousness swirling about his body in all manner of ways, nothing yet touched his Guiltless Mind. The world's affairs were as the spokes of a rapidly turning wheel, Sanyi was the center.

So, it went this way, a day would turn to dusk, dusk to dark and dark would yield again to the relentless heat of the all-consuming day, and the men would gather, and under its protective coolness to discuss the day's events and coalesce.

Three months into their training, it was time for Sanyi and Vibius to be initiated into the gladiatorial ranks, or be sent back to the quarry. The initiation was a solemn ritual. Each initiate must do battle with an established gladiator on a 10 x 10-foot platform ten feet from the ground. There, they would do battle until one of them was thrown to the ground or forced to surrender. Even Vettius, who hardly glanced askance at the training sessions of his own investments, was duty bound by custom and honor to attend.

In preparation for the event, the gladiators were spared the two grueling training sessions, held most days. Instead, the men bathed, received physical therapy, and rested. And now, the hot day had given way to dusk, a pleasant breeze from the East, and in the West there descended a blood red sky. The first two gladiators summarily dismissed first two initiates, but as Vibius scaled the ladder to the platform to fight, Doctore's hopes began to rise, and it was not in vain.

Vibius did not attack instantly as an inexperienced fighter would. Rather, he offered a low fake with his wooden blade. When the gladiator lowered his weapon to block, Vibius grabbed the wrist with his free hand and brought the point of his blade to the man's throat, holding it there, less than an inch away. In a live match, it was a sure kill. Swift, efficient, and overwhelming, it was Vibius's way.

Sanyi's way was much different. He could feel the ladder creek under his enormous weight as he climbed up to the platform to fight. Instead of being the aggressor, it was the gladiator who confidently attacked. Sanyi blocked the thrust with his blade but was slow. With his thrust blocked, the gladiator hit Sanyi hard in the face with the butt of his weapon in a back fist motion. But it put him in too close.

With blood flowing from above his eye, Sanyi was able to wrap both of the gladiator's arms in his free left arm from behind. Then, as if pointing to himself, he was able to bring his wooden gladius up to the gladiator's throat and hold it there. In the arena, it would have forced the gladiator to appeal. Although he was indifferent to his fate, Sanyi had won and would be a gladiator.

There was a ritual whereby the new gladiators were gathered in the square and honored by the Doctore, the other gladiators, and then by Vettius. This event represents the first indication of a return on his investment.

At this time Sanyi, politely expressed all of the correct sentiments, as the world would have him do, but it did bring back to mind one of Jesus's most difficult lessons, that to the dreaming Son of Man, praise was at least as dangerous as punishment. The io would use praise and love, and the appearance of joy to keep the Son distracted and dreaming. Of any kind or degree, judgment was equally distracting to the Son of Man, and this Son gently determined not to be deceived.

Also, the new gladiators received their arena names. Sanyi would be called Pompilli, and then they would be branded with the V for Vettius emblazoned on their right forearms. Virtually, every man let up a gruff, grudging scream, the pain too great to be contained within the body, but at his appointed time, Pompilli did as had Christ upon the cross and put peace to the pain in his arm. When the branding was concluded, Pompilli had not uttered a single sound, though his body reacted violently. He was dizzy, rising to his feet after the procedure which had put a raised ugly V where before had been bare skin.

After, Sanyi joined Asinius and Vibius on the patio lying on their backs looking at the stars. "We are looking at the stars inside of our heads?" Asinius asked jokingly.

The 13th Disciple

"Yes, I am seeing stars inside of my own head, even when I close my eyes,"Sanyi replied, holding a blood soaked cloth to his bleeding eye as he sat down with a groan. All three men laughed.

"Hispania is out there somewhere," Asinius said, pointing to the west. "And were I to be there, I would be a king."

"But you were captured instead," Vibius retorted. "You could have fought to the death or killed yourself, but you allowed yourself be captured."

Asinius grew agitated at the obvious truth. To Asinius, the world was unfair, as he was royalty forced into slavery. Sanyi correctly noted that it was not being captured that distressed Asinius, but his judgment that something was unfair about it, his judgment of it at all.

In the kill or be killed world of Vibius, the world was just as it should be: ruthless, and unforgiving. By not judging it, the entire world failed to even annoy him. In fact, Sanyi noticed that mighty Vibius judged Asinius much more than he did the Romans, saying, "That is why he is so arrogant," while pointing at Asinius.

"His arrogance is your judgment of the form of his pain," Sanyi said, still smiling with a gash over his eye, but not his arm. "But the true cause is his false belief in guilt of separation from the source. It is the true cause of the world's pain, the only cause."

Asinius and Vibius stared at each other in questioning puzzlement, laughed, and looked back up at the sky.

One night, shortly after their initiation, Vibius and Sanyi were summoned from their quarters and taken to a party of some Roman nobleman in the profusive upper portion of Vettius ludus. When the guard informed them that some important Romans wanted to meet them, Vibius became agitated and suspicious, while Sanyi was as always, unaware of lurking treachery, but untouchable in his right Mind.

The guards led them down too long rows of head high torches, that disperse light in waves rather than rays, which led to a lavish spread on the far end. Sanyi was surprised to see Vettius in attendance among the unknown number of noblemen. It was the first time he'd seen him up close.

Vibius already knew what was afoot and paid no attention to the scowling old man. They were each handed a sword and instructed to prepare themselves to do battle.

Vibius had felt this way many times before, blindsided, helpless. The first time was when he was eight, and he watched in helpless horror as his father was killed on the battlefield. He was hiding with his mother, not fully comprehending, as she beseeched the gods to let her see her husband just once more. They did not oblige. The battle had gone badly for their side.

Vibius' father had come on horseback to rescue them, but so had the enemy tribe. He had barely dismounted when an arrow found him in the middle of the back, and he fell dead with a muffled thud in the grass.

Is that all? little Vibius wondered. He could still hear the hiss of the arrow even though it was buried firmly between his father's shoulder blades. Just one final gasp, where did his father go? Tonight would be like that all over again. Now Sanyi did perceive it too. He had not reasoned it out as Vibius had; rather, it had been revealed to him.

It was an inner certainty that one of them would die by the hand of the other. How he wanted to console his friend, how he wanted to tell him, how unnecessary his anguish was, and how much it didn't matter. But it was Vibius who took control of the situation. They were allowed 10 minutes to stretch and prepare during which Vibius instructed Sanyi to fight as absolutely hard as he could. The reasoning was sound; if the men put on an entertaining bout, the loser's appeal was more likely to be granted.

As the men proceeded to the center of the floor to fight, the only flaw Vibius could find in his plan was whether the big man would respond with the requisite aggression and fury; such fears were quickly allied.

Before he could even get his sword pointed straight, the big man was charging him, thrust, thrust, horizontal slash, thrust, and vertical slash, thrust. All the while bringing his massive bulk forward at a speed

Vibius had never imagined he possessed. Now, Vibius found his sword arm pinned between his own body and Sanyi's.

Sanyi's sword arm, however, was quite free, which posed a problem for Sanyi as well. The last thing that Sanyi wanted to do was kill his friend. In that same instant Vibius connected with a stern left hook, Sanyi shoved with all his might, freeing his friend's sword arm, but sending him in mid-air, crashing and sliding across the floor on the other side of the room.

Spectators scattered as Sanyi followed up. Vibius escaped the first downward slash which clunked harmlessly into the stone floor, by rolling to his right. Sanyi followed up with a second downward slash that Vibius partially blocked and by rolling to his left was able to stand. Vibius felt his counter-attack stopped from behind, by the big dark hand of Doctore, who proceeded instantly between the two men to keep them separate. It had worked; the crowd was mightily pleased, and Vettius was proud as a peacock. Rather than let them destroy the palace, he stopped the fight.

As soon as he was breathing normally, the first

curious thought Sanyi had was that his premonition had not been fulfilled, that one would die at the hands of the other; the next one was, *Where is Vibius?*

It was just now he noticed that the Roman guards were returning him to the gladiator's restricted area of the ludus alone. Once safely returned there, Doctore informed him that Vibius had been sold. So, after all the invented drama, it was just a demonstration—just business. Had he known Vettius, it would make perfect sense to him. As Doctore would later inform him, Vettius would've never pitted two of his investments against each other. But Pompilli was soon to know Vettius well enough for himself.

Vibius was astonished, how easy it had been for him to forget that he was chattel. Pompilli, firmly ensconced in his right Mind, experienced the apparent separation from his friend differently; he did not partake of the io's offering of loneliness and isolation. Instead he used the Holy Spirit Vision to realize that no separation had really taken place, that in Heaven they were both truly one with God.

He missed his friend just as fiercely, but in a

completely different manner, one that brought deep joy to him for each of the many memories of his friend. The mock battles during training, the long talks at night. No sorrow—just joy. *"Some men make heaven from Hell, others make hell from heaven."*

If Pompilli had any regrets, it was that he had never taken Vibius to Jesus in this lifetime. It was not so much like regret as wondering what if.

Not bad, Doctore thought, as Pompilli deflected the opponent's gladius in a crescent-shaped block, then retraced the same arc, and with his fist at the level of his own chin and blade vertical, sliced through the throat. The only sounds were banging of the wooden swords and the muffled sound of Pompilli's own into the opponent's flesh. Not bad at all.

Vibius had been gone for six weeks, and it seemed as though Sanyi had suddenly learned everything he taught him, on top of Doctore's own teachings. Most men learned their lessons little at a time; some learned them all at once. Doctore had seen this before, but Pompilli was the most extreme.

Now, Doctore considered Pompilli worthy of himself, and he was set to let the big man from Judea know it. Doctore had a way of moving without being seen. It could only be experienced, all the men talked about it in a mystified manner, even Vibius. Now, Sanyi saw that they were right.

Most men lean, shift their weight ever so slightly, or flinch just before they attack, but not Doctore. Doctore hit Sanyi on the head from ten feet away before he could blink. There in the hot sun, on the burning sand, Doctore went at him, using the very same attack again and again and again. A choppy 45 ° diagonal cut, at Pompilli, that no man could catch up to.

"Block me," Doctore demanded, attacking again and again with his right arm like the spokes of a chariot.

At once, Pompilli did successfully block the attack while, at the same instant, experienced the cracking of the wooden sword against his skull.

Again and again, Doctore attacked, and Pompilli never feigned, never shied away. Doctore was impressed, experiencing that he was being blocked in nearly half of his attempts, but he could not have known that Pompilli experienced every outcome of each attack. But in either outcome of each, in all the many worlds there, in each of them, it was time for Pompilli's first contest, but not before he came face to face with his Dominus.

He had not seen Vettius for nearly two months since the night he fought Vibius at the party held for noblemen, and then only scantly, this was his first meeting with his master. Now, standing in his office, watching the little man toil at the desk, Pompilli wondered if he would ever speak to him.

It was easy to see why the men thought he was so mean and greedy. He was not unlike the money changers. But Pompilli remembered what Jesus had said of them: "We all act in service of our own perceived needs." It was a lesson that Vettius would bring Pompilli back to.

Once, as they were gathered around, Jesus said to Peter, who had his legs folded in front of him, "Why are you sitting in that way?" Peter, perplexed, wondered what profound teaching would come from such an innocuously posed question and struggled to respond.

So, Jesus answered for him, saying, "You are sitting in such a manner because it pleases you to do so. You will change position as soon as you deem another more suitable." And as if unable to help himself, Peter stretched out his legs and put the palms of his hands on the ground behind him. Everyone laughed, including Peter.

And Jesus said, "Judge neither the villainous nor the virtuous, for each acts selfishly as the other, and trust not your own good intentions. It is not possible for any to act in opposition to his perceived needs. We are all equally selfish, we are all totally selfish. Concentrate, therefore, not on good deeds in the world but rather on proper thoughts in your mind."

The 13th Disciple

Vettius

"I wish to congratulate you on your progress," he at long length offered. "Doctore informs me you're progressing, and your fine battle with Vibius shows me it's true."

Pompilli was shocked to hear such a booming, baritone voice from such a diminutive frame. It was clear that this was a man who carried authority, who was accustomed to giving orders and having them obeyed, to having his way. It was also clear, by the way, he had yet to look up at Pompilli, that he was possessed of ample portions of that noble Roman virtue of arrogance. *In reality, we all suffer equally from the thought of separation, which hides itself in many different forms in the dream.*

Vettius suffered from one of the cruelest hoaxes. Vettius stopped what he was doing, placed both of his palms flat on the table, and, staring blankly at the space between them, remembered—no, more relived than remembered—foot races with his brother in childhood.

Growing up as the youngest son of a powerful

The 13th Disciple

Roman nobleman, Vettius labored under a far more crushing weight; he could never overcome his older brother, Tiberius, nor live up to his father's utterly unrealizable expectations, and yet mightily did he try.

He had been set to war against Tiberius from almost the day he was born. Tiberius was older, bigger, stronger, and by far the more suitable heir to his father's fortune. Tiberius was exemplary of everything that a noble child should be, while Vettius—smaller, weaker, and timid—was what remained.

His earliest memories were of playing gladiatorial bouts against Tiberius, which he always lost. Later, as a small boy, he would lose foot races as well. The boys would race around the outer walls of this very villa with their father looking one way as they took off, then the opposite as they returned. But there was never any doubt as to which boy would return first, and Tiberius always finished before Vettius could be even seen running wearily around that far corner.

Growing up in such a way made him believe that he hated Tiberius when he really loathed his oppressive father. But young boys do not despise their father. So, deep in places that he did not know of, little Vettius began hating himself and condemning his brother; the io's methods are subtle.

Vettius became steeped deeper still in the lies his mind told him on the day when his father punched Tiberius in the face as punishment for not winning by a large enough margin. His father then turned and left, abandoning them bloody and dishonored to endure their mutual shame alone. But their father's sons did not endure their shame alone; they rather embraced it together.

Tiberius was still lying face down in the sand with blood streaming from a gash high on his forehead, which made it appear that his entire face was a mask of blood. Vettius weeping, dropped to his knees at his brother's side and helped him to sit. With Tiberius leaning on his shoulder, it was all he could do to hold him up, but with all his might hold him up he did. Tiberius groaned, but he never shed a tear, and between the two of them, they built one fortress against their father.

The following day, Vettius again tried mightily

to keep up with his brother. He saw his Tiberius disappear around the first corner, but when he cleared the third corner, Vettius found Tiberius standing there, waiting. Together, the two brothers jogged around the last corner and stopped finally in front of their father.

Their father said not a word, rather calculated coldly and cruelly. He had too much invested in Tiberius to strike him down again. Without the slightest warning, he backhanded Vettius across the face, turned sharply, and left them again. Vettius could not forget that moment for years. He remembered the ringing in his ears and warm feeling in his head, but not his feet leaving the ground nor his tiny body flopping down hard. This time, it was Tiberius helping his battered brother.

Their father continued pitting the brothers against each other. The intention was to build Tiberius's confidence so that when he competed against the sons of other noblemen, he would have the mental advantage. This tactic didn't take account of Vettius at all. Even with the aid of Tiberius not defeating him as completely as he could, Vettius began not so much to enjoy losing but to become comfortable with it. And as the beatings continued, his mind told him, "You deserve this. But a small boy's spirit isn't killed by a single blow; boys are resilient. It takes many blows to break him. Once broken, however, no amount can put that which was made wrong to right."

Tiberius was set for greater glory. At 11 years old, he had already been fighting against grown men in his father's sandy arena. But now, as set forth by his father, came his greatest test. He was placed alone in a large patio with high walls with a spear in his hands and a large male lion. It seemed obvious now that he should have perceived his father's treachery. He had been training against a mock lion for several months now. His father had hired two soldiers to train him, but here he stood, alone and frightened with his spear that may as well have been a twig.

When the lion roared menacingly, Tiberius could detect no discernible confidence gained by all the victories over Vettius. Their fathers plan failed miserably. The beast's foul breath wafted through the air and assailed his nostrils. He was stunned to be standing here now with his father and his trainers looking down from high above, too far away to help if needed. It was needed.

The lion attacked and mauled him, but Tiberius, all alone with his spear, struck the beast in the eye socket and killed it. The lion died on the bloody marble patio floor. Tiberius died in his bed the following day.

Vettius who had been noticed by his parents as only the darkness against which Tiberius shined became now completely invisible. And while his father descended into grief, it was he who lost a brother, an ally, and a friend. Maybe, he thought, maybe now they will leave me alone. To a small boy alone in the world, the wish was not unreasonable, but it was the first brick in the wall. It was the first instant when Vettius cared about only Vettius.

For Vettius, it would have been better than he remained so. But his parents did not honor the silent wishes; they simply transferred their ambitions. The darkness he had been into an all-encompassing eclipse, enough light for two sons.

The 13th Disciple

Vettius began spending much time around his father's gladiators. The same man who dedicated his life to crushing him into the sand now dedicated himself to reach down and pick him back up. But small boys are not like puzzles; rather, they are more like a sheet of glass. Once broken they can never be fully repaired. Some pieces never fit, some shards are always missing. And Vettius the small boy who would always crave his father's attention never received, now despised it being heaped profusely upon him some cuts are just too deep; younger wounds never heal.

Before his 13th birthday, Vettius knew all the techniques of all the styles of gladiators. But to him, they were just empty movements, just like the steps he took walking. What Vettius needed to learn from his father was not how to be a gladiator—he could never be one—but the gladiatorial industry, the business of a ludus.

Vettius watched his father's fortunes rise on the blood tide of his gladiator's victories. The investment of blood and coin paid dividends in fame that his father could cash in political clout, the unparalleled clout of greatest power. Perceiving scarcity on the inside he sought fulfillment from without, his curse becoming his remaining son's heritage.

At 15, Vettius was thrust into position of charge when it was his father's turn to host the gladiatorial games. As unnatural and awkward as he was physically, he was as adept and capable as an administrator. It was he who arranged the competitions among combatants against each other in such a way that his father's had the best chance of victory. He wrote the stories which the gladiators fought to. He promoted the event nearly a year in advance so that by the time his father dropped the white linen to commence the games, that name was on the tip of every Roman's tongue.

Vettius' games began with a roar. Blood sprang freely from the gladiator's veins, his father was a staggering success, and Vettius himself, always from behind-the-scenes, had come of age.

The coming-of-age arrived with conflict and confusion. Vettius was dismayed to realize that he paradoxically adored the adoration of the man who had murdered his brother. And of that brother who surely

The 13th Disciple

must have been sacrificed then to procure his success now. If it were that he could change it all again, would he? He did not think so. He knew so.

The roars of the crowd were for his gladiators, however, coin and the attendant political power was now for him alone. He was not envious, rather contemptuous of the gladiators, and he believed that he had the right to sacrifice them to the crowd and gain its crucial favor.

And because his father preferred leisure in this stage of his life, he granted to his only remaining son the entirety of his land and estate.

Vettius now literally had as much control of his father's fate as he did a gladiator's, and he was only 15. Vettius acted almost exclusively for Vettius, but when he saw his father's rival Augustus stagger alone, drunkenly into the streets, Vettius saw a way to act exclusively for himself.

Augustus was drunk, attempting to comfort himself for he had wagered much on the games of the house of Vettius and lost much in coin to that same house with that suffrage extending accordingly and much more importantly to politics. The younger Vettius was positively beseeched by Augustus for relief of debt. In a seemingly benevolent deed, Vettius arranged to negotiate repayment for Augustus.

And it was obscenely easy to lure his unsuspecting father to Augustus with the expectation of contracting humiliating terms for Augustus. As a reward for putting on the games, his father had let him remain in charge of all of the affairs of the house of Vettius. While he did forgive the most debilitating aspects of Augustus's debt, all the coin repaid to the house of Vettius was to be paid to that house's youngest member.

Vettius was delighted by the shock and betrayal that was the last lingering expression marking his father's face. Yet, he remembered picking his brothers bleeding face out of the sand, helpless and diminished. But now, here he stood, master of his father's house with Augustus's indebtedness too. He could not help feeling that now that the circle had been completed. But it wasn't a circle that was finished; rather, it was aught but the final brick in the wall, the decisive crushing of the gentle spirit of a small boy into the dirt. As a seed becomes a tree and is a seed no more, so it is when a small boy becomes an angry man. From henceforth, Vettius acted solely on behalf of Vettius.

"Pompilli, let me come directly to the point." Pompilli, expecting nothing less, stood dutifully silent as the little man continued, "Doctore wants you to fight in some of the smaller venues outside of Roma, while I wish to maximize my profits by having you fight in more lucrative events in Roma. But I want to know what you think."

Pompilli was still struggling with the Roman accent, but it was obvious that the little man with the big voice was lying. *He couldn't care less for me*, Pompilli thought, *or my needs for that matter*. But Pompilli was already at peace with itl it was forgiven, which was Jesus's way of making himself impervious to the world and its horrors.

The situation before him now was beyond tricky in worldly terms, for it would indeed be impossible to satisfy both his Dominus and his Doctore. "Well,

Pompilli?" he demanded. "Are you up to it?"

"Dominus," he began, "Doctore is a master instructor. It would be wise to obey his counsel, nor would I be profitable to you, dead after the first match." Pompilli had dutifully kept his eyes down to the floor, but now, reflexively, irresistibly, he raised them to examine his Dominus.

So, this was the stingy little ludenista all the men hated so. Vettius glared up scornfully as he prepared a scolding, but it was never delivered. The response was polite and proper and appropriate for the situation, but it simply was not the one he wanted. So, he refrained, paused from writing, and looked at Pompilli simply to size him up.

So, this was the gladiator Vettius had heard so much about, his gladiator, the one with such a different way, the one who was a follower of a crucified rabbi named Christ.

Pompilli, realizing his mistake, offered up his obedience, saying, "Dominus, your will be done of course."

The 13th Disciple

"Of course Pompilli," Vettius replied, "of course."

The silence was long, but for Pompilli nothing was uncomfortable. His Dominus demanded not a response, rather the correct one. He could understand why the gladiators distrusted and disrespected him so, but Pompilli remembered what Jesus had said, "Forgiveness is still and quietly does nothing."

He was not disquieted in the least by the little man who could have ended his body's life on the spot, at the wave of whose small hand half a dozen Roman soldiers would have instantly impaled him with their spears. "I am prepared to do your glory, Dominus," was the reply. Pompilli had understood, and Vettius was appeased.

Then, Vettius asked, "Is there anything I can get for you?"

"I have a wife in Judea," Pompilli said halfheartedly, thinking that it was too much to ask.

But Vettius replied without hesitation, "If you are alive, I will bring her to you."

There it was again, Pompilli noticed. He did not say would try to bring her, rather he would bring her. The man was accustomed to getting what he wanted. So, he would see his wife again if he was alive.

"Your Latin is good, but you seem to have difficulty with our accent. You will improve," Vettius added.

Pompilli nodded in agreement before understanding the statement for the accent. When he did, he smiled to himself. Jesus taught that language was aught but symbols of symbols. "There are no words in Heaven," Jesus had said, nor need of them.

Vettius looked back down at his table, where his flattened palms remained on its surface and made straight his arms, then relaxed and looked up at his gladiator.

He had much to ponder about in this regard. Used correctly, he could win much coin with a minimum of risk. But he wanted more than just a coin or even political profit from this particular investment. Until now, these were his guiding principles, his only principles regarding his investments in gladiators, but he was growing weary and older. Weary of losing gladiators in their prime and worried about much more than that which was likely to guide him upwards toward the pillars of the Senate, Vettius was growing fearful of his place in the afterlife. Perhaps, his Doctore was right. Though impervious to the cost in coin, perhaps, he was not maximizing on the quality of his capital. Perhaps, he could let his ludus mature, strengthen, rather than sacrificing one for the short-term approval of the blood lustful and mercurial crowd. How he had come to despise their hold over him. So, from this particular gladiator, he desired more than arena winnings, much more.

From this, he would gain what even his mighty father and superior brother could not: acceptance into the elite of Roman society, true power, political power, and a place above them in the afterlife. No less than this he demanded for himself, of Pompilli. Vettius, never looking up, considered all these things carefully, then dismissed the gladiator.

Pompilli had been dismissed and returned to his

quarters. There, he stretched out his big body on its back, put his hand under his head, and bent one of his massive knees. He considered his Dominus. The little man was obviously a liar, and he would gladly sacrifice his life for short-term profit.

Before Jesus, Sanyi had little patience for liars; they even made him ill, the illness of judgment. But now, nothing made him uncomfortable. He remembered Judas and the way they did distrust him. Perhaps, Christ distrusted him also, but Judas too had his lessons to learn. It was also obvious that Vettius was a quick student. He also knew he was more interested in Jesus than himself, but as yet not why; there could be many reasons. It was true what the others had said, and now he was sure that he would likely die in the arena at the greedy hands of Vettius. He considered all these things quickly, then the gladiator closed his eyes and fell into a deep comfortable sleep.

The 13th Disciple

The First Contest

The night before his first contest, Sanyi received an initial lesson in the full decadence of the Roman orgy. There were nude women dancing in pits on the marble floors, the gladiators were permitted to feast, drink wine, and have sex with wealthy noble women who could not wait to get their hands on them. It was debaucherous, but most of the gladiators welcomed the diversion, from the looming threat behind tomorrow's sun.

Tonight, there was only one who was unappreciative; he was Asinius, the nobleman captured in Hispania, the eastern part of the empire. Asinius told Sanyi, "The gods would punish the impure, who indulge in excess."

Sanyi thought, *Then the gods must punish us all, for we each indulge completely in our own needs, the sinner and the saint are equally virtuous.*

"Tomorrow, they will all die," Asinius said.

Sanyi knew that Asinius too was satisfying his needs, and even as he moved away to get some wine for himself, he did so not with judgment but remembered fondly when Jesus had turned the water into wine.

Smiling, he thought how much Vibius would enjoy such frolic as this. Joyfully, he thought of Lucilla. Anathema to some, bewildering to all, but blissful was the only ways he could think of things, the only way he could long for those loved, but not close, the only way he could be, it was what he was, what he had known he was since knowing Jesus.

Following the frolic of that night, Sanyi stretched out on the bed in his cell, thinking not about tomorrow, but the evening as it was here in this room, his cell. Then, he remembered Lucilla. He thought of her not in terms of the past, which does not exist, rather as blooming in blazing portraits, erupting through the sweeping river of time and the eternal now.

And he lived on each of those portraits to re-experience each as though he lived it for the first time again. Contented, Pompilli fell into a deep sleep.

He was awakened the following morning by a Roman guard clanging at the gate of his cell. Behind

The 13th Disciple

the guard was Doctore. Doctore made sure to let the men sleep as long as possible. He wanted to minimize their wait and its strain on their nerves. This was unnecessary for Pompilli.

When all of Vettius's gladiators had gathered, Doctore led them into the arena. There, they paired off and did light sparring with each other. Across the arena, gladiators from the other ludus did the same. It served as a warm-up for the gladiators, and a snack before blood, for the crowd.

For ruling noblemen like Vettius, pleasing the crowd was everything. Individuals were of no importance at all, but controlling the imagination of the collective was the key to power. To a lanista like Vettius, the games meant nothing; the power he could garner from them meant all. He was as nervous as any of his investments.

When the warm-ups were concluded, all for gladiators could do was return to the areas and wait. Asinius was the first to fight. Sanyi did not watch the fight; he focused on the crowd. Although the contest lasted a full 25 minutes, the only parts Sanyi saw of it

The 13th Disciple

was Asinius's appeal to Julius Lentulus and Vettius. The fight was well contested by both men, and the crowd had been appeased. It was Lentulu's games, and he was given to mercy, but Vettius was not. So, with the thumb pointed toward his own throat, Vettius gave the signal, and Asinius was no more.

A dark pall was cast instantly over all the gladiators. Such was the nature of Vettius, their Domina, and their owner. Sanyi made no judgments, nor was he affected by the elements of a dream. He was to fight next.

As Pompilli emerged from the shade inside to the unsheltered blazing sand of the arena floor, he was not invested in his fate. Rather curious, he shared one but not both of Christ's pre-crucifixion sentiments. The glare cut his eyes like glass, forcing him to squint hard. He was aware that the shards of light and furnace of heat made the sun enemy to both men.

Sanyi was a secutore, a heavyweight, and he was fighting Brutus, a Samnite with three victories in the arena. The three men in the arena—two gladiators and a referee—acknowledged the sponsor. The gladiators faced each other, and the referee signaled the bout to begin. Sanyi was fighting for his life.

The two men circled first. The Samnites was another heavyweight but slightly less heavily armored. Pompilli knew that a long fight was not to his advantage. However, as he circled the arena with the din of the intoxicated crowd surrounding, there appeared to be no opening to his opponent. Keeping his shield tight, Sanyi shuffled directly in, making a vain stab with his gladius that attacked only Brutus's shield.

He heard Doctore. In practice, Doctore was severe to the point of cruelness but not beyond it. He was mercilessly critical, and only the best-executed techniques went unpunished. But today, Doctore was uncritical, forgiving, bellowing advice in an even, encouraging tone. "Try to open him up," was the part of what Doctore had proffered, and it seemed like a good idea.

Brutus moved in with a couple of diagonal cuts, one cutting downwards toward the left, followed rapidly by one downward toward the right. Pompilli blocked them both. But as Brutus retreated, he stabbed back at the giant opponent who was trained to attack any retreating fighter. Additionally, he cleverly changed the timing and made a deliberately slower attack with the horizontal stab, catching Pompilli with his shield up and sword arm extended in a wimping miss. The point of Brutus's blade punctured Pompilli's gut and drew blood. Pompilli withdrew and circled around until he felt recovered. Confused, Pompilli circled as Brutus moved in. As Brutus got closer, Pompilli lashed out with a horizontal cut at Brutus's exposed forehead because of his shield held too low.

To no avail, Brutus quickly and easily bent his knees, and the errant gladius wooshed overhead. His errant attack failed to open Brutus up, and, worst of all, Pompilli failed to retreat after his attack. He was flat-footed as Brutus moved in.

Brutus's sword delivered a slashing diagonal cut, hitting Pompilli hard in the head and bending his neck at a 90° angle, sending him stumbling backward. Then, Pompilli noticed something. After weeks of training with Doctore, Brutus seemed to be moving in time slowed down. In that time slowed down motion,

Pompilli could see that Brutus dropped his shield ever so slightly just before he attacked.

Brutus did attack with a barrage of cuts which were swift and sure, and it required all of his speed and attention. But Pompilli successfully endured the onslaught with only a superficial gash to his left shoulder. Confidently, Brutus closed the distance for another attack. Pompilli pulled his shield close, with the tip of his blade pointed at the Samnite's throat. Then, flat-footed, Pompilli waited.

Doctore thought that Pompilli was dead. Instead, Brutus dropped his shield as anticipated. Pompilli pushed it all the way down with his own shield, and, with lightning speed, thrust the tip of his gladius against his opponent's helmet. It entered the left eye socket and snapped the man's head to the right in a twisting motion. In agony, Brutus dropped his sword and shield and writhed on the ground holding his eye. Brutus never appealed, and it was unnecessary. Vettius signaled the referee to stop the fight, and the match was over. Pompilli had won.

The following morning, they buried Asinius, in

The 13th Disciple

a sandy graveyard outside of the ludus. His body was wrapped in white linen, and he was carried on a stretcher from the ludus to his grave. Burial was another solemn ritual for the gladiators. Another mechanism by which they bestowed respect and honor upon each other. Another ointment to the open wound of slavery.

Asinius had no family in Italy, so all the gladiators together bought his gravestone. Thousands of years later, the gravestones would be the treasure troves to archaeologists.

Pompilli noticed he can just see the ocean off to the horizon. He knew that Asinius would have approved of being buried near the ocean, toward the setting sun.

Returning to the ludus, the men were sad about the death of one of them. Even if he had been aggravating, he was still one of them. But in total, Vettius had done well, having only lost Asinius, and everyone else won.

Pompilli, as usual, was not saddened, having only happy memories of Asinius, having never judged him, secure in the knowledge that not only was Asinius not really gone but that he had never really been. But even after the quarry, after the time spent in the ludus and just risking his life in his first, even so far into his right Mind, there was one worldly thing for which his body was completely unprepared; it was the astonishing outline from the side perspective of the petite and lovely Lucilla. Indeed, Vettius was well versed in the language of reward and punishment.

She stood there in the archway of the gate to the villa, pestering one of the soldiers as to his whereabouts which the soldier had already informed her he knew nothing about. But if not for her beauty, the soldier would have arrested her already.

Even at a distance and under the shade, he could not mistake her outline. So absorbed was she in interrogating the guard that she did not see him until he was almost close enough to touch. She didn't so much see as feel his presence about her at first. As everything seemed quiet around her, she looked down at her feet for fear of what she may find behind her, Pompilli slowed his advance, and everything for a time slowed for him. It was a feeling he had never forgotten, one he could never take for granted: her tiny body against his, her soft skin and marble hands. He stood there, holding her with her face buried in his chest, and he stroked her hair gently as she sobbed. He remembered what a child she was, he remembered how he loved her, but was still surprised by how sublime she now felt.

When she finally looked up, he could brush the hair away from her cheek and the tears from her eyes. He looked long into them before kissing her. Then, he looked at her again, and there were no words. This was a potent portion of the dream. He noticed now that being a good husband toward his wife, doing the best for her that a slave could, he understood that the pain of separation cut her deeply. She believed it was real, yet even for her, he did not surrender the peace of God. Further, that peace still covered the entirety of the Sonship, Romans and Vettius included. It was the surest sign that he was still in his right mind.

But on the worldly level, as the growing impatient Roman hurried them in, he was only too happy to comply. With his winnings, Vettius provisioned a private room for Pompilli in the ludus, and one for Lucillia in the city. It was to the one in the ludus that he ushered his wife now.

Reunion

After so long, Lucilla hadn't nearly enough time to adjust. Sanyi still didn't seem real to her, not as real as the sounds of combat clangoring up through the window from the ludus down below.

A half-oval window, through which the fading daylight feebly cast out the remaining darkness, was the sole source of light after he closed the solid wood door. Stone ran from wooden floor to the wooden ceiling which her husband's huge frame nearly scraped. When she turned so that the closing door was behind her, she beheld a rectangle containing a small writing desk on her left. There was no no chair; Sanyi was too big for one. At the opposite end was a bed. She did not want him to take her to it yet. She had her prize, but not in perpetuity. She could not yet relax into what was, as it was now.

Her defenses against joy relented stubbornly. Her resistance to love acquiesced not at all. She plopped rather than sat on the bed. Staring at her hands on her knees, she heard her heavy bag falling against some wall or corner or other having just been casually cast there by her husband. As he came to her, she relaxed even though what followed couldn't help but be etiolated by the constant whisper of the subtle and deceitful io.

He sat gently beside her, and the pillow of the mattress caved in bringing her to him. He who was ready for her, while she already regretted the future moment when she would be torn from him. When and only when she could support the io's way of thinking, temporarily at least, no longer, only then did she fall into his loins and allow joy to ensue.

Unlike the unencumbered peace of their lovemaking before their separation, before his capture, her passion was panicked, fearful, and impossibly apprehensive. Rather than live in the lovemaking of the moment, she sought to save it, to keep it like a coin to spend again and again at a later date. So, it was that she sought desperately to hold on to that which cannot be grasped, digging her nails into his back again and again and again.

For him, it was the simplest they had ever had.

The 13th Disciple

Pompilli could always enjoy the moment, any moment, even more than could Sanyi. It was a skill he had honed with Jesus, and practiced expertly now, enjoying her exquisite, long-missed, and mightily desired body in full absence of the fear of the near and unreal future, that she would soon be taken from him. Rather, he took her in his huge hands, took in every delicious drop of her, living only in the purity of the moment. For a long time, there were no words.

When they finally spoke, though three years apart, it was as familiar as yesterday. Sanyi was sprawled out on his side as Lucilla sat up cross-legged, looking at him. She seemed almost embarrassed now, halfheartedly giggled and spoken to his shoulder when she did speak to him.

Although she was certain that he had endured unspeakable horrors, visible scars were on his face and body, still, she wanted desperately to know that nothing really horrendous had happened to him. She tried to believe in the reality that wasn't.

She looked at him, his entire body. My big gentle husband is so strong, she thought. "How do you do it?" she asked. "How do you endure all this pain and suffrage?"

He understood that it was truly her suffrage about which she spoke. But he spontaneously surrendered the introspective glance, which she instantly recalled meant that, right now, he was focusing everything on her every word, on her very next word.

"I was told that just yesterday you killed a man, yet you could have been killed yourself. When I saw you, you were just returning from a funeral of your friend. I don't understand how you can go on another day in this place, and you are called Pompilli now? I hate Roma, and I will never call you such. To me, you are as you have always been—Sanyi. I'm sure I should have killed myself long ago." She finished her statement weeping.

Seeing her in such a state, he decided to keep secret his time in the quarry as such knowledge would surely incapacitate her. He understood again, but more deeply, how much she desperately needed him and that he already had everything he needed and nothing else.

It was he understood also that was what everyone found in Christ, why they all craved to be near him, while Christ craved nothing.

How simple it seemed to him now. Everyone has everything they need; they simply have to surrender the excess, to drop to the ground that which is so heavy and have it waft lightly up as mist and disappear. Is Lucilla willing to surrender what she does not have? It would not be easy but he would have to try to reach her. He loved her too much not to make the attempt. He did not think it possible to convince her utterly, but perhaps she could take a few tiny baby steps, obtain a subtle shift in perception, a slight lessening of fear. Of this, she was at least worthy, and it could be a beginning.

He wanted to tell her that fear and pain were unreal, just as the past and the yet to come. He wanted to say that no one has killed anyone, because no one was here, but he was aware of the power of the illusion. "Oh my dear, don't you understand it yet," was what he thought, and his expression must have betrayed him because she went from looking at him lovingly in her childlike manner, to flashing anger, in another childish way. She couldn't believe what she was feeling, anger. Here it was years later, after all, he had been through, and all she had done to get to him, and she was actually getting angry at him. They were squabbling as though no time had passed and nothing had happened.

"You sound just like Jesus," she snapped at him. "If Jesus is real why don't you try speaking to him?" she scolded, then she paused, feeling horrible for what she had just said and intended. Softly, in a whisper, she finally said, "He's dead, didn't you hear?"

"Lucilla, Jesus is the only thing that's real," he reassured. "The one real thing in our dream, and he still speaks to me, and I take down every word." He waved his hand and turned his waist, pointing to the large pile of bound and unbound books he had written in pen and ink—some on papyrus, some on parchment.

"They crucified him," she insisted slowly, letting the significance of the word permeate his thoughts, "Crucified. How could a loving Father allow such a horror to His son," she added.

He could understand her confusion. To one who

believes that Christ was a body could conclude only in a most unloving Father, but the Christ saw himself as a Mind in Heaven rather than a body on a cross. Sanyi recalled his own experiences in the quarry and the arena where he saw himself from above the battlefield, where the truth in the falsity of the illusion was laid bare. Lucilla holds no such perspective.

"I know how it appears," he said compassionately. "They crucified his body, but Jesus was not a body. He who saved others would not save himself to show that the *guiltless mind cannot suffer.*" Then he related how he had perceived Jesus' intentions at the last supper.

"I saw it myself," she persisted as if she had not heard him.

"Tell me all that happened," he bade her finally.

She told him about the horrible crucifixion, of how she could not see Jesus' body on the cross, even though everyone else could. How she was too terrified to look back upon it for fear of not seeing him there.

Sanyi quietly understood his wife's mistake.

Had she looked back upon the cross until she could have seen the body of Christ, then she would have been saved that very instant. Yet, she did forsake salvation for the sake of the io, further escaping the net of salvation desperately of her own accord, that she alone was responsible for the surrender of love in favor of the preservation of thy self, the all to terrible defense against love.

He did not judge his wife, knowing that she had done only that which all had done, himself included. Terrified at the loss of the false sense of self, the illusion of a self, something that was not God, nor of God, she would suffer through an infinity of horror and misery in the nightmare, before at too long last giving up that which she never had. But he did not tell her that. Instead, he lied and told her it was nothing. And then, he was infinitely tender to her for the remainder of that night, for he knew that she had nowhere to turn but to him who had nothing else.

The 13th Disciple

The Promise

That night, the ludus fell dark and silent. But she knew she could not keep it from encroaching with the sunlight. Lucilla looked out the window as the first rays dappled the sands of the ludus below. She felt Sanyi behind her enveloping her like the ocean around a rock on the shore. He held her there, and she already dreaded having to leave, having to leave him there to the horrors of the day and days ahead, which she was powerless to save him from, as well as leaving absent him. He turned her toward him, and putting his hand gently under her chin, lifted it until her eyes met his. "You are sad. There is aught else you can be, it is understood. I cannot remove your burden from you," he said. They each were equally powerless to save the other, the difference being that Sanyi accepted it. Yet, something came upon him now for which reason there was not. He stood up, the act of raising his big body taking some time and changed the viewpoint of the room very much in so doing. But he kept his eyes fixed directly upon his wife as he made ready his words. She raised herself to her knees on the bed, then sensing the correct moment lifted her eyes expectedly toward her husband's. He held her gently by both shoulders then bent his body so their eyes were inches from one another. At last, he said, "What is important is not what happens here, but rather that you understand that there is no here."

She was unsure which was the greater absurdity, that which her husband spoke or his surety of its correctness. "Your grief can be overcome with the certainty that it is impossible to be separated. We are in Heaven, we are as one there, so much so that there is no place where one of us ends or that the other begins, a oneness so complete that bodies cannot accomplish it." As she protested, he interrupted her gently, saying, "You will see this when you awaken from the dream, when you realize (the only way to know anything) in actuality, you already have, we all already have awakened."

And now, she stared up at him in such a way that she could never look away, and he said "When we awake, none of this will matter. I know you don't believe me, but I swear you'll see that it's true. And when I do awaken to make it out, I'll find you, I'll find you and make straight your path, just as has Jesus, I promise." More firmly rooted in his right mind than ever, he said it with such tenor and authority that she was inspired, took courage, and grudging believed finally. If great and mighty Sanyi came to Jesus, so then could she, perhaps today.

Still looking straight into his eyes and believing every word she said, without knowing what she was saying, or how she would accomplish it swore: "And I promised to let you know when I awaken from mine, when I make it out."

Before now Lucilla had never thought of waking from a dream; she knew nothing of it. Indeed, despite her husband's beliefs and Jesus teachings, she was unaware of being in one. But now she swore solemnly, and hoped that she meant it.

It was implicit, of course, that Sanyi would be the one to make it first, and he would return to rescue her. Then, she would be with him in the afterlife forever, and Jesus be damned to hell; that was all that she wanted. She took comfort in that, but she resisted it too. For Lucillia wanted not the oneness of Heaven, rather the specialness of a blissful dream of forever alone with her wonderful husband.

"Don't die," she beseeched him in a whisper, interlocking her fingers behind his neck whilst peering into him. "Please don't ever die." She could not be aware of how desperate she sounded because she was unaware of how needy she was.

Body's need, he thought, *and she thinks she is a body.*

Trying in vain to speak through the tears, she instead wept openly, fully into her husband's great chest instead. Gently, he pulled her, brushed her hair back from her face and lightly kissed her cheek. Then, he pushed her back onto the bed, holding her until she finally was to sleep.

For Lucilla, it was the only cessation of her intense grief she would find, and yet she still could not know what a curse loving the gentle Sanyi would continue to be.

The morning did arrive, and Lucilla left the

ludus. Sanyi watched his wife depart through the gated archway. Watched himself from above the battlefield and knew that most men could never have watched her walk away with such peace. Most men would have felt deep pangs of want, born of loving from lack.

Sanyi lacked very little, therefore, he loved almost purely, the absence of missing her, but a symptom of his pure love for her. He was not concerned for her welfare, because he was aware that as himself, she was a dreamer in a dream. But he was curious as to whether or not she would attend his fights, well aware that she could watch him die before her very eyes. Such a thing would intensify her nightmare, but it could not harm her, the dreamer. He decided that he would bring these things to Jesus.

As for Vettius and his ludus, he judged neither. He simply noticed how they as did all of Roma depended entirely on slaves who needed nothing from Roma in return. Yet will be the day and is already when the master shall be free of his slaves, he reminisced Jesus words.

She exited with those melodious words from her

husband's tongue, reverberating, and rebounding off the inside of her brain, "So close that there is nowhere one begins or that the other ends. An oneness so close that bodies cannot accomplish it." This was the closeness she craved forever. Being so close to him felt like the only thing she could ever endure, and nothing else would suffice. Yet, she was still kept from him.

It was the especially dangerous trap of the special relationship of which Christ had warned Sanyi. Where her husband's feeling was inclusive of the entire world, even the Romans, even the money changers, her sense of that infinite expression of closeness excluded every single thing in the world that was not her husband. Such a sense of specialness, born of the bloody hands of the io's defiant, defense to love, was what necessitated and would continue to necessitate for her unreal centuries and the death and rebirth, of pain and suffering, the stubborn holding onto of a world which never was. A world which her husband, following Christ's example, had so gently and insouciantly cast aside, but now bitterly persecuted her.

With a victory fresh under his belt, Vettius was

anxious to maximize his returns on Pompilli who was correct when ascertaining that his master was far more concerned with Jesus than himself.

Vettius now sought to appeal to the Son of God for redemption in the afterlife. Redemption for the severe punishment which he expected for the extreme guilt which he perceived. Pompilli was brought to him, and Vettius dismissed the centurions leaving him alone with his property. They greeted, and Vettius led Pompilli in a slow walk out of his office, past the main indoor court, out of the main building, to a timber and vine-shaded patio on the western wall of the ludus, through which they could view the Mediterranean Sea.

The vines crawled and curled around the long, two-foot diameter timber, to provide ample shade to a fountain flanked by several cool marble benches close enough to the walls to be leaned against. There were no bright colored plants that Pompilli could notice anywhere, only palms and unripened grapes.

Vettius sat first on the bench facing west toward the sea, acutely aware of the weariness of his body after such grueling training sessions. Pompilli wasted no time in sitting when allowed to, the weariness of his possession going unnoticed by its possessor. Pompilli put his big palms down on the bench beside his thighs and propped himself up. He noticed that he was tired, too tired and should be resting. He noticed that his owner did not notice, and he noticed that despite all of this his heart was light, his mood cheerful as he wondered, *What does my Dominus want?*

Looking demure sitting beside his gladiator, Vettius came characteristically directly to the point. He was almost certain that receiving redemption in the afterlife would be more difficult than favor in this life. He was shocked at Pompilli's answer.

"You need do nothing, for it has already been done, rather it has all been undone. Remember that you have never left your home which is in Heaven. Do you fear death, Dominus?" the gladiator asked.

Vettius immediately nodded in the affirmative, then craned his neck. After a long moment, the gladiator turned to his left and spoke down to the man at his left saying, "No you don't, my Dominus."

The 13th Disciple

Crossing his mighty elbows and bringing his mouth down to his master's ear, he spoke softly but powerfully, "You don't fear death, my Dominus, you love it, you embrace it, you call to it, you beg to it, 'Come save me, save me from a most unmerciful disaster'. Which unmerciful disaster? God? We, each and every one of us, singularly and in total, we all do."

Looking up and to his side, Vettius remained silent knowing full well that Pompilli would soon prove his startling point. Then, the gladiator straightened himself, looking straight but speaking to the man at his side. "Death," he continued, "proves we are real. God is Love, God is Almighty. He can only create, not destroy, but we die and by so, doing seemingly do destroy that which He created, thus putting ourselves above Him, conquering Him in a sense. The Son says, 'In death I destroy that which He hath created', placing myself thus above Him. Therefore, if death is real, then God is dead. If I cannot die, I cannot kill God, if I cannot kill God, I cannot be real for only God is. If God is, then I am not. Death is the bloody proof which says I am, and God is not. Remember that the Son's terror is that he believes that he is, which is his greatest error for he is not; only God is. God is, and we cease to speak.

Until the Son remembers to laugh at the tiny mad idea, we must believe we die. For if we do not have death, we did not have life, which is to say we do not have a self apart from God, which is our true terror. Yet to have a self says that God is dead, how silly."

"Death, my Dominus," the gladiator summarized, "is neither to be feared nor favored, it should be treated as nothing for it is nothing, but there is the mistake of thinking that death is peace, but you cannot awaken and see Heaven if there is even a speck of fear in your mind."

Dominus paused, absorbing his property's words, and that property knew that where his wife could never comprehend. His Dominus understood, implicitly and immediately, grasping his own words even as they were spoken, filling the air.

"And tell me of my enemies, Marcus Aurelius and his ilk," Vettius said, then he asked, "Must I pray for them?"

The 13th Disciple

Pompilli flexed his huge thigh, still surprised by the booming voice emanating from so small a frame still sitting next to and below him. "You deal with them on the worldly level as you see fit, save that you simply must not judge them. Recall that difference—love or hate—is what the io uses to confuse us, to make us believe that we are each separate one from another. And were you to deny a brother's entry into heaven, then you would deny your own. And consider how futile, for it, Heaven is already here. You and I have never left it; we but sleep, dreaming our dreams of exile."

They would continue to meet and talk everyday, sometimes more than once, usually just at dusk as the blood-colored sunset dimmed to dark. These meetings occurred after the intensive training sessions, when the gladiator should have rested, but his Dominus was as greedy a student of Jesus as he was an able one. Whereas to Lucilla, he would explain a simple concept in several different, equally unsuccessful methods. Sometimes, he found his Dominus finishing his sentences for him.

The Mystical Match

Vettius considered his options regarding Pompilli carefully, which was characteristically unlike him. Normally, Vettius was considered bold for risking his investments so easily. It was a strategy which gained him favor in the eyes of the populace and, accordingly, grudging recognition by the political class.

What no one understood was that in his mind, Vettius risked nothing. His gladiators were mere chattel, and his wealth was vastly unknown and underestimated by all. But regarding this piece of chattel, Vettius was already unknowingly guarding against friendship, the io was slipping in.

Regarding the threatening friendship and the victory fresh under his belt, Vettius had an ever more delicate balance to maintain in order to maximize his returns on Pompilli. Almost in defiance to that balance, he determined that Pompilli would fight in the ludus of his political rival, Gaius Aurelius, against his best gladiator. Both men were anxious to court the crowd and, through it, political power.

The 13th Disciple

Vettius was in the enviable position of not having to field the winning fighter. Aurelius was younger, but Vettius was politically unknown. To gain status, he merely needed to satisfy the crowd, which could include either sparing or sacrificing Pompilli at their whimfull delight. Aurelius had not only to please the crowd, but his men were expected to win. Either way, as always, the gains and losses to the owners were denominated first in the currency of blood of the gladiators on the sand.

Vettius had always been insouciant to the outcomes of matches, calculating coolly the fate of his fighter by a cursory judgment of the momentary caprice of the crowd. The gnawing at his stomach was new and different to him; it was more than unwelcome. It was something which hitherto unknown but presently beyond his control. That knot, Gordian and distended at the pit of his own stomach, was beyond his touch and out of his control.

As Pompilli emerged from the shade to the glare of the arena, it pulled so tight that he feared it would bend him over. He had to straighten his arms against the plush rests to prevent it.

The match would be held without shields. It would be to Pompilli's detriment for he was by far the bigger and slower man. As anticipated, the Thracian brought the fight to him, trying to negate his superior reach. Pompilli deftly blocked a series of diagonal and horizontal slashes with the same attitude that he would pick flowers from the side of the road. Then, the Thracian thrust straight at Pompilli's midsection. Pompilli brought his blade down in a counterclockwise half arc, and he clearly heard and saw the thrust being easily blocked. He also clearly felt and saw the blade run him straight through. Both, disparate acts, occurring in slow dreamy motions. That was interesting, he thought.

Pompilli retaliated with a horizontal cut, which missed entirely when his opponent ducked under it, simultaneously cutting the Thracian's head off. From above the battlefield, Pompilli could see his dying prostrate body, could see himself appealing to Vettius for his mercy, could see the Thracian appealing for the same, and could see the dead Thracian. He could see all the dreams as they were, happening all at once.

It was as Jesus had said, and he could take any of them he wanted, or none at all. But unlike Jesus, he could not hold all of them at once, any more than he could see both near and far simultaneously. He had to focus on one soon, or it would be lost to the random collection.

The Thracian cut him across the belly, horizontally, not deep enough to cause internal injuries, but deep enough that if he wanted to do anything more in this lifetime, then he had to act soon. The Thracian was leaning forward and off balance, as he finished the slicing cut.

Pompilli, with more agility than such a big man should have, had already recovered and was moving in. With both hands on the hilt, he sliced vertically with all his might. The dull blade struck the Thracian in the back of the head with a blunt thumping sound, splitting it from the crown to the base of the spine.

When the man fell on his stomach at Pompilli's feet, a cloud of dust was the only movement his body made. The helmet was all that remained to keep the Thracian's head together. The match was over, and Pompilli had actually won, and the weight which was lifted off of Vettius had nothing to do with senatorial ambitions.

Once inside, Pompilli was again attended to by the finest standard of Roman medical care. Roman doctors had pioneered physical therapy techniques that would be practiced for thousands of years. They could reset broken bones perfectly. Only severe internal bleeding was beyond their competence, and fortunately, Pompilli had none of that.

His quick backward jump, along with the extra layer of fat afforded by his bland bean diet, had protected him from the worst of the Thracian's blade. He was still safe from things that weren't, things within the dream. He had just seen the multitude of illusions; now, he wanted to see beyond them all. He had no idea how soon he would. But that little bit of wanting would make him wish he hadn't.

So far, it had all been going well, for he who had nothing else. But he was about to learn just what a distraction being too close to what he always wanted could be. The io shifting tactics from savior to the most subtle and diabolical, to the special relationship of awakening from the dream itself.

Lucilla was no longer so naive about what a gladiator does and what he must do to return alive. She waited, panic-stricken, for her husband's return, her mind and brain terrorizing her with all possibilities of the impossible.

When the horse cart bringing all the gladiators from the arena came back to the ludus, she leapt with blind terror to see if her husband was in it—and thank God he was. The smile that came across her face was one that only pure joy could form. She was not even disappointed by the fact that the gladiators would be put straight to bed, the hospital, or the ground.

For now, she was delirious with joy simply that he was alive, safe, and close. She went to sleep that night with something that she had lost the night Sanyi was captured with Jesus, something she was sure she'd never hold again. It was the most precious of things to lose, but the most dangerous thing to hold close to—

hope.

Lucilla knew that a gladiator was never truly safe, ever. Safety came only after the granting of freedom, only after the wooden sword and the green wreath. Yet, for just now, all things did seem possible.

Pompilli had seen his wife from the slave cart but feigned that he had not. It was not for lack of what the world would call love or caring anymore than splitting a man's head open was what the world called brutal. Pompilli simply "realized" that from the many-faceted experiences of his most recent match what Jesus had taught, that which he had so recently experienced on the sandy stage of the arena, from above the battlefield—that all of this, this world, was over long ago. It was over before it ever really happened; it was over even now in this moment that seemed to be.

This realization was how he could watch his beautiful wife leave the ludus, taking with her all the delicate touches and scents that any man craved, that his body craved as it craves the air. But in his mind, he had nothing else.

The 13th Disciple

When the cart stopped in the court and Pompilli got out, he was aware of some pain at various points of his body. But he wanted to be alone that night, not answering the inane questions of the physician. So, he went to his cell—not the room he had spent with his wife, but one still paid with more than enough coin for, and lay on his back on the hard cot, staring straight up at the fungus on the ceiling. It was not thoughts but clarity that flooded through him.

He fully understood now what Jesus said that night in his garden and his determination to be crucified. It wasn't that the Mind of The Son was healed by Jesus when he was crucified; it was healed the instant that it seemed to be apart from the Father. That was what became so clear to him in his top-down view of the battlefield—none of what he thought he saw was real. For how could it be? How could the atonement be accepted and the world, which was aught but the result of guilt for a sin that never really happened, be real for even an instant.

He shifted his body a little on the cot and then put his arm across his brow without blinking. He possessed utter faith now in all aspects of the teachings of the Christ: that the world lived only in a dream of time that was already over. Time was what the io used to make the dream seem real. Jesus came not to forgive a crime that never was; Jesus was to remind us of our place beside the Father from which we could never really leave.

"This world is long since gone," Jesus said on that night. This was a terrifying thought to the io, which created the worlds of illusion and strived to keep the illusion real. For if the world was long since gone so too then was the io, but it was infinitely healing to the Son who was mistaken belief was the io's device to keep the dream alive. But Jesus said that the io would not allow the Son to simply wake, because like a trick of magic, once it was known, it is undone; once it was undone the io is dead.

Pompilli didn't stir for the remainder of that evening. He simply lay on his back with his arm across his brow, trying to scheme the io's scheme of keeping the Son asleep and his dream of separation alive. He understood that the io would do anything to keep him in the world, but what he was trying to understand now was precisely how.

On the following morning with him, Vettius plotted Sanyi's next contest. Being severe was seen as a sign of strength in the Senate, but Vettius was feeling uncharacteristically weak on this day. He liked the gladiator, felt, as did Lucilla, comfortable and comforted in the giant's presence. Were he capable of the sentiment, he would have even said safe.

In the business of pitting gladiators, the Lanista was always assisted by his Doctore, which often led to full-scale warfare between Vettius and Doctore, who was no longer a slave but a free man able to speak his mind to his employer—an employer who needed him more than he needed the employment. They each had an equal, but different kind of investment in the fighters.

For the politically motivated Vettius, the investment was always purely political more than financial. Now, with the presence of big Pompilli, it was becoming ever more complicated than that. For Vettius, the trick was how to feign indifference, to

The 13th Disciple

himself at least.

While on the one hand, Vettius was accustomed to treating each of his gladiators as an expensive piece of equipment, a strong mule or a good cart. He was good to them so long as they won in the arena. But sometimes, to curry crowd favor and the associated political clout that it bore, he would over match or outnumber his gladiator, heartlessly indifferent to the outcome.

Whereas Doctore had forged a personal bond with each fighter and cared for all, even loving some as a son, neither man's cause was more correct than the other, nor more or less selfish. Each was completely selfish: Doctore in attempting to make schedules which maximize his fighters chances to live, and Vettius in maximizing his financial and political return. These two men were as selfish as they were different, and they were as different as they were disapproving of each other.

Vettius had always lived the privileged life of a Roman nobleman. He looked down upon Doctore as unworthy and unappreciative, who was, after all, neither Roman nor noble.

Doctore had been a gladiator, a slave. He had escaped the horrors of slavery by the blade of the gladius, knowing that Vettius could not have prevailed for a single day in his place. Also, he was too well aware of the stingy manner to Vettius's nature. Doctore had won an incredible 23 bouts for Vettius and still not been awarded the wooden sword and green wreath. Where it not for intense and vociferous public disapproval, Doctore knew that he would have remained a slave still.

Doctore had not any awareness of the burgeoning friendship growing between his pupil and his employer. He held on to things as he still believed them to be. What Doctore really needed now was to buy time for his large and largely inexperienced pupil. A gladiator was like fruit on the vine; it needs time to grow ripe.

Vettius needed a new champion to showcase at the games he was to host in the coming months. Each year, the gladiatorial event was hosted by a different ludus, and this year, it was Vettius's turn to host the event. For politically ambitious Vettius to curry favor with the crowd, it was not critical that his gladiator would win, but that he appeared generous to them. Willing to sacrifice his valued property, his champion, at their whim and for the overall event to be spectacular. As of now, that champion was the promising but inexperienced Sanyi, whom he now called Pompilli.

Vettius insisted that he fight the rising new retiarius, Tetricus, from the ludus of Maximillian. Doctore stubbornly refused, insisting that Pompilli needed more time to develop. He even suggested that they enter the lesser venues outside of Roma to allow Pompilli to further both his skills and reputation there.

"Nonsense," Vettius said, raising his voice. "My champion fights only in the grand events."

But Doctore saw through Vettius's feigned pride. Vettius was taking shortcuts with his gladiators again. When Doctore was still a slave, he had been forced to accept Vettius decisions, decisions which were the thread by which his life hung. Doctore often wondered how he had survived it.

Vettius pushed him too soon as well. And even once he was established, Vettius made him fight while still badly injured, often made him fight two other gladiators at once, and even made him fight a retiarius without a sword or shield.

Then, there was the lie, there was eternally that. Vettius swore to Doctore that he would grant him freedom as soon as he had accomplished ten victories in the arena. Doctore did not complain after he had won his eleventh or twelfth matches. Even after the 13th win, Doctore simply asked Vettius if he remembered what he had said about freeing him.

Vettius didn't hesitate to say, "Of course I do," looking away as though he were not worthy of being spoken to. That was what a slave was. But when he defeated two Thracians at once, the crowd in that arena chanted, "Libera, Libera, Libera," demanding freedom for Doctore, who was then the gladiator called Mordax. Vettius was forced to grant it immediately, for Vettius was a slave too, to his ambition.

Doctore would never forget going from the body of the second fallen opponent to where Vettius was seated to get his wreath and wooden sword. It was unreal to him at the time because it was so unexpected; he had always resigned to die in the arena at the stingy hands of the greedy Vettius.

Doctore never noticed how he became accustomed to being a slave. Most men didn't. Sooner or later, they simply accepted it. Slaves could see the past human failings of their Dominus, but men could never go unappreciated. Even a slave had to feel that his life was significant, albeit in service to another.

But Doctore was so aware that for all his sacrifices, Vettius remained completely indifferent, and it was against this indifference that Doctore, now a freeman, could at long last retaliate.

When Vettius promised to free Pompilli if he won all the fights through his tournament, Doctore did not remind Vettius that he was a liar, but he did demand that Vettius contract it legally, cleverly extending his free rights to a slave and forcing Vettius to do what he otherwise would not have. Vettius did not get angry; he had baited his Doctore into the maneuver. Feigning practical indifference, he made the contract, but in doing so, Vettius felt torn into two.

So, Doctore had secured Sanyi's future at the expense of his present. The contract would spare Pompilli from Vettius's treachery after the tournament, but nothing put down on scroll could save him from the fights in the tournament nor the upcoming match against the retiarius, Tetricus, of the ludus of Maximillian. The salvation, if it existed at all, was to be found squarely within the walls of the ludus. But Doctore had no idea what true salvation was, nor that there wasn't anything he could do to spare Pompilli from what lay in wait in the darkness all around, to be revealed in the arena.

As he dismissed Doctore, Vettius demanded to see Pompilli immediately and privately. Doctore was sure of treachery, but in fact, none would be revealed. Vettius would simply use the occasion to do what he had long wanted: to broach again the subject of Jesus with his champion gladiator, Pompilli.

Pompilli entered wearing a red toga, the gold V on it indicating that he belonged to the House of Vettius, thus signifying his status and rank among the slaves. It was an unwanted distinction, one of which he neither approved nor disapproved.

Accompanied by a spear-carrying Roman soldier, Pompilli was escorted into the office. The oval opening covered with a thick purple curtain, separating it from the main house, was readily dismissed by Vettius, who had just risen from his laborious desk. Waving his arm over the tabletop to clear it off, Vettius then feigned a laugh.

"Dominus," Pompilli said with a respectful bow of the head.

"Let's go outside," the little man boomed in his deepest baritone.

Pompilli thought that they were going to the balcony overlooking the practice arena directly behind the table, but they walked off to his through a door to his left into a portion of the complex on the top tier which he had never before seen. It was a large rectangular court so cluttered with green leafy trees that he could not determine if they were inside or out, only the prodigious columns rendering a clue. His eyes were dutifully pointed down toward his Dominus.

"You were a follower of the crucified Rabbi named Jesus, one who said that he was the son of God," Vettius said in a tone as close to low as he could.

So, this remained about Jesus, Pompilli correctly perceived immediately. "Who said that? All of us are," Pompilli corrected when he thought it correct to do so.

Vettius stopped and looked up at his slave. Pompilli could almost hear the little man's thoughts. "Let us sit," Vettius said, moving toward a stone block for that purpose.

As he sat down, Pompilli looked up at small birds flying around one of the columns.

When he did perceive that Vettius wanted him to explain, he did so. Pompilli explained to his Dominus what Jesus had taught, that the world was aught but a dream, and that our purpose was but to awaken from it, to make it. Pompilli had explained this to many others, his wife included, but unlike all of them, Vettius instantly understood.

"There is only one Son of God. That is all of us," Pompilli finished. Vettius hadn't even noticed that it was fully dark out, and the only light was the flame from the torches. "So, Jesus was aught but the first to awaken from the dream?" Vettius asked, surprised.

Pompilli reflexively smiled broadly, nodding his head in the affirmative as he did so. Vettius did not even notice how much he enjoyed the affirmation. It was not an affirmation that Pompilli wanted to communicate, but merely the correctness of his master's conclusion.

Then, in a little while, Vettius asked Pompilli how he could pray to Jesus to gain favor for things of this world. Pompilli considered his answer carefully. Vettius was a man accustomed to getting what he wanted, but this time he would not.

"I have done as you were doing in there," Pompilli said, motioning toward the office with his head. "I have toiled for coin, plotted to vanquish my enemies—in Judea, they were the money changers. But you see that I am here. Jesus did not enter a plea to the Father or intercede on my behalf, nor would he, for to do so would be an admission that the world is real and of consequence, which is a lie, save for the fact that he knew that they believed their dreams to be true. The Christ was never concerned about the dream; he loved only the dreamer.

You can ask Jesus to help you in this dream world, but because he loves you, he will not answer, for to do so would make the dream seem to be real, and you would be doomed to never escape it. You have ambitions, as did I. But you need no ambitions any more than I did. At this moment, we each have everything. The only difference between us now is that I have nothing else."

"But Jesus performed miracles prodigiously," Vettius countered. "One of the many charges against him was that he did perform miracles on the Sabbath day."

"That was Magic," the gladiator continued. "Magic is anything having to do with the body, and he performed it for his own purposes, to instruct the disciples. Otherwise, Dominus Jesus would not heal a crippled body because, in truth, there is nobody to heal."

"He did seem cruel," stated Vettius matter-of-factly.

"This may seem cruel to a mind that believes it is a body, but to the Mind that knows it is a Mind, it is redeeming," the gladiator gently corrected.

Vettius remained silent for a long while, astonished at the gentle authority of his slave, unknowing of how to proceed in the unassailable truth of the gladiator's assertion.

Pompilli perceived his master's quick comprehension without judgment, nor did he judge his wife for her lack of comprehension. He remembered the warring factions in Sidon, how one chief understood and the other did not, but Jesus judged neither.

A most amazing man, Vettius thought again of Pompilli as he dismissed him. Once back in his chamber, Pompilli stretched out in his usual manner: on his back, with one leg up so his foot rested flat, and one hand under his head. He had already summed Vettius up. His Dominus understood Jesus implicitly. In fact, he was not surprised when the thought occurred that Vettius was well on the way to waking already. Another thing apparent to Pompilli was that his Dominus was and always would be in deep personal pain—the pain of seeking approval from others, a skill he had honed with his long-dead father.

It continued in this manner, that Vettius would call Pompilli to him in the early evening, as soon as he could. Sometimes, his champion was still breathing heavily from practice. They would take long walks in the gardens, sit on the balcony, and watch the brilliant sunsets to the west. Vettius was always impressed by the rapturous beauty of them, while Pompilli remained indifferent to their worldly, dreamlike nature.

Vettius would talk—talk of his desires to become governor, of his treacherous methods to obtain it—and always, Pompilli would listen without judgment or scorn, the only man Vettius could trust to do so. Gradually, by steady degrees, their relationship became more and more revealed for what was the true nature between master and slave: namely, that Pompilli needed nothing from Vettius, not even his freedom, but Vettius needed everything from him.

Back To The Open

With his wife pacing desperately outside, Sanyi hung his huge leg over the end of a table as the physician removed the retiarius's trident, which had broken off in his left thigh. The pain was excruciating, but it was not what was making him quiver with cold sweat. The lightning bolts of pain that shot through his body barely registered. It was remembering the dark sky and the falling off the world that made his fingers dig into the tabletop when the physician removed the trident's single embedded prong in one swift motion.

Pompilli, aware of the pain, wished it was all that there was to worry about. With the trident removed, he lay down his head and with his arm covered his eyes as the blood which spurted from the wound, mixing with sweat and sand into a soupy brown mud that oozed into tiny rivers, ran down his leg, then dripped down on the ground.

What was that, what was the world coming to get him? Was that Heaven? Jesus had said much about the world being an illusion, but he had never said anything about the darkness, had never prepared him for anything such as that. What was that? Pompilli didn't know.

But in trying to make sense of it, he made the subtle and terrible mistake of remembering not to laugh. And in remembering not to laugh, this Son knew again that which he had not since he had known Jesus—doubt.

After he could walk again but before he could resume training, Sanyi went to meet Vettius in his office. There, Vettius disclosed what he and Doctore had previously agreed upon. The agreement had seemed clear at the time, but his injury had now cast some doubt upon it.

"How is your leg Sanyi?" Vettius asked.

"Well, I think it bends in both directions now," he answered dryly, trying not to make anything of it.

Vettius straightened his arms out on the desk, leaned back in his chair, and studied his man. Without either of them knowing it, in the next few minutes, they would both make a critical decision for themselves and each other.

"Pompilli," Vettius began, "you've done well. You've risen quickly, and with just three victories, you've won coin and fame. Of course, you've also gained me coin and influence with Maximillian and other political vermin. He almost begged me to sell you to him."

He said it as though he had done Pompilli a favor by not selling to him but was thrown off when he realized that Pompilli did not get the implication. Actually, he did get the implication; it just didn't register with him.

Vettius lived by the double-edged sword of reward and punishment, success and failure, friends and enemies. Pompilli understood those concepts and understood the falseness of them. He understood they were just devices of the io to keep our attention on things in the dream and not having, at least he once did.

"I didn't sell you, but I did pledge you to fight in Maximillian's games in three months. I know you are still injured and Doctore tells me that three months is not enough time. But if you win, I will gain his patronage for the Senate, and I will grant you your freedom immediately."

Now, Pompilli sensed a slight touch of pleading in Vettius' voice that Vettius himself was unaware of.

"You don't have to answer now, give it some thought," Vettius added.

Pompilli did perceive his master's treachery, but what Pompilli did not perceive was his master's hesitation. Vettius knew that he was verily risking this gladiator's life for one last match. He also knew that he wanted so much more from him than the last match, so much more than that.

He even intended to build a house for the freeman and Lucilla to live in once he was retired. The ex-slave would be his new teacher. But the io dug in; old ambitions die hard.

At this moment, their constantly evolving master and slave relationship became more completely entwined. It was the master pleading to the slave for something that only he could give. Their relationship crossed the well-marked line of master and slave to man to man. Vettius could, in principle, command his slave to fight, and it would be done, but Vettius had a favor to gain and had to appear to be magnanimous. His gladiator had to seem to be willing to give his answer to fight in the affirmative. Then, more importantly, once the answer was rendered, to win or at least force an appeal.

The Sanyi in the temple, which the money changers had turned into a market before Jesus had entered it, would have yearned to do good deeds. Thus, he would have agreed to risk his body for the other man's sake. The Pompilli that was before the dark sky opened up would not have trusted his own good intentions, knowing that they are not enough. He knew the misleading desire for doing good deeds, understanding that none truly existed. He was aware that nothing good or bad could happen in this world, for it was aught but a dream.

But the Pompilli who answered was not the same as the gladiator before the darkness appeared to him or as the man in the temple. He was a mixture who remembered, but once again had the old desires, the desire of the io, to do seemingly good deeds. So, even before he was aware of it, his decision was made, oblivious to the influence of the io. As he observed Vettius studying him, "Dominus," was Pompilli's only remark, but given with a slight bow of the head, and the answer had been given.

Doctore was not the only one worried about Pompilli's next match. Vettius, who was usually self-centered, also found himself preoccupied with Pompilli's final match. This concern was unwelcomed, new, and frightening. It was selfish, but it was love in the only way Vettius knew how to express it.

Pompilli himself was still badly shaken by having seen the sky, and the world, drop away. It was not what he had expected, if he had expected anything at all. He had no idea what it was or what it meant. Against his will, he cast judgment upon it for he judged it as vile.

Jesus had said that the absence of the illusion of separation looked as pure bright light. But the reality he thought that had just woken to was completely dark, and it was in that shifting darkness that the io went to work.

Every organ in the body did its job. The liver secreted bile, the brain thoughts. Since it seemed the sky fell away, Pompilli's brain had been excessively secreting thoughts, successively secreting, evaluating, and eliminating ideas before most of them made their way to his consciousness. Each idea was a toehold into understanding what he had seen.

Of all the thoughts that capricious randomness could give him, the only idea taking form now was the one that was unthinkable until now—Jesus was a sophist.

The thought popped up and was immediately suppressed before it could become a full-fledged idea. But like everything else in the dream, it fought to live, fought to make believe it was there, fought to make the Son believe it was real and he was false. In doing so, the io fought to kill that which gave it apparent life. Yet still, it fought.

Worst of all was the silence from Jesus. In all

the days since he had seen Jesus, not once had Jesus failed to scribe his course for him. But once discovered for his treachery, the Christ had abandoned him.

Pompilli, who could not train, had plenty of time to think. His thoughts weren't the only thing working against him. Claudius Maximillian, in his quest for redemption against Vettius, had a new gladiator in his employ, but not his ludus. None of Vettius' spies could discover him, but out there, somewhere in Roma, a healthy, highly accomplished, technically polished gladiator was training. Training as though he were fighting the gods, he would be fighting the wounded and shaken Pompilli instead.

It was already a month after his match with the retiarius, yet Pompilli was preoccupied with the darkness and his doubts about Jesus. His injured left leg could scarcely hold weight and was being manipulated by the physical therapists.

At this point in his career, painful injuries were commonplace to Pompilli. In the past he had always ignored the pain and chatted with his doctors and physical therapists attending him. But now, he sat with the shoulders hunched and stared at the floor, beyond the floor.

He needed the help of two other gladiators to scale the steps to his room. Once there, however, he noticed Vettius had left a small, very big gift for him: Lucilla. He was overjoyed to see her, but as her visit lingered, a new idea entered his mind, one he had never known before.

As he saw her sitting there on the edge of the bed, her beauty and desirability overwhelmed him with an impending sense of loss for the first time in his life. Now, he wanted to hold her more than ever, but when he stepped toward her, he could not hold back the grimace as the leg sent a screaming message of agony to his brain, and he stumbled.

Lucilla rushed to him, and together they hobbled over to the bed. Once there, Lucilla realized that she was not going to make love to her husband today. She could feel his fever burning and see that the pain in his leg would take predominance over all.

Lucilla, barely 22 years old and still very much

a little girl, gently stroked her husband's forehead. As she propped up the pillows for him to lean against, her senses heightened, becoming aware that there was something very wrong with him, and it wasn't his leg.

Sanyi reclined against the pillows, only to immediately stretch out in full repose. His wife looked down at him, into his gentle eyes, and he told her, confided in her about the darkness. And as doubt weaved its way deeper into Sanyi psyche, his wife's response turned it upside down.

"It was nothing," she said. "It was just nothing, just as Jesus always said."

"Listen to yourself now, quoting Jesus," Sanyi said, laughing painfully, and then fell asleep. Lucilla spent the night in the V shape between her husband's arm and body. She cuddled his burning hot arm in hers and lay awake all night. Though there was no way for them to know it, she had just taken the first baby steps toward her own enlightenment.

Three months later:

"Jupiter's cock," Doctore screamed, the

paroxysm made manifest by the sheer frustration of incompetence. Somewhere in Roma was a fierce and seasoned gladiator who had been training for three months, while Sanyi could barely recover and could only limp. For all the spies that Vettius and his money could buy, that Maximillian's gladiator was in Capua was the only information they could glean.

Doctore informed Pompilli of this and mentioned that Vettius had even promised to double payment to the one who could name or at least garner some useful information about the unknown gladiator. But for Pompilli, it was completely unnecessary; he instantly knew who his opponent was. Pompilli kept this knowledge to himself; there was no need for Doctore to know, yet.

But on this day, it wasn't just Pompilli keeping secrets. Doctore had been with Vettius many years now, and he perceived Vettius's treachery. Earlier in the week, he had pleaded with Vettius to delay the fight, or substitute another gladiator in Sanyi's stead. But Vettius steadfastly refused for Maximillian insisted on Vettius's champion, and that was Pompilli.

Doctore still did not realize that Vettius now had great affection for Pompilli. He perceived only Vettius' treachery, believing only that Vettius was deliberately sacrificing Sanyi to the altar of his own higher ambitions.

Politically, Vettius believed he could gain more with the aid of the gods by losing to Maximillian, a notion that stirred him politically like no other. Sacrificing Pompilli would allow Maximillian to save face while Vettius would secure patronage for his political advancement. Though painfully obvious, he thought to spare Pompilli such knowledge. He was wrong.

Vettius summoned Doctore and Pompilli togethe, making them both a solemn promise that Pompilli did not have to win. Rather, he merely had to fight long enough to force an appeal.

"Pompilli, if you can force an appeal, then I, as the guest at Maximillian's ludus, which, as you know, means the appeal is mine. I swear to you that I will grant it."

The 13th Disciple

As Pompilli finally began his training, he perceived Vettius's treachery and forgave it, but he did not forgive it as would the Holy Spirit. He did not forgive it by making nothing out of it, because it was nothing. Rather, he forgave as one who had been wronged, thus judging Vettius as a brother. Having seen the darkness within himself, Sanyi could only see the world through the eyes of his separated mind rather than the eyes of the Holy Spirit. Thus, he had slipped back into the rescuer personality of his boyhood, and now he would rescue Vettius. The promise to grant an appeal was no small thing, but it was useless unless he could fight well enough to force it.

Doctore must now train Sanyi such that his strength and stamina returned, while ensuring that his injured leg also heals. With two weeks to go, there seemed to be no good way to achieve it. Yet, Doctore was amazed, for Pompilli had progressed beyond all he could have imagined. Despite everything, he might yet emerge victorious.

In the evenings, after the injury-shortened training sessions, Vettius did not see Pompilli but let him spend the time with Lucilla instead. They engaged in intimate moments, where passion and love intertwined seamlessly. He remembered it not ever like this. Lucilla's shapely form snaking rhythmically on top of him, changing positions again, tasting all her beautiful juices, and she and him reaching ecstasy together, his inside her. It was an experience that made the dreams seem very real and not one he wanted to wake from, and he wondered what Jesus was really talking about anyway.

The 13th Disciple

The Final Day

The games began early the following morning. First, lesser-known and lesser-skilled gladiators were paired against each other en masse. From between the vertical bars of his cell, Pompilli could see the men entering from opposite sides of the arena and walking purposefully toward each other at its center. He was painfully aware that each man began the morning with high hopes of moving down his road to freedom.

But neither Vettius nor Claudius Maximillian was in a mood for mercy. The men who lost and appealed were slaughtered; the winners were paired against each other again. Before the sun's shadow was lifted from the arena's floor, not a single gladiator was standing, all their high hopes cascading down to bloodstained sand.

Pompilli adorned his armor in the manner of a man accustomed to doing a particular task, unconscious that he was even doing it. It was the same manner in which Doctore had taught him to fight. Warming up, he felt the pain of his injured leg, moving from unbearable to something just slightly less. To save both his stamina and leg for the match, Doctore kept his warm-up abbreviated. The gladiators would enter from opposite sides of the arena and walk briskly toward each other. Doctore didn't want his man limping into the arena.

As the gates swung open with a clang, Pompilli stepped onto the sand into the din of the cacophony of the crowd noise and walked calmly toward the center of the arena. There, he was astonished not by the vision of his old friend, Vibius, which had been fully anticipated, but by the revelation that Vibius had changed his style completely, he was now a Thrax.

He fought now with a shield and a sword curved like a J, allowing the sword, when blocked to still snake around and slice an opponent in the back. Pompilli had never faced a Thrax before. A morsel of intelligence on the matter would have been worth all of the gold in Roma had it been obtained in usable advance. Now, however, all of Doctore's hard work just crumbled like grains of sand spilled onto the ground.

He made eye contact with Vibius for just a second. If Vibius recognized or was surprised to see him, it didn't show. He simply turned to Vettius and bowed; Pompilli followed suit. It wasn't surprising to Pompilli. Gladiators lived, trained, and grew together, just like Original Sin—separation set in, scattering loved ones like dust in the wind or opposing grains on the sands.

As Vettius dropped a white cloth to signify the beginning of the bout, a cool dusk breeze blew it away before it hit the floor. To Pompilli, it was a good sign. But Vibius was quick, barely had Pompilli turned to look what he felt the impact of Vibius's curved blade against the shield, staggering him. The rumor that Vibius would be granted his freedom for winning was obviously true; he fought like a man possessed.

"Pompilli, put your head into the fight," he heard Doctore roar, and he determined to fight in the center and make Vibius use more energy and move around him, like spokes about the hub of a wheel.

Vibius charged viciously, Pompilli had never seen his old friend in this manner before. It felt like he had ten arms, but Pompilli's shield, sword, and own massive body absorbed and sprung back after each powerful blow. Vibius's frontal assaults weren't working, so he shifted, moving around in a large circle as Pompilli had hoped. It was Vibius, who was using more energy, but it was also he who possessed more energy to be used.

Still, Pompilli was well aware that Vibius was much too good to continue using something that wouldn't work. Pompilli shifted to his left, to his right, keeping pace with Vibius moving in a wide arc. Then, Vibius attacked, but unlike the previous times, this time, when he stepped back after his failed attempt, he moved right back into Pompilli, slamming his shield and shoulder into Pompilli's massive torso. Pompilli was slightly unbalanced, but it was Vibius who was knocked off balance.

Pompilli hesitated not an instant. He jabbed, reaching with his right arm for all he could, nearly stabbing Vibius in the rib cage and ending the fight, but pushing off with his injured left leg made him a second too slow, and Vibius regained his balance without injury.

For a cruel, hopeful second, Lucilla thought her

nightmare was over until Vibius straightened up and squared off against her husband.

Pompilli took the standard position with his left leg forward now. It wasn't that his leg didn't hurt; he was just too busy to pay attention to it. As Vibius charged in like lightning, this time, he gave Pompilli something else to think about.

Vibius struck diagonally down, and although Pompilli blocked it, he was a second late with a shield too close to his body. It was then that Vibius's oddly curved sword did its dirty duty. It reached like a claw around Sanyi's shield and sliced the tissue of his left shoulder to the bone.

The intense pain was worse than his leg had ever been but not enough to stop the attack he had already commenced. While fending off Vibius's blade with a clang, he lunged in with several short chopping jabs. When his blade returned bloody, he knew that at least one of them had found its mark.

Neither man knew how badly the other was wounded, but each of their bodies recognized their limits against the cold steel of the other man's blade.

The calculation had changed from preserving stamina to saving blood. Each man would have to kill the other before he bled to death.

Pompilli's agonizing shoulder left his shield noticeably low, and Vibius sought to take immediate advantage. He attacked with lightning speed, but the surprisingly big man sidestepped and bladed his body to the attack, nicking him on the sword arm as he flew by.

Suddenly, both men realize that although Vibius entered the arena with more stamina now, he was the one losing the most blood. Pompilli didn't have to do anything but wait, and Vibius knew it. But Pompilli's shield was now down by his side, and when Vibius sliced at his left side, it cut a gash across Pompilli's left arm midway between his shoulder and elbow.

Pompilli dropped as he brought his elbow into his ribs, holding himself, comforting himself. When Vibius attacked again, he had only his sword to block with. It might be enough; Vibius was slowing down. Those who were in the fight to the death were now in a race to it as well, and the winner would likely not survive.

Had Vibius looked at his injury, he would've seen a stream of blood, but instead his eyes focused like an eagle on the huge target offered by his one-armed opponent. Then, he did something desperate. Vibius inched in slowly, cautiously. Pompilli was confused, yet never seen such trepidation on the part of Vibius. He was sure that Vibius was on the verge of death or treachery.

Then, he noticed Vibius's shield held low, down to the rib cage. With every fiber of strength remaining, Pompilli drew back his sword and sliced horizontally at Vibius' head. He was sure that Vibius would be too late to raise the shield, and he was right. Vibius dropped his shield entirely, bent his knees, and let the blade slice the air harmlessly above him.

In a split second that seemed like an hour, all he could see was Pompilli's huge damaged left leg. Remorsefully but viciously, he cut it to the thigh bone. Pompilli screamed and dropped to both knees, his blade fell ineptly into the sand.

The 13th Disciple

Vibius, bleeding badly moved in for the kill. With his left hand, he pulled Pompilli's head back hard with his right hand placing the point of the blade on Pompilli's throat. He was poised for the command that both men knew was coming. Pompilli could feel the slight pressure from the tip of the blade as he raised the two fingers of his right hand to Vettius.

Vettius, in turn, appealed to the crowd, and it was in a frenzy. He extended his right fist with the thumb pointed out parallel to the ground. Pompilli could see Vettius's head pivoting slowly back and forth in its full range as he scanned carefully, deliberately all the choices came down to the only one there ever really could have been. And then, with a final glance at Claudius Maximillian, Vettius did what Jesus said we all do. Acting against his word, but in his own self-serving best interests, Vettius put his pointed thumb on his own throat, sending the command to Vibius to take his old friend's life. There was only one frantic heartbeat when he saw the sign.

Again training took over, but not so much that he didn't miss his wife. He desired desperately to take care of her now. So, it was in desperation that Sanyi tried to change his dream. In the times when he had been indifferent, he could change the dream at will. But suddenly, when it deeply mattered, all the choices vanished like dust into the air, the mere wanting of any one instantly rendering a doing away with all of the infinitely many.

Betrayed and blindsided, as his old friend rammed the gladius through his chest, forcing a gag reflex that he would never live to experience, Sanyi's eyes locked onto Vettius. But it wasn't Vettius's treachery that he perceived, nor even Vibbius'. The final, ill-formed thought which was never completed was, "Jesus, why, my Lord, have you forsaken me?"

"Nooooooooooooooooo!" Lucilla screamed, louder, longer, than she had in her life, or ever would again. Leaning over the rails so that her feet came off the floor, she wailed for a minute continuously without drawing a breath. She shrieked so loud that it could be heard even above the roars of the drunken obstreperous hordes. She screamed the life, vibrancy, and beauty of youth right out of her.

The 13th Disciple

When her feet hit the floor again, she turned her back, bent her knees, collapsed, curled up on the concrete floor, and stayed there till her weeping became shallow raspy breaths, stayed until she was the only one there, until the pale sun came out under a rainy sky.

She staggered down the stone steps and out of the arena in the drizzly dying light. She meandered the lonely cobblestone streets, blank in thought with her jaw quivering in slanting rain that was turning cold.

Aught for what to do, she returned to the dank apartment that Vettius had provisioned for her. It was there that she resolved to end her suffering, but with dagger in hand, Vettius's men summoned her. So, concealing the knife in her gown, she determined another way to join her husband and take Vettius to the afterlife with her.

Lucilla did not lift her eyes, had not lifted her eyes, since seeing Sanyi murdered for spectacle and sport. She did not look directly at Vettius sitting at his desk. He began speaking, saying all the polite and appropriate words. What a great champion Pompilli was, how sorry he was that he was gone. He said it as though he had nothing to do with it. But when he slid coin that Pompilli had won across his desk toward her. She reached into her gown, pulled the dagger, and sliced down at the ugly little man.

It was the most futile and desperate act she had ever done. The guards were upon her instantly. They seized her harshly, leaving the dagger stuck in the desk. Vettius stood up, walked around the desk, and bade the guards to release her. She fell like a sack in his arms, weeping. He nearly had to hold her up, but for a reflexive act of revulsion was she able to pull away.

"Don't touch me!" she screamed in a guttural tone as loud as she could, that could barely be understood.

Vettius told her that she could stay in the apartment for as long as she lived and had the guards deliver her and her coin to it. But she never heard him; she fainted, and unconscious was the manner in which the guards had to deliver her home.

Lucilla didn't remember much in the days and weeks that followed. They buried Sanyi along with

Vettius's other fallen gladiators. She did not attend, nor did she purchase a headstone. It was the expected thing to do, but she would not dishonor him so.

It was an ugly and inhumane practice that took her husband who was himself a savior of lives, a physician, and a philosopher. She would not do that which was wrong simply because it was proper. She would not leave his name for eternity on a lonely gravestone on a sad hill outside of Vettius's ludus. She would not!

The days and weeks flowed into weeks and months, but for her, nothing changed. She ached for Sanyi, who was gone, and gone with him all hope. It was an incomprehensible but undeniable mechanism: that a thing available, however much wanted or not, when made unavailable, became so much more in value. And now, for Lucillia, that mechanism cast a cold pall over her, the melancholy growing deeper breath by crippling breath.

She had always seemed to her husband as a gentle thing, a flower. But some flowers dis not blossom in the dark, and could not thrive in the cold.

So, lost and alone and seeing no way out, she took the only way out she knew. The one she knew she would eventually take the instant he died. And though she lived in crippling anguish, she did so without fear. She feared not to be alone, for companionship brought no relief. She did not fear death; she welcomed it.

She studied the dagger, like the one she tried to bury into Vettius. She did approve at long last of what she was to do. Being left alone without him was unbearable, more unbearable than the uncertainty of death. Hopefully, she could be with him once again in the afterlife.

Being in his presence was all that she knew since she first saw him. She had loved him unquestioningly with neither motive nor purpose and been in longing of him since. She followed him from Judea to Roma for love's sake, and now, for anything, even death, to stand between them seemed unfitting. Without him, her life was unbearable.

Since his capture, she had lived in fear of losing him, but here in the certainty of that her fear dissolved easily away, and in her fearlessness she can say that the cost of Sanyi had been too high; loving him had not been worth it. There, she had said it, she had said it and not loved him one bit less for saying so. But being apart from him was always meant to be.

"I cannot live with myself," was the thought her mind spoke to her. As without hesitation, she prepared with both hands to drive the blade home. If her thoughts had ceased there, she would have been dead in seconds. But one singularly odd thought emerged which made her hesitate, but with sudden clarity compelled her to stop altogether.

It was a simple thought really, an obvious one overlooked daily by the masses and multitudes, but it stopped her like a stone statue. Somewhere between the last thought and the next one, there oozed in a slow elongated moment the thought that most never perceive, the one that said, "Who is the me with whom I cannot live? Who do I speak of when I refer to myself?"

She felt the cold dull blade in her hands, but it was upon the far wall that she fixed her gaze.

As she looked at the wall across the room, she

beheld a small dark oval in its center. The voice in her mind said, "Look away," it said, "be terrified."

But she was beyond that now, and so, as quietly as defiantly, she stared at the darkness. She challenged the darkness, threw her dagger at it with a groan, seeing herself as it left her hand and disappeared into the ever growing void in the space in her room.

In that instant, she knew she was not in her body, that she was not a body. She could see the room both inside and out from any perspective and all perspectives at once. The oval was now a large dark sphere, and she knew that though it looked to the eyes of the body as the world falling away, through the eyes of the Holy Spirit she could see that it was the world that was not there.

There, in that holy instant, she forgave the world as Jesus would. Knowing that it wasn't there, knowing that it took nothing from her because of an illusion. Nothing was all there to take. Then, staring at the blade with the body's eyes, she said regretfully, "Oh, my poor pitiful Sanyi, my poor husband. There's nothing to fear. It's just the nothingness that isn't."

But those were the last words of regret she ever spoke, and after she looked back up, she would weep no more forever.

The Promise Remembered

To Lucilla, it was an odd thing that had happened to them. One of them had set off upon a journey, and the other had finished alone. She had awakened from her dream before him, but she could not have done it without him.

Whereas, he walked a disciplined path of daily Forgiveness and non-judgment, she had been shaken awake without trying, without even wanting to, abjectly defiant, yet was she awakened. She simply saw her body throw the dagger, and then she knew forever that she was not a body. That was all it took, a simple shift in perspective and salvation was hers for always.

But she knew one thing that he did not. Not to judge the darkness, but to see beyond it, that was what she must tell her husband. *It was so simple*, she thought. *We spend our lives tripping over it, never noticing.*

Gentle Sanyi had found it. He had found and lost it as suddenly as she found it. So, as unlikely as it seemed at the time when they made the promise, it now fell to her to find him and show him his way home.

But how? She had only to ask, and it was answered.

One of Vettius's guards knocked upon her door. They had been coming by every week, and until now she had avoided them. But on this day, she opened the door. The soldier very formally asked if there was anything that she needed, and she said that she only needed to speak to Vettius for a moment. So, on the next day, Vettius's soldiers returned to take her to him.

Lucilla could hear all the familiar sounds of the ludus as they drew near the arched gate. The clanking of wooden swords, the grunts of men struggling under the midday sun. She smiled to herself as she observed the part of her mind that still thought that she was a body attempting to draw her back to sadness and the feeling that she was alone by mixing the familiar with the missed to create the sense of loss.

But the io would not have its way as the inner smile made its way to her slightly upturned lips, and she gently forgave it all. She did not allow the io to make a tool of the ludus, which would make her remember her missed husband and mourn him all the more. The ludus was just a ludus, that was all.

This ludus by sight and sound was the same as she remembered, but there was something different. The men there pitched in mock battle and all stopped to see her going into the main house.

Once in there, she could hear the sounds of battle resume. She knew that she was the reason the men had all stopped. Some out of respect for her husband, and others just because she was beautiful. But she made nothing of any of it as it was just the illusion of bodies all around.

She watched her body going up the stairs with a guard before and after. The sudden unawareness of the body becoming as common as an involuntary hiccup, she gave it no thought. At the top of the steps, they turned sharply and made their way to the office of Vettius.

Before they passed through the broad doorway, the guards searched her. They had no need to as a folded paper was all she held. They led her into the office and stopped as soon as they were inside. Vettius looked up from his desk. He was all the way across the room, but she could see relief so strong in his eyes that it felt almost like gratitude. Despite his outward demeanor, Vettius was a deeply guilt-ridden man, and whatever he saw in her face obviously assuaged his crushing sense of guilt.

He motioned to the guards to let her go and immediately got up. They met on the side of his large desk and embraced. For Vettius, it was reflexive. When they parted again, Vettius was just as amazed by his own actions as that of Lucilla, that she had even allowed him to touch her.

The shattered little girl who had previously left his office had gone. This woman was, what. She just was.

"You look well," he told her.

"You, not so well," she replied, and they both chuckled.

"I noticed that Doctore was not in the training yard," she said, knowing that was what was different about the ludus.

"Yes," Vettius replied. "Doctore retired and returned to his home country, and he will live there for the rest of his days a wealthy man." He said it as though to justify himself but knew all too well that it did not.

Vettius was having a crisis of conscience that he could not recognize. Lucilla recognized it, and though she knew that everyone is all innocent in the eyes of God, she understood that Vettius's pain was an unavoidable part of his path to salvation.

She remembered seeing her body throw the dagger and realized what her pain had helped her to do. So, taking his hand, she said, "I want you to know that you didn't do anything to anyone." It was the kind of thing that can only be said only by one not with faith, but one with Knowledge. Such faith comes only to one completely in his right Mind.

Vettius thought how soft her hand felt. He let it go and waved his hand in protest, but she stopped him and looked into his watering eyes and said, "No, we are all dreaming this dream in order that we awaken to the peace of God." He still tried to pull away, but she wouldn't let him and continued saying, "And we, each and every one of us, has already awakened."

With this, Vettius stopped in amazement, saying, "My God, now you sound just like your husband. He lives inside of you."

Smiling, she answered, saying, "He lives in us all." Vettius nodded in agreement, but he did not know that she was speaking of Jesus now.

With his hands on her elbows, Vettius pushed her gently.

"I've decided to get my husband a headstone after all," she said.

"I have already seen to it," he confessed.

"That is well," she answered, "but I want you to inscribe something on it for me. It must be exactly as I say in a tone indicating it must be precisely thus."

She reached into her dress pocket and retrieved the parchment that was crumpled now since she had been searched. She placed it directly into his hand, saying, "Promise me you will do this for me exactly as I have written it here."

Never taking his eyes from hers, he nodded in agreement, and she let go of it and stepped back.

"You have my solemn oath," he said.

"Thank you."

They looked at each other for just another second.

"Why don't you stay in Ostia or Roma at least?" he asked.

And she answered, "Maybe, maybe I will."

But Vettius knew that just as had Doctore, she would leave, leaving him alone. *But where would she go?* he wondered. *Where would she roam to? And what would she do?*

At one moment, he wanted desperately for her to stay because she as did Doctore reminded him of Pompilli, but for the same reason, he wanted her to leave just the same in the very next moment.

Life for Vettius would be such until the end of his days. His sacrifice of his friend and teacher gained him the political power that had been his lifetime ambition and appointment to the Senate, but discovering that having was not as wonderful as wanting, he repudiated it.

He continued the ludus as a matter of course, but he never sacrificed another gladiator and freed all of his slaves after three years, regardless of position or status. Some left while others remained, but to Vettius it was all the same.

The constantly ticking ambition and conniving ceased; his desk became clear, and it was his brain that became encumbered by his broken heart. He became as Lucilla had been; he even realized it for himself. He lived in the afterglow of the flame that he had extinguished by his own hand, that flame which had rested upon the gladiator and cast its cold pall over him never to be reignited.

Vettius lived a very long life.

He lived in the shade.

He lived it alone.

Vettius had indeed kept his word, Lucilla thought. There was a headstone on Sanyi's grave, which was on top of the sad shifting hill where all of Vettius's losing investments lay.

Lucilla sat on her knees, running her fingers lovingly across his name Pompill in the cold stone for a name which prior to she could not utter, but what was a name, aught but a symbol of symbols. The inscription on it was just as she told him that it had to be.

Then, she felt a clean, gentle spirit. Was it Sanyi's? She could tell only that it was clean. Then, she saw herself on the hill by the eyes of the great eagle circling high overhead, in the cool gray, misty sky. The big bird was high, so high up that she could scarcely see its huge body, yet by its eyes could see a gentle young man kneeling to read the precise inscription carved in the stone.

He was tawny and blonde with the Roman sun emblazoned in bronze across his bare back and chest. Then, she was on her feet again, where he was reading the inscription.

She regarded him as a brother, touching his blonde hair gently. As she turned and raised her gaze, she beheld the bluest eyes framed as a lion's mane. She swore that she perceived the blondest of Jesus Christ there could ever be, not for his appearance, rather for his gentleness. The meaning of such, she knew not, save that things were as they should be.

Sanyi would have enjoyed a day such as this, she thought from this point of view, from above the battlefield. His big body had always been so hampered by the heat. The remembrance brought not even a small pang of remorse, the old Lucilla, the one that had never been would have languished, constricted by grief, but the io could not touch her here, fully in her Christ Mind. Then, she kissed his name and smiled, finally realizing as he had for a time at least that this was all illusion that was long ago undone. That the body which she thought he was had never been, the truth that He is can never be destroyed.

Then, she returned to reading the inscription.

The promises they had sworn to each other in the world of form had reached beyond the dream to their truth as one. It was an unlikely journey, though one all made. Theirs began by one of them and yet accomplished first by the other. She exchanged his faith for her lack thereof and had awakened before he could, yet knew she could never have made it at all without him, just as he could for now at least not find redemption without her. So, she would continue to scribe his course, would suffer as he had, to be reborn again and again into the world of illusion, so as to find that lost little lamb and set straight his path until God Almighty would reach down and lift him into Himself.

Book II

Lost

And the load

It doesn't weigh me down at all

He ain't heavy,

He's my brother.

— Paul Russell

The world I see holds nothing I want - Lesson 128

A Course in Miracles

Whenever I've died, it's always been the same. I like it for a while when I'm living, but then get tired of it and die. I decided to die before I was born—you know how it is. And afterward, when I'm back in my Mind, I like that for a while, but then get scared, shit scared, 'cause you know who is there, and *think not that he has forgotten.*

The 13th Disciple

You remember that, don't you? Yeah, sure you do. We all do 'cause we are all part of it—the big it that never happened. That's just the way it is back in the Mind; that's why we don't hang out there too long, because, *an angry Father pursues his guilty Son,* blood on our hands, murder in His heart—kill or be killed.

How long can you wait under that kind of pressure? Not waiting as in time going by—you know how it is when you're in the Mind, there is no time. But waiting as in, "Let me get past another one, another nightmare, another movie. Let me get one step closer to getting out of it." Fuck that, let me get 1,000 light years closer.

But there is no time, and it's not just the lifetimes you gotta clear; it's the lessons you gotta learn. *We leave the world not by death, but by Knowledge.* How many have I lived by now? Millions? Trillions? I don't know. How much closer did I get? How do you know? All I know is I can't take this anymore. There's gotta be another way, I want to get outta here so bad, I'll take anything.

And just like that, just like ordering Chinese

takeout, just like nothing at all, I got it—one of those that comes along every 10 million or so. When I started dreaming again, I dreamed I was a soldier.

But this time it wasn't just my dream. We are all connected, sure, but he was as much the dreamer of my dream as me. His conflicted with mine, adding truths as uncomfortable as they were undeniable, but he simplified a lot of things.

So, how then do I tell my story without telling his? How can I tell you of the transformation from the man I never was, toward the Truth that we all are without telling how he did it? One is not possible without the other. Our story is not one of doing, but one of undoing.

He told me as much. He said, *"You cannot do this without me, but together we have already undone it."* But done it, undone what? I am losing it again. Let me tell it while I still can, let me tell you how, but I can't tell you why.

It was 1975, and Nixon was pussying out of Vietnam. As I said, I was born a soldier this time—just a killer really, an assassin. I'd already done three tours and was barely six months into my fourth when, somehow, the war just came to an end.

In my last battle, I got the shit blown outta me on some piss-anthill outside of Da Nang. It was one of those shit piles that command fought to the last man on, resupplied with new men up to platoon size, then abandoned, but only after the VC gave up and withdrew—anything to say that we were winning.

As I said, I wasn't a real soldier or even a sniper anymore; just an assassin by then. I had just come out of the jungle where I'd smoked some guy command thought was a spy for the VC. He wasn't a spy for the VC; he was a drug dealer. HQ didn't like competition. "It was a sin," they said, "competition, that is." Anyway, he won't be profit-sharing with them anymore. I didn't mean to take his whole fucking head off, but it usually happens with a 50 cal from three-quarters of a mile.

I was held up at some shit hole outpost north of Da Nang, waiting to be choppered back to HQ for the debrief when the gooks hit, and the little fuckers hit us hard. I didn't mind the chance to kill more gooks, but it was a close one.

The gooks poured over shitty sandbag walls and into the base. By the time my ammo ran out, they were so close that I could feel their brains splatter on my face. The last one I got; I stuck him to my elbow with the bayonet. I could smell his bad breath and hear the dry raspy sound that came outta his throat.

I held him up against a wall of sandbags and smoke and gunpowder filled the air so thick I had to lean into where our noses touched just so I could look into his eyes and see the light going out. See, I never minded killing people this time; I liked it. I liked seeing the life go outta their eyes, just like throwing the lights off in a room; it doesn't happen right away 'cause there's always a slight pause before the certain fade to black. See, there is nothing purer than killing a guy—he was dead, you were sure of it, and he was too.

I didn't really mind if they killed me either, then or now. The difference is that then I didn't give a shit, and now, I realize that nothing really matters. Day one of that schooling came just a few minutes after that last raspy stinking belch of hot air left the fucking gook's lungs; it was *subtle, just a shift in perspective.*

As I said, we were being overrun. The VC were coming outta the ground like rats, and I thought we were gonna buy it; I thought that I was gonna buy it when all of a sudden, the shit just hit us.

I could hear the screeching sound of our own jets and remember thinking they're dumping it all right on top of us, right here, right now. I was right.

The last thing I saw was a wall of fire rising from the jungle that looked just like the fountains at Cesar Palace—blue, red and hot orange climbing higher and hotter. The concussion sucked, rather than blew, my eardrums out. The fiery orange and white-hot scorched my face. The flames went so high up that, standing, I had to crank my neck 90 degrees and still couldn't see the top; the Empire State Building looked like a toy next to it. I never heard a fucking thing—the shit just concussed the brains outta me and just kept coming.

Then, I was out cold, but I could feel the

bombing and fighting like a dull blade trying to cut through my unconsciousness, sawing away for hours.

When I came to, my head was splitting worse than any hangover I'd ever had, and there was a lotta blood dripping down my head and arms I couldn't make out if I was ok or not. I was completely caked in mud; only where rivers of blood mixed with sweat could I see pass the mud to my body at all.

When I tried to get up, my legs felt like I'd just run a marathon yesterday. I could barely see, couldn't assess a fucking thing, but somehow was able to stagger in the foggy smoke. Then, dirt mixed with gunpowder made a soupy gray haze that you had to swim through and from somewhere farther off I could still make out the smell of napalm.

Napalm blows up and burns orange and black, but everything here in this soup was gray changing to black. I was sure I was dead; this must be what it's like. How could anything survive this? How did I survive it? I stayed up, but barely. I figured I'd go to the top and wait things out up there, but I felt someone watching me, watching every aching step I took.

The 13th Disciple

I tried to shake it off, but when I saw the outline of a body down the slope behind me, I dropped and started feeling around for a piece of shit M-16, or better yet an AK. Jesus, my palms hurt just patting the ground. Nothing. I lost sight of it and thought it was my imagination, but then just like that, he was behind me again, this time, uphill.

Now, I really wanted something hot, but a knife was all I had. Who the fuck was that? I could make out the dark form through the gray haze perfectly. How'd he get up there so fast? He must not be hurt that bad, if at all. Was he here through it all, or did he just show up now? I was sure as shit here through it all, and I hurt like fuck all over to prove it. I reached down my leg for the knife, but whatever he was, it was going to take a lot more than a knife to deal with him.

I was still looking up at him. I couldn't get over how dark and 2-D he was. I thought I would be able to make out some detail as he got closer, but instead, l just got scared, scared like I dunno, like I could just fall through him like cracks through the universe. Fuck that, how was he armed? I wanted to know. I never found

The 13th Disciple

out. I was staring more into rather than at his dark 2-D shadow when suddenly it was lights out. I wasn't unconscious that dark shadow poured itself out into the smoke and dirty air and just swallowed me up. I just couldn't see a goddamn thing. I can't describe it, but I'll never forget that feeling. It was more than just being surrounded by darkness; it was like I had stepped completely outside of the universe, twilight zone shit.

I was fucking scared. Like when I was a kid, and my stepdad beat the shit out of me, and then nailed me inside the doghouse. I remember shivering in there, and he'd come by every few hours just to kick on the sides—it rattled the fuck outta me. Then, one time he ripped the plywood off just long enough to throw the dog's head still warm inside. It rolled up in between my legs, then the motherfucker nailed up the door dark and tight, leaving it trapped in there with me.

Until then, I used to like the dark, I used to like to hide in it, feel safe in its form, in its fiber, but in the nanosecond when that dog's head landed between my legs, I was more terrified than anyone can stand. I ripped and kicked at the door, but I was too fucking small and weak, and the darkest dark leaves no place to hide with a hot leaky dog's head right next to you. I didn't get out until he passed out and my mother found me. And it was nothing compared to the protracted and prolonged terror I felt in that black hole on the napalm blasted hillside in Vietnam.

Whatever this was, I wasn't anywhere near ready for it. The last thing I remember was thinking I can't take this anymore, *there's gotta be another way.* And then, there was no more shadow, no more blackness. I was back in the gray soup with the acrid smell of napalm running up my nostrils. It was weird. It was like it never happened, but I still remembered it.

I was glad to be back in the war. I never thought napalm could smell so good. The worst that could happen to me now was getting killed. I remembered it, but I couldn't be sure that it had really happened. But before this was over, the answer would be so undeniable that I would never ask it again.

After I came to, the medics found and carried me, one under each shoulder, through that nasty fog to a triage area they had set up right there. They cleaned me up, then ferried me out to a hospital ship sailing in the Gulf of Tonkin just as ass wipe Nixon declared a ceasefire.

They choppered me in at night on one of those light observation jobs that were more glass than a chopper, and you could stand right under as it lifted off, and it wouldn't even shake a mosquito off your nose.

This was a cramped two-seater job that left my balls swinging in the wind. We went east from the coast. It was pitch dark after take-off for most of the flight up to the thick carpet of cloud cover.

When we got into the clouds, I almost thought I'd be able to walk across them. I don't know how he kept us straight without instruments, but he did, then we busted through the top, and the full moon lit it up.

We leveled off and skimmed the tops of the cloud breakers for about 30 minutes, and you couldn't see a star in the sky, just the full moon in all its silky brightness. But every inch of that brightness was soaked up by the wave tops of the clouds below. We descended back into the soup this time to burst out from beneath.

You could tell the war was over because the ships were all lit up and never would have been during the war. The fleet looked majestic from up high, like big city lights, for 360 degrees from horizon to horizon—the biggest damn city you ever saw.

The napalm and my rattled brains made it look weird, like from outer space. Practically, my ass was the only part of my body strapped inside; the rest of me, partly unconscious and ready to puke, hung sometimes with both arms overboard, with nothing but miles of air between me and the water. And every time I threatened to heave, you'd better believe the pilot made sure I stayed that way.

When I looked down, I could see the entire peninsula, and we just stayed that way for who knows how long, waiting for clearance, I guess. It was busy; there were lines of choppers going east on their way to their appointed destinations, to various ships over the edge, partly on the other side of the world. Finally, below the dark blanket of cloud cover and above the carpet of lights on the great cirque, we began our

The 13th Disciple

descent.

Judging by the way we came, it musta been pretty still out there because he brought her in by a long 45-degree downward slide, like we were sliding through a long narrow chute. The boat itself was a huge tanker converted into a hospital ship, bigger than an aircraft carrier, but it looked like a postage stamp from up here. I musta still been pretty groggy because when we began our slide, it was like a soupy black mist came around the descending bird, and all I could see was in that tunnel.

The ship, invisible at first, was in that tunnel. As we dropped and my stomach came up, the ship came with it, as the long descending slide continued. The bird itself was like a pee dropping onto the huge back of an elephant in still air, but I couldn't see around the tunnel that was just big enough for the ever-descending blades to scrape through. The ship was coming up at me, and when we were about halfway down, it was like there was a lens, and I could focus in and out of it, but I could only zoom in right now.

We slid without a hiccup, down, down till I

could make out the conning tower, down till I could see clearly the bridge, but I was still way up there; you wouldn't want to fall from there. Finally, I could make out the people on the darkened decks, save only the landing lights. Finally, we touched down, and no sooner had the skids touched did my boots hit the deck, with the few contents of my stomach in a close second. I was able to keep a lid on my stomach, and there was a faceless person who asked, "Are you Captain Ballard?" But he said rather than asked. I didn't even acknowledge, just followed him, glad simply to not throw up.

I didn't bother to look where we were going, just followed his heels with my eyes, through doors and ports and bulkhead down metal stairs you could see through. I reckon that we hadn't gone more than a third of the way down when I finally went lights out. I don't know if I hit the deck or he caught me, but when I came to, I was in a huge cargo hold converted into a recovery room.

There must have been 1000 beds or more and each one was filled with some kid screaming for his

The 13th Disciple

mama. Outside, I could hear the choppers. I knew that they were evacuating US Embassy personnel. I'm not too bright, but even I could figure out the war was over. Fuck that pussy Nixon. Shit, another half step closer to home and nothing to do with the rest of my life. What the fuck was I going to do now,? Become a bounty hunter?

I had to get out of there. I did a quick body check and figured that I could still walk, so I swung my feet over the edge of the bed rails. My feet were bare, but I didn't give a fuck. Some nurse started to give me some shit, but I gave her a look that said think again, and she did. My legs were ok, I could walk, so I made my way topside.

At each set of steps, I counted my blessings that I was able to climb them. For most of the guys down there, all they could do is lay and hurt.

Outside, the sun hit my face hard, and the wind nearly blew the little flap they gave me to wear up over my head. I didn't give a shit. It felt good to be up there.

The first thing I noticed was the thin line of

helicopters retreating from Vietnam. I didn't care about losing the war, but I did hate being left out in the cold.

What the fuck am I going to do now? I asked myself again. This time, I must've muttered it out loud because there was an answer, "Become a bounty hunter." That kind of frigged me out. It was a civilian walking the other way. He said it just as we drew even. I stopped and turned around, feeling that fucking flap blowing off my ass again.

It was a civilian, a needle-nosed little prick, probably CIA, who even made me creepy. The tall grey-haired fuck next to him was a naval officer in full-dress whites, but the suit did all the talking.

"Are you Captain Jack Ballard?" he asked. I thought for a second before I answered. Were they gonna debrief me right here?

"Sure I am. What's this about?" The two glanced at each other, and then the suit started talking again.

"Captain, we have a mission for you, and you'll have to take it or leave it right now before you know what it is. If you take it, you'll be briefed when you're ready. Otherwise, this conversation never took place."

I muttered something, playing for time. "I apologize for the suddenness, Captain, but discretion and time are of the essence here. But if you agree here and now, all of your past transgressions will be forgiven. It seems like a shame to let a man of your tastes and talents go to pasture simply because the war is over."

"Transgressions," I muttered. "What transgressions?" I looked at him, and then at the officer for just a second, but then back at that creepy little CIA guy in the business suit. "Your transgressions, Captain," he said, pausing a long time between words. I was getting a sick feeling that we both knew exactly what he was talking about. He went on.

"Let's begin with Private Sean Mattingly, Captain?"

"Who?" I muttered, then I knew who. Sean Mattingly, I'd forgotten all the fuck about him. It was easy for me to do that after I'd killed a guy. The suit could see it register on my face. He fucking had me, dead to rights, but how?

Mattingly was a stupid little piece of shit who should have just kept his big mouth shut. He and his fat fucking girlfriend, Todd Olbermann, had a bad habit of falling behind on runs. Todd was a fat pig, but he never seemed to lose any weight. To me, he just seemed to keep getting fatter. It pissed the drill sergeant off and kicked our asses for it. And that pissed me off! So, after lights out one night, I stuck a sock down that fat fuck's throat and beat his ass. I thought I'd get away with it because I just hit him in his blubber belly and left no marks, but Mattingly ratted me out. I lost it. I made up my mind I'd get that pencil prick back before the end of boot camp, and I did it.

The last week of boot camp, we spent doing drills deep in the Okeechobee swamps of Florida. The swamps and heat were supposed to acclimate us to Vietnam, but it also allowed a little space between the sergeant, Mattingly, and me. Enough space for me to kill him. I just had to do it. I didn't even give a shit about getting away with it. I just wanted to off him so fucking bad.

So, the first chance I got, I took it. During a live fire drill one rainy night, I put a bullet right in the back of his fucking head. You should've seen it open up, just like the watermelon I used to blast when I was a kid. The force shoved his whole body into the mud so deep they almost couldn't find him.

I thought shit sure they'd know it was me. But this was 1963 and we were going to Vietnam, they didn't even bother to ask. They ruled that an accidental shooting by persons unknown and a week later I was dropping out of a chopper into a hot LZ in Vietnam. I had forgotten all the fuck about it.

"We've had eyes on you for a while now," he said. "We have eyes out for people like you." What he really meant was that we have weight on you. The sun was in my eyes, and I had to squint pretty hard to look at him.

"So, what you want from me is to make a hit?"

"Oh no," he protested in his most bureaucratic way. "We are just a private enterprise operating in the free market for our own messenger." Private enterprise my ass.

"You want me to deliver a message," I said, "just tell me who." I didn't bother to ask what the message was.

"No need to lean on me," I added over the salt wind that kicked all around us.

"No one is pressuring anyone to do anything captain," the creepy little fuck said.

I'm a mass murderer. I have no idea how many hits I've done, but even I hate fucking liars, I almost said. It was true. Of all things, they really made me sick, and I don't even know why. But I wanted the job and to keep the weight off me, so I kept my mouth shut.

Anyway, as a soldier, I'd kill people for free. So, to get paid for the same gig, to me that sounded really nice. And that's how it happened. That's how I went from being a soldier to being a full-blown hitman, standing on deck in my pajamas, talking to some pencil prick with the wind blowing up my ass.

I stayed in the hospital ship for about a week, getting better. Other guys came and went, some in body bags, but the ship stayed just off the coast of Vietnam moving north as best I can figure. What were we waiting for? The choppers that had been ferrying men and material offshore were gone now, but we stayed. Why? Everything and everybody coming and going.

We came to a dead halt. I felt like an asshole doing laps around the deck while guys were screaming and dying inside. But we stayed another week. They offloaded more patients and bodies onto a troop carrier, and I was practically the only one aboard, but we stayed put just doing circles day and night in international waters off the Gulf of Tonkin.

One day, as I was in the aft having a smoke and catching some rays, some sailor came by to take me to that creepy little civilian. I followed him into the tubular maze that was the guts of the ship. You could always hear the hollow sound of footsteps that sounded different than they did on the ground. He took me down the crisscrossing cobweb of metal steps into the bowels of the ship.

He opened the door, and I stepped into a cabin about 20 feet square. There was a general, an Army captain, and a naval officer, sitting around a big round table with a green tablecloth. There was glassy silverware, a pile of bright white plates, and sweaty water pitchers in the middle. With all that brass in there, you'd better believe that I gave the sharpest, smartest salute I ever had.

I never really looked at him, but he was there too, the needle nose little prick. Forget about the brass; it was the pricks show. He was in charge of seeing that it was carried out and, more importantly, making sure Walter Cronkite didn't know fuck all about it. The captain introduced himself, but I honestly don't remember his name, and the General, well, I'm not supposed to say his.

The civilians, to this day I still don't know it. I was told to stand at ease. I removed my Barrett, held it in one hand, and folded my hands behind my back.

We were all standing just inside the doorway, but the General led the way, and they all followed him to a table and sat down. I remained standing.

"You're rated as a sniper. Is that correct?"

"Yes, sir," I responded to the captain.

"Can you use a 50 caliber?"

Yes, sir, I sure can sir," I said.

"What's the range of that thing?" the captain asked.

"Well, sir, I've hit a melon from a mile out before."

Everyone broke out laughing, but it died when that little civilian fuck started in.

"So, it must have been really easy plucking off Mattingly. How far were you, about 20 yards?"

I cleared my throat and started to answer, but fuck it, I don't have to answer to civilians. Then, the captain asked so, I cleared my throat again and said, "Sir, I have no recollection of that event."

Why the fuck did they keep bringing that up? What did they want me to do so badly that they had to blackmail me into it? They don't have to blackmail me into killing anyone, shit, just give me another target, I always said.

There was a long silence. It was the General who broke it, asking, "How are you feeling now, son? Are you fit for duty?"

"Sir? The war is over, sir."

The General told me to sit down, and I did. Then the general offered me a drink, and I took it.

After the drink and the chow, they assigned me to a small cabin. The long side had a bunk hanging off of it opposite the door. The short side was small enough that I could touch each bulkhead with my fingers.

You open the door and turn left to see a small desk with one of those snake headlamps. There was the thick dossier that I expected planted squarely in the middle of it. I closed the door and shut off the overhead, and it turned pitch black, not even light from under the door, just the way it is on a ship, especially in cabins on the lower decks.

I pulled the chair in the dark and sat down. I didn't pull the string to turn on the lamp, just sat there enjoying the darkness. This darkness was different from the one on that blasted hill that was coming at me. This was the kind I was used to, the kind you could hide in, that other shit was like a black hole there to swallow you up.

Five minutes later, I was studying the dossier of a North Vietnamese General, General Gu. The most recent picture of him was at least ten years ago. They said so themselves when he was just a Colonel. So, this was the man they wanted me to kill, threatened to charge me with murder if I didn't, murder in this madhouse. What the fuck was this shit about?

Mean-looking mother fucker, I thought. He had a square face, and he was big for a gook, bigger than me.

Snipers are usually smallish; I go about a buck fifty soaking wet. Western-trained medical doctor, it said, the University of Paris of all places. Psychiatrist, that started the bells ringing. I heard rumors for years, we all had. Some gook had supposedly come up with some new psycho-torture, interrogation techniques no one could resist. They said he could shrink wrap your head real tight, fucked some guys up so bad they joined his side, and some mother fuckers even quit the war altogether. They weren't prisoners of war, but they got captured, tortured by the good General, and just stopped fighting. What the fuck was that about?

Maybe that was true, maybe that's why they wanna off him so bad, but as I read on, I got the meat and potatoes. The good doctor who has since made General had a nasty habit of massacre. Now that might not seem all that bad, given he was at war, and we had done it to them lots of times. Mi Lai wasn't the only one believe me, but the way HQ sees things, it is all about who massacres who.

The general had been at it almost 20 years, 20 fucking years! Man, that's a long time in the bush. See, our guys came in and did their crappy little one year of combat duty, then went stateside to fuck off for the rest of their enlistment. Not the gooks, rich man, poor man, private, general, or psycho psychiatrist—they went into the jungle and didn't come out until the war was over, or they just didn't come out.

He was doing it to the French before we even got there. He'd move his men from the north down through Laos and Cambodia, cross over into South

The 13th Disciple

Vietnam, and hit our guys hard from behind. They'd isolate a company or platoon and annihilate them; I mean to say dead to the last swinging dick.

Then, they'd slip back into the jungles, cross the border where we couldn't touch them. Sometimes, they'd just drop their uniforms, put on civilian clothes, and walk right off the battlefield. Getting all the help from the good fucking citizens of our ally, South Vietnam. Command hated him, but the more I read the more I admired him. Fuck who was I to knock a psycho butcher? They hated him but were powerless to stop him. Nixon even invaded Cambodia, trying to find him and his men. Don't believe that bullshit you heard on Walter Cronkite; we were out to get this guy. But just like always he'd vanish.

Also, it looks like I'm not the first one they sent after him. The other guys didn't do so well either. Some were killed, some became loyal to him, psycho torture no one could resist, and none returned. Holy fuck. Ok, so I could figure out why they hated Dr. Death, but wasn't the war over? Well, their war was but mine lived on.

The 13th Disciple

They had my gear—piece of shit M-16 rifle, pistol, sniper rifle, grenade sack and machete—packed on a chopper for me. But this was no small recon job; this mother fucker was a Huey, a full-blown gunship. She had a pilot and room for six swinging dicks, locked and loaded. But now, there was only a pilot and one Navy SEAL aboard to escort me in.

The SEAL is a decent fighting man, the best the squids could put up for sure. I had a brawl with one once, six-five and 250 pounds and it took the motherfucker nearly an hour to beat me down.

Wanna know why? Because I can take the beating. I can take the best beating anyone can dish out. I've taken so many. I'm not afraid of them. I'll take as many as it takes, but if I ever get up—I'll get you.

I have been taking beatings my whole life. It started with my stepdad; it started when he used my arms for an ashtray. It started when I was so young I couldn't remember.

Everyone thinks the burns on my arms are battle scars. Fuck that—they've been there for as long as I can

The 13th Disciple

remember. Like this one time when I was six, he grabbed my left wrist and nearly broke it off, then he yanked so hard it practically came out of the shoulder, then he buried the cigarette right into my arm until smoldering. It went out with a singe, and there are hundreds of those singe marks on that arm alone. I think it made me a better soldier; I wasn't afraid of a goddamn thing.

You could hear the WIR of the big bird's engine starting up and the weight of the massive blades as they gained their gaudy angular momentum and feel the equally opposing recoil from the deck as he held her there against the big bird's angry protest, held until she couldn't hold it a second more, then with a lurch we leaped into the black sky.

We choppered inbound on the darkest, the most moonless night they could find—the kind of dark I liked. The kind you could hide in. We were headed to a spot in North Vietnam that I only knew as coordinates on a map. I'd know the terrain; it's the same for all of Vietnam, but not my way around. All I knew was that it was going to be hot. They had tried all war long to kill this man, failing that they figured he'd have his guard down now that the war was over. I figured differently.

And nobody believed in payback more than me, but the war was over. Why was it bugging me? It never would have before. What fucking happened to me up there during that hill bombing? Ah, what the hell, I was still gonna kill him, wasn't I? Knowing it was a mistake, I stuck his picture in my shirt pocket as the blackest night closed in on my mighty Huey.

Less than 30 minutes later, it touched down near the river bed. The chopper's rails hung about six inches off the water in the pitch black, and I was up to my knees in it when I splashed into the soup. Of course, I didn't hear the water. All I heard was the hurricane force of the Huey's huge thrust bear down as it lifted off.

That's when I caught the full-force rocket blast from the huge blades cutting the raw air in pulsating spasms, pushing the mangoes and jungle evergreens flat into the river.

As the beast rose like a bird, like a vulture, like

The 13th Disciple

a condor whose huge wings pounded you down, that's when I caught that sense, the sense unique to Hueys, the scatter and backscatter pummel the air, the water around my knees, my entire body, and the fluid shock resonating from my head through my feet in the river and back again.

Then, the huge beast shockingly summoned me with a pale green landing light, in my haste I had forgotten my grenade sack. They dropped it to me, and there in that silky iridescent strobe of light, I saw the young coconut palms slamming back and forth over me, around, in the savage pressure wake that I thought they would kill me right there.

And then, as those chopping blades forced lower even the black water, pushing it in pulsating spasms into the earth and with nowhere to retreat the viscous liquid lifted itself savagely into the night sky in an upside-down torrent of hurricane-force until at last, the Huey jumped out of there sideways, treetop level and I lay flat on my back in the water, not to be shot, adrift, alone, staring in the most intense of blackness up at the carpet of darkness in the sky.

The 13th Disciple

I'd spent a lot of nights alone in the jungle in Vietnam, seeing a lot of starless skies, but I never stopped to look at them before. I could see myself on my back in the water, the space between the jungle flattened only by the river, then on either side the jungle took at last dominion again.

I lay there, on my back, my hands and feet helping me stay afloat in the shallow waters until a mosquito bit my exposed cheek, then I knew it was safe to move.

"See you here in a week, Captain," one of the men said. But we each knew that probably wasn't true, and that's when I knew they weren't even coming back for me. That's why they picked me, and that's why they used leverage on me because this was a one-way trip for me. I should have known.

I wondered if anyone else aboard the chopper knew that. I would have blown it out of the sky if I thought they knew. I hated anyone getting over on me. But, really, it didn't matter to me either. I could be one way or the other. It was another strange and subtle shift that I couldn't explain.

The 13th Disciple

Then, my mind went back to that dark thing of how I could see it or see the world papered over it. That thought lingered and then faded away like the sound of the chopper in the distance. It was pure dark now, and I had to get my shit together.

If my intelligence was right, the General's command base was an old French colonial plantation. The fortress itself was built by the French to serve as a villa and a fort. It was about 40,000 square feet standing on roughly five football fields.

It had four squat columns of reinforced concrete that were about four stories high and 80 feet square, independently viable with munitions and stores for 10 men each if the main building were taken out. The columns were connected by concrete walls over a football field in length themselves, each had arched passageways leading to a large inner square open to the sky.

In the original design, there was even a European hedge maze outside of the southern wall. The inner square was still wide open, but you don't need to be really smart to figure that those archways were filled with red brick and the maze. Well, that's a long gonner.

Running under it all were huge wine cellars that made perfect munitions stores or bomb shelters. Red brick by now filled in the space between the floors of the old covered walkway connecting the columns to themselves, but only on the outside. The inside was open to the air. The brick was only to keep shooters like me from seeing in from the jungle, but as for protection against my sniper rifle, well, you may as well be holding up a brown paper bag.

The recon photos showed that the ground itself was essentially a huge plate of reinforced corrugated steel. What served as the roof for the four great big columns was unknown. I was not so concerned about the building itself, but its surroundings. How thick was the jungle, and how close did it come up to the compound?

I had been dropped about 5 klicks out. The jungle was thick, and moving through it undetected was easy. But when I got to the edge of the jungle and saw what I was up against, I couldn't believe my eyes. The house had a perimeter of about five football fields of cleared ground surrounding it. The fucking gooks had burned the jungle to the ground and then ripped it out by the roots just to make the house unapproachable. They had done a pretty goddamn good job.

I might as well turn back now, five yards, five hundred yards, may as well be 500 miles. I didn't have to get into the villa to make the hit, but I did need to be within a mile. The war might be over but I'd bet they'd still be mowing the grass out there, probably extending the radius too. I wondered whose command was trying to kill him or me.

I was just lying on my stomach in the grass, covered with leaves and branches, like a kid in bed, when I could hear two VC moving in the woods behind me. I lay very still but very comfortable as they came up and stood on either side of me. They smoked, one of them passing a cigarette to the other nearly over my head.

They spoke in Vietnamese, I understand Vietnamese, but I couldn't make out their dialect. They finished their cigs and left. You get used to lying in the grass so close to the enemy that you can see his boots.

The 13th Disciple

What you didn't get used to was a suicide mission with no way of completing it. I needed a cig myself.

I spent the next day and night in the jungle thinking things over. There was a road that went from the jungle into the camp. You could be sure any vehicles going into the base were searched real good, but I was wondering about the cars coming out. I knew that sooner or later, the General would have to leave.

With the war over, maybe security would be light, and maybe I could wait for him to come to me. I'd figured to set up out by the road and then ambush the car. But even if I could tell a decoy from his real car. How could I be sure that he would even be in it? I'd have to hide in the trees to see how the General moved around. Shit, I could be here a year, but it was the only way.

I moved in the night through the brush along the side of the road for about 2 clicks. I was looking for a place where a car would have to come to an almost complete stop. I didn't find that, but slipping around like a snake through the grass I got a risky sick idea. Even though they had cleared the jungle to the dirt around the villa, out here the brush moved almost up to the edge of the sloppy mud road.

I knew exactly what to do. I chopped up part of a blown-up banyan tree, which is everywhere out here. It was only about five feet long, but half as thick again, so that it would force any jeep to come to a complete stop. It nearly wore out my machete in the process. I left it standing and had it leaned against the brush so that I could push it over easily. Then, I packed my rolled-up sniper rifle in the deep grass, cut up some of the biggest elephant ear leaves, and fashioned a pretty damn good camo suit for myself. I could slip right into it, covering myself instantly in the glossy rubbery leaves so that a gook could look right at me at high noon and never see me there.

If all went according to plan, I would have to pull off this ambush no more than 20 feet from the road. Fuck me! Then, I moved back toward the camp, climbed the tree that I'd already picked out, watched the camp, and waited. I knew that I would probably have to wait for an insanely long time. At first, this didn't seem so wacky to me until sunrise when I got really hungry.

The 13th Disciple

It's not that I couldn't come down out of the tree, but I would have to wait, hunt, and forage inside, pissing off the enemy. That would be a pain.

This was Mattingly getting back at me from the grave, I thought. Then, I realized he wasn't the only one they could have used. How much weight did they really have on me? It was just a matter of how long or closely they'd been watching. Shit, most of the hits I'd made were under direct orders. It was the indirect ones that got me in trouble, I guess.

I moved down into the shade and fell asleep. I didn't wake until it was early evening and that was only because I was being eaten alive by big gnarly Vietnamese fire ants, each one big enough to bite your handoff.

As I escaped down the tree, killing the ants on my body as silently as possible, I realized that I might have missed the General leaving the compound while I was catching some Z's. But I thought it more likely that he'd move by night instead. Sure, the war was over, but here I was anyway, and maybe he was expecting someone like me to be here.

The 13th Disciple

When you live in war, uncertainty is the only constant. You learn to live by your feelings, and right now, that's what my gut was telling me, that he was still in there.

I was careful as I moved. I knew there were VC around, and I didn't even want to disturb the Macaws. There were virtually no, I mean to say zero, big animals left. No tigers or other big cats.

On my first tour, I'd seen a lot of big animals. I came across a coiled-up jaguar in the south once. I was a regular Army then and just on routine patrol. The big cat was coiled up in the base of a blown-out palm. It exploded from the tree in the fullness of the moonlight, the savage streak of its blasting past me in full fury a mear half-second before I carelessly stepped on it while trudging through the jungle. I fell back by the pressure wake alone and turned on my stomach just in time to see its streaking blackness soaking away into the shimmering night. I had also seen more than an occasional black bear in those early days of the war, but they are long gone now. The fire ants, well, they're doing just fine.

The 13th Disciple

The forests of Vietnam are two kinds: evergreen forests, which include banyan, and rubber tree forests, which was what I was smack in the middle of. In that evergreen woodlands architecture, the massive rubber trees with their coarse beige and brown bark served as the column beams going easily 100 feet or more and 10 feet in diameter.

Some of the trees consisted of colonies of trees whose huge immovable trunks wrapped and twisted as viciously as snakes in a mating frenzy so that even dead still, they looked like they were spinning at 100 miles an hour. Ten stories up the rubber tree barks opened to their giant evergreen elephant ear leaves that canopied and softened up the sun for the misty, mottled jungle floor below.

All in all, I approved of the brush. The trees were high with broad branches that made climbing easier than riding an elevator. But those columns were spread far apart making movement easy, and easy to detect. There were other woody plants on the jungle floor, ebony, teak, palms, and bamboo all entwined with evergreen leaves, not the best for cover but it would have to do.

Once I had everything figured out, I moved away from my position. As soon as I was clear, I dug a hole and took a dump and then made my way to the river where I took a swim to dislodge the remaining fire ants, got some water, and even stabbed a fish with my army knife. I cleaned it fast and ate it cold.

Then, I made my way back, collecting up some bananas and mangoes as I went. I returned to the same location, but this time, I made my way up to a different ficus tree. I figured it was far enough away from the ant motel of the last night that I wouldn't get my balls eaten off.

As I made my way up, it became obvious that this one was perfect. I was in a sea of big green leaves where you couldn't even see the ground or the sky. The branches were big and comfortable, and as dusk settled in, I wrapped myself around one and waited for night. Once it came, I climbed up high.

The branches were still very thick all the way to the top. I swam my arm around a few large leaves and cleared the top of the canopy, it was as if I broke the surface of the deep ocean. There, in the bloody tropical twilight, and for 360 degrees, all I could see was a thick canopy of lush green leaves and the diffuse dying sunlight that was half absorbed and half reflected off of them.

As the sun set, I settled in. I found a nice Y-shaped branch at the top of the canopy from which I could see the dim lights from the compound. If a car left that place, I'd be sure to see it.

When it got dark and the sky had a million stars out, I still couldn't see my hand in front of my face. I turned over on my back and put my arm under my head and crossed my legs in my habitual repose. I could just as easily be lounging in a hammock at a Club Med somewhere as on an assassination mission in a war that was over. It's all in how you think about it, I always said.

Some guys go out on a mission, and they are all uptight all the time, just because they are in a war. There will be time enough to be uptight all right, and you'll know what to do and when, but until then, save

The 13th Disciple

your energy and relax.

Right now, I thought that a cigarette and a bottle of rum would really complete the picture for me. Booze and cigs, some guys wouldn't touch them. They were too afraid of jonzing out and giving their position away when they got into the bush and had to go cold turkey. I'd seen it. Before, they couldn't hold their hand straight after three days. Not me, I was disciplined. But just like killing, cold turkey never bothered me. As I said, I kinda liked it.

Sometimes on R&R, I'd go cold turkey with a bottle of Jack and a pack of Marlboros right next to me. I'd wait all night and way past noon of the next day, get real good and jonzing for them, I'd torture myself. I liked it, I liked wanting it and waiting for it at the same time, knowing that it was only me who could cause and end my torment. It was the only thing that made me feel alive. And when I finally did dig in, I don't know. I mean it was good, I guess, but never as good as it seemed it was going to be when I was waiting for it. What was the point of having it if you could get it, I guess?

The 13th Disciple

The point is you have to be in control of your shit. Ahh, that's bullshit too because I could never not pour it in as fast as I could. Sure, I could deal with not having it, could handle not having it now, but if it was around, I would have to go all in. And why not, life is so fucking shitty, I can only take it, can only take the pain with the gentle anesthesia of inebriation.

It was the same way with women, I guess, a little different maybe. I'd been married once. I didn't see the need to stay that way. I didn't need love; well, I knew that was a lie. But I always lied about love. I lied to my wife when I said I loved her, when we got married, then I lied again when I said I didn't when we got divorced. Love, what a bunch of shit, still don't know what's worse, loving or being loved.

All I know is women were different than booze and cigarettes. You had no control over when it was that you couldn't take it anymore, they had it. I had only enough discipline to stay away from rather than deal with them. Besides, I could always get laid, bullshitting them was always easy.

Guess I felt that way about people too. They

were too much to deal with, all the lies, all the bullshit. Like I said, that's why I liked killing people, it was final, he was dead, and you both knew it.

Usually, while waiting, I don't think about a thing, and time crawls. But tonight, my brain was yacking away. I took a look at the compound, but there was nothing. I could feel the wind shifting and a stiff breeze blowing from the east. A few minutes later, the low rumbling of thunder came into the jungle. Soon, it would be raining, and that would be all right too. If I had to move, the wind and rain would muffle my sounds; otherwise, I'd just stay up here and enjoy it. And that is just what happened, it rained, and I didn't move.

When the first strong gust hit, it felt good. It made the big floppy leaves rustle around and blew the mosquitoes out. It felt so good that I actually dozed off up there until the first few sprinkles woke me up. I knew then that this was going to be a big one. The entire milky galaxy was behind some deep mean black clouds. I couldn't see the clouds, but I couldn't see the stars anymore.

The 13th Disciple

I sat upright with my legs crossed Indian style and rode the steadily swaying branch. As the droplets grew fatter and dropped harder, I remembered how much I liked the rain. As a kid, I used to run into any one of the old rusted cars around our place just to listen to it hitting the roof. Once, I got away from a beating by my step-dad when I bolted out into the rain. He was too fucking drunk to follow me out. Didn't mind beating the shit out of me, but he wouldn't get his knickers wet. He stopped at the front porch like it was a wall. Guess he was afraid it would sober him up.

It was raining that day too, the day when I blew the back of Mattingly's head through his face. It was coming down in buckets. It took only a split second to do it, to erase all he was, and all he'd ever be. And all over what, because he made us run, in boot camp no less. Fuck, that's what boot camp is all about. The drill sergeant is a professional asshole paid to find shit wrong and to make it up when he can't find something. But Olberman was a fat fucking jelly belly who disgusted me. That I judged him made it easy to kill him, not what I thought he'd done to me. So, it all came down to how I thought about it, not what it really was. Well, that will make him feel better, I guess.

Now, it was streaming down in sheets. Several flashes of lightning lit the jungle like a strobe light, and I could see the canopy top waving back and forth. I pulled the leaf of an elephant ear toward me and curved rather than folded it into a trough, then put it to my lips and drank as if from a fountain. That water was cold and pure.

It wasn't until the storm moved off that it got light and then it got hot. By 09:00, it was over 90 degrees and sweltering. I'd had plenty to drink the night before so, I wasn't thirsty, rather I was starving, jonzin too, who am I bullshitting?

All I'd had for the last 24 hours was a cold fish, some bananas, and mangoes. I wanted to find some breakfast really bad, but something just told me to stay put. Then, I didn't mind being hungry.

In my mind, I was in the game now, "lean and hungry", out for a kill. And I knew one was on the way. I didn't expect him to move by daylight, but like I said, in a world of uncertainty, I listened to my gut and stayed put.

The jungle was a sauna now, and I was forced to stay in the sun on top of the canopy to survey the old plantation house. I could talk my mind out of being disturbed by hunger, cigs, and booze, but not the heat.

By 14:00, it was brutal. But suddenly, all consciousness of that dissipated like the steam off the leaves when I saw two cars coming down the road out of the plantation and toward the jungle. I wasted only a second to be sure that cars were actually on their way out. I had no way to know that the General was on board. I just knew.

I dropped below the canopy as a diver below the waves. I was vaguely aware of the relative coolness in the shade. My shirt felt much hotter than my body as I used the branches like an expressway, sliding down smoothly in the streaming shafts of light to the sun-dappled forest floor below. It felt like I was gliding like a sailor down the rigging rather than falling. There was a moment when I forgot about the mission, my guilt, and everything except my body sliding down the jungle.

I jumped the final ten feet and bent my knees so that my butt touched the ground, and before I could stand up, my good fortune occurred to me. Not only was the ground still wet, but because it had just rained the tree that I was going to use to block the road would draw no suspicion. They would blame it on the storm. I sprang off to the ambush point, intending to drop the branch across the road as planned.

I can't remember a single step I took on the ground. No sooner did my boots sink into the still-moist earth and a carpet of leaves made it seem that I was in a race against time. It was the sound of two cars that wafted through the woods and told me I was going to be too late to block the road. I really had to turn it on to get to that tree and hope it was where I'd left it, tied standing up next to the road.

I got there before they did. I cut it loose and watched as it fell across the road. I swear that the mud was still splashing up in the air when the cars made their way up to it. They were going slow because the road was muddy and that gave me time to slink back away from the road, giving my position in the deep shrubs along the roadside.

My sniper rifle was right where I left it. I got down, unrolled it, and sat in a three-point position: right knee and both feet together on the ground, with my left knee up off of the ground as the cars passed. I already had the butt firmly in the crook of my right shoulder with the barrel down.

If I got lucky, all I had to do was to raise the barrel and shoot. I wouldn't even have to stand up. As for the camo suit, there was no time, and I didn't need it. The brush was thick, and the mud was sticky. I quickly smeared healthy portions of grassy mud across my forehead, and it stuck.

They came to the overturned tree blocking the muddy path and stopped. If there had been only two soldiers, I would have engaged them first before killing the General. But there were three, and they were being cautious. They were speaking a mix of Vietnamese and French. The French I could make out.

"Attention, attention," one of them said very

slowly. As expected, the blockade drew no suspicion; they pulled right up to it. Three men got out and began inspecting every nook and cranny around them. The one who was speaking French was looking up in the trees, while the other two were bayonet-ting the shrubs along the side of the road. I was fucked.

I had anticipated two or three cars with the General in the second car. So, the General's car was stopped right in front of me, and in my line of sight would be perfect if I could just fucking stand up. But like this fucking VC just knew I was in there. He scanned the low bushes back and forth again and again over my position.

My face was caked in camo and cloaked behind the leaves, but somehow, we actually made eye contact, and he didn't make me. I closed my eyes to make it go away, but I could hear him stabbing his bayonet past my left side and then my right. It was ten inches on either side. Then, the men sprayed the bushes and up in the trees with long explosive bursts that had flaming red leaping from the barrels of their AKs.

I jumped outta my fucking skin, but my body

didn't move. It was frozen, much too afraid to. When it stopped, I opened my eyes. Only the gunpowder hid the smell from my shit-stained shorts. But now, I couldn't believe my luck.

As the soldiers cleared the road, the General sat up straight or something because I could see his head from where I was. I wouldn't even have to stand up. It took a second for me to slightly adjust my rifle and get his head in my sights. It was a task I had performed a million and one times, but this time, something happened that had never happened before. Sometime between when I pulled the trigger and the round exited the barrel, I felt it. I was him, and I felt the bullet go right through my brain from one side to the other. And just as if he felt it too, he ducked.

I have no idea where that round landed, but I'd sooner answer that question than figure out how the fuck he knew I was there. The sniper rifle only holds a single round. They are not meant to miss. So, I dropped it and, without even coming out of my crouch, picked off the shocked shit less corporal who had tickled me with his bayonet a minute ago with my pistol.

The 13th Disciple

Still, without ever standing, I was able to roll out of there and back into the jungle just before the machine-gun fire from the other two VC obliterated all the brush in my old position. The last thing I heard just as I came to my feet and flew outta there was the car door slamming shut.

As I jetted out of there, it wasn't me I was worried about; it was my mission. I was OK, right now. I was fast, and the compound and all of the VC were behind me. All I had to do was make it to the river. But my mission was dead. There was no way to take the General now.

By now, every VC gook on the fucking planet was looking for an American running through the jungle, and they'd be all around the General. I was as fucked with HQ as I was sure as shit fucked here.

I dropped down and lay flat on my back in the deep grass so the two VC on my ass could catch up. They did, running full bore and straight up. Even with just a 45, I was able to drop them in mid-stride, and they never even knew they were dead.

The 13th Disciple

Now, for the General, maybe my mission wasn't screwed. If I knew this guy like I thought I did, he wouldn't be cowering back by the car. He'd be chasing me too, and that car door I heard slamming told me that I knew this guy.

I needed more than a 45. I went over to one of the dead VC, a kid who didn't have a face anymore, and pulled his ammo belt off. Then, I picked up his still-hot AK47. Now, I'd hide and wait for the General; I knew that he was coming. But I was wrong about that. He was already there waiting for me, a big mother fucker.

As I stood up with the kid's AK, I heard him coming up behind me. How the fuck did he do that? No one did that to me. But when I turned around, my weapon was already leveled, and his 45 was still rising up. I had him. Dead to fucking rights, I had the son of a bitch, but I never fired my weapon.

As I faltered, he took two steps and put the muzzle of his 45 to my forehead. It was cold, hadn't been fired. I can't say why, but that told me something about him, I don't know what, but something.

The 13th Disciple

I turned my head to the right and brushed the 45 away from my face like I was putting out a cigarette, then a second later, gave him the best-left hook anyone has ever seen, right on the button.

It rocked him, and he dropped the gun and staggered backward. I moved in, but he kicked me in the balls. It was all I could do to bring both hands down and block him. But that left me exposed. I watched helplessly as his other leg came around and caught the side of my face flush.

I kept fighting, but can't remember much after that. We were mixing it up there when I saw in the grass off to my side an AK. I jumped down and grabbed at it, but when I rolled back up to my feet, it was with empty hands.

I fell back to the ground with my hands behind me, palms on the ground. I could clearly see that the General went for a gun too and got it. He had his 45 again. I looked straight into his eyes, and they were focused tightly between mine. He told me in Vietnamese to get on my knees and put my hands behind my head.

Instead, I raised slowly to my feet and gave him the universal finger for fuck you with my left hand. He gave me another straight kick to the groin with his right leg, and I turned my arm over to block it with my middle finger still up as the block was going down to meet his rising leg, but I never touched a thing. In the same smooth motion, his leg kept rising, his hips twisted, and his foot turned over. It was the most beautiful thing I never saw. The round kick caught me flush, spun me around in mid-air, and dumped me lights out in the long grass.

The second that I came to, I wished that I was dead. There was a light, like the headlights of an oncoming train. It was only a flashlight, but it might as well have been a freight train.

I knew what was coming next. See, I'd straddled both sides of this fence before. And the more awake I became, the more pain I realized that I was in. I was sitting upright in a chair in the middle of the room, my feet chained down and hands taped behind me, all standard operating procedure. As I said, I'd been here before, and all you gotta understand is that right about now, it pretty much sucked to be me.

    The tape across my mouth went from ear to ear, and I actually thought that it alone was holding my jaw to my face. That big fucking gook kicked the shit out of me, and now it was really beginning to hurt. But I knew the real beating was about to begin. I had already let go. It's just pain, I said, it's just a feeling like any other. No need to stress over it, and sure as shit won't do a bit a good to freak out.

    It worked whenever my stepdad cornered me and beat the shit out of me, and it worked in the field too. You'd be surprised at how well it works. Sometimes, it's all in how you think about it.

    The only light was from the flashlight on me, but I could hear people in the darkness that enveloped it. The cong always thought men didn't like the dark ring that a spotlight forms around the man being interrogated, but I like the darkness. I had always taken refuge there, and it did my spirits good that it was so close to me. Normally, the worst thing they could do to me would be to turn the lights on.

But now, for the second time in my life, the darkness terrified me. Not because of the unknown held within, but because of the known. He was out there, maybe not in the room, but close and aware, not just of my body, but thoughts as well. I couldn't pick up his, but he heard everything I was thinking.

Usually, this dance begins with some sort of sparring to decide what they think you know before things go medieval on your shit. If they thought you were of no use to them either because you didn't know anything or because you wouldn't break then things went to def-con 5, they'd be feeding the pigs with your ass.

The trick for someone in my shoes was to make them think I knew something more than what I'd told them. The one thing about the VC was that they believed and, with such good reason, that they could break anybody. Even, if you could take the beating, you could maybe last long enough for headquarters to work something out, a prisoner swap or something, anything to get you the fuck out of there. But now the war was supposedly over, and I wasn't even here officially, so by my math things looked pretty fucked.

Suddenly, there was a gook in my face. He pulled the tape from my mouth, and it peeled off with a loud tearing sound, which I know must have hurt, but I didn't feel a thing. It was fucking hard to talk. He started off in very bad English, so I answered in Vietnamese, which I hoped would make me the tiniest bit more human to him. I don't know if it did, I didn't expect to be saved, but I did want to know if I felt what the General did just before I took the shot at him. But obviously, I could die without knowing that now and probably would.

Most of it went on in Vietnamese, but he was taking orders from some fuck back out of the light, and they spoke in French. I didn't let on that I understood French.

He started off with the normal warm-up bullshit—name, rank—but the guy in the dark told him to get to the point, and that was fine by me. Might as well give them what they want and get it over with.

They asked me if I knew the war was over, and

said yes, then I shocked them. I told them the name of the General who had put the hit out on his General. They asked me if I knew why, and I said I didn't care.

They went back and forth for a little while in French and Vietnamese. I didn't follow it all because I was blacking out. Fortunately, my hosts prevented that by taking a handful of my hair and pulling my head back until I could see upside-down behind me.

When he saw that he had my attention, he looked back at his boss in the dark and asked me if I worked alone. I nodded, and I could tell he believed me because he moved on. Next, he said "How many more assassins are coming? The war is over. How many more are coming?"

I replied, "I don't know."

Then, he hauled off and back-fisted the lights outta me. So, that was the last thing I said before he knocked me out, saying that I wasn't the first and probably not the last.

I had no idea how long I had been out for. When I came to again, it was dark. I hadn't seen blackness like this since that hill bomb in Da Nang. I said "come to" but I wasn't really conscious. Maybe because they beat the fucking daylights outta me, or maybe it was something else. All I knew was that it was dark in there, so dark I could not see the floor, and I was laying on it, sprawled out on my left side with my swollen left jaw on the hard stone or rock. The only sensation I had was that of a faint sound of water gently trickling somewhere and the cold of the stone floor, which felt good on my jaw but chilled the shit outta the rest of me. I felt around some more and noticed I'd been stripped down naked. That too was all SOP. I lifted my head as best as I could to look around, but I couldn't see a fucking thing no matter what.

Down there in all that stank, it occurred to me that killing a man wasn't always such a shit thing to do to him. It takes just the subtlest shift to see it, to see that the forced march of life itself is the curse, death the escape. *There is the mistake that death is peace.* Shit, if I'd known that I'd never capped my stepdad; he was the most miserable son of a bitch alive. Yeah, that's one stank body no fucking creepy CIA limp dick was ever gonna dig up.

It took me years to do it. I'd decided to ever since that night in the dog house. Who knows? Maybe I could have forgotten about that, but I could never forget about him. Shit, I saw a reminder of him every time I looked at my arms or legs, loving reminders of every time he used them for an ashtray.

It was when I went home from my first tour. When I was a kid, that SOB always tried to get me to go hunting with him. But I knew two things: first was that he always got drunk when he hunted, and second, what always happened to me when he got drunk. So, I never went when I was a kid, but after my first tour, well, he didn't have to ask twice.

That dumb fuck never saw it coming. I waited till we were in the deep woods, and it was dark, just like with Mattingly, but this time I told him what I was going to do. "Hey, fuck, wanna say goodbye? Because right now, you're gonna die." Then, I decked him, with a crack. It sounded just like a shot and felt good when he collapsed into the leaves. He was just coming around when my saw cut through his Adam's apple. I had his hair in one hand, and, with his head held back, I was sawing through his throat with the other. My first stroke ripped through his Adam's apple.

I remembered the skin opening up. There wasn't a lot of blood at first; it would come later, hot and sticky. But that first cut musta woke him, he knew exactly what was happening. He tried to tuck his chin and grabbed my cutting arm fiercely with both hands, but I kept his throat exposed and kept cutting. It wouldn't even take a full stroke now.

That's when I saw him cry, and it made me stop. I saw the fear in his eyes and the spittle in his quivering mouth, just like a helpless boy about to get a beating. That's when I got it, that he was just like me. I didn't pity him at the time or show any mercy. I sliced his fucking head clean off and threw it between his legs. I saw his headless neck steaming in the cold. I turned and left him there for the animals to finish off. If anyone found anything it would just be his clothes scattered to shit and back. I was sure that no one would ask a lot of questions; he didn't have many friends, but he had one that I never thought about, never thought to give a fuck about.

I could hear the sound of the water had changed. Before it was just an unobtrusive trickle, but now it sounded like a rocket at take-off, thunderous. *My brain is playing tricks on me,* I thought. Fuck that it was torturing me, yakking at me even down in this hole, bringing up shit buried so deep I forgot about it. Why?

When I got back to the house, I came in through the back door and went right to the kitchen. I peeled my clothes off, threw them in the sink and started cleaning up, cleaning the blood off. That's when my mother showed up, standing in her puke pink robe in the hallway just staring at me.

What the fuck was she doing up at 6 a.m. anyway? She's usually passed out till noon. When I turned and looked up, all I could see were her eyes. That's how it was with us, whenever she knew something about me, no words were needed, and this time was no different. She knew exactly what I was doing, exactly what I had done, and exactly to who.

What had I done? Didn't I just get rid of her

problem and save her from another 10 or 20 years of beatings? Not really, I guess, I really just got rid of my own problem, my own need to get back at anyone or anything that had ever crossed me. How many beatings had she taken for me, how many times had she stuck her face in front of his screaming fist intended for me, how many scars on her once pretty face should be worn by me instead, how many?

I can still regard my mother from the Mind, above the battleground with no way to know how many dreams we shared or what we were to each other if anything at all, I only know that she was a stick figure with no real body or emotions, but as a dream figure myself it tore me up.

From the dream, I looked hard at my mother for the only time, ever, and saw the scars. They seemed so heinous at first, like the ones over both eyes, too rugged for makeup to cover, but time blended them seamlessly, and gradually, they became part of her.

She sure as shit took the bastard home like a stray dog, but he'd fucking killed me if it weren't for her. I took my hands out of the sink and shook them off as she walked over to me, staring at me, her eyes were all I could see.

She came over, never blinked, not a tear in her eyes, she came over, stopped still seeing right through me, and spit right in my face. It was the worst fucking half-second of my life.

I walked around her, changed my clothes and left. *Oh, fuck it! I guess I can see things her way.* If I tried, if I wanted. After all, there weren't many choices for a woman like her where we lived, and I had just removed the only choice she ever had, and I did it for me in spite of her. Still, I'd never admitted that I did something wrong, not even to myself. But now, I felt rats biting at my ear, and fuck it.

I was still thinking about that as I was driving to my wife's house right after. I was supposed to sign the divorce papers. I thought it was going to be simple. Drive over, leave the engine running, go to sign on the line, and split.

I was one of those bizarre kinds of husbands who completely dreaded showing the slightest bit of emotion. I even once had a panic attack after a particularly tender round of lovemaking and got sick when I attempted vainly to gasp the words, "I love you".

She never caught on. She thought I was just choking on something, and I was. But when I saw her there, I didn't know how to put it, but she just softened me up, and I almost lost it. I'll spare you the details, but as I took the pen to sign my name, she touched my hand and that touch gave me a rail spike in an instant and set off a brush fire of emotion coursing through my soul.

Her hands were so soft, and this time so were her eyes. She said, "We don't have to do this." Looking at me like that with the sun coming up and through her dress, my heart was pounding, my gut churning, I was bursting apart at the seams, exploding to tell her how there were no words to say how much I love you, how I could have made love to her forever right there, in that room, on that couch, forever ourselves melding into one, *a oneness so complete that bodies cannot accomplish it,* that I imagined growing old with her right there in that room.

"If you don't love me, then leave, but I think you love me, and I love you." When she said that, I got weak, and it was all I could do not to start weeping like a baby.

But what I did was to put one hand on each of her slender shoulders, feeling that softness of pure skin, push her at arm's length, look straight into her soft blue eyes, and told her a bald-faced lie as I would to the enemy.

"I don't love you," I said and walked outta there without leaving her a clue. I high-tailed it back to Nam to die. Shit, the only thing you had to worry about here was getting tortured and killed.

And here I was, near death, sprawled out on a stone dungeon floor, and what was I thinking about; shit in the past, none of which could hurt me anymore, or could I do shit about?

Yet, those thoughts roared so loud. When I passed out this time, it wasn't from fatigue or a beating or even starvation. The truth was that I just couldn't take any more of myself. The last thing I remember before passing out again was the cloud of mosquitoes biting and more rats and roaches coming in a swarm from a grate in the floor.

The next time I came to must have been a long time. I thought it was the mosquitoes that finally woke me up, but the first thing I thought about was my stomach. I was jonesing, more than starving, but I was thirsty more than that.

As far as I could tell, I was in the same position, on my side spread on the floor. I rubbed my hand across my belly, and it felt small, but so too did my jaw. In fact, I think I'd actually healed a bit from the beatings I got from the General and the interrogator.

It was like my body was numb. I could make out the proportions, but I didn't really feel anything in detail. And I still couldn't see a fucking thing, between the darkness down there and my eyes swollen shut.

I could still hear the water trickling again. So, I decided to go to it. The standard operating procedure now was to orient myself. The sounds came from behind me, and it was a huge fucking big deal to exchange the positions of my ass and my head right there on the floor. But somehow, I managed to rotate 180 degrees.

My body didn't hurt as bad, but I was weak now, and it made me really fucking tired. So, I rested for I don't know how long. Maybe I even fell asleep, I don't know. But eventually, I began to crawl toward the sound of trickling water.

It was funny. Back in the war, I tried so hard to stay alive, and now I was going to die in here, and I didn't give a shit. I didn't give a shit about dying, I didn't give a shit about the rats and roaches and mosquitoes, I didn't even feel the pain my body was in. I was somewhere else, I was everywhere else, but there was nowhere else. And then, I was back inside him, inside his head, just like when I took the shot—I was him.

I was him, sitting in my chair pushed back from my desk with my legs straight and feet crossed. I was staring at the glass of Jack Daniels with both hands cupped, resting on my lap and the bottle on the desk. Shit, the gooks drank Jack, go figure. I could sure use a shot of Jack myself. I could almost taste and feel the sweet mahogany texture of it flowing, coursing, and collecting like water in the lowest parts, the most badly deprived, habituated tissues of my dream body. There it coalesced in my imaginative fury, relieving me of my agony, of my banishment from the seductive substance, and vomiting up violently my massive delusion of self-control. I could see everything as if I were him, and I could move in and back out again. This was fucking weirder than anything I'd ever known before. Anything except that fucking dark star that I fell into in Da Nang, or the bullet before it went through his brain.

But there he was thinking about me just like I was thinking about him. I guessed he could read my mind too, so I tried not to think about anything that would give me away. I thought I wouldn't think anything at all.

Then, I realized how stupid that was. How the hell did you not think? It was like not breathing. You could only decide what to get hung up on or not, but the brain was always secreting thoughts, like bile from the liver—the shit just dripped. Like now, my brain thought, way to go, asshole, getting captured on an assassination mission that didn't exist, in a war that was over, by a man who could somehow read my fucking mind. I couldn't stop thinking it, but I could kick the shit outta myself for it or not. I kept crawling.

As I crept closer and heard his thoughts, I could tell that, just like me, he was scared. But instead of freaking out, he was beginning to make sense of things; he was actually starting to understand it. I didn't understand it—I didn't understand a fucking thing. I lost contact with him when I came into contact with a wall.

Finally, I began to think that I was in a dark, immaterial desert outside the universe. But then, finally, I found something of this world, something I recognized: a wall, cold, hard, and slimy. I painfully raised my bruised torso and leaned back against it. I felt roaches scatter and heard mosquitoes buzzing, knowing full well that rats were close. I took comfort in them, for they were things I knew about, but I had no idea what I was experiencing.

I turned my face to the wall and ran my tongue

across it, collecting every precious drop of tawny moisture. This was where he left me to die, and I wouldn't have thought to blame him if I could have thought about anything else but sucking every last drop of slime water condensing on the stony wall. Maybe it's because all I was thinking about was that water on the wall, the here and now, but that's when it happened. Or maybe it's always happening, but I was just able to see it—a subtle shift.

That's when the wall that I was pressing my aching face against just wasn't there, then it was there, then it had never really been there at all. It was only partly gone, then completely gone, then back again. I opened and squeezed my eyes shut repeatedly, but it wasn't my eyes that I was seeing with. At that moment, I was in that moment and no other. The shit that had happened or would happen to me ceased to exist, just like the moments themselves. The next second seemed no closer to me than the next century.

None of them existed anymore, so they were in fact unreal. It's not that they didn't happen, but that they aren't happening, and thinking otherwise seemed an illusion.

I was a murderer and quite possibly would be once again, but right now, I was just the body of some guy struggling to sip some slime juice off of a wall that was never there to begin with. When I saw things in that way, I felt, I dunno, innocent.

Innocent—that's a big word to a guy like me. I mean I know not in the world of illusion, in that world my body had done terrible things to all sorts of other bodies, but all of that was in the past or was to come, not now.

INNOCENT—in the moment, what else could I be?

INNOCENT—I rolled the word in my mind, across my tongue, and formed each succinct, savory syllable. I-N-NO-CENT, I took each precious letter to taste and savor, to hold onto in the darkness, in the forever now.

INNOCENT, I AM INNOCENT, INNOCENT IS WHAT I AM. And when I perceived things that way, there was no wall, no floor, no pain, and no fear. It was like when I let go of my life, but this was letting go of everything—life and the universe surrounding it.

Time was just like the wall. I mean it didn't stop; it just wasn't. Of course, the past and future are both fake, just tricks of the ego, but I wasn't supposed to know or remember that. But I got it now, beaten to a cunt hair of my life—I got it all by myself. Or maybe I just remembered it: that no one can harm anyone in a dream.

I went on that way, going back and forth, in and out, just making subtler and subtler shifts in perception. I could sense fear when I came back to what I thought was reality. And when the universe dropped away again, I felt Love.

Man, I wanted to stay there, stay with whatever it was keeping me in Love, but then I don't know, I couldn't hold it. I panicked and lost it. And at the moment I did, I wondered if it had ever really been. Like a dream, you tried not to wake up from, and couldn't hold onto once you did.

I was about to die and had finally found

complete peace. Now, I wanted to keep that peace, more than I ever wanted anything. I wanted to keep just a slice of that peace.

But just like the passing moments, and the breaths we take, just like the lives we live, going like dust into thin air, just like everything else in the dream, and just like the dream itself that never was, just like that it was gone. Replaced by the clanking of metal and a shaft of light that made the roaches scatter in their millions of scaly steps.

I turned around and leaned against the wall. The light hurt my eyes and I shut them and passed out.

I don't know how long I was out for this time, but when I came to, it was in a small hospital unit of about a dozen beds or so. There were no guards, no bars on the windows, and the door was open. The inside wall went only halfway up, and I could see people walking past the corridor.

Shit, I was in the mansion and I could get up and walk away if I could get up at all. I did another body check, wiggle toes, check, then I noticed that I was clean and that my jaw was almost back to normal.

I sat up in bed and just stayed there a minute, trying to clear the cobwebs. Obviously, the General had a change of heart regarding my fate, or at least a change of tactics. I had completely forgotten that feeling of peace, unaware that I had even had the dream of innocence.

After a couple of minutes, a male doctor saw me and came in, waving for a female nurse to follow. It struck me how even in North Vietnam the doctors wore white, and the nurse was female.

He asked me in Vietnamese how I felt as though he knew I could speak it. I answered that it was the best I felt in a long time. I didn't bother saying since I got blown up in Da Nang. I said that I was getting hungry, and he checked my pupils.

By the time he'd finished the nurse had dutifully returned with a tray of rice and mango. That's what I remembered hating about the gooks, the way they turned every daily task into some life-or-death mission.

Now, I wondered why I hated them for it, why I

hated everyone for everything. For just a second, I wasn't judging, for just a second I felt a little piece. I even smiled at myself a little, unnoticed.

The food was bland, but it made the space that it occupied in my belly feel a lot better nonetheless. I finished off the mango and thought about the ones I'd eaten in the tree I didn't know how many nights ago.

I laid back in the bed as I had that night in the tree, with my right hand under my head, it was a natural position for me. I looked up at the ceiling and wondered when. When would I be meeting the General, and what would that be about?

There was a late afternoon thunder boomer erupting outside, the kind that rolls infrequently in Nam. The day turned to night, temperatures dropped 20 degrees, and it sounded like a fire hose got turned on in the sky.

I jumped a little when the rain exploded against the tin roof like machine-gun fire, and that's when I finally knew what it was made of.

A guard, the first I'd seen since waking in the

hospital, brought me some clothes. They seemed to be my greens, cleaned and repaired, but I didn't care enough to notice. I was too nervous about meeting the General.

The single guard instructed me that I was indeed going to see the General. He escorted me to the inner square that was open to the bullet-sized raindrops, and they made a distinct cracking sound as they impacted the courtyard.

I thought about the bullet that didn't go through the back of the General's head. It was midday, but it looked dark outside. The cool rain felt good. The guard opened an outer door, and I went into a short narrow corridor, down three or four flights of steps that ended at the door to what was once probably a servant's quarters, below ground level. He opened the door for me and followed me inside. There were no windows, only a small green banker desk lamp spotted the room, the walls were red brick. The desk was against the far wall, and behind it a bookshelf. Not so much a bookshelf as three holes in the wall where books were deliberately put. They were about six feet long. On a low shelf immediately behind the desk chair was a bottle of Jack Daniel's I'd seen him drinking in my mind.

Where the hell did he get that from? I sure as shit would have loved to make a toast to any fucking thing at all, but not just now. Now, my body's needs came second to my own. The carpet was red and halfway up each wall ran strips of teak, an expensive wood that comes cheap in Vietnam. It was an ordinary office with a hint of cozy to it which I would have recognized if I recognized cozy.

The guard put me in the chair and stood at the wall behind me. As I waited, I studied books. There were some on military history and theory written in Vietnamese. The I-CHING was in French, the Holy Bible in English, and as a bookend, a statue of a gladiator—a Murmillo, of all things.

I was just thinking about how nothing should surprise me when I heard the door open. When the soldier saluted, I knew that the General had just come in. Out of a ridiculous habit, I stood and started to salute. The guard didn't know how to respond.

The 13th Disciple

I could hear him approach from behind as I came quickly to my feet, then clumsily aborted my attempted salute. I really didn't know what to do under these circumstances. I mean, how do you respond to the commanding officer when you're a prisoner in a war that's over?

"Old habits die hard, don't they, Captain?" he said in Vietnamese about my gaffe. His voice was deep, belonging more to a General than a doctor.

Then, he stood behind the desk and looked me square in the eye, and up and down, then back in the eye. He was just as big as he'd looked in the jungle. I noticed some scars on his face that I hadn't seen before, old scars.

His tone was strong, but even. I was curious, not worried, if he wanted me dead, I'd have been fed to the pigs long ago.

He motioned to the chair for me to sit down and we sat down together, formally and very politely considering that I'd tried to put a bullet through his head. He told the guard to wait outside and sat down just as the door shut, put his elbows on the desk, and clasped his hands. They were big and gnarly. He looked right through me with coal-black eyes while stating matter of factly, "You were captured just outside the Villa nine months and one day ago." So, that's how long I'd been here.

"You stated that you acted alone, but with the knowledge and under the orders of members of the US military and your government," he said as he was shuffling some papers. He was asking the right-sounding questions, but it was all bullshit, he only really wanted to know about me. Me, I was dying to spill my guts and didn't even know it.

"Yes sir," I said.

"How many more will needlessly follow you, Captain"?

"I don't know sir," I said. I really didn't. I didn't even know why they sent me, but it would help me if I knew what they wanted from you. "Is this revenge? Didn't you kill someone close to General, whatever the fuck his name was?

"We have all killed our fair share Captain," he cut me off. "I know what they think they want," he said. I wondered what he meant by that.

"Now, you, Captain, will stay here until I decide it's time for you to leave," he said in Vietnamese again. "And then I'll give you something to deliver to your superiors."

"What, sir," I hesitated. I couldn't fathom what he could mean, but my curiosity was killing me. I had come here, dying to know about how he could read my thoughts, both in the bush and in the hole, but now this piqued it to a rivaling degree. And while I hung on his next word, the General looked down and busily signed more papers. I suddenly realized that this was going to be just a get-to-know-your-first session. Fucking great, great to meet you, stop by anytime you decide to put a bullet in my head.

With so much to say and nothing being said, I played it cool. I didn't look directly at him but at his desk and at the bookshelf behind him again. He kept looking down at the papers he was glancing through and signing, but he was watching me. When my eyes settled on the murmillo, he stopped, looked up at me, and said, "You have interest in gladiators?"

"Yes, sir," I said. "I studied all about them when I was a kid."

"The murmillo was your favorite, wasn't it"? His body relaxed a little, and he turned halfway around to look askance at what he'd probably seen a thousand times as if he had no idea that he had no way of knowing that.

If he saw my jaw drop, he didn't act like it, just played it cool, and went on about the murmillo. "The perfect balance of speed and size and power," he said. "That statue is nearly two thousand years old. It was discovered on the site of an ancient ludus on the western outskirts of ancient Rome, on the coast in a place called Ostia."

Ostia didn't ring a bell, but I said, "I had toy gladiators around my room from Christmas when I was six. By the time I was sixteen, I had read every book there was on gladiators. They were the only books I did read, and the murmillo was my favorite."

The 13th Disciple

"So, is that how you become interested in soldiering?" he asked.

"Well, I never really liked being a soldier," I admitted, "but they don't have gladiators anymore."

"Yes," he said, "armies are too big, too messy, they have to be maneuvered, coordinated with sea and air components, and too complicated. For the gladiator, things were simple, he could depend only on himself. His opponent was always in front of him, not hiding in the grass. And he didn't have to worry about being attacked after the battle was fought."

I must have been squirming a bit, but I also thought, okay, bring it on, let me have it.

"Is that why you became an assassin, Captain? Because you're on your own, no orders to give or take, no excuses to make to anyone. Is that why, Captain?"

"There are no excuses for the things I've done, sir, some of them anyway."

"There are no excuses needed, for any of us," he said.

The 13th Disciple

Now, I really wondered what he meant. I finally realized that he was not angry. I just expected him to be. In a second, my pounding heart would be relieved. I wondered what he knew about me, what he did not.

"Relax, Captain, I have spent these last nine months not thinking about you. Despite the fact that you were able to get so close, and that you did not kill me when you had the chance. But then you reminded me of some basic Truths that I'd forgotten during the war. But I am in touch with the Truth again, and so I Forgave you, and I haven't had ill-thought about you since. And please understand, Captain." He was speaking in English now. "That when I use the word Forgiveness, it is not as so often in a superior manner, nor as one who feels rightfully wronged and who condescends to graciously forgive his offender from the perch of moral superiority, but in the truer sense. Namely that I am reminded, reminded by you that no one really hurts anyone, *nothing is ever done, only undone.*"

"Well, if dropping by to put a bullet in your brain after the war is over is not offensive." I had no friggin clue what he was talking about, and I couldn't read his mind anymore, but I could sure as shit read his face.

He was getting ahead of himself now and saying shit that he had intended to wait to say. He was about to break it off now, and I didn't want him to. It seemed risky, but I had to do it.

So, I asked, "Sir, how did you know when to duck?"

He leaned back in his chair clasped both hands behind his big neck and seemed massively relieved like he had a horrible secret that he didn't have to keep just to himself anymore. "I felt a spiritual bullet go through my brain just a second before you pulled the trigger, and you felt it too."

"Yes sir I did sir," I said. What the hell else could I say? Either we were both crazy, or we could both read the mind of the other, and neither one of us was sure which was crazier.

"Captain, you undoubtedly know of my profession before the war," he said, leaning forward and putting his gnarly hands on his desk.

I nodded, and he continued, "I was a psychologist; I had my own practice in Paris, which may surprise you. I had a good reputation among my peers, was sought after, and successful.

But psychology is more like the weather than gravity. It can be absolutely correct and still denied. I had a client who I was sure was evil; the clinical name was sociopath. He was a high-level sociopath, very intelligent, and steeped in deep denial. It was my job to both diagnose, i.e., judge him, and then treat him.

Sociopaths do not like to be called sociopaths. They, by nature, resist criticism of even the smallest degree; their very low self-esteem simply cannot accept any. Well, with my patient, it was locked combat three times a week.

One day, after he'd left after a particularly grueling session, I went and lay down on my own couch, thinking about the standard therapy that I had been taught in medical school, and I immediately realized why it was so unsuccessful. The standard therapy was steeped in judgment and criticism. Diagnosis is, of and by itself, a judgment. Now, I was not a religious man, but I suddenly and unknowingly cried out loud, 'God, there must be a better way. There must be a better way of dealing with clients and treating people in the world than by judgment and criticism, I hope that I can find it'.

Well, to make a long story short, my client exited therapy, paid his bill, and I never saw him again. I had almost forgotten it, but one night about six months later, after another long day of seeing clients, I poured myself a scotch and sat back in my chair. My desk lamp was on, this very lamp," he tapped at it, "other than that the room was dark. I was just nursing the Scotch, not really thinking anything when I was shocked by a voice coming from inside the room. I was startled, but when it spoke, it sounded reassuring, and it said the most astonishing thing. It said, *"This is A Course in Miracles. This is a better way."*

Then, he went on to tell me how he scribed the course over the next eight years from this inner voice, which he claimed to belong to Jesus Christ. As he went on, I could almost believe we were in another universe where I was just another one of his clients, but hopefully not the sociopathic one.

I could imagine him just as he was now, leaned back, hands clasping, wearing a white doctor's coat instead of fatigues, and maybe a little less of those thick muscles. He'd still have the graying temples, but maybe that roundhouse that nearly broke my jaw would not have been so well practiced. I never wanted him to stop. I was completely at ease with him, and I had never been at ease for a second in my life. I would have agreed to anything, but I never dreamed of what he had in mind.

"Anyway, the war broke out, and even the rich privileged had to return to Vietnam. I had almost lost it all. The Course almost became just another casualty of war, and then you, Captain, tried to put that silly bullet in my brain, and I woke up. I should thank you for it."

"Thank me, sir?" I repeated, confused.

"Indeed," he affirmed. "I would like to treat you, Captain. I would like to treat you as a client, but to do so not by the personality theory I learned in university and have used exclusively since, but rather using Course principals."

I think my jaw was hanging, it must have been, and I had no idea what he was up to, but like I said, I was at ease around the man, and I'd never been at ease a second in my life.

"Do you have any religious beliefs, Captain?"

"Well, sir, any God who made this universe is a pretty fucked up God," I said and noticed that I wasn't completely at ease anymore, hoping that I hadn't said the wrong thing.

"Then we are in complete agreement, Captain," he said. "Please make yourself comfortable in this compound, Captain. There is no need to attempt to escape. You will leave on your own accord when you are ready."

He stood up, and I stood up after him, and again aborted an attempted salute. It's just a habit. I'd been in the military so friggin long I have to salute just to take a shit. He cracked just the tiniest smile, and there it was again, that "at ease "feeling I got from him.

He called the guard, who entered immediately. Just before leaving, I said, "How the hell can I run? You'll know where I am all the time anyway." We both chuckled a bit, knowing that we were the only two people on the planet who knew what we were talking about.

When I returned to my quarters, I still had that easy feeling of peace. It permeated unseen from behind closed doors of rooms I'd never see and into the broad corridors of both levels of the Villa.

I was choosing to see again, and I would later learn. I didn't get it. I'd been sent to kill him, and here he was helping me. I didn't get it.

At first, I thought it was because he felt guilty for the things he'd done, the people he'd killed. Of course, he knew better, that we weren't our bodies, and no one killed anyone, *nothing real can be threatened*.

Shit, time seemed to fly. What in my mind was only about a 30-minute face to face must have been hours because now it was dark. I wondered what it would have been like being his patient, what kind of

The 13th Disciple

therapist he was. He said he'd been the normal kind.

Originally, I doubted it because I had dealt with plenty of those. Maybe it was that nonjudgmental way of dealing with me. Anyway, I knew that I was still in a war, undeclared it may be, and things will change fast, but I unknowingly felt untouchable in the here and now.

The following morning, there were a lot of activities. Supplies coming in, troops rotating out. I was worried because I thought the commotion could help conceal a sniper or a bomb. I didn't even eat breakfast. I just threw open my door and asked my surprised escort, in as polite, but urgent Vietnamese that I could muster, to see the General. But to my surprise, he wanted to see me too. He took me to the General in an ammo depot deep in the center of the house and underground.

The way down there was not unlike my descent through the bowels of the hospital ship when I got this insane mission in the first place. The exception was that while the ship was cavernous and metallic, this was crooked, narrow, and dank. These were the old wine cellars, a safe place for the General to hang low while the logistics went on overhead, or an attack, but I could not help the thought that surely we were headed down, and down was the only direction where lay my old hole.

We hit the bottom, and I was back down in the cellar. The corridor was more than ten feet wide but dimly lit, and I couldn't tell how long it was. It never ended, just disappeared into the dark about ten feet ahead no matter how far I walked.

There were large doors spaced about twenty feet apart on either side and oak crossbeams I nearly cracked my head on every 20 feet or so. I can still remember the distinctive sounds of our boots echoing against the stone floor as we walked inexorably toward the General, who was standing in front of one of the doors.

I can't believe this, I thought, *after all this, he's locking me back down in the hole.* The General was standing almost in the dark because of the interference patterns of the corridor lights, which hung sparsely on the walls all the way to that point that vanished seemingly at infinity.

The 13th Disciple

When I finally stopped in front of the General, his face was the last thing that I saw. I couldn't read it. We stood there for an eternal second it seemed before he sent the soldier away and I could catch my breath again. He waited until the sounds of the guards were fading up the stairway before he began speaking.

The guiltless mind cannot suffer, the body can feel no pain, it is the Mind which tells the body that it stuffers rather than the other way around. "You have to believe that you are a body and that body is in pain to notice that you're injured," he said. "Pain is the body's way to tell you to stop walking, or don't eat any more of that, it will make you sick. It tells you to stop before you do more damage to it. You won't notice the pain during the battle, but when the threat has passed your body screams, 'Pay attention to me, I need your help.'"

We were about eyeball to eyeball now, and I had no idea where this was going, but I was mesmerized. But when still looking at me, he reached out his right arm and pulled the door open. I wanted to run; I was terrified of being back in my old hole. Instead, I followed him into the half-darkness. He walked inside, leaving me helpless to move in the hallway. He had almost completely disappeared inside before I could manage to follow. As I stepped in, I thought I heard the last of the rats scattering away. I had almost completely forgotten about the rats.

"It's the same way with the Mind," he said. "You've got to be in pain; you've got to hit your knees." Then, lowering his body to put one knee on the ground, I followed suit. He put his big and gnarly hand down and let it hover just above the stone floor. In that moment of silence, I heard the water trickling again.

"That is what you were doing down here," he said. "That is the point in your life which you have come to, the point that says there must be something else, something other than this. There must be a better way. When you were down here in the dark, your mind is free to suffer out loud. In the dark, there was no place for you to hide. What can you remember about your experiences down here, Captain?"

Actually, I could remember plenty, but I struggled to bring them up, and then lost focus and I wasn't thinking about anything for I don't know how long. But he didn't rush me, he didn't say a word, and eventually, I did.

"I remember feeling claustrophobic," I said. "It was like being buried alive; I felt like I was suffocating in the darkness, like I was in a coffin. But it doesn't make any sense," I said, looking at the huge space, thousands of cubic feet of space we were standing in.

"I had plenty of space, but it felt like the weight of water was crushing me. Thousands of gallons of water on my face, on my mind. I don't know what it was, and that got me scared. It's like there's this darkness all around me. Most of the time I can't see it. It's like a door that I'm not supposed to look behind, but every once in a while, I walked past to find the door open. I didn't want to look in—I just did. I couldn't help it, and I can't take it back. Do you think I'm crazy, sir?"

I remembered all of that, but I could not have told him about the last thing I felt, that abundant peace. I'd forgotten it entirely, like a sweet dream that leaves you feeling better when you wake up without even realizing it, or remembering the dream which left you that way. I looked at his face when I said that, and I could see him studying mine intently.

"And how do you feel right now, at this very moment, Captain?" he asked.

"I feel terrified and even traumatized," I answered.

"But you are safe in the here and now, nothing to be terrified by. And I dare say that you were traumatized in the past, traumatized by me in this very place, but at this moment nothing bad is happening to you, is it?" he asked.

"No, sir," I answered, not sure where he was going with this.

"And if I could remove all memories of your ordeal down here, do you think that you would feel either terror or trauma?" he asked.

I studied the question, went over it like a scientist would a moon rock brought to Earth. I turned that rock over again and again and came up with one inescapable conclusion.

"No," I answered in a low, even tone, as much

to me as to him.

"Then, Captain, how can you possibly feel terrified or traumatized in the here and now?" he asked.

I answered him immediately, "It's shit that I bring with me," I answered easily, "shit that's gone, in the past which doesn't exist, and I let it fuck with me."

"That is correct, Captain. You and you alone let it fuck with you, and your brain let it fuck with you. And realize, Captain, it is all unnecessary because it is all under your control."

I did realize it.

"But who or what am I?" I asked.

"You are a Mind or Observer above the battlefield, beyond space and time," he answered me.

All of this went on with no judgment of either one of us for the other. Nothing of what was done in the past by either of us in the act of warfare was held against the other. The future, however, was a different matter. He must have recognized my unconscious guilt because he said, "The past is beyond your control. You can no more excuse it than you can alter it. You must simply forgive it." I think here he meant in both worldly ways and from above the battlefield. "I have done terrible things in this war myself, but I did so of my own accord. I do not blame the exigencies of war for my crimes; I properly blame myself. I tell myself that those were the things I was into then, but not now. In the end, it's not good deeds that are important; it is proper thoughts."

    I told him about my dark follower on the hill outside of Da nang and asked him if he thought I was crazy. And then, he stood up slowly, stretching his legs and said, "No, I don't think you're crazy, but I think you've seen something you're not ready for yet." That was the most significant thing that I could not yet understand. To even think to follow up on it escaped me for oceans of time that never were, the broken dreams, the needless seeming suffrage of millions of dreaming lifetimes, the agony of the ages built on a foundation of mist, and I missed it. I missed recognizing it, over and over again, missed undoing it seemingly forever.

The 13th Disciple

He paused a second and then said, "Come on, Captain, let's get some fresh air." Well, that was about the best idea I've heard in a long time, so I said, "Sure, let's go." Then, I followed him out into the pale corridor and upstairs to the green leafy and red brick courtyard.

The air up top felt good, and we took a couple of good lungs full of it. Then, he lit a cig and handed it to me. We shared the cig, but I could have taken or left it. When it was done, I didn't want another. I guess my body did a little detox too because I wasn't jonesing out, but that wasn't it.

I took a long drag, and the nicotine felt good coursing through my deprived lungs and bloodstream. I raised the cig to my lips for a second hit, held it there in my bent left arm, realizing that I didn't need the second hit any more than I had the first one. Then, I took the hit. He noticed my hesitation and studied me. "How long was I down there—about nine months right," I said, answering my own question. "Is that long enough for my body to completely detox," I asked. He studied the question; I could see it in his eyes and face which could be at once stern or compassionate. Then, a wry smile came to him, and he said, "It doesn't matter whether it has or not." Then, he took a final drag of his cig dropped it to the ground and stepped on it. I followed suit. "Addiction is as any disease, it is a decision of the Mind beyond space and time for the body. We don't abuse drugs, we don't abuse alcohol, and we use those substances to abuse our body, to remind ourselves that we have a body, that we are a body, addiction of any form is the bloody proof that I chose the ego instead of God, that I chose it instead of Him. So, no healing can take place, no therapeutic principles apply until we surrender our false selves to Him." Therefore, young Captain,

"Seek not to change the world, but choose to change your mind about the world."

He saw the confused look on my face, realized that he was getting ahead of himself again, and smiled. "More on that later he said," and there was such compassion in his voice, I can't even describe.

The cig was good, the air felt good just because it was, not because I was relieved to be outta there, I was no longer living in the past, right now at least. I was shocked to notice that I had not been paying attention to things. I had been trained to keep track of things, but I didn't know what time it was, only that it must be late afternoon, judging by the thunder in the distance, I didn't know if the logistics were still going on, I didn't even notice that the General and I had been uninterrupted. It must have been by his instructions.

There were two stone railings that met at 90° angles we used to sit on. I put my elbows behind me like I was leaning back on the bench, but the General put his elbows on his knees and leaned forward at 90 degrees to me as he began speaking. It was going to be quite the speech.

This was where the General broke it all down for me, about how none of us is really here, that the universe is just a bad dream, *a tiny mad idea* we made up to escape the punishment we think is coming for a crime that we never did. That would've sounded crazy to me nine months ago. Crazy before that bullet that never went through both our brains. Crazy like him clearly reading my mind and me reading his. But all of that had happened and it was the old world or my old way of looking at it that seemed crazy now. I understood him immediately, he didn't have to explain it twice. He gave me as much as I could take at a sitting like he was in a hurry. He didn't want me to know, but there was an urgency about giving me His Course, but I didn't get that, because man for the first time in my life I was chill and I liked it. He told me how he scribed A Course in Miracles via an inner dictation over seven years and when he heard the word Amen, knew that his Course which was just the beginning was concluded. What he did not tell me was that the very next day as he shaved in the mirror there was a loud urgent voice that could not be ignored, it said there is one here for whom you have been sent, find him, he didn't tell me that part yet.

He told me about the lessons I had to learn. He said, "You don't make it out of here until you learn your lessons." So, that's what it's all about. This was my spiritual boot camp and the General my spiritual drill Sergeant. It was a long day. We said goodbye in the courtyard and I went back to my quarters.

I was tired but I couldn't sleep. I was trying to

remember everything the General said, going over it again and again in my mind. I didn't want to forget just like the dream that slipped away. Guilt was heavy on my mind. I was guilty of so much, but to hear the General tell it, nobody really kills anybody. We are all just characters in a mad dream from which the dreamer has already woken up. He could read my mind so who the hell was I to tell him he was wrong?

We didn't really have regular sessions; the therapy just sorta broke out. The closest thing to what I'd call a regular office visit was one of our first and down in his office. As I said, I've seen plenty of shrink wrappers before; they think all your problems come from some subconscious, unresolved conflict. They were always trying to dig shit up from your past, and I didn't like it. I have a lot of shit back there. So, I'd lie and figure out what they wanted to hear and feed it to them. I even fucked one of them right there in her office between sessions. Yeah, some court-appointed bitch I made fall in love with me just before my second tour. I think I even knocked her up, but fuck it, I can't remember.

The 13th Disciple

But the General, he took that game right away from me. That early session, I was sitting looking at him, the bookshelf, and gladiators behind him, and he said, "Close your eyes," and I did. "Now, Captain, don't open them until you don't hear a single thought. You can hear all the sounds from the outside world, but nothing from the brain. In other words, Captain, no inner voice, no inner dialogue." What the fuck did he mean? I sat there with eyes closed, not trying to shut off the light, but my brain. Was I allowed to talk? I heard him laugh and gratefully opened my eyes. "You would have been sitting for quite a while, I am willing to bet, Captain," he finally said. "You see, that constant drip from the brain cannot be turned off; there is just no valve, just like the heart. Most people, at least, cannot control it, but the issue for us is this: that voice is not you; it just comes from your brain the way CO_2 comes from your lungs. You are not your thoughts, young Captain; rather, you are the Mind or Observer of those thoughts."

I was okay with it. "The brain undirected," he continued, "is like a car without a driver." Like my fucking life, I thought. "But properly obedient to the driver, The Observer, or Mind, which is beyond space and time, it is a very useful tool. What happens to you means nothing; how you deal with what has happened to you is everything. That is the crux of my method of treatment. So, you will simply learn to control, to gain dominion over your brain, and most of that comes down to bringing things to where you are safe, in the here and now. That pit I put you in from which you have emerged cannot hurt you; the past does not exist."

As if anticipating my question, he said, "If you think otherwise, please show it to me." He was right; a second ago isn't any more real than ten years ago; there is only now.

"Ok, I get it," I said. "I have nothing to fear in the past, but I'm so fucking mad about it, all of it. My stepdad... I killed the fucker, but it still enrages me, and there's nothing I can do about it. Talk about the now... shit, all I have to do is look at my arms, and I can almost count how many times he used them for the ashtray. What do I do about that? Just say fuck it, and it's over?"

"No," he said firmly, evenly. "There is nothing healthy or spiritual in denial. You acknowledge the pain, you acknowledge the rage, but acknowledge also that you can surrender the past with all of its pain and guilt and rage for the perfect peace of God this very second."

"How?" I asked.

"The first step," he answered, "is to love yourself."

"Love myself?" I exclaimed, shouted, shocked, astonished, and laughing. "Love myself? What the fuck is that like? That is something so far outta my wheelhouse, shit, I never even considered it. 'Love myself.'" I put my hands on my knees and stared at the floor, then I spaced out.

We sat there silently for I don't know how long. He didn't rush me, but when he thought the time was right, he said gently, "I think that is enough for today." He was right.

See what I mean? There is no point in bullshiting, you only got over on yourself.

The 13th Disciple

I walked around for a while in the broader corridors of the complex, upper and lower, as if I was taking a walk in the park. I bounced off a few people but kept my head mostly down. Then, when the darkness of the inner court finally told me it was dark, I went to my quarters. There, I continued to ponder that most amazing concept: "Love Myself". What did that even look like?

I opened the door, turned on the light, then shut the door and flipped the light off again. I wanted to be alone now and quiet my mind. I made my way in the dark to the bed and sprawled out on my back with my right hand under my head and my left leg crossed over my bent right knee. I lay there until my eyes adjusted, and even when they did, I could barely see a thing.

Then, I flattened out on my back and, even though I had failed miserably just hours before, I tried to turn off my brain, turn it as dark as the room. I wanted to see if I could stop all thoughts from coming through. Instead, they crashed my flimsy barricade like Niagara Falls. They came in the shape of my wife. I could see her there, so lovely, so loving. That is the only way I could have gotten over on her—that she was so loving.

What the fuck did she see in me? The uniform maybe? She could be simple that way. But love, and especially her loving—the pure, uncomplicated, austere, and lofty offices of it—wasted on the cowardly and corrupt such as me? All I thought of was me.

I can see now from above the battlefield the day I dumped her, ran out leaving her crushed and broken on the floor in the stunned grieving tantrums of one uncomprehending of deliberate human cruelty. Cut by the bloody thorn of a traitorous heart, I strove now too late to protect her, to heal her from that most egregious traitor, to heal all her past afflictions and protect her from all yet to come. But there were none, for that one was gone.

And me, my voice ready to crack, tears filling my eyes, my heart exploding—what did I gain? What did I attain in my cowardice? I broke the very being of a comely, lovely girl, and never thought I felt a thing. Never felt my constricting soul engage the world in all its murdering madness.

The 13th Disciple

How many times had I pushed her away, terrified of the desperate loneliness which could ensue if she abandoned me? And so, pushing accomplished the very thing. But I never said, "I love you". How do you marry a girl without saying that? She never said a word about it, she never complained, not that I noticed anyway. That's what I knew that I got—no, that I deliberately attracted—a sweet, concupiscent for and only for myself. Then dumped her before I got too close. I was already too close.

I pounded my fists with my closed eyes into the mattress a few times. She loved me only because she could love someone like me. Everyone's gotta love someone at some time, I guess. But how could anyone possibly love me? How could I possibly love anyone? How?

I had only loved one other person this time around—my mother. And you saw how I left her. It was like when I left her, I was coming apart. Exploding to say those three simple words. I hadn't thought about my wife, just the dull, chronic bitterness nagging at me from somewhere. That I responded to with shortness of temper or further drawing in. She never knew I loved her, and I denied it constantly. She deserved so much more. Deserved to have love dumped on her in buckets. Deserved to have it piled on her as it should be by a husband. I wanted to, God, I wanted to, all the time.

I love you; three simple words, and I was too chicken shit to say it. I said it not once in all those years. But now I need desperately to. "I love you," I shrieked to the dark and pounded on the mattress with my fists again. "I love you; I'll always love you, I can't not love you."

I balled in the dark to no one there, and now the heels of my feet joined the assault on the sorrowful mattress. Intoxicated with grief and guilt, and the desperate loneliness I alone initiated, I screamed. I yelled at the top of my lungs, "I love you," over and over again, while pounding the mattress with my fists and heels digging in hard with my arched back lifting my flapping body completely off the mattress again and again and again.

I don't know if anyone heard me or not, and I don't know how long it went on. All I know is that she still never knew that I loved her. She never heard it from me.

The following morning was like a hangover, except that instead of wondering what I had done or to whom, I wondered who had heard me or had I been broadcasting my tantrum to the General by my brainwaves. I was glad that he wasn't there to see it, embarrassed, I guess. I needed coffee just now. Interestingly enough, I had not since jonzing out down in the hole until now needed anything—no booze, no drugs, not even cigs, but now I needed coffee.

I got up, and there was just enough light to see that someone had placed a three-ring bound and a one-sided typewritten copy of A Course in Miracles on my small desk. Horrified, I wondered if they had witnessed my display unbeknownst to me. You might wonder why I would be embarrassed by anything, but I was relieved when I realized that it had probably been put there before I returned to my room from my session with the General. I remember that I never even turned the light on when I entered last night.

I sat down and began reading A Course in

Miracles. I opened to the introduction and perused through the 50 principles.

I am not a strong reader or a highly intelligent man. I had somehow gotten through college, the only way I could get a commission. I learned English at home and French and Vietnamese at the CIA, I mean by their methods. See, they didn't want their spies or assassins to move around without being fluent in the languages of the region they were in. Man, they could teach you a whole language in a month.

It was the General, though, who pointed out something about languages that I never noticed, no one does, that we all learn it without being taught, which blows my mind. But more than that, languages were developed for over 8,000 years by the ruling class to command the subordinate class and were inherently violent and deliberately lacking in the expression of human needs.

But I read the first 99 pages of his three-ring bound manuscript without looking up. I never even thought about a cup of coffee. I would have kept reading, probably the whole 669 pages of the text, but there was a knock on the door.

I left the book there and opened it; it was him. I smiled when I saw him, not embarrassed but surprised. I nearly shouted that I had just read the first 50 principles of Miracles.

He asked me which one I liked best, and I said without hesitation, the one that says there is no order of importance to the order of Miracles. He broke out laughing.

And so there came to be a feel, a texture to those steamy jungle days of necessary pain and healing, of introspection and non judgment, I would rise and read The Course, His Course, His Course in Miracles, absorbing every word on those yellowing, cracked, dingy, typewritten pages as *droplets of rain on a dry and dusty place where parched and hungry creatures come to die,* where I freely opened up my indrawn soul to my non-judgmental confessor and subjugated my ego whole to the unambiguous authority and nonjudgmental truth of A Course in Miracles, where I saw finally that I alone am responsible for my fate and solely capable of my Resurrection, where I at long last put to Peace the misperceptions called sin and guilt and fear and realized that it is impossible for me to be alone for I am one with God and *there is no place where I begin or that He ends, that nothing real can be threatened that nothing unreal exists.*

I cannot say for certain he preferred any topic more or less than any other, but if you forced me to say, it would release me from my needless obsession with my body, the appearance of life in my body, anybody.

"I am not afraid of dying," I had defensively stated. But he gently corrected that the Mind must be returned to, in a state of peace. "Death should be neither feared nor embraced. And the day of your death should be no different from any other."

This was probably the crucial point to be learned this time. The body, he continued, should be respected so long as it is useful, to be gently laid by when it is no longer needed.

"So, when I die, it's because it's time to?" I asked.

"When your body appears to have died, it was

never really alive to begin with. It is because it was agreed upon before it appeared to have been born," he answered.

"Guilt demands punishment," he told me. Even my regular shrinks knew that, but we believe we are guilty, that we believe our *tiny mad idea* is the crux of the problem. We raise our arms in defense against the mighty blow from God which will never come, we demand punishment for a crime that never was. But there is nothing to be guilty of, so nothing to be punished for. "

Notice that he did not absolve me from things of this world, the dream world. The things that my body had done to other bodies, could never be forgiven, I am beyond redemption. But in the Mind, in Heaven, I am still completely innocent and I am so close to God that there is no place where I begin or that He ends, God is. Returning to the Mind in peace is crucial. I get that now.

I told him how I tried and failed to turn off the incessant engine of my brain, how I could not control or stop my thoughts. He advised me to never try again, and that it was never his intention to recommend that I do so. He simply advised that I relegate it to its proper position, namely as background, or white noise. "You can no more no more shut off your brain then you can stop breathing, the brain is just a car, you are the driver." He repeated.

Regarding my wife and my guilt overall, he recommended against denying or burying it, deal with it he said, and forgive yourself or you are doomed to live in the seeming world of illusions forever, guilt and romance, are dramas of the ego designed to keep the Mind of The Son distracted from the only true 'cause it has, return to Heaven from which it has never left. I suppose the same is true for my mother, Oberlin, Mattingly—shit, the list is long. But the point is to snap out of it, the ego that isn't.

He conjectured that because of my early abuse there were ancient injuries that stressed my infant brain with dopamine or some shit and altered it, rendering talk therapy useless. Most of my Army doctors gave up on that shit too. They would bring me in, sit me down and ask me a few questions, but end up just shooting some shark piss up my nose and pronouncing me cured, cured enough to go back into the jungle and kill people anyway. Fucking Army, always covering their limp dicks. What I really need is some jungle-fighting techniques to handle the latrine that drips from my brain. I am a Mind beyond space and time, an Observer of thoughts, I am not thoughts, I cannot control thoughts, only observe them and most importantly I must not allow myself to be controlled by them.

I had been in my quarters reading A Course in Miracles most of the day and it was well afternoon when I put it down to walk around the broad upper corridor and let things soak in. I had completed the entire circuit and returned to the small living room and noticed it was completely cleared of my contents, including my ever-worn three-ring copy of The Course. I panicked immediately. Talk about a special relationship.

I hadn't seen the General all day, and it just occurred to me. Depleted I sank to the bed and sat there motionless with my heart pounding. Eventually, a guard knocked only once before opening the door and stepping through forcefully summoning me. The General stood tersely holding a thick envelope about the size of a phone book.

"I am sorry to interrupt Captain," he said. "But as I'm sure you'll remember I told you that when it was time, you would leave with a message to your superiors. Now it is time. Please deliver this to your good General, with my regards and this message. The war is over. If he wants, we can end it once and for all. If he wants to."

He looked me square in the eye all the while he was talking to me but turned away immediately after he stopped. He turned his back to me and tersely left, the guard closely following him.

I didn't even bother to stammer for an explanation. I didn't want to leave, but whatever he was up to now he had his mind made up and there was no changing it. He didn't even let me wait, we left immediately.

They were going to ferry me down the river in a kind of transport boat that they have used for centuries around here. Smaller than our P T boats, 22 feet to be exact, but quiet. There was a tiny wheelhouse covered with some sort of palm leaf hut, something that I could hide in, and down below in the bow, there was even a mat laid out. It was all per my original mission. I was originally supposed to make my way down the river to the coast, not aboard their boat obviously. Of course, that was probably bullshit, I was never supposed to make it out alive. None of that really mattered now, any more than it did that the war was officially over, or that I didn't even know who the enemy was anymore, myself I guess. But I knew there would be a destroyer or sub out there for a week, a month a year, forever. And I knew how to make radio contact with it. I got into the boat at just about dark. I went below the first thing. And holding a flashlight in my mouth I opened the first folder, it held the decomposing three-ring-bound copy of A Course in Miracles, my copy of His Course In Miracles, thank God I thought.

I opened the second folder pulled everything out and put the entire stack on my knees. I had to balance a little bit as we shoved off, but as soon as the flashlight beam landed on it everything came into focus for me.

There were pictures, testimony, and confessions, but mostly there were lots of pictures, pictures of war crimes. So, that was it, atrocities! And it wasn't just a few isolated events like My Lai, this had been going on for at least a decade, this is tactical, it was planned. There was no way that headquarters to not know all about this shit, there was no way that they weren't directing this. Oh boy, the General had them all right, dead to fucking rights. Who knew how far up this went, the Pentagon, White House. We had heard all about his "atrocities", but what about ours, oh fuck me. Who knew how high-up heads would roll, would heads roll? Yea they would, it would go high up this time, not as high as it should, but higher than it ever had before, higher than it was supposed to, that was shit sure.

The General had hit a bull's eye on something else too. Projected guilt and expected punishment. I've been in the Army half my life. I know all about how command thinks. And if it had been them, if they had the goods on the General then they sure as shit would've used them. So, of course, they expected him to do the same. Oh man, it was just like he said. The bullshit we made up in our minds and projected out into the world piles up so fast. Here, they were trying to kill this man terrified of what he never even thought of doing, giving him no other choice but to do it. I didn't need to see anymore. So, I packed things up, went topside, and made up some stories of my own.

It was dark up there as dark as it was below, you could see it better from above the battlefield, the sky was as dark as the river and you couldn't tell where one began and the other ended. I dangled my feet off over the edge, knowing there was water near below, but I could just as easily have been dangling them over the edge of an airplane.

It was beginning to bother me now about the General. The way he just cut me loose like that, man oh man, the bonds of friendship wrap themselves around us so stealthily. Expectations grow like weeds in the grass; you don't notice them until you sprint full speed and bam, they drag you down unseen.

After all, he had taught me about Forgiveness and Judgment, living in the now. There I was doing

The 13th Disciple

what I had always done, being a servant to my expectations and brain. And what had I done my entire life? All the rage and bitterness, all the violent self-destructive habits—all of them, a defense against Love?

How many fights had I picked with a marine twice my size with no chance of winning? How many suicide missions had I eagerly volunteered for? How many ways had I allowed my stepdad to beat and burn me? And make no mistake, I did allow it. I relished in the injustice he heaped on me, and threw back into the face of a God I didn't even believe in, pointing my accusing finger saying, "There, Father, at your hands I suffer," only to preserve the ego's insane illusion and my own mistaken tiny mad idea. Fuck me!

I grabbed the thin rail and pulled myself up. I propped my right foot on the lower rail and reached thoughtlessly for a cig when I realized I had none. I didn't miss the cig anymore; it was just a habit.

I was sad, no doubt. No, fuck that. I was pissed. I didn't try to hide it from myself. "There is nothing healthy or spiritual about denial," he had said, and I didn't like the way he just cut me loose. I didn't like it, but there was nothing I could do about it, any more than I could my past. The crimes committed there were beyond redemption, and I could never be forgiven or punished sufficiently for them.

But here, in this snapshot of one moment in time, here in this forever now, I moved away from war and toward a new old life. Guiltless and Forgiven in my unblemished Mind, to learn its lessons of Forgiveness and take baby steps toward Heaven until God Almighty would reach down and lift me into Himself.

I did it with a burgeoning Love for myself and a grudging Forgiveness of the world. I was the living redemption of the most reprehensible yet with no intention of ever killing another dreaming human being. Nor would I have. I might have even made it this time, but then I heard Hueys, Gunships, six if I was right, each loaded with SEALs, and I was right.

I felt their body shattering backscatter of the leading edges of their long blades chopping the air into pieces. As I said, the back-scatter reverberated in your gut for minutes, but I didn't have minutes. I screamed at the General's men in Vietnamese to turn the boat around, but they refused. They said they had strict orders to deliver me to the coast, no matter what.

Then, I realized what should've been obvious: the General sent me away to save my life. Maybe he figured command would be getting impatient after not hearing from me by now, maybe he got some advanced intel, or maybe he just had a feeling. Whatever it was, he sure got it right! To him, life was unreal, so then was death. But he wanted me to get away to learn the lessons of this dream and get out of it.

Fuck, what was so special about me? It didn't matter. I was still fully invested in the very dream he wanted me so badly to leave, and that I thought that I had partly awakened from. I was going back to save him. The kid at the wheel must have been 15 years old. I brought my weapon up to his head and told him to turn the boat around. He didn't flinch, nor did anyone else, and we kept going downriver.

But when I jumped overboard and started swimming for the shore well, he spun it around, fished me out, and we went back upriver. I was still dripping wet on the deck when it hit me again. What the fuck am

The 13th Disciple

I doing? The brain is so silly, so willingly caught up in an ego drama designed to distract. He didn't want me to save him; he had already saved me. If I could just give him the time, but here I was going back into a war that was over on a spinning blue planet of guilt and grief and misery, born of a tiny mad idea during a long desperate eternity that never even was. But shit I went.

We hit the shore and began to run, the two klicks or so from the river to the Villa. I was loaded with all my weapons but still must have broken a world record. As I ran through, I couldn't figure out how I was going to clear the distance from the brush to the villa without getting picked off by the Hueys, but when I got there, I knew exactly what to do.

Two of the birds were on the ground in the empty space between the villa and the jungle. They were waiting with their props rotating. It looked exactly like what I knew it was, an extraction. All I knew was that those birds didn't have a clue I was there; they were sitting ducks.

I pulled my sniper rifle and set it up in the Y section of my elbow, about shoulder high, took aim at one of the pilots and squeezed off the round. All you had to do was see the chopper spin out of control and roll over to know I was dead on. The blades broke off against the ground and debris from the resulting explosion sounded like a Saturn V rocket at liftoff, and it took down the second chopper as it tried to lift off.

The explosion was ten football fields away and still scorched my face, making me turn away in pain as it roared blazing upwards. The fireball kept the other choppers away and everyone's attention while I was able to haul ass into the villa. Odd thing was that all the guys inside were my guys now.

When I got to what had been the wall around the compound, I had no trouble climbing through a hole and into the compound. The Hueys circled around, but I knew they weren't going to fire into the compound again. They were waiting for their own guys now who were engaged in a firefight with the General who was isolated behind some burning rubble.

I could see some of his soldier's bodies strewn around, but I couldn't tell if he was dead or alive until I saw one of the SEALs take it, his head just exploded off the shoulders. Then, I knew that the General was alive and kicking. I also knew that he was outnumbered four to one and the other Hueys would be touching down with reinforcements at any time.

Then one SEAL tried to circle around behind the General. I picked him off from on the dead run. The shot went right through the back of his head. You could see his body slam face-first into the ground and he was dead before he hit it. The other three Americans couldn't figure out what had happened and never did. They each died without ever seeing the shot that killed them.

Finally, I was able to get to the General. I called out to Him. "You idiot," he said in English, "Get outta here!" Well, needless to say, it was too late for that. As soon as the other Hueys lost contact with their SEAL, they recommenced their rocket attacks.

"Get outta here," he barked again, "I have reinforcements." And sure as shit, I could hear Migs. I knew there would be VC ground troops, probably choppered in from Hanoi, close behind. All we had to do was hold on. But some things are best let go of, and

The 13th Disciple

I never should have come back here.

I never felt the shot that killed me. I never knew if it came from one of the reinforcements from the remaining Hueys, or even a surviving VC who mistook me for an enemy American. The bullet came through my back, lifted and spun my body, and pounded it into the grass, leaving it there as though there was a tank parked on the back of its neck.

All that I knew was that I was dead. My last words to the General were, "I tried to tell them the war was over, but I never got the chance." I died there in his arms.

No sooner was I dead than the fighting stopped. There was the sound of secondaries, and the remaining Hueys flying away. The General held me there that way, not sad but just studying the situation. He looked like a mathematician who had found a flaw in his proof, but what he really found was the terror in my mind. Just like he'd said, "Don't judge." He held me with one hand behind my head and shook it hard just as the lights were going out.

"No, no, nooo fear, nooo fear," he said. "Everything is as it should be (it has already been), but the next time, my brother, next time the ego becomes, I simply ask you to choose again."

The 13th Disciple

Book III
The Last Pope

In the dream, the voice was reassured and reassuring, and said, "Congratulations, you made it that time."

- Dr. Helen Schuman

Never see yourself as a victim, and you will never be angry.

-Dr. Ken Wapnick

The problem is mind.

-Dr. Bob Shenk

Ian Spencer choked, then gagged as though a blade had been run up from his stomach and cut him through to his throat. The black fog enveloping him tasted like bile. Dense and unrecognizable to the human senses, it was dark, darker than anything he had ever known, darker than the tannin water he had swum in as a boy in Australia—water so dark that it hid the hand completely beneath the surface before the wrist entered it.

The 13th Disciple

With no sense of up or down, his body or not his body, absent a sense of self or non-self, and with the ego obliterated, he began to panic again. *This is nothing like before*, he thought. *I never knew it could be this bad; it never had been before. This time it really is indubitably attacking me. What is this, where does it come from, and WHY ME?*

He could feel a cold hand push hard on the back of his head, could feel his body being constricted as if by a Boa, then he could not feel his body, not even the weight of the constrictor. He opened his eyes, but nothing. No light, no body, no self. He tried to scream. The words which would not come out were, "I am here, I am. That was it—I am, I still am." He whimpered plaintively in his thoughts, vainly trying to scream, but there was no sound, no light, nothing, not even time.

Now, he would beg for the pain of cracking ribs, would welcome the anguish of death just to prove what he could not say, inside this darkening, his darkening, just to know that I am even if for so ephemeral a passing, such as a lifetime, to be or have been, to scan the mighty heavens from the insignificant perch of a sky ablaze with a million candelabras, each of them lit by the mighty hand of God, then to be painfully disposed of as a pitiful body.

How much better it would be, how far superior it would be to the sense of no sense or sensation, no inkling of I or me, no self, only the black fecal foul disgusting stench of every putrid evil human deed, semen mixed with bile ejaculated onto him, the revolting spillage submersing his body, until exhaustion overcame the terror, until resignation set in.

Still, the dissolution continued, divorcing from the self, dissolving into nothingness. The death of the body seemed imminent, the death of this body he struggled so vainly to preserve. He would now let go of instead of accepting salvation; he would once more slip through its fine mesh.

Somewhere in another universe, he could hear his cell ringing. The chimes followed him down the long dark well into which he had fallen, again. It was an unseen place by the world, but an undeniable one by him. One of those weird places where universes rub, wearing themselves thin against each other.

The 13th Disciple

Where time stops in one and spills over into the next. Where there are no thoughts. Maybe it was hell. When a thought finally did come, after an instant or an eon—he could not tell—the thought said, "DON'T DO THAT AGAIN, DON'T YOU DARE." Fear boiled over. What was natural had now become unnatural, a warning from the devil it seemed.

The cell chimed again, faintly, far, light years away, yet just next to his hand. His hand—he had a body. Part of that body was close enough to the outside to hold on. His hand was not part of his body now, not really part of him.

In his panic, he unthinkingly forced his body back onto himself and himself back into his universe. His hands flailed, found the cell, found the earth. Now, if he could just squeeze the earth tightly enough, he could stop falling, climb back out. It was only inches on the outside, closer to him than the headstone, but from in here it was light years away. But he could do it; he had to do it because the alternative was unthinkable.

The cell—concentrate on the chimes, he thought. But the thought said, *it's too far for you, you can't reach it.* Then, defiantly, he did reach it, felt it vibrating through the dirt as he felt the grass on his face. He wasn't embarrassed, didn't look to see who was watching, just collected his cell phone and backpack and fled down the slightly sloping sandy hill without having even seen, let alone read, the inscription on the headstone.

He had to endure the rattling bus ride from Ostia for three hours before he was back on the Via Nomentana on the northern side of the city, a place which before the war had been called Talenti. There, he could sit in the poorly air-conditioned cafe and drink. The paleness left his face as the dark red vino poured in.

He needed something stronger, he thought, but he would have to wait until he got closer to the city center before he could find any. There just wasn't that much available way out here. He pondered his predicament. "North 13, and west nine," Nancy had said so nonchalantly, neither of them could have dreamed it would have caused him such distress. It was only a gladiator's headstone, and she only needed him to translate the inscription carved on it some 2,000 or 3,000 years ago.

Two hundred years ago, or even just before the war, such a discovery would have been a huge big deal in the archeology of the day, but to the archeology of today such a find seemed not so significant at all. The world was still in recovery, more pragmatic than academic. The headstone would remain where it was, only the inscription, which was in the old Latin, would enter the database. The accompanying ludus would be unearthed to reveal its accompanying treasures, but not by him. He wasn't going anywhere near his, scholarship be damned.

Still, this was his second attempt to read the inscription, and the second occurrence of his old childhood menace, what he and his mother called the darkening, it would not take another attempt for him to put two and two together. But as he sat there, slowly recuperating, Ian Spencer could have had no idea what Roma had in store for the world, nor the ego for him.

The world had slowed since the war. It had come to a crashing halt in some places. Gone now were the quantum computers and mag-leve global transportation systems. Digital computing was the best anyone could hope for. Cell phones, oddly, were abundant. Near large population centers where the Vatican held control, it was a serious offense to be caught without one. They had become a burgeoning defacto global ID card.

Asia had been nearly obliterated, and on the North American continent, there remained only the blasted skin of what had once been home to billions. No life there was or would be sustainable, nor was there a place on the planet with electricity 24 hours a day. And even after three-quarters of the earth's population had been wiped out in half an hour, Roma stood as it always had, defiantly upright.

There had been the British Empire, the Rothschild's and the Rockefellers, but behind the scenes, from out of the shadows, the planetary puppeteer—the holy priests of power, the dark order of the Jesuits—had been pulling the strings from Roma all along. Ever since the reformation an angry church had pursued its guilty flock.

The 13th Disciple

Now, with blood on its hands and murder in its heart, the pursuer drew within breaths length from the oblivious pursued. It was fight or flee, kill or be killed. It was all or nothing. But only the Vatican knew the score. The church was out for revenge, and the people were in for tribulation.

Until this morning, the Vatican was Ian Spencer's singular obsession. Until the headstone, until the darkening, he schemed exclusively for disseminating the Vatican's centuries-long secret war against humanity, with or without being caught.

To complicate things, even as he fretted for the world for its fleeting future, Roma yet yielded up treasures of its unalterable past, a gladiatorial ludus. The dichotomy of Roma could not be more starker; it was at once a gift and a curse on mankind, and it was with that gifted curse and hardened defiance that Roma bound him to itself.

He paid and then washed in one of the ancient public fountains that had fed the city pure mountain water for centuries. Beforehand, he took the cell phone from the shirt pocket to see who had called and saved his life. The display said "MOMMA". Of course, it was his mother; who else even knew? Since he had returned from Australia, she was likely to call or text at any odd hour of any day. He could read her texts, but he never spoke to her, of course.

Unlike the headstone, he didn't need to read the text to know what it said. He closed the cell and slid it carefully into a pocket of the green backpack that contained his digging tools. Fully clothed, he bathed in the clean cold water that came to the wall all the way from the Italian mountains. The stark coldness of the water felt right to him, as it protected his skin from the raging Roman summer sun and the onsetting symptoms of heat stroke.

That dark tan skin was the Italian in him, his unknown part, his father coming out. Only when finished did he remove his khaki long shirt and ring it as dry as he could, revealing as he did the lean physique many mistook for that of a gymnast. The shorts could stay wet; there would be no chance of getting even a dirty seat on the bus. Anyway, the damp khaki would help keep him cool for a blissful short term.

The 13th Disciple

He was still fit, but not as tanned as he was before he went back to Australia. Then, he put on his damp shirt and took the cell from his backpack; it was wet but not dead. It could never be dead.

The Nomantanna was a clusterfuck, he thought, as he rattled his way down toward the city center, past the Colosseum, and the Vatican. Between the Nomantanna's cobblestone-paved north and south roadways was a vast median where the remains of the old maglev, a causality of the war, a visible relic of a past technologically superior to the present.

As he bounced around the sweltering old autobus, he could taste the sweat and exhalation of the other passengers. He rubbed against an old Italian lady carrying a large cloth sack, a large Nigerian man holding the rail high with both hands, sweat darkening the armpits of his bright multi-colored shirt. Everyone stared blankly at their surroundings, disinterested, hopeless, only the sensation of discomfort registered.

He could easily imagine the same a thousand, two thousand years ago. Outside, motorcycles and bicycles buzzed like bees around a hive. As the fatigue set in, it anesthetized him more so than the alcohol he was in search of. All he needed was a little to take the edge off, just to buy a little time. Just as when he was a little boy, it would pass. It would not be forgotten, but it would become bearable.

The stark terror of it was like a choke hold, deadly, but not dangerous if removed in time. In the past, it seemed that whatever it was applying, the hold would release it more readily, but whoever sent that cloud at the headstone made it clear they were taking no prisoners. It wasn't a who or a what, or a nothing, it was an insidious non-thing, the ego, but he could not know that yet.

He still knew more than most that this was the dawn of a new dark age, an ephemeral time between the end of the last nuclear war and the blue-black twilight of the emergent global police state, run, as it had always been, by the Jesuits. The last of the Great Wars had as designed killed almost 90% of the human population. From this intentional chaos the Vatican elite who created the war had emerged from their bunkers prepared. The rest of mankind came up like rats.

The 13th Disciple

For now, the Vatican and its minions lay inert, still organizing their final solution, and there was room to run. But in less than 100 years, the technological advance of the masters would catch up to those who were mastered, and then the brutal boot would come crashing down on the face of mankind forever.

Standing there in the cold afterlight of civilization, Ian Spencer would soon have to choose between saving what was already forsaken and that which never could be lost. Confronted there on both levels by two great conspiracies: on the worldly level a satanic, transhuman one stretching back for centuries, that of good vs. evil, the first cause of telluric conspiracies, the reason for any of them; the second, an older, more insidious one, an omnipresent one, the one of the always unknown, undetected ego, the non-part of the non-self, the part believing in sin, guilt, and separation from God.

The first one could not touch Him, but what the ego conspired to do with that other conspiracy could send this Son of Man into an infinite loop of unreality from which he may never escape.

The 13th Disciple

He could not understand his mother without knowing all of her history here. He couldn't understand his mother, nor forgive her. His mother was a joke of a mother, yet as a small boy he thought she was the most amazing person in the world. He was not the only son to be so utterly wrong about that most formidable and damaging of special relationships.

Knowing her history meant knowing his father's too, but that was different, a difficult thing to know. To know who he was, what he had done, and that had been a terrorist was to know himself, who he was. He could have easily been stigmatized by his father's past, but brilliantly and in one simple stroke, his mother had protected him from both of them. His father, via an act of martyrdom worthy of comparison to Christ, had protected them both.

Simply by keeping her maiden name, he could stand on an autobus, walk down a street or sip café at a bar without drawing fierce attention, both favorable and otherwise. His parents were born in the afterward, 300 years after Pope John Francis, the last Pope, the last Jesuit Bishop of Roma, as foretold by St. Malachy nearly 1,000 years prior. In the time before the global police state controlled by The Holy See, his parents' generation was the last to rise up, to fight back against the Pope-less church.

The bus clamored to a stop at Piazza Venezia, and he nearly leapt to his feet to get off, despite fighting the crowd in the aisle all the way out. He rushed with the other ants across the vast via to the stand under the balcone where Mussolini had launched several famous tirades hundreds of years prior. From there, he went right, then left, where the Nomentana narrowed to accommodate only bicycles, and pedestrian traffic.

There was a dark and cool restaurant he knew. He frequented it often, and although he had just about given up on the pretty young waitress working there, it had all the necessities: alcohol and air conditioning. He drank a double rum and aranciata and opened his cell. As it buzzed to life, he went to messages received and clicked on "MOMMA". He read it, and it said, "My Son, choose again."

"How is she doing this?" he whispered to himself, "She's dead."

The 13th Disciple

MOMMA - Nicole

Nicole Spencer's life had been sheltered by standards of the afterwards, pretty and petite with doting parents she had, had a magical childhood filled with many imaginary friends, fairies and ghosts of her parents' old farmhouse who helped fill the isolation a young girl would otherwise feel in the lonely Australian countryside of the afterwards—the time after the good times, before the times when you would own nothing. Her parents initially encouraged her fantasy life, believing she would grow out of it. She never did.

Most people had occupied land of the deceased after the war, and farming was the major means of support for most in rural places. Most places were rural, especially in the massive and sparsely populated former prison colony of Australia. They were back to hunter-gather in the most isolated places.

As a little girl, Nicole became fascinated by living things, by life itself. Whether plants or animals, whether Dogwoods exploding to full bloom in the orgasm of spring or the ancient and deadly approach of the black widow to a luna moth struggling in its silvery web, she was fascinated by and non-judgmental of it all.

When her parents' horse gave birth on a late night in early spring, nine-year-old Nicole was beside herself with excitement. From one, there came two. In the years that followed, she doted over the little colt named Splash and rode him in splendid ecstasy all throughout the known boundaries of her world—a deep and enchanted forest under fiery sunrises and spectacular, golden twilights, all wrapped in a luxurious and lordly canopy of green and mist.

The horse grew strong and with a shimmering coat of black coal. She could walk up to him and scratch his forehead in the little splash of white there and named him Splash. There was always a response, a connection with her like electricity through the ether, a unique identifier, pure and clean and she speculated to her parents that animals were just as loving as people.

But one day when Splash was five, he lay on the ground and was not roused by her gentle ministrations and he was cold. She cried softly, called her parents and sat on the ground beside him, petting the white spot, without a response. As her mother approached, she was not simply sad; she wondered what is different about Splash now.

"What is the difference between life and death? What is life? From whence does it issue, to where does it go?" she asked. It was neither the first nor last time that this little girl left one of her parents speechless. Yet, this was the only thing that pretty little blond-haired, blue-eyed Nicole Spencer wanted now to know. She sought to help life and save life as naturally as to draw breath.

So, she studied medicine. Psychiatry appealed to her because of its potential healing effects for the whole of mankind. She recognized immediately how the long, clean lines of formal logic and Boolean algebra were disdainfully smudged to the edges by the psycho-logic of Freud. In the former, everything was clear and a statement was either all true or all false; in the latter, they were blurred. It was possible to love and hate the same person at the same time. It was possible for the psyche to be in both states of existence at once, but one must recognize the unavoidable and unwanted byproduct like heat from friction.

She learned shorthand on her own and applied to university in Roma but was summarily denied. Higher education in the afterwards was not wasted on young girls who had fairies in their minds and dreamed of embroidering life; that was reserved for the dark dreams of programmers and weapons researchers. This young girl's dreams were shattered by a refusal letter delivered, as it was in the afterwards, by horseback.

She never forgot the way she waited breathlessly for the reply after sending in her application. Even the dreary bureaucrat of a postman took notice of the pretty young girl who ran to the fence where the post box was with the expectation of life in her beautiful blue eyes. He was gone before those eyes ran with tears when she read the blunt words: "Miss Nicole Ann Spencer, Address, regarding your application to do course work at the Jesuit University Roma Italia, Rejected. Sincerely." Then signed by an innocuous associate Dean.

Until Splash died, she had never really been sad,

had never known heartache. Now, she was overcome with the strangest sensation of her life—not in her body, nor in the room around her, but where? She breathed heavily, then shortly, suffering the sensation of severe melancholia unrecognized, deep despair unknown to a young lady.

In keeping with her nature, she sulked silently to her bedroom. Once free from sight of her parents, the tears came. Despair flooded in gushers, and then they ceased. Her tiny body heaved, and then it relaxed. Her long blond hair tangled into knots around her body until she felt her body floating, and for days or weeks, she knew not. Finally, she felt that she was not a body, and there alone in the darkness and safety of that Knowledge, she received her purpose, gently and with virtuosity by the voice of Jesus.

The voice was not alarming; rather, reassuring and kind. She wanted to do what it said. What it said was, "This is A Course in Miracles. Please take notes." And so 15-year-old Nicole Spencer transcribed A Course which declares with pristine clarity and unambiguous authority that there is no world, and necessarily that God has no fists. Love cannot hit, nor is Salvation a bargain in return for obedience; it has already been granted. It can be refused, but never rescinded.

For two years, she transcribed The Course spoken by Jesus. Then she heard the word "Amen" and knew that she had finished. So, it was with some surprise that on the night after the day she heard "Amen," she heard the voice one last time. It said, rather emphatically, "There is one for whom you were sent. Find Him." It was the only thing of urgency that had been expressed, seemingly incongruent with the bulk of the text, and was received separately from the text.

Roma

She wasn't thinking of boys when she left home against the strongest objections of her parents for the epicenter of the world, Roma. They thought she could never survive such a thing being so young and frail, but she knew that she was not a body, that what she was,

was invulnerable, that what is real cannot be threatened.

She had not told her parents about the Course yet; she didn't know that they would both die before she would get the chance.

There were only a few boys around, and it was expected that she would marry one of them. But in the backwaters of Australia, they were just that, boys.

Since having scribed A Course in Miracles, she was experiencing a new sense of purpose. The past disappointment over acceptance to university was utterly forgotten; the only purpose Roma could serve now was to launch Christ's word from the most populous place on the planet.

So, she had no idea what to expect, heeding another voice, the one calling for change and also perhaps in obedience to the odd demand to search for and find that chosen one. Thus, when she was only 17 years old Nicole Spencer left her secluded town in the Australian countryside and went to the greatest metropolis Earth had ever known, and then known again: Roma.

The 13th Disciple

Her journey was made, as were most voyages in the "afterwards," by ship and train. The Vatican had told the population that airplanes didn't exist anymore, which everyone knew was a lie because they could see them in the sky but flying was strictly reserved for the owners—the Vatican.

Beautiful, blond, and 17 years old Nicole Spencer hit the Italian peninsula at Calabria by ship. Then, in the dark of night, she took the train to Stazione Termini in Roma. She couldn't see the astonishing Italian Alps through the metallic darkness enveloping the small engine as it groaned and strained its arduous way uphill. It came more than once so close to a full stop she could have easily stepped out and walked faster than the train itself.

The night was cool, and she was not perturbed. She fell asleep leaning against the window as the train rolled down through the starless darkness toward the glimmering, but blacked-out coast. When she woke, it was because of the heat as the train was crawling in the direct sunlight to its ultimate destination: Stazione Termini in Roma.

The 13th Disciple

Had she not just recently scribed A Course in Miracles, she would have been overwhelmed, as most people when viewing the cavernous interior of Termini. The shade provided some relief, but it was hot as she stepped with her small backpack, which carried only a change of clothes and her handwritten copy of The Course, still in shorthand, onto the marble platform. It protruded like finger piers from the enormous main building.

Looking left to right, there were platforms, some attending to trains, others bereft of any, from horizon to horizon. Then, she made her way, through the cacophony of heat and sonance, and random chaos, from the station to the sinuous and turbulent Via Nomentana.

She went south toward the city center in her blue jeans and white tank top, and felt the burn on her delicate skin where it was exposed, but it was too hot to cover up. To continue with her random walk through the sun emblazoned ancient via was all that she could do.

She had never seen such continuous commotion,

never seen such grandeur as the fountains and thousands of years old buildings and the decadence on the street as in the first few minutes walking down the Nomantanna, toward the massive Piazza Venezia and the Piazza Nuvona, whose massive expanses lie slightly further south. She took refuge in the arched shade of a 3000 years old government building with its glossy terrazzo floor. She rested sitting Indian style on the floor leaning against the wall until she felt a delicate but undeniable change in the quality and spirit of the air. It was just cool enough to continue.

As she neared the city center in the modestly cooling heat, the buildings seemed grander, and there were even gasoline-engined cars. The buildings, statues, the ancient superimposed upon the new modern, the postmodern, as she walked under dome of a blood red sky which hung ornately across the Tiber, as it descended boldly beneath the Castel Santa Angelo and the Vatican behind, by all of it she was equally unimpressed, by the grand or small, by the good or bad. For as The Course which she was the most current scribe had taught her well, this was all illusion.

The 13th Disciple

But later that night, when by light of the streetlights she saw Spurio Pompilli throwing stones at the advancing Vatican guard she was not so dismissive. Her Course had not adequately prepared her for him. Shirtless, jean-clad, and sweating every lean muscle seared its imprint through streetlights into her memory. There may have been other good-looking Roman males in the mob, but her eyes were directed nowhere else.

She made her way pensively toward him. She went on autopilot as she stepped blindly into the ancient street. She could easily be arrested if mistaken for a protester but was undeterred and unaware of the prospects. She could get close to him, unnoticed by him, each time he reached down to pick up a cobblestone that had been part of the road for thousands of years, then launch it toward the Carabinieri and the Vatican guard line, she could see the jet black hair fly backwards as he leaned into the throw, then wrap around his face with each recoil, could see the lean muscle ripple, the tension and release of tension, that made her aware of her inner thighs, was aware of them as she watched him unaware of her.

The 13th Disciple

He had no hair on his back and shoulders, but she could see a clear line of it that ran in a V from his chest all the way down below the low-slung jeans, over a well-defined set of abdomen muscles as it did. Closer, she moved still closer, so close that she could just barely touch his outstretched and sweaty rib cage, just below the right lat muscle.

Then, she thought that she could gently stroke that rib cage, then step behind him without removing her hand, run it down his fine abdomen, feeling the hairs and sweat all the way down to the beltline, then lower. Dreamly, she would have done it she thought, but for the fact that as he turned to retreat before another volley, he stared directly at her. They were stunned by each other. She by the brutal masculinity of him. She had never even kissed a man before. Not boys like Allan White or Tommy Christen, whom she had let kiss her only to see what it was like, then never again.

She had never thought twice about attracting men. She did not realize that she had never seen a real one. Just the few boys scattered about the small backwater towns near her parents' farm. But here in the midst of the street riots that ran almost like clockwork, she was face to face with a true Roman. She immediately dropped her eyes in embarrassment, but she ran the length of his body in doing so. There was that devastating V shape that disappeared from sight below the low-slung belt less waist, there was space between his skin and the denim that opened and closed rhythmic with his heavy breathing. Down there was where her shy blue eyes came to rest.

Spurio Pompilli had turned only to retreat in anticipation of the onslaught by the Vatican Guard and Carabinieri. It was then that he came face to face and was stunned by the pure, petite beauty of the slight biondo child before him. Her raw beauty took him away from reality—the reality of the riot, the reality of everything.

"Cosai fai qui? Coasi sei qui, troppo pericoloso. What are you doing? It's too dangerous," he finally said in a language she could understand. Then, almost as he would to a child, without permission, gently took her hand and ran, guiding her as gently as possible down the Via del Corso. She saw him run, legs long like a soccer-player; she felt his hand large and safe around hers, the perfect amount of pressure. He took her securely but gently.

Spurio slowed down, yelled something in Italian to who knew who, then took up flight again. She tightened her backpack again and let herself be towed by him. *This is all very interesting,* she thought, as much a spectator as a participant, certainly different from Australia.

They had not gone as far as the Via de Croche before the tear gas was launched. Everyone took out handkerchiefs or medical masks to cover their faces, Spurio gave his to her, she almost confused pressed it pensively to her face. Seeing this Spurio stopped, yelled in Italian again, as the mob and Carabinieri continued their way down the Via Del Corso he took a 90 degree turn onto the Via Tomacelli, bringing Nicole along across the Ponte Cavour. Only then did he slow their pace, she finally noticed that she was breathing hard, a lot harder than Spurio.

They eventually came to rest on a stone bench in the Piazza Cavour. They waited less than three minutes without saying anything, Spurio looking around as if for someone. Just as she was about to catch her breath a car—an old, small car, a Volvo maybe—accompanied by an entourage of motor bikes stopped. Taking her hand again, they got in on the passenger side back seat, and the car went south along the broad tree lined road that wound itself east on the south side of the grand Tiber River. It's gushing waters black now with the night and shimmering in streetlights guarding the length of both sides of its meandering expanse.

Inside, someone handed Spurio a white long sleeve shirt, which he drenched as soon as he pulled it over his head. Someone else gave him a wallet and some keys which he put away skillfully. No one said anything, but Nicole felt as safe as she did sweep away. This must be a movie, she thought with a slight smile emerging on her lips. She leaned back and just enjoyed the show. The car did not stop until they had gone all the way down to where the river rested against the wooded enclave of Trastevere.

They got out together, and the car pulled away. Still without saying a word, as if waiting until it was safe, he guided her down the steps of the Ponte San Butco to the broad walkway that curved with the Tiber.

There was no electricity just then, but by hundreds of torch lights she could see the makeshift shops that had been set up with everything from aluminum to cardboard boxes.

They sold shirts, fruits and vegetables, candy, tobacco, and some wine with prepared food. It had been this way on hot summer nights on the banks of the Tiber for thousands of years, she felt that instinctively.

Still holding hands and still not yet having said anything, she was looking up at him from the left side wholly unaware that she was smiling broadly, beaming.

Once she did realize it, she wiped it away embarrassed, from her mouth at least. Finally, he turned to her and said, "What were you doing there? You should be more careful."

This, his natural voice was lower and softer than she expected, concerned. Then, she saw his face up close for the first time; it was more attractive than she had imagined, chiseled, Roman. "Where are you staying?"

"I just arrived from Australia a few hours ago, I was lost I guess," she answered, looking down slightly as though embarrassed, but not really.

But he was aghast. "Who could let such a young girl travel so far alone? How can this happen?" Then he spoke in Italian, then went suddenly silent. He could see her just looking at him, and he wanted to just look at her. Then, the electricity came back on and with it the lights.

"Are you hungry?" he asked. "You must be. I know a place close."

"A restaurant?" she prompted.

Of course, unless you want me to cook it for you myself." His English was just flawed enough to sound exotic, if not downright sexy. *No, it is sexy,* she thought, *everything about him is.*

"Well, aren't you afraid of the police?" she asked coyly, though not trying to."

He laughed, but there was a slight desperation in

it. "The Carabinieri will arrest only those they catch on the street, or a few blocks away from the protest place."

She noticed he did struggle a bit for the words, but his English was very competent. "By the time the lights come back on, they have changed shifts and do not even know or care who we were or what we were doing. As long as we don't attack them with guns or make any riots afterwards, they will leave us alone. It's an informal truce. That's good, no," he said.

"No, yes," she answered confused, but engrossed. She hadn't even noticed that they were sitting down to a small outside iron table with only a tablecloth to cover it and an umbrella over them. There was a carafe filled with water, two water glasses, a bottle of red wine and a basket of bread already out.

She was suddenly aware that she was famished. A waiter arrived immediately and provided two wine glasses. She could hear the clinging of the glasses together in his hand before he placed them on the table and left.

She had no idea of what he or anyone else save

The 13th Disciple

Spurio looked like, just taking in Spurio as he skillfully uncorked the wine and poured themselves a glass, hers first. She had not had any more glasses of wine than kisses with boys, but she was thirsty, and drank the wine straight away. She felt a gush of warmth right through her limbs.

When the food came, Spurio ordered another bottle of wine and before dinner was through, she had finished more than half of it with him. She didn't know what they had eaten or for how long, an hour, or all night. All she knew was that she was thoroughly satisfied by what she had eaten, drank, and who she had done it with.

They got up leisurely to leave. She did not notice Spurio pay, but he hugged several of the staff as they left. Then, he took her away down the maze of streets in the tree-dappled jurisdictions that made up Trastevere. Streets that had been in Roma for thousands of years, streets on which people walked, fought in and made love on. Streets that raised families who grew up, grew more families, grew old, struggled mightily and passed on unknown and unnoted, without a trace except for what it left behind, the human race, the passions and providence of the species seeming so urgent seeming so solemn all only to be washed away by the tempestuous torrent of time.

The streets just seemed to be conspiring toward that end tonight. Gradually, step by step, by steady degrees they seemed narrower, darker, more intimate, more and more ready, ready for them. In the distance, she heard thunder. Ahead and to their left opened another narrow corridor just barely separating apartments facing each other, so different from the wide-open spaces of rural Australia.

That is where he is taking me, she thought, she hoped. He slowed, let her pass in front, then stopped. Looking around and seeing only a few souls about, he guided her with his big hand on her back down low, the narrow street which was no more than a walkway. His hand felt large there, and she did not protest when either by design or mistake, she did not care when it made its way down to her lower lumbar and rested boldly there.

Walking behind, he seemed as much to be

pushing her gently in the direction he wished. She accentuated the sway of her hips in turn. The street was so narrow she could almost reach across from one vine encased wall to the other. The path came to an end at a stone wall no more than three feet high running the narrow width of it.

The wall was the only place where they could sit, but they stepped over it instead. There was lush grass that sloped gently to a stream on the other side, with green-leaved oak trees covered by vines as thickly as the walls. It was private, only the red barrel roof tiles to spy down upon them. In the sky, rain threatened, but they were not.

She dropped her backpack, feigning that it was heavy, glancing down as she did. When she looked back up, he leaned down to kiss her. It was gentle at first; she took it flush on her mouth. She could taste the mixture of wine, a hint of tobacco, and him. He put one heavy hand on her lower back, very low, and pulled. She felt him throbbing and lost all control.

Pulling madly at his shirt, she nearly ripped it. Only by slipping it over his head did he manage to save it. Then, she clumsily made for his belt. She managed to undo the buckle, but could not unbutton his jeans. By her clumsy eagerness, she made it clear that she was woefully inexperienced. By the way he skillfully undressed her with one hand, unbuttoning both her jeans and his he showed that he was not.

She wanted to see him, feel him, explore and experience, to do too much at once. But the sensation she felt when he got down on his knees in front of her defeated her imagination. She had no comparison. He had just succeeded in slipping her panties smoothly down around her waist. She expected him to stand, but he just stayed there, on his knees in front of her, his shoulders broad and tan.

She had never had such a sensation; she could not describe it, but it was power. There was this powerful man on his knees in front of her, caressing her slender inner thighs, kissing them, up one across, and down the other. He kissed her belly button, and she unknowingly pulled his hair. She kept her eyes down as he stood, took her slim hips in his broad hands, and turned her around forcefully. She arched her back to him and grabbed those huge wrists, and that touch sent shockwaves of desire as electricity in both directions.

For her, who had never been within a continent of any object of such raw masculinity, so beyond anything she could conjure in thigh-massaging evenings of her girlhood in the outback, her central nervous system disconnected. For Spurrio, the unbelievable softness of those luxurious palms and long slender fingers sent an adrenaline rush of lust, nearly forcing him to shred her jeans in his bare hands on the spot. Instead, he slipped them gently and efficiently off, the fabric coming to rest soundlessly in the grass.

She commanded her hands to remove the white, tight apron-like shirt, through whose sheer fabric the nipples of her small breasts violently protruded, but they would not obey. Instead, they pulled at the bottom edge of the shirt. She stared embarrassed down, with both arms and legs crossed, frozen as a deer in the headlights. Spurrio encapsulated her quivering wrists in his one massive hand and lifted them gently skyward, efficiently removing the offending garment completely unnoticed with the other hand.

The 13th Disciple

As he took hold of her silky smooth hips, the size of his hands excited her even more just as he pushed in again. *So, this is what it feels like,* she thought, and she didn't have another thought. Only living in the ecstasy of each of the individual moments, multiplied one after the other.

She could not remember each or perhaps any of the individual pushes and lunges. Their bodies curving and coiling rhythmically into each other. She screamed, and didn't know it, scratched, and didn't know it. She was elsewhere. Even as she saw his back before he put his shirt back on, she was aghast when she saw what she had done to it. If he ever had complained, she could not remember. Instinctively, she reached to touch it as she would a wounded kitten, but pulled back embarrassed. For his part, Spurrio displayed no knowledge or concern for his condition. Partly dressed, they rested in the grass and vines. He lay on his back with his hands under his head; she lay on her back with her tiny head on his shoulder, then she curled into him prompting him to put his arm around her.

It was with the greatest satisfaction that they

casually dressed thinking of nothing but this moment, this tuft of grass beneath the oak vine, and each other.

Some people were coming near; they could hear voices carried through the air but not yet the footfalls. Presumably, it was people returning home. Spurrio showed no embarrassment; only laughed a little under his breath and helped her on with her backpack. His non-response at once encouraged her and lightened her mood to the point where she giggled. Spurrio took her by the hand again; they stepped over a tiny wall and walked past the middle-aged couple going the other way as if he owned the alley. They politely smudged themselves to the right side, allowing the older couple more room to pass.

They continued to laugh and giggle to the end of the corridor and they turned back the way they came. She did not know from which way they had come; she was lost. Spurrio put his arm around her as if to protect her from the first few droplets of rain falling. She could not believe it, but was immediately turned on again and swayed her hips a little more hoping that it would somehow tempt him to put his large hand there. It tempted a lot more. Whether by her hopeful flirt or because of his own prior design, Spurrio led her across the Ponte leading to the island in the middle of the river Tiber, on which for centuries stood the old ospidalle.

They ran across the ponte to the island before he gave up the attempt to keep her dry, she was thoroughly soaked. There was a spot of grass where a huge oak had pushed up through centuries of old cobblestone, to become as much a natural phenomenon as the ospidalle itself. The leaves were full, but they cast no shade there, for one of the only spotlights still remaining in the post-industrial world was planted at the river's edge of the cobblestone sidewalk, and shed its light around the tree and on upwards to the top of the walls of the hospital 24/7.

The old hospital was a military installation, and behind its walls humans for centuries had been subject to all manner of unspeakable experimental horrors. But such things were unknown to the two lovers outside of its walls tonight. The rain came down cold, it soaked them close to the skin, revealing the skin, exciting both of them once again.

The 13th Disciple

Spurrio, as he had just done so very recently, removed her backpack letting it fall soaking to the cobblestone. Then kissing her cheek with his entire body, he pushed her up against the old oak tree. By the time he got her to it, her top was already off. It didn't matter that he had just seen her less than an hour ago. It was as though a new mystery was being revealed. He dropped to his knees in front of her. She was shocked and terrified by her unexpected sense of power.

He slipped her jeans around her waist again as she lifted each foot slightly helping them off. She quivered as though from the cold as she felt his large hand gently caressing her inner thighs, kissing them. But when she felt them around her buttocks lifting her up, then pulling himself with both hands into her, she screamed. Her scream did not stop him, it did not stop them. With her legs locked around him their bodies lean and snaking into each other until she felt the soft wet grass beneath and him on top. He held her gently, with one hand on her buttocks, and the other protectively behind her head.

As she felt him cum again, that terrifying sense

of power returned for just a nanosecond. It was accompanied by the realization of just how bold and tender he could at once be. As she lay on her back in the grass, the rain ebbing, slowing, to the rhythm of her own breathing, coming gently to a sprinkle, she softly stroked the back which before she had clawed for, and quivered in ecstasy.

As they dressed again, each of them thought they could do it again. Instead, he took her back across the ponte and into the winding bewilderment that was Trastevere. As he took her home in the blue-black light of twilight of morning, the route was so circuitous that she thought he must be lost. Only later did she learn that he was taking standard cautions against being followed.

When he finally took her home, it was up the exposed stairway at the rear of the building. Had she been an expert in espionage, she would have thought it amateurish. But she was not yet a seasoned terrorist and noticed no such thing. What went more alarmingly unnoticed was that she was just beginning the most dangerous of special relationships, romantic love.

The 13th Disciple

Once in the apartment she immediately understood why he didn't take her there to make love. The place was as congested as the Via Nomentana. Some bodies were just beginning to wake, others weren't about to until well into the afternoon. There was the sound of snoring, and she thought she recognized some of the people from the restaurant last night.

There were two pots of espresso smoldering on the small four burner stove. Among those awake hugs were given all around, and words spoken in Italian. Some said hi to her, most in Italian, but some in pretty good English. DeStefano, the waiter, said good morning in English. Now she noticed him for the first time. He was young, about 20, with dark hair and black eyes. He was taller than her, but shorter than Spurrio. His eyes seemed to be kind to her, and he was generally good looking, but not distinguished like Spurrio. The former was Italian, the latter Roman.

Everyone who was awake was talking about something, obviously some were talking about her, she wondered only in passing what they were saying. There were only two girls there, Adrianna, and Fabrizia, who were both in love with Spirrio, but he was promised to neither. Later, she would meet Piero, who would regularly fight with Spurrio, they would argue over some cause, tell each other to fuck off, then go drink.

Some would come and a few others would leave, but these in this cacophonous home would be family. For now, she was just being introduced to those awake and the ones just awaking. Lorenzo got off the couch, introduced himself in perfect English and bid her to take his place, shyly she did, looking at Spurrio as she sat. He was still arguing with Pierro, but smiled at her after she sat. Across from the couch was a bed that folded out from the wall. About four bodies were strewn across it.

She hadn't eaten since dinner and now she was treated to her first Italian breakfast, caffe and colnini. She gobbled the coletto, but the espresso was strong and bitter. Before everyone else woke up, Spurrio took her into the bathroom with some towels. She did not feel strange about going alone with him into the bathroom in front of strangers, she thought of nothing but him.

The 13th Disciple

The shower was just an old white tub with a spigot coming out of the wall and a cloth curtain drawn around the top to keep the water in. The hot water felt good as it cleaned her skin, but she didn't want to clean anything inside of her.

He came over to her with his wet hair dripping on her, she drank it in. He turned, and she washed his broad back, taking her little hands from his shoulders down to his tapered waist. He turned around, and she did the same thing, but slower now, caressing his chest gently, his tight abdomen, and then lower more gently around his steadily rising part.

His body was now a huge toy, and she couldn't wait to play with it. She went to her knees in front of him, but Adrianna pounded on the door. She and Spurrio argued in Italian. She was still saying something to him in Italian, and he started to laugh, took Nicole's face in his big hands and kissed her full, softly on the mouth. They finished their shower quickly. Spurrio took their clothes to the laundry which was back in the bathroom and overheard Adrianna announce to one and all in Italian again that, "She was so thin you could put her in the folding bed, put it up and not know she was there. At once, Pierro told her to "Shut up'." But DeSteffano said that was precisely what Spurrio liked about her. Everyone else laughed.

As their clothes washed, Spurrio and she sat at the table. They, the Italians, began to argue. For Nicole's sake, they tried to do it in English. They had much success and even though about three fourths of the conversation was in Italian she could still get the main gist. She noticed, first of all, that Italians seem to think of debate as sport. It was always passionate and loud. Although the faces changed, the seasons changed, the subject remained the same, the Vatican, the Vatican guard, and to a lesser extent the Carabinieri.

Andrae complained, "The Vatican is becoming even more bold. Soon, there will be a microphone in every room and every apartment in Italy, then the world."

Eduardo speculated, "They must be getting worried pretty soon. Look at the size of the protests."

DeStefano cut Eduardo off, saying, "They don't

give a shit about the size of the protests. We have rocks, they have guns."

Lorenzo repeated an often-stated maxim, "We must get our own guns, only one thing happens when people with stones meet people with guns."

"Which is why we must keep our protests peaceful, like Gandhi or Martin Luther King Jr," Piero countered.

DeStefano suggested, "We should get the colonel and that old mafioso to organize us."

"Are we going to turn into the mafia now?" Piero said. "And reinvent the military?"

DeStefano added, "We should just listen to them; they have experience organizing. And all the guns in the world won't do us any good if we can't shoot them." He countered. It was getting louder, but Spurrio was going to make it louder by shouting over them all.

Spurrio boldly proclaimed, "All of you are right, and all of you are wrong. So far, our protests are peaceful, we throw a few stones and the Carabinieri pretend to chase us. The crowds cheer like a football game and throw us money, but it's all theater. If the Carabinieri or guard of the Vatican were really worried about us they'd shoot us in the back as we ran away. The Pope and the Cardinals like it, they know it gives people an outlet, and it makes them believe falsely that something is being done. They would love for the crowds to double again, as long as they can raise their taxes again, tell us who we can make love to and how, and put the cameras in every room and toilet in the world. It's gladiatorial."

Andre said, "He's right. We must convince people to stop paying their taxes."

"Oh, how is that going to work? When the Guardia Svizzera Pontificia, The Vatican Guard," he said in English for Nicole's sake, then continuing in Italian, "come pounding down the doors. And they will have more than stones in their hands. We must have guns too. Gandhi had guns until they took them away from him," Eduardo said emphatically.

Piero insisted, "We must not get guns. It will escalate not to bloodshed, but to a bloodbath. A bloodbath we cannot win." They were all yelling now.

"Fuck off," Spurrio screamed.

"Fuck off," Piero screamed back.

They were at each other's faces, with the others gathering around. Then, as if a referee had blown a whistle with the boiling point reached, they each turned away making some gesture with their hands.

Piero made a fist and punched his other hand. Spurrio put his hands on his hips then ran them through his hair. The fighting woke no one up; everyone moved about the room as they were going to begin their day.

Spurrio looked at Nicole, feeling not embarrassed that she had seen him getting mad, just hoping that she didn't misjudge the Italian way, that everyone there loved everyone else. They all had the same cause.

He sat down on the folding bed next to her, resting his elbows on his knees and she with her legs crossed massaged his back. For the first time, the tiny room seemed to be its size. It had always been full of bodies and noise and now that the cacophony had ceased it seemed more than empty. There were some sleeping bags and pillows on the floor against the wall. He took her hand, lay with his back against the wall, and she curled her body instinctively into his, they slept until it was dark.

Nicole was awakened by Spurrio's gentle love making. She was never aware of him kissing her neck or removing her top. She awoke to the sensation of him kissing her belly button. She let him slide her jeans off. He parted her thighs, caressing and kissing them.

They made love on the floor against the wall, coming to a sweating climax together. They rested, breathing heavy, then relaxing. Some people, who she did not know, had returned. Spurrio simply covered their naked bodies with the sleeping bags, and they giggled.

Then, her tiny stomach erupted with a hungry growl; they were both hungry.

"Let's go," Spurrio said.

"To where?" Nicole asked.

"To the restaurant to drink with the others," he

replied, laughing. Then, she smiled at him, and he smiled at her for smiling.

At the restaurant, if anyone remembered any part of the verbal warfare in the apartment, it was far from obvious. Spurrio and Piero hugged. Spurrio gave him a gentle headlock, and punch in the head. Eduardo and DeStefano rose from the table and joined in. They hugged Spurrio, they hugged her. They weren't yet drunk, but already well on their way.

She sat back and drank it all in, pinching herself to see if it was just a dream or a dream within the dream. She wondered briefly again if she could be dragged back into the nightmare. It would be ironic indeed if the one she was sent to find could bring her back down. But then she remembered that "nothing once given is ever taken again."

For the rest of that night, she relaxed and in an ocean of wine, joy, and laughter, that was at least equal in magnitude to the seeming conflict at the kitchen table earlier.

All night long, Spurrio attended to her, filling

her glass, her plate, translating for her, and constantly taking her face in his hand or gently petting her head. She loved it. Later that night, they were first back to the apartment, so that Spurrio could make love to her once more. But they took too much time. When the others came back, Spurrio simply covered themselves with the blanket, and no one seemed to mind. With any other man, she would have been horribly embarrassed, but with any other man, she never would have been there in the first place.

Later that night, instead of going to the protest, Spurrio collected some money from his friends. Then, with his beautiful new girlfriend, he took the train from Stazione Termini to Napoli. Arriving early, he intended to take her to the beautiful beach where they could play in the clean, cool water. But by noon, she was beginning to burn, so Spurrio bought a huge umbrella, which he stabbed into the burning sand at an angle to protect her from the sun's burning rays. All day they lay under the umbrella, drinking wine, eating bread and cheese, and devouring each other. He was wearing cutoff jeans, and she was topless in a bikini. He never thought blonde hair and fair skin could be so sexy.

When it got hot again, he carried her into the cool water to cool down, to cuddle each other, and to make love. He began teaching her Italian, and she learned surprisingly quickly. They got a room for the night, drank wine, had snacks, and made love until morning. Each time, their bodies digging into each other, leaning, straining, finally collapsing into each other.

The following morning, with an umbrella in hand, Spurrio led her to the beach to repeat the process. For them, there was no other place to be, no other time to worry about. There was no future or past, no Vatican or protests; they were light years away from Roma. There was here, now, each other, and that was all there needed to be.

After three days, they left the umbrella on the beach and took the train from Naples to Italy's spectacular mountainous interior. Although she had never seen anything like it before in her native Australia, she was at least able to see it for what it was not. She noticed how she could not see Spurrio in the same way. He mattered to her. It frightened her, and she wondered if he might not bring her back into the world of dreams. But she remembered again the words, "nothing once given is ever taken again." Still, whenever she made love to him, she was not so sure.

They camped on a spot so high that she could see both the Mediterranean and the Adriatic Seas. There he asked her to marry him. She was so shocked that she could not respond. Only the tearful nodding of her head up and down told him what he wanted to know.

After she was coherent again, he explained that the marriage could not be legal, that only the Vatican could make the marriage legal. It was a serious crime to have sex out of wedlock, and only the church could marry. It gave the Vatican tremendous control over people's daily lives.

"You mean I'm a criminal?" To which he wryly smiled and said, "Yes, Mrs. Pompilli, you are." Then, he kissed her gently on the forehead.

He produced two plastic toy rings, placed one on her left index finger and the other on his identical one. "It might be dangerous to wear these," he said. "If any Carabinieri, or Guardia Svizzera Pontificia guard asks for documentation of marriage, just say that it's a joke. When we get back to Roma, they will all be very surprised," he told her.

After that, he took her to San Giovanni, a northern factory town near Milan, to meet his parents. When she saw them, she could not believe that two such ordinary people could produce such an extraordinary son.

When the door opened to the small apartment in which he grew up, it revealed parents as ordinary as the dwelling they inhabited. His father, with a full head of gray hair, opened the door and hugged his son. He stepped back into the apartment, and his mother reached for him. For a long moment, all three were embraced. Spurrio said something in Italian, and they smiled, beckoning her to come in. She did, and his father closed the door behind her.

Spurrio introduced her to them in Italian and translated their greetings to her in English. Outside of their gray hair, his parents did look extremely young.

The 13th Disciple

Their skin was taut and smooth, especially for ones in their 50s. It gave her hope for their children, not even noticing how much she had slipped.

Spurrio showed his parents their rings, and they immediately understood. The joy across their faces was instantaneous. They ate pasta, bread, and wine. They wanted to know all about her, and since Spurrio hardly knew her, they had to ask. Spurrio became exhausted by translating. They avoided the subject of his protesting.

"I'm going to teach you Italian," he said.

"You promise?" she asked.

"Yes, Mrs. Pompilli," he answered, smiling.

They stayed the night. They did not make love under his parents' roof. They slept together in what had been his bedroom. She slept on her side curled into him. She could not have felt safer. When they woke, breakfast was already being served. They had espresso and cornetti. His mother was begging them to stay, but he wanted to show her Florence. Spurio promised they would return straight from Florence. As they left the small apartment with hugs all around, Spurrio paused to ask his father a question that both pleased and surprised him. It was whether he could still get a factory job.

The 13th Disciple

-Il Fronte Popolare -
The People's Front

In Florence, Spurrio acted as tour guide. He was able to explain all the history to her just as in Roma, as only an Italian could. They stayed with his friends who spoke English well enough that needed no translation.

In the three days, she could not remember all the people she met, but she remembered that Spurrio told all of them that she was his wife. She thought she would never get over that. Then they returned to San Giovanni, where Spurrio told her he was going to give up the protests and take a job. She didn't know how obvious her joy was to him, but seeing it made his show through.

As they made their way from the train station to the bus, Spurrio explained the protests could do without him, and he without them so long she was beside him. She never dreamed such a simple sentiment could make her cry. But simplicity would not carry the day, for by the time they returned to his parents' apartment, it had already begun.

The 13th Disciple

His father was the only one to greet them at the door. When they entered his mother remained on the couch glued to the scratchy black and white TV. His father closed the door and silently the three of them sat. His father in the lounge chair, Nicole and Spurrio on the couch. From the TV hanging on the wall issued forth sights and sounds of gunfire over easily recognizable streets of Roma.

While they were still on the train returning from Florence, the crowd gathered in the city center of Rome for its daily dance with the Carabinieri. They carried signs and placards and chanted, "You don't change tyranny, you end it." Some carried signs saying, "You don't defeat the government; you change the minds of the governed."

There was a swarming sea of red flags; some bore the likenesses of Che Guevara. Some wore masks; others simply used their shirts to cover their heads; most didn't bother. Some carried sticks, some stones, and others carried large wrenches. They marched in surprisingly straight lines toward the Carabinieri.

At the appropriate distance, they released rubber

bullets and tear gas. The crowd returned the tear gas and answered the rubber bullets with stones. When the crowd reached the point where the Carabinieri customarily charged, the police unexpectedly parted, like hair down the middle of the scalp, to one side of the street or the other.

Then, the Vatican guard advanced, moving only a few meters before raising their rifles and firing live ammunition into the crowd. The instantaneously recognizable sound brought screams of fear, some of pain, for many were hit, and death was quick. The Vatican guard threw more tear gas, and as the crowd tried to help its casualties, they fired upon them.

Paolo was one of them. While helping one of his fellows to his feet, and putting the man's left arm across his shoulders and carrying him by the hip with his right arm, he was shot in the back. Both men dropped to the ground in a pool of blood as flowing eddies of tear gas floated around like fog. Paolo screamed that the pain of being shot was unbearable.

Susanna was there; she was under an arched doorway when she saw Paolo shot. Forgetting all risks to herself, she ran to his aid. As she arrived, she could just see the faint glimmer of recognition leaving his eyes, and all that he had ever been or ever would be fading away.

That was how he died, like the blood leaving him; he just faded away. Bullets continued to fly down the stone streets, echoing off the marble canyon walls and gas. She did not move, she did not flinch. Comatose with grief, she held Paolo and rocked him on the stone street until someone finally rescued her from her predicament before she was herself shot.

At his parents' apartment, Spurrio was stunned. All four of them watched TV with blank faces. Nicole knew that some of his friends were in the crowd, were down on the street. If not for her, he probably would have been there too. They watched the TV as though it were a funeral, shocked, saddened.

He and his father drank grappa, while the women drank more wine. Spurrio was not angry but overwhelmed with anxiety. His only desire was to return to Roma to see who was hurt, and how it had happened, why it had happened.

The 13th Disciple

The Left Hand of Power

It had happened because in a cool, dark room in the bowels of the Vatican, whose only light came via monitors and backlit keyboards, Massimo Barrone had just taken his seat at the Left Hand of Power, as it was called. Too tall for a chair, he stood rather than sat in the center of that room, mission control. By simply putting the microphone on his ear, he was taking charge of all the sophistication and power the Vatican had developed to keep the people in line. But all that machinery was useless without a man, the right man, the man he intended to prove himself to be. In fact, such proof was simply a formality.

For Massimo Barrone, just a month shy of his 30th birthday, the rise had been meteoric. Holding now a position previously held only by men decades older, he was eager to show those on the inside and those on the outside, especially those who had denounced him (for none had doubted him), that he could do it. He would do, without hesitation, that which they could not, and all they had invested in him would pay huge dividends.

The Vatican had decided to expand its police state, but first, they had to crack down against those who refused to be brought into line. Massimo was the whip. Other men, wiser and more seasoned, had been seated in the Left-Hand Seat. They were stern men, but age, temperament, and the fact that they were Roman and had kids down there, as well as friends who had kids down there, made them willing to crack the whip, but not actually to use it.

Now there stood in that place a man without family, bereft of friends, compunction, or regrets. Where the older generation had cracked the whip, this younger man would use it.

No longer would the protests be tolerated like a soccer game, no longer would there be little consequence to being without a fully charged cell phone, or having sex out of wedlock, there would be nothing exterior to the Vatican's jurisdiction, to the reach of The Holy See. Devoid of empathy, impervious to human suffering, insouciant to any consequence of his own actions, Massimo Barrone dispassionately dispatched the orders to shoot to kill.

The 13th Disciple

At six feet five inches and 250 pounds, Barrone was not only physically the epitome of the leader of the Vatican's police state, but psychologically combative, and more importantly just intelligent enough. Barrone was intelligent enough to be at the top of the entire Carabinieri, and Vatican Guard forces, but not so intelligent as to be disinterested by law enforcement outright.

He had huge hands, but could type rapidly and efficiently. He spoke perfect Italian and English with a perfect British intonation. Barrone's father had been a Judo champion of Calabria and muscle for a local mafia chieftain, which was no longer the real mafia as many were wont to say, but a thug nonetheless.

Possession of firearms was a capital offense and immediately after the war anyone found in possession of one was arrested by the Carabinieri and executed by firing squad. In the absence of firearms, the reputation of the Judo champion of the region preceded him. Rarely was he even required to actually use his impressive bulk against someone.

When he was only 12 years old, Massimo, already over

six feet tall and 200 pounds, would sometimes follow his father as he accompanied the mafia man on various troubleshooting visits. Usually, Massimo would take care of the problem himself. He liked it even then, at 12 years-old, putting a grown man on the ground and making him submit to his own 12-year-old will.

Then, he would relive and relish in it again and again in his own mind. Once, however, a troublesome, young upstart rival, had hired his own Judo champion. Massimo remembered vividly how the other man was not intimidated in the least by his father, but was nonetheless thoroughly beaten by him.

Massimo's father threw the other, larger man with an over the shoulder throw so hard that it broke the other man's ribs with an agonizing scream. Massimo had heard men grunt before, or even whimper, but until then he had never heard a man scream. Before the man could stop screaming his father deftly took his back and silenced the screams by choking him to death.

Then, his mighty father took both of the upstart's hands and held them behind his back as his own employer produced a pistol, put it to the man's temple, and blew his brains, partly against his father's grass-stained shirt. His father never flinched, but before the body had hit the ground, he looked his son cold into the eyes. To Massimo, the message could not have been clearer, be brutal, be dirty, be overwhelming.

Before his 14th birthday, Massimo was running with a crew of his own, each one big and mean. But whenever they were themselves accosted by local police, or the Carabinieri, all of the men, even the one of highest rank, was obedient to even the lowest of the policemen, for a while, for appearance's sake.

Sometimes, they would beat up an off-duty policeman, one who had crossed them, by taking money and then not performing the required task, or more often by trying to steal the business be it drugs, or guns, from the gangs, but when the Carabinieri or police snapped the gang healed obediently.

It didn't need to be explained to him; the Carabinieri carried their guns openly on them, the gang judiciously decided not to. They would always have to retrieve their firearms, and men with guns always killed men without them, no matter the size or stature of those involved. It was an obvious law of nature.

The point was further driven home later that same year. He was standing at a bar sipping espresso next to his father when suddenly his father's massive head crashed into the bar with an explosive impact. But it wasn't his head exploding on the bar, it was the bullet exploding his head. It was as if a huge hand had grabbed the back of his head and slammed him into the bar. There was almost no splatter. A few minutes later a hit was made on the mafia chieftain in whose employ he had so long been. Once his Judo champion bodyguard was removed the chieftain was an easy mark. The hit had been disguised as a mafia war, but everyone knew that the mafia was well into its decline, the Carabinieri had simply set it up in service of their master, the Holy See.

With his father's blood still wet on his shirt and body, Massimo at 14 was taken into custody. He did not feel too uncomfortable about seeing his father blown away inches from him, but he intensely disliked incarceration. So, when his uncle, a Carabinieri Captain adopted him, he felt rescued. But for the best of all concerned Massimo didn't live with the family, instead his uncle sent him at the not so tender age of 14, to the New Italian Military Academy at Velletri. From there he would proceed to the school of the Carabinieri, and then to the academy of the Vatican Guard or Guardia Svizzera Pontificia. It wasn't prison, but just two weeks shy of his 15th birthday Massimo Barrone quietly became an institutionalized man, a man with a mechanical will, and a heart of stone, with a honed narcissistic temperament willing to do anything.

After graduating from the school of the Guard of the Vatican at the age of just 19 years, Massimo Barrone was assigned to the Vatican's diplomatic corps. The Vatican was having trouble with the nation of Ireland. It seemed that in the aftermath, some nations still didn't get it—that there really is a New World Order and you don't shy away from it.

The diplomats to the Vatican enjoyed diplomatic immunity in all of Italy, not just Roma, meaning that they could not be arrested for anything, but they could be harassed for everything. This proved to be a very unfortunate state of affairs for the Irish diplomat when Barrone was required to verify the diplomat's credentials.

Officer Barrone spotted the diplomat's black Mercedes Benz leaving the Prime Minister's palace on the Via Nomentana. The prime minister had always been a token, but even now, bureaucrats kept up pretenses. So, it was easy for Barrone to know where the ambassador was and when he was leaving.

Barrone pulled his dark blue Alfa Romeo up behind the ambassador's glossy black limo and turned on his siren and lights as soon as it entered the Piazza Venezia. The shocked driver pulled to his left, bringing the heavy black Mercedes to a halt at the island in the center of the grand expanse of the Piazza. Barrone waited, not patiently, but expectantly, imagining the diplomat's annoyance and relishing how he would turn that annoyance to fear once the tiny little bureaucrat realized that he was no longer the one in control.

The officer stepped out of the car and walked purposefully toward the diplomat's car. Using his flashlight, he rapped hard on the bullet proof windows of the driver door and left passenger door. He motioned both occupants out. The driver readily complied, but the passenger behind the dark glass gave no indication one way or the other.

Barrone pointed to a spot on the sidewalk, and the frightened driver, never having seen a man so large and imposing, went obediently to the direct spot that Barrone had randomly pointed at. He rapped his flashlight hard against the roof this time, so hard that the driver was positive that his poor passenger must be concussed, and kept rapping until the door as if by its own reluctant initiative opened itself.

At last, the moment the giant had waited for. Pre-empting any protestations of the diplomat, Barrone motioned him as curtly as he had the lowly driver to another point on the sidewalk. "Sir, do you have your diplomatic identity card, sir? May I see it please, sir?" It was all grotesquely polite, spoken in the Queen's most perfect intonation—a curt kind of formality that was deadly serious.

The words written would seem fawning, falling over themselves, but delivered aloud with a nascent whiff of threat rising, which hung heavy like gunpowder in the air. Once outside of the safety of the limousine, even the experienced diplomat was visibly intimidated. Barrone loved every second of it, knowing he was in control, and now he poured it on. He examined the diplomat's credentials. "Sir, please step to the curb, sir, and stay at least ten feet from your driver, sir."

"Sir, yes, sir. I'll beat the living shit out of you, sir, right here, sir, in front of God and the whole fucking world, sir, and I'll leave your pissed stained driver stinking right here to tell everyone how you shit all over yourself, sir," was what the diplomat all too well understood.

Barrone spent the entire remainder of his shift in a state of glory. The Irish consulate protested, and after a public reprimand, the Vatican Guard promoted Massimo Barrone.

Massimo Barrone had never intended to kill Andrea Lorenzi, however.

It never even occurred to him to do it almost until the moment it was done. Lorenzi, about half the size of Barrone, was milder by nature. He had more of ice water cruelty in his veins. Utterly devoid of empathy, ambitious, and fitting easily into an Armani suit, he was the new prototype for the Guard of the Vatican.

He was first in line for the soon-to-be-vacant Seat of the Left Hand of Power. After Barrone received his promotion, they became barracks mates at the school of the Guardia Svizzera Pontificia, high up in the astonishing mountains to the south of Roma in the tiny village of Velletri.

Lorenzi never dreamed that he had anything to fear from the giant, Barrone, whose intelligence he respected. Indeed, it had been established that Barrone would be his right-hand man when he ascended to the Left Hand of Power.

Late December was the slowest time of year, and the massive academy was barren. Both men, more through lacking family and friends than devotion, remained at their residence in the academy.

Barrone had gone for a run into the woods on a

trail which wound its way wildly in steep, astonishing cliffs and evergreen around the academy far below. It had been snowing lightly for about an hour when he came upon Lorenzi where the trail turned near the top of the steep-sided mountain.

"Race you to the top, old man," Barrone said good-naturedly.

Lorenzi, a year older of the two, retorted, "You are on shortie."

As with everything, Barrone first toyed with Lorenzi, letting him pass to the inside first. Then, he sprinted up to Lorenzi on the outside, fell back, and played catch-and-mouse again. Lorenzi, who had been slowing down, now gave it his all in a mad dash for the top.

Barrone could have just as easily made his way around Lorenzi on the outside, and Lorenzi would still be alive. But by chance, he made his way on the inside. Not so much intending as not, he just edged past Lorenzi with his massive left elbow extended a bit. He wasn't even sure that he meant to do it, but he was sure that it had been done.

He didn't look back or slow down or even call in order to look for Lorenzi. No one would know that he was the last one to have seen him alive. Barrone just jogged in the now fast falling snow, back down to the base.

Still, he never would have gotten away with it had it not been for the fact that Lorenzi had reported himself off base for that day. He had gone to Napoli to be with a prostitute. When he returned to the base, arrogance got the best of him. He berated the gate guard for doing his job and would not tell where he had been. The guard did not allow Lorenzo entry, and he had to sneak back into the barracks.

When he went for a run on that fateful morning, Lorenzi was listed as AWOL. No one ever found his body, and Barrone had gotten away clean with a murder that would never be discovered. He took full control of the Seat of The Left Hand of Power.

When the train pulled into Stazione Termini, the TVs at the stations displayed the news: 88 dead and 117 injured.

Spurio returned with Nicole to the apartment, taking some perfunctory evasive measures, but basically going straight there. Once there they realized what happened, Paolo was not there, and Susanna was psychotic with grief.

"He's dead," someone told Spurrio. "He's dead, and they have his body."

"Are you sure?" Spurrio asked.

"Susanna was the one who found him."

Judging by Susanna, Spurrio figured that at least, she was sure.

Later, people came and went, they walked stunned and grieving into the streets, still putrid with tear gas wafting lazily in the air. Spurrio and Nicole did it with them. She could understand grief in any language.

No one seemed angry yet; that would come later. For now, they were just in a deep state of shock.

As that day had changed into night, changed

into the day after, and the day after that, the debate changed with it. Paolo and Susanna had been dead set against armed violence. Now, she was one of those proposing it. Piero was still against it, but Andre, DeStefano, and Eduardo were now for it.

Spurrio said, "It has to be all or nothing. The strength of reasoning isn't working. We must stop it altogether, and move to the reasoning of strength."

Susanna, looking catatonic and staring at the wall, asked DeStefano, "Can you get the Colonel and the mafioso?" DeStefano simply nodded in the affirmative.

So it was that in a language she could not understand, in a tiny room filled with fear and grief turning to rage, surrounded by mostly strangers whose cause was alien to her, that Nicole bore silent witness to the secret birth of Il Fronte Popolare, The People's Front.

From the strength of reasoning, to the reasoning of strength. It was not the kind of shift which her course talked about. She was non-judgmental of it all, in her mind it didn't matter who won, The Vatican or the people, it was all a tiny mad idea made up by the psychotic split mind of The Son Of Man. All that mattered to her now was that she had found the one for whom she had been sent, and was to guide him gently home as he had done for her so many centuries before which never even existed.

Because she could not understand Italian, Nicole was largely unaware of the nuances by which The People's Front grew. To her, it was like watching water boil, all of a sudden it just was.

"The mafioso gives us the money," Spurrio explained. "It's supposed to be a 50/50 split, but no one knows how much he is really skimming." She could see the stinging judgment in his statement, but did not judge.

"The colonel," he said with less judgment, "provides the trainers and training. But he already warns that most training is on the job." She sensed her husband's dismay. He explained it to her succinctly, "Experience is a cruel teacher. It gives the examination first and the lesson last." What he could not know then was that it was he who would be that cruelest teacher's most frustrating pupil.

Spurrio was already a guerrilla, he simply had to know that he was. One lesson was usually all it took, be it shooting, explosives, even driving. Moreover, Spurrio was unknowingly a master strategist whose intricate far-reaching plans born instantaneously in his head would be more than a match for the greatest power structure the planet had ever produced.

Nicole's single-minded purpose during this time was to learn Italian and concentrate on translating her course into it. She had many willing teachers, not just her husband, Piero, DeStefano, Andrei. And she reciprocated by teaching English to the Italians. The People's Front did not remain a mystery to her for long.

Her husband explained, "We will kill people, I will kill people."

She explained that she did not share their view. To her, bodies were not real. Then, she stopped speaking because she realized she was no longer so sure. That bodies were not real had been obvious to her since she had scribed it directly from Jesus—until she encountered Spurrio's body. The illusion of his body was indeed strong. Who was she to say?

All she knew for sure was that this special relationship was intense and especially dangerous. She knew that, even if only in the dream, unless she took control of it, in the end, it would crush her.

"I don't like it," Spurrio said repeatedly. "Since we've become The People's Front, there is too much traffic in the apartment. In and out, everyone can see us coming and going. It seems like we were more careful when we were unorganized." Everyone agreed, but no one agreed to do anything about it. It's not that they discounted his warning, but there was simply nothing that could be done about it.

But Spurrio figured a way out of the building in case of emergency. During the day, when the people in the apartment below were out, Spurrio ripped up the floor in the closet, so that they could at least escape into the apartment below. The family that lived there were opposed to Vatican rule, so it was easy to convince them. The little boy even offered up the fact that there was space between the walls. Enough space Spurrio found for a man to shimmy all the way to the end of the hall.

It took about a week for Spurrio and Piero using a hammer and chisel to weaken the wall, so that a man could push through it and jump to the street below. If the time came that it was needed, the escape route was ready. He instructed Nicole, whether he was in the apartment or not, to make her way straight there in the case of any emergency.

The daily protests had been reduced to no more than a dozen people throwing stones at the bulletproof Vatican Guard police cars and fleeing before being shot. Soon there would be none. Since becoming "The People's Front," Spurrio and his friends had dedicated those hours formerly spent protesting to training with the colonel.

They had just returned to the apartment from training which the colonel had arranged. Nicole sat lotus style on the bed studying Italian with Paola next to her. DeStefano was making espresso. They were just beginning to relax, when machine-gun bullets raked the apartment through its two windows facing the street.

Paola's body was slammed as if hit by a truck, against the bed. Her brains splattered against the ceiling and rained down upon Nicole before she had any chance to duck. DeStefano scalded himself with espresso, but did not notice it as he dived flat against the floor. Nicole did as she was instructed and this enabled Spurrio to concentrate on his aim.

Spurrio drew his weapon and blasted the Carabinieri who was first to crash through the apartment window via a rappelling rope. The sound of shattering glass being submerged under the thunderous cannon blasts of .50 caliber machine gun fire from the street. The Carabinieri dropped with an unheard thud. The next two repelling police were dead before they were able to breach the apartment, their bodies cracking to the ground outside.

From his back, DeStefano raked the door with a machine gun. While Eduardo and Spurrio lay down suppressing fire through the windows, everyone escaped through Spurrio's pre-planned route. Spurrio had just killed his first three men. He knew he would be a target for the Carabinieri and The Vatican Guard, but this was not what concerned him as he ran to join Nicole at the per-arranged rendezvous point. What concerned Spurrio was the certain knowledge that already there was a traitor in their young group.

The Operations

As summer turned to October, then a cold November, Spurrio, Nicole, and Susanna moved to Naples. Spurrio and Susanna were acting as a husband and wife team. They bought rings, left in the morning, and did not return until evening, keeping regular hours so as not to draw attention. All the while, Nicole was content to hide in the apartment to cook meals and study Italian and translate A Course in Miracles into it.

They were joined by Dominick, who, despite being Italian, was the palest man Nicole had ever seen. He looked like he hadn't been in the sun for years. Despite this, he had high cheekbones, a chiseled chin, and shoulders as broad as Spurrio. Spurrio's first thought was, "I hope I don't have to fight him." In fact, both were dedicated and capable; they would be brothers.

During his entire time in The People's Front, Spurrio never asked Nicole for permission, nor sought her approval, nor did he lie or omit any detail of the actions he had done or was planning to do. So, she understood well why everyone was so tense. They were in Naples to attack a Vatican Bishop.

This Bishop was in charge of the Vatican bank in the region. He was responsible for writing mortgages to people who had no way to repay them. It was an old mafia default-by-design scheme, where the Vatican bank lent money it was able to create from thin air to people who would have to work to provide real goods and services to repay it.

The bank was more successful if the people defaulted on the loan and the bank repossessed the house, making more profit than if they actually repaid the loan. As always, the acquisition of land, buildings, and hard assets, not repayment of the debt, was the true aim.

The People's Front was outraged over this, and they meant to put an end to the custom formerly called usury, and anyone who practiced it.

The bishop's office was in a square; there was an archway leading in and out. Dominick could easily see his breath as he stepped from the car, and hear his footfalls reverberating loudly off the cobblestone streets against the drab and fading stone walls of the square.

The Uzis fit neatly under his coat, and his swift advance on the four bodyguards flanking the bishop went unnoticed until they were under the arch. Suddenly, his arms, which had swayed naturally, came up with a machine gun in each hand. The two bodyguards on the bishop's left side were dead before they hit the ground.

The third one drew his own machine gun and fired a blast at Dominick, while the last bodyguard rushed the bishop back into the square, covering his body with his own. Dominick returned fire, eviscerating the bodyguard in an atomized mist of blood. Spurrio and Susanna, seeing their own breath, leapt from their own car and advanced rapidly but deliberately on the bishop and his remaining bodyguard.

Dominick dropped his spent clips where he stood, reloaded, and then stood his ground in the center of the archway. Spurrio and Susanna moved with deliberate speed toward the bishop now, their bounds in their step intensifying, their footfalls echoing and being drowned out by the gunfire. Susanna pulled her weapon first; her right hand moved fast, but her draw was long coming all the way across her body. By the time she straightened her arm and twisted her right shoulder forward, the bodyguard nearly had her.

But Spurrio was swift and sure; he shot the bodyguard twice in the right temple as he turned and drew down on Susanna. The bishop lay prostrate on his back, raising his hands to protect himself from the inevitable bullet that was soon to kill him. Spurrio stood over him, aimed the gun at his head. "We do this in the name of Il Fronte Popolare for all those you made homeless." Spurrio looked into the man's eyes just before he pulled the trigger and felt something wholly unexpected: empathy. No one watching, however, would have noticed the hesitation, for Susanna shot him four times in rapid succession in the heart. The gunshots were still reverberating off the cobblestone as they jumped into the car, and Dominick sped them all away.

Massimo Barrone was furious. In his mind, he was murdering all of his subordinates by crucifixion. "How could this have happened?" he asked in a matter-of-fact way, in a normal tone that belied his murderous intentions. If not in full control, he had to give the appearance of it. More of the latter was needed, less of the former. Deceit being the core of his nature, he knew how to do this instinctively. He knew something else by instinct: that Spurrio had done this. He could not prove it yet; he had his rat and would confirm it later. But for now, he knew it in his cells; he simply could tell the cat by the paw.

Spurrio considered his unexpected attack of sympathy as well as Susanna's spontaneous ruthlessness. It was already clear to him that both trends would continue; it was not so obvious what the repercussions would be. Vengeance had taken full control of Susanna, as she was becoming one of the most violent and fearless members of Il Fronte Populare.

Quickly, The People's Front was planning its

next attack. They would target another heavily guarded Bishop, but the real target of the attack was his entourage of Guardo de Vaticano bodyguards. They sat on a couch, with several lounge chairs brought around a small table with a mock-up of a Milan Street on it. Some people stood, but everyone was focused like a laser light on Romano Prodi. Dark, slight of build, but as intense as he was brilliant, Prodi pointed to the map. He would have been an engineer or scientist in the pre-war days, in the time before the global Holy See. Matter-of-factly, he stated, "The light changes here or here. If the first one is green, the second is always red. The bishop will have at least two cars of bodyguards, one in front, one in back. Maybe some in the car with him as well. There may be some more in the windows and on the rooftops of the buildings along Via Colleti, so we will use smoke for cover. Any questions?"

"When?" Andre asked, holding an unfinished glass of red wine in his hands. "It will be dangerous; we need at least a week to prepare," Spurrio responded, sipping the last of his grappa.

I hope it's not a trap, Spurrio thought as the

bishop's car passed right on schedule. Two cars accompanied the bishop's, one in front and the other behind. In each, there sat four heavily armed men. As the last one turned up the Via Colleti, Dominick and Eduardo, as if to trap it, stepped into the traffic lane behind it. They followed up the one-way street, dropping white smoke that streamed and then billowed along the way. It blended well with the light sprinkle of falling snow and the gloom of fog accompanying it.

Parked cars lined both sides of the street, and through the smoke, Spurrio and Romano Prodi walked deliberate steps through the intensifying gloom. The simultaneous racking of the machine guns reverberated through Spurrio's guts and rose up and wafted into the smoke and mist swirling around them. The light changed, and the first car pulled through the intersection as Spurrio and Romano emptied their machine guns into the passenger side of the bodyguard's car. The wheels on the bishop's car squealed, and that sound was followed closely by the sound of chunks of metal colliding. Spurrio and Romano had both found their mark, and the driver was dead instantly. The bishop was still alive. They only killed him after his car had come to a complete stop.

What had been the lead car attempted to escape straight down the Via Colleti. Machine-gun fire came from all four windows as it sped away. But perched on the rooftops were DeStefano, Eduardo, Giovanni, and Paolo, trained their machine guns on the speeding car. It was only a matter of time until it met the same fate as the bishop's. When it came to rest against parked cars on the side of the road, Dominick lobbed a hand grenade through the broken window. The fiery explosion echoed up and down the Via Colleti, and they all disappeared like smoke into the wind.

Massimo Baroni was livid when he learned of the extravagant and brazen violence The People's Front was engaged in. He would take his revenge on them, but not before using them for his own purposes. He made the public statement that "the massacre was an act of terrorism." But then he got an idea of how to use it to his advantage. He called on the Vatican to write more stringent laws regarding terrorists and terrorism.

His current problem was that the public not only

would not condemn The People's Front's attacks on the Carabinieri and the guard of the Vatican, but it also approved of them. Indeed, it was public support and secret donations alone on which The People's Front survived. Everyone knew well that they would never attack innocents; they never had and were even known to call off an operation if it risked the lives of the nonpartisan. However, he knew just as assuredly that his own guard of the Vatican would readily commit any variety of heinous atrocity at his direct order. Then it would be an easy matter to blame it on The People's Front. The false flag was as old as the ages, as ancient as Roma itself. No matter what he intended to do, he had already identified Spurrio as an enemy to be reckoned with.

In less than a week, they were in Sicily. Spurrio left Nicole with his parents near Milan. He couldn't shake the bad feeling since the Carabinieri attack on their apartment in Roma, that there was a traitor among them. If things went south, he wanted Nicole to be safe and as far away as possible.

This time, they were going to attack the Vatican

The 13th Disciple

Guard barracks in the desert-like interior of the island. About the time they were blowing holes through the doors of the bishop's car on the Via Colleti, there had been a demonstration in Palermo, and a certain Martial of this Vatican Guard barracks ordered his men to open fire, killing 119 civilians. The People's Front was enraged when they learned of this. The Vatican Guard had the most sophisticated and numerous firepower in the world; the protesters had stones. Spurrio was eager to address the injustice at once. The Vatican Guard barracks in Sicily seemed to be the perfect choice. They had never struck so far south, and it would be both a shock and a demonstration that no one was safe.

Prodi was again using a pointer and sitting in front of a mock-up, this one of the army bases serving as The Vatican Guard barracks. Situated on a desert island flanked on one side by a freshwater lake of more than a mile square. There were always armed guards in the five-story high gun tower at its center. "The tower guards change shifts twice a day, at noon and midnight," Prodi said, tapping the mock-up with his pointer. "But there are perimeter lights as bright as day, so it is always daytime. There was absolutely no approach," he concluded dejectedly.

They all circled the mockup in their individual faded deco chairs, staring in silence at the problem before them. It was not until the desert air had gone from cold to hot that Spurrio finally had a question, then an idea.

"Can our chemists cook up a batch of ricin?" he asked, almost offhandedly.

"Sure, they can," Dominick insisted.

"Good, look here," he said, pointing to the lagoon on the model on the table. Water was supplied in Sicily as it had been for centuries in Roma, via aqueducts from the surrounding hills.

"This is the water supply, and once we are sure that it does not supply water to anyone else, that is when we will put a little ricin in the lake."

"How much will be enough?" Paolo asked.

"We will have to find out," Spurrio replied, sipping red wine from a plastic cup.

The 13th Disciple

"I will do the homework," Podi volunteered.

"All right, it's on you," Spurrio agreed.

The day was hot and dry, and the cactus and flowers reflected vividly off the sun-blasted hills in hues of art deco as Spurrio spied with binoculars, cranking his head 90 degrees from behind the steering wheel more than a mile away. He was young, and it was supposed to be simple.

Willy, just 17 years old but already dutiful and committed, had just to hike to the lake, remove the ricin from the backpack, spill it into the lake, and pretend to go swimming if necessary. But he was alone all the way to the lake. Spurrio could see him clearly through the binoculars.

Tall, almost as tall as Spurrio, but skinny as a rail, with a frock of thick black hair he wore perpetually in his eyes. They all wondered how he could see a thing. It was supposed to be easy, but the gunshot exploded like a cannon in the dry desert air, and the bullet seemed to cut his skinny body in half.

In stark contrast to the gently muffled thud of

the boy's body as it fell in slow motion, coming to a dead stop on the desert rock below with a cloud of dust suspended for an eternity about it.

Spurrio, stunned, slowly removed the binoculars, pausing them above the steering wheel for a second. He was sick to his stomach, but now he knew who the traitor was amongst them.

"You were the only one at the apartment in Roma, and here, and they are the only places the Vatican Guard and the Carabinieri were waiting for us," Spurrio said matter-of-factly to Andrea.

"Don't deny it!" Susanna screamed.

"I don't trust you, bitch," Andrea said just loud enough for all to hear.

Spurrio punched Andrea hard; it sounded like a gunshot, and Andrea ricocheted off the wall. He landed on the floor on his stomach, groaning. Spurrio hoisted him high and slammed him down again with another tremendous thud. But as Spurrio drew back his fist again, he saw the villain was unconscious. Then that old part of himself, the part that could not attack anything that was helpless, took over. He dropped him like a sack.

But Susanna, who no longer possessed such a part, raised her pistol to end the pathetic little man's misery. Spurrio's cat-like reflexes took over; he was able to deflect Susanna's hand just enough to blow a hole in Andrea's leg and puncture everyone's eardrums in the room.

They fled the apartment and Sicily with their eardrums banging, leaving the traitor to bleed to death on the floor.

Spurrio was sick to his stomach. He was only trying to avoid the video surveillance of the train stations and city centers by taking a motorcycle through the countryside, adorning the required safety helmet, which protected his identity better than it ever could his head. After filling his tank without removing his helmet, he went into the bar to have an espresso. He paid for it but never had a drop.

What he saw on the TV first made him nauseous, then terrified, then made him doubt everything he was doing with The People's Front. Nicole had been arrested by the Carabinieri and was being held for terrorism. It was the Carabinieri who made the arrest, but it had Barrone's fingerprints all over it. Spurrio could recognize a paw print or two himself. They had seized her from his parents' house. Andrea, that little rat, he should have killed him earlier. He was once again the only one who could have told the Vatican Guard she was there.

Barrone had foiled him in Sicily, and now had kidnapped Nicole. It was a ploy designed to provoke a rash response; Barrone wanted nothing less. But for Massimo Barrone, it was truly a case of be careful what you wish for.

"Un gaze, " Dominick exclaimed, "even the mafia never did such a despicable thing."

"They know she is a civilian, it's an outrage," Susanna joined in.

For the first few days after it happened, Spurrio could not eat, sleep, or hold a thought. With bats in his belly, he roamed in the woods, rode his motorcycle aimlessly, and paced restlessly indoors as the storm roiled within. But when all his swirling, nervous energy coalesced into a white-hot plan for recovery and revenge he remained tireless, but was aimless no longer, once he knew what had to be done and now he became as eerily calm as he was ruthlessly determined.

He would respond on two fronts; the first was coldly not to rescue his wife, rather to kill Barrone solo, then hook up with Il Fronte Popolare and break her out of the prison.

The People's Front had been investigating Massimo Barrone for some time, probing. They had discovered no one whom he loved, no parent, child or lover, he was that kind of man, but there was something he held more dear than he was ever capable of holding a human being, it was his vanity.

Massimo Barrone was in love with his good looks. He did have a chiseled Roman face with curly dark hair. Add to this the fact that he was six feet and seven inches of statuesque muscle and you could see the theory begin to hold water, what you could not see was that he was a remorseless psychopath psychotically devoted to devouring each and every entity within his sphere, bringing it down to his level, only in that way could he accomplish anything at all. He could not just take a woman, though he could take them by the dozens, he had to rape them, or love and then leave them heartbroken, diminishing them, he did not have an orgasm, he had her orgasm.

Barrone had sent notice to Spurrio that he would keep Nicole, and keep her in the most desperate of circumstances until he turned himself in. Spurrio played for time. "Tell them you can't find me, that I've gone into hiding," Spurrio told The People's Front.

Then, he rode his motorcycle with his helmet on and his sniper rifle into the clean mountain air of Velletri to insult more than Senior Barrone's vanity.

Il Fronte Popolare had intelligence indicating that Barrone traveled on odd occasions from the Vatican to the Carabinieri base in Velletri to train in Judo with the best of the Carabinieri. It was the closest thing he had to entertainment. Sometimes, he went by helicopter, sometimes by train, always changing up his mode. This time it was by the Vatican-issued Alfa

The 13th Disciple

Romeo.

As Massimo Barrone maneuvered his dark blue, almost black Alfa Romeo down the snaking, twisting road of the spectacular Italian Alps, he paid no attention to the stunning vista passing by him. Not the windshield full of trees, nor the deep gorge beside the road through which crystal-clean water roared with white foam, exploding into the rocks and wafting up and away in ephemeral mists. He was incapable of such things.

He could not see the man who had parked his motorbike about a mile away from him across that deep abyss. The man balanced with one knee on the ground, beginning to lift a sniper rifle level with himself. Barrone could not hear the report of the rifle, nor the cracking of the bulletproof window, nor the fragments of glass across the left side of his face.

Spurrio watched the car drive off the road. He could hear the screaming of glass and metal and feel the concussive blast and heat from the explosion that followed as the Alfa Romeo rolled over and over in flames down the deep ravine.

The 13th Disciple

Now that Barrone was eliminated, it would act as a distraction, but he realized that he must act quickly to secure the escape of Nicole.

"She is being held in the prison for women on La Gudica in Venice!" Spurrio told the group, including Romano Prodi, looking studious wearing wire rimmed glasses and Dominick gathered there.

Indicating a model of the prison with a pointer, he continued saying, "One long wall, the south wall, is right up against the water. They think it's protected that way, but only from land. We go in at night. Once the electricity is cut, the auxiliary power will come on at the prison, but not for the rest of the island. We will have plenty of time to take to the roof tops before the security cameras come on. From there, we lay down suppressing fire until the boat with the dynamite can tie up to the wall. It won't be able to tie up exactly. We will have to drop anchors for and aft. This will be right under the guard tower, so lay that suppressing fire, down heavy. We already have the boat, the C-4, and the Carabinieri uniforms for the ones on the boat." Spurrio slapped the prison mock up with the pointer producing a crack louder than intended. The plan was ready.

And so it was that four men in Carabinieri uniforms aboard a Carabinieri disguised water bus slowly drifted to the prison dock, with its heavy diesel engines belching as they slowed reluctantly to idle. The wake pushed high up over the seawall and then retreated.

The guards in the tower trained their high-powered weapons suspiciously on the vessel as two of the Carabinieri jumped off and pretended to tie up to the dock. It was precisely then that the lights went out and the suppressing gunfire that Spurrio had begged for exploded. His compatriots came through better than he could have dreamed, so thick was the bombardment that the guards could not stand up to take a shot.

In her cell, with other members of Il Fronte Popolare, Nicole heard the gunfire and knew exactly what time it was. But no one was prepared for the tectonic explosion that followed. It was so powerful that it knocked those standing to the cold cobblestone ground, Nicole among them.

The 13th Disciple

Nicole and Abby grabbed the female guard and wrestled her to the floor, pushing her face until the guard's cheeks were cut against the scratchy stone. Nicole kicked her in the back of the head, knocking her out cold, then Abbey disarmed her.

Spurrio and Dominic were firing into the guard tower as Prodi drove the small speed boat up to the gigantic hole now blown into the wall. Once inside, using their knowledge of the prison layout, they began their systematic search for Nicole and the others, blasting holes in anything that wore a uniform as they did so.

Bullets ricocheted in sparks off of the ancient masonry as Il Fronte Popolare members calmly sprayed halls with Uzi's as though they were watering gardenias. They didn't have to go far. Nicole, Abby, and another woman he didn't recognize, obviously someone they had befriended, came running toward them from smoking, crumbling walls.

Spurrio tossed Nicole a pistol, which she caught flawlessly in midair. They all turned and ran back the way they had come, toward the sea. As they turned their back to run, a guard appeared from around the corner behind them. Without hesitation Nicole turned, shot him in the head as though she had swatted a fly. The force hit him like a truck, and his brains exited through the back of his head and splattered against the ancient stone behind him.

Without hesitation, she followed Spurrio and Dominick back through the smoke-filled and battered prison until she could hear the water lapping against the wall. She wasn't sure of which direction they were headed, but suddenly there was wood instead of stone under her feet. They were on the boat dock, and she could hear the angry vibrations of a diesel engine's discontented guttural rumbling only meters away.

She followed Spurrio and Dominick aboard. Instantly, the huge beast stood up on the water like a great stallion on its hind legs and took off into the night, she was not aboard it. Spurrio had pushed her overboard and followed suit. They were back at the sea wall of La Guddica and Spurrio was pushing her down, his big hands on her head felt good, comforting to her even here. She trusted him implicitly. She trusted him.

The 13th Disciple

Finally, she understood what he was doing and was able to help. They were swimming under the boats that were tied up at docks alongside the sea wall. As they came up for air one time, she could see the Carabineers boats in pursuit of the one they had just abandoned. Then, Spurrio submerged his body, tugged gently at her hand, and she was in the darkness again. At last, they came up next to one boat, which had the letters "va benne" across its transom, and they scurried aboard soaking wet.

Suddenly, a huge fireball rose from the water, from the boat they had briefly been aboard. It had been controlled remotely, and Dominic had waited until the Carabinieri boat pulled abreast in order to board. Once they did, he blew the whole thing up. The blast blazed like a red teardrop on the dark aquamarine waters as it rose like a mushroom cloud into the night, and then the agonizing screams of Caraibbinieri being burned alive cut like razor blades through the cold misty gloom.

Spurrio and Nicole admired the show, then shivering, stripped, donned dry clothes that were waiting for them there, along with Susanna, and followed her onto the stone island known as La Guddica. The cobblestone streets were dripping with age, mist, and were narrow, more like corridors, as the streets of the oldest city of Europe should be. Fog and smoke filled the air, but the night itself was so dark she could not see them. Only their sneakers gave a clue that anyone was about, and Spurrio's strong hand, which she held like a child. He, in turn, followed closely behind Susanna, who finally opened a narrow door and led them up a narrow spiraling staircase to the apartment at the top of it. They were safe.

After she caught her breath, Spurrio kissed her full on the mouth, and it was one of the best memories either of them could remember. She also gave Susanna a hug. Susanna explained that this apartment belonged to her grandmother, who had just died. "It is yours now. You'll be safe here. I have people—people unknown to the Carabinieri and the Vatican Guard—who will attend to you. You two are safe here."

After Susanna left, Spurrio took his beautiful young bride, the one he had ignored for a greater cause, and made love to her. From that moment on, she was not merely his first cause, but his only.

For Massimo Barrone, the appropriate response could never have been message received

It was not the outcome that arresting Nicole was intended to provoke, but it was still Barrone who would have the last laugh. Because what Spurrio could not know was several hours after he put a bullet into the left side of Barrone's face that unwitnessed, a terminator of a man climbed, burned and bleeding, up the sheer face cliff in the dark. He staggered onto the roadway to await help, which he was sure was coming as soon as he failed to report in at the Vatican.

He had not miscalculated; a Guardia Svizzera helicopter discovered his wreckage within an hour after he had climbed defiantly up the scorched embankment and collapsed on the roadway. With bloody bandages around his head, shards of glass embedded in a face burnt and ripped to shreds on its left side, still in uniform, Massimo Barrone took charge in the control room of The Seat of The Left Hand of Power on that very night.

The 13th Disciple

Now that he and Il Fronte Popolare had made a break for his wife from prison, Spurrio discovered that his true devotion was to her. Their time together in the upstairs apartment in Venice became the honeymoon they'd never had.

Often, they would just make love all night, falling asleep to the sun streaming through the curtains as it rose over the beautiful Venetian landscape. Nicole could gaze down upon the now abandoned prison, which thanks to their handiwork, had no walls. The Vatican guard had no choice but to abandon it.

The burned-out building, which could have looked like a blight to strangers, was beautiful to them. For the time, they were prisoners in this apartment. But the time together was filled not simply with intense love making but also with loose and fun moments that genuinely cheered them both up.

Neither had any desire to leave the apartment, nor did they for several months. All that they needed was delivered by unknown people through a doggie door in the front door. They had vino, bottles of Lambrusco, and baskets of bread and cornetti still steaming and falling apart in their hands for breakfast. Ground espresso beans whose aroma romanced the olfactory glands as it swirled boldly down their nostrils.

There were fresh green and red shiny vegetables grown in private gardens in Litorale di Lido.

They had discovered paradise; they had discovered each other. Soon enough, Nicole began to vomit in the morning. Initially, she thought it was just something she ate, but Spurrio said, "No, my love, I think it's something else."

Nicole had never considered the possibility, never considered that it was a possibility, that she was pregnant. Now that she was, she was genuinely confused.

To further add to her confusion, Spurrio wanted her to have the baby. Nicole would gladly have had 10 of his babies, but she said, "Terrorists have to travel light." They laughed, and he held her, and she knew that it would be alright.

Then, he said what she thought he never would, that forever on he would put her above all things. To her, this was the most special gift of all. It was also the ego's proclamation of victory, undetected. She had never doubted his love for her, only her place.

It was an absolute impossibility that he could ever look at another woman. He was gentle and kind and would never hurt her and had now proven that he could protect her from an enormous power structure of absolute tyranny, in a fiery and explosive display of devotion. But until now, she had accepted that she was and always would be second to some other cause, that he was the kind of man who would always love himself or some greater cause more. But now here he was, him of all men to declare without provocation, that he loved her, and would always hold her above all things. As he said this to her with one knee on the floor next to her chair, which could have been a throne, she heard, and believed him. But neither of them could have known how horribly he would soon prove it.

Although the apartment was small, and they would have liked to walk around, they were far from desperate to leave. They were merely being prudent by staying in. La Guddica was inhabited by Venetians who

The 13th Disciple

could recognize and trust only their own. Spurrio and Nicole were known to be there and were still safe; no one would tell the Carabinieri, let alone the Guard of the Vatican. But now that she was pregnant, either a doctor would have to come to Nicole, or they would have to go to one. They chose to go out to one.

Doctor Taz was sleeping in the examination chair when they walked in from the narrow street, which was really just a corridor. Spurrio feigned a cough to wake him up.

Doctor Taz was about 60, small even for a Venetian. He wore dark slacks as nondescript as himself and a red sweater. Over the back of the chair hung a white lab coat associated with doctors. The room had the drab art deco hues carried in by the drab light of northern Italy in winter.

He turned on the overhead lights, and they were dim even at maximum obeying the Vatican's strict laws of conservation for all. As he rose and turned around to face the young couple in his examination room, he could scarcely be sure which of them was more nervous. He had faced thousands of such couples as these, before and during the afterwards. That part of human nature which was his specialty was as old as the species, hardwired into its DNA and by providence, little evolved from it.

After the doctor pronounced Nicole and their baby fit for motherhood and childhood respectively, they walked all over La Giudecca. From the Riodi San Biagio near the burnt and gutted remains of the prison that used to be, all the way to the monument laden San Giorgio Maggiore. She was able to get Spurrio to think about the prison as she did, remembering how it had been, and seeing it as it was now.

Noticing how it had once inspired fear and detest, but now they had to try to notice its gutted hulk, so insignificant was it. She said seeing it differently helped point out how it was possible to change your mind or choose again the way in which you viewed it. He said it was easy to change his mind about it because he had blown it up. They both laughed.

Then, she admitted that she was uncomfortable but never terrified because she knew he would come for her, not that she was sure, but rather she knew it. "So, did I," he said. They could have made love sitting there on the canal wall with their feet hanging over, but they waited to return to the apartment.

And so, they went on making love, roaming La Giudecca, and being drunk in each other's company. Spurrio kept enough money to take care of them so, on that front there was no pressure, but what built up on the outside was more than enough to replace it.

The Vatican controlled all tv programming so most Venetians did not bother to have one, but most of the businesses did. So, Spurrio and Nicole would watch tv in the bar as they walked around La Giudecca. It was like being struck by lightning when over the tv they saw that Eduardo and DeStefano had been arrested for, of course, terrorism. Nicole felt her knees buckle, and then Spurrio took her by the elbow.

They returned to the apartment but felt claustrophobic once there. So they went to the broad walkway on the long south side that looked over Murano for clarity. Spurrio found it instantly, stating, "Barrone is alive and still coming after me, this time through Eduardo and DeStefano," he said to Nicole.

"Aren't they supposed to be out of Italy?" she asked.

"Well, obviously they didn't make it. The question now is who else have they got?" he answered. "I don't think they are actively rounding us up. I think they have all of us they are going to get, but Barrone will play it as though he is rounding us up in an unstoppable, systematic fashion. He'll use this to make—"

Then, Spurrio stopped talking because he did not want, could not let Nicole hear his thoughts. Nicole stared questioningly at her husband, but then reached for her stomach, bent over in sudden pain related to her condition. Spurrio took her still long and silky hair in both of his hands and pulled it gently behind her. He held it there until he was sure she would not throw up. Then, letting it flow rather than drop to the ground, he put an arm high around her shoulder so as not to hurt her stomach as she leaned into him. With the other hand, he gently stroked her head.

Thinking that this was his wife's reaction to Barrone's arresting Eduardo and DeStefano made his anger boil, but he could not let it show, not to his wife. Instead, he held her, gently rocking until the pain dissipated, and he could help her to her feet. Being careful not to broach the subject, he took his wife home up the stairs. He filled the tub for her with hot water and bathed her. As she was falling asleep, he put her gently to bed, tucking the covers under her body tightly as though she were a child. Nicole was already asleep before he finished, but all that long night, Spurrio did not sleep.

Spurrio knew what he had to do, and he would do the only thing he could, what he had always done since before joining Il Fronte Popolare, he would sacrifice himself for others, but it was the one time he should have sacrificed them instead.

Nicole barely noticed that she was even getting fat until the eighth month. This was what she thought was making her irritable. For an entire week of that month, she was so irritable that she lashed out at Spurrio, one even accusing him of only wanting her for sex.

For his part, Spurrio grew feathers, and it all

rolled off as water on a duck's back. He let her pregnancy explain her behavior, and for that matter, she did too. But one night, as she lumbered her girth up the stairs to the bathroom to throw up, the pain was especially intense. It was so bad she thought that she must be having a miscarriage.

She pulled her hair back from her face as she stood up from the bowl she had just been vomiting into, then went to the sink to wash her mouth. As the pain attacked, she patted her stomach with her still elegant left hand, then took a mental picture of what she saw in the mirror there: red painted nails on her elegant shaped left hand, incongruously placed against her enormous pregnant belly, the dark blue sweatpants and the stale white tank top.

She had never heard that voice, the one that had dictated A Course in Miracles to her, the voice of Jesus, since it had finished and directed her so emphatically to find the "one for whom you were sent." And she did not hear the voice now, but the realization and accompanying cessation of pain made the message clear, that it is he, the one you pat in your womb. It is he for whom you have been sent.

For all of its complications during the pregnancy, once the message was clear the short remainder was smooth and Ian was born in the pre-dawn hours in their apartment. The delivery was so swift that Doctor Taz had been roused from his bed. But by the time he arrived, he was no longer needed.

In fact, Ian cried so sparingly, a behavior that would mercifully continue, that Spurrio, bouncing his newborn, blanket-donned son on his two knees facing him, remarked that he could not see what all the fuss had been about.

Nicole was not amused, not simply because she had done all the heavy lifting; she had an entire new reality to consider. Namely, it was her son and not her husband for whom she had been sent. There were problems and advantages to this new situation.

She did not yet know her son, but she doubted he could be any more intractable than her husband when it came to The Course and its teachings. It was a relief to know that she didn't have to focus on Spurrio.

The 13th Disciple

He would teach their son the ways of the dream world, and she could focus on saving him from it, without noticing that she was already losing her own way.

In the weeks that followed, she noticed that Spurrio, would leave in the early morning darkness, and with a hooded sweatshirt, just in case his face might be caught on a drone fitted camera, jog entirely around La Giudecca, she would sometimes catch a glimpse of him in the distance, between the buildings. She was safe in the certainty that he would always return to her, not simply because La Giudecca was an island, there were a lot of boats in Venice, but because for each other they were the only ones, it was as undeniable as gravity, a relationship as special as it was dangerous. Soon she would be jogging herself, but for now she was content being a good mother, fat and breast feeding.

A few months later, Nicole felt good to have her figure back. According to Doctor Taz's scale, she was exactly her pre-pregnancy weight. Time to start jogging with Spurrio, she thought as she heaved the baby seat up onto the bar.

The barmaid was already making her

The 13th Disciple

cappuccino the Venetian style before she had come to the bar. The TV was on above the bar maid. That was when the Venetians in the bar and the street heard such a guttural, frantic, prolonged scream that they could not believe that it erupted from the frail young blond on the floor. But that was precisely the origin of the exhaled inner pain. Nicole's knees bent, then she grabbed her stomach as though she had been kicked by a horse. It was too horrible to be true, too horrible not to be, Spurrio had been arrested for terrorism; he would shortly be executed.

She would never love again, never let another man touch her, would never experience joy, would never be happy again. Laying there on her side on the floor, refusing all aid offered, she simply wailed and cried, in a semi-conscious stupor. It was hours before she could be moved. Eventually, Dr. Taz was summoned and he administered one of the rare doses of sedative available in the afterwards. It was only then that she and her son could be taken into the apartment of one of the old women.

For Spurrio, the deal was an impossible one,

impossible to take, impossible to refuse. During his long dark jogs around La Giudecca his thoughts were not only with the Il Fronte Popolare members being rounded up, but also for his wife, which was to say himself.

He could not deny that he couldn't be certain that he could protect her and his son. Hadn't her capture seemed inconceivable before, yet he had to change everything, and rejoin Il Fronte Popolare to break her out. Who was to say it couldn't happen again? It was unlikely that they would be again taken, but that is far from certainty and when it came to Nicole there was simply no room for chance, he had to protect her at all costs. Leaving Italy was not the answer, there was nowhere they could run and they had no resources outside of Italy. It was to be guaranteed by Cardinal Rossilli no less. No, the deal, which was too terrible to take, was too terrible not to take. So, he took it.

Once he did, things moved fast. He was taken from La Giudecca to the Vatican by helicopter. With his hands handcuffed behind his back, he was taken through one of the wide corridors there, up to the largest man he had ever seen in his life. There, in his Armani suit, he stood. They had never met face to face before, and it was still shocking to see this six-foot-seven monster in front of him, with the unmistakable sign of his own handiwork on the giant's face.

With lightning speed, Barrone balled up his right fist and punched the handcuffed man in the face. Spurrio was lifted off his feet and knocked unconscious, not by the blow, but by hitting the back of his head against the stone wall. When he came to, Barrone was gone. He was sitting in a large square room with stone walls and floor. The ceiling had some sort of wooden beams. Spurrio was about to face the wrath of something much worse than Barrone's: that of the woman he loved, the only one he had or could ever love.

The door was opened, and she made straight for him.

"You had no right," she said with gritted teeth and pronounced in English, "NOOOO RIIIIGHT."

"No right to decide for both of us, none, no

right, you bastard." In that nano-second, she had white-hot hate for the only man she could ever love, and blinded by it, she hit him with flailing punches. She even gave him a small scratch until she saw the lump on his jaw and realized that she had not put it there. Then, lovingly, softly, she touched and stroked his face, sobbing as she did. Spurrio was still shocked by the silky softness of her hands. He tried to respond, to defend himself, but could not. She had just done what no part of his turbulent life ever could, not life under tyranny, not war, nor even the Vatican. If only for a second, she had broken him.

What a terrible deal he had made indeed. This was regret he had never known before, not of losing a football game or missing an opportunity, but deep-seated, non-recoverable regret. He had thrown both of their lives away. His knees were weak, but for her sake, he held onto the appearance of strength.

Then the door creaked open, and a female Carabinieri walked in with a baby and handed it to Spurrio. He took the child, but he really wanted to be holding his wife. He was afraid to look at her for fear she would see his weakness, not for his sake, but for hers. He knew he was about to die, but she would be forced to continue on for the sake of their son, and this was the last she would see of him. He needed, no, she needed him to be strong for her.

They held each other there, falling to the floor, Nicole weeping inconsolably. Spurrio could not even lift her up. Then they were torn from each other by several of the Vatican Guards. Nicole was dragged, with her eyes shut, out of the chamber to the waiting room where Spurrio's parents waited. They were not allowed to see him. She forgot even where her son was. Somehow, when she opened her eyes, he was there, but she did not reach for him. Instead, his grandparents did. She sat on the floor with her back against the cold, scratchy stone. She was too far removed to politely acknowledge his parents, too comatose with grief to make polite promises to see each other, which they all knew would never be kept.

The single gunshot seemed to go right through her body. A few hundred feet away, perhaps just in the next room, all she loved and truly cared for had just vanished in the split second that it takes a bullet to enter and exit the human skull, and was probably being unceremoniously discarded as a fallen gladiator's body at this very moment.

Nicole stopped crying as if stopping in midair, rose up, and put on her backpack. Standing, stunned and confused but for the vague remembrance that, "this is he for whom you have been sent," she would have walked out of The Vatican and into the cobblestone streets of Roma and killed herself on the spot. Instead, she took her son from his grandmother's arms and walked blankly out of the Vatican accompanied by several guards all the way to the street.

Then she walked that way, blank, stoned, suddenly indifferent all the way to Trastevere. She passed along the way the restaurant where she and Spurrio had eaten, a few meters from the street where they first made love. She walked into a negocio, bought some things and train tickets. Then, blankly, with her son, she walked to the ponte, in front of the Ospedale, where she and Spurrio made love again on that first night.

The 13th Disciple

She stood there in the center of the ponte facing the darkening twilight. She put down her son and pulled out a pair of large shears she had just bought at the negozio. She yanked her hair very hard with her left hand until she felt it pulling hard and ripping at the back of her scalp. With the shears in her right hand, she tore rather than cut a jagged line that left her hair short, above the middle of her neck. Then, like sand, she let the silky blond that used to be her beautifully rare and exceptional hair pour into the turbulent, murky Tiber, and be swept away. She did not follow it with her eyes to see where it went.

With sweat still on her arms, holding the shears in both hands, she pointed them at her chest. She moved as though to strike herself, but her son cried, reminding her of her mission, of her duty. So, angrily, she stabbed herself in the left cheek until the metal hit bone and blood poured. Then the shears went the way of what had once been her own beautiful hair. In the last embers of that final twilight in Roma, she yanked up her son and walked without blinking or focusing on any single object to the Via Nomentana all the way to Stazione

The 13th Disciple

Termini.

She took the train that went northwest, to Genoa, avoiding Venice. She rode the trains in silence with her son all the way to Paris. From there, since air travel over what had been the U.S. was forbidden, she took passage on a boat to Australia. At such a great cost, and unimaginable heartbreak, she had found the one for whom she had been sent. To find He who was lost and set straight His path, but she had found and lost the love of her own life in this dream world—and now was herself lost.

The 13th Disciple

End Il Fronte De Populate

Wandering the darkened streets of Roma, still trying to anesthetize himself from the terror of the darkening, Ian didn't eat much. He preferred to allocate those portions of his stomach to alcohol.

In one of the nightclubs, his favorite pretty young waitress didn't even try to wait on him—a fact he was aware that he could either ignore or let it bother him. He let it bother him. When he was just drunk enough, not to be too drunk he paid and left.

Not wanting to be alone, but with anyone either, he walked down the winding Nomentana to Trastevere, focusing on every physical thing he could. Every single thing to reassure him that the world was real and he is part of it, that he was safe here, in the skyscraper structure of this universe, in no danger of falling out of the window, through the darkness of a non-universe to smash headlong into the nothingness below. The ego could not have been more pleased. It was, in fact, what it had intended.

He focused with effort to walk on this hot

summer night, wanting no headstone, no darkenings to haunt him. Once he crossed the Ponte Cestius to Trastevere, he decided to stroll along the banks of the Tiber. He could see the island on which was the Ospedale where, unknown and unknowable to him, was the second place where his parents made love on the first night they met.

Darkness had settled over the sky like a blanket, but here in the city center, Roma, it was bright. While the rest of the world struggled to recover, Roma never really suffered. He was aware of this and felt guilty as he descended the stairs to the brightly lit, cobblestone banks of the ancient Tiber. It wasn't his fault; this was just Roma. There were cafes, bars, restaurants, and even temporary summertime nightclubs down there.

There were women down there, Italians mostly, his favorite, but he found himself talking as usual to someone other than a favorite. When sober he would often wonder why this was the case. Why his most favorite and favored must be wholly unaccepting of some significant part of himself or lose that specious title in his mind at least.

The 13th Disciple

That Freud would have a field day with this was as close as he could come to admitting that he had a shit for a mother.

Judging that he was as drunk as he could possibly be, he walked out of the temporary nightclub. But before he could make it home, something woke him stark up out of his buzz. It was a man, or a devil, standing on the Ponte Sisto, threatening to jump into the Tiber.

It was a man, a Romanian he judged by the accent, but then, as if someone pulled a string, the man was a bright white neon skeleton. The man yelled to the crowd in his bad Italian, "I want to die."

The skeleton whispered to him, "You want to join me?" Ian scanned rapidly up and down both banks, not for any one thing exactly. *I must be going crazy,* he thought.

"I want to die," again to the crowd, "You want to join me?" the flashing skeleton again asked him. "It's right, you do want to die," the thought said about him in the third person. By the time he heard the gunshot ringing around the cavernous Tiber, he was almost sober.

He watched the man fall, stiff as a board, doing a three-quarters rotation in slow motion, and smash into the water broadside. He could hear a muffled sound of a dead body hitting the water, which encased his body in slow motion as a fluffy blanket, drowned out by the sound of the gunshot. Then, music filled the vacuum left by the gunshots, and the acrid gunpowder clouds rotated and wafted away up into the clear summer sky.

The Vatican guard had already dispatched a boat into the water, and it was the platform from which the criminal was disposed of. "You will wish you went with him," the voice said from outside of his head. He turned in both directions, but only the acrid odor of gunpowder still dissipating in the music filled the air. The party went on; this is Roma.

"Well one thing for sure is, if you want out of this forced march called life, then the Vatican Guard will help you right along," the thought both comforted and sobered him. "I do not want to die," he realized. "Better to have never been born at all."

"Fuck it, now I gotta get drunk all over again," he thought.

He would do that, then go home before it got too hot, rinse the taste of bad booze out of his mouth with bad booze as he had done before, and ponder again how she, his dead mother, was still able to text him. Maybe he would use the Vatican Guard to kill himself too, but most definitely he would never go near that headstone again.

The 13th Disciple

Ian

When she finally arrived back to what had been her home in Australia with her young son, to an empty house that had been her parents', in the full knowledge that they had been dead for how long she knew not, she didn't actually feel too guilty. She was just too hurt herself to be hurt over anyone else. She had already endured a lifetime's worth of pain in fewer than 30 years. There was just so much to go around for each, and hers was well spent already.

The farm was as she thought it would be: dusty, dirty, but operable. Although there was no electricity for lights or a refrigerator, there was enough solar to run the pump so they could have running water. She had, after all, grown up there; she could get it working. But that was the way it was afterward, especially in such far-removed regions such as hers—Australia, a former and current prison colony, now designated Vatican Region 11.

There were fewer than 10,000 people in as many square miles, most concentrated together near a town center. You could leave your house empty for years and return to find it unmolested by humans; there just weren't enough people to molest things out there, not even bureaucrats and enforcers of Vatican law, so she hoped.

Her son was raised much as she was: lonely and isolated on many levels. He had to invent magical make-believe friends as she had. But she was not the doting parent hers had been. She could not dote; sometimes she could not even stand her son. Sometimes all she could do was stare, crying out of the window for hours. She knew that if not for the extra baggage of him, of his life, that her husband would never have surrendered. Now that extra baggage was hers.

She knew that was not his fault; she knew that somehow it would be felt, that he would know that she really didn't love him, that she was just doing her duty, raising him and teaching him The Course.

"My mind can change all things that hurt."

"Fuck you it can," she answered back, and meant it.

The 13th Disciple

Ian remembered bits and pieces of his childhood, whereas other children already had continuous memory streams. He could not recall beginning karate, taught by an old vet who had been in the Australian Special Forces, before Australia was dissolved into Vatican Region 11.

He could recall getting the crap kicked out of him in a tournament by a 10-year-old named Roger Smitts when he was only eight. He would never forget the shock of the blunt force of the older kid's round kick, banging against his head. He could not forget the discombobulation that came with the ringing ears and spotty vision, an unknown and terrifying new sensation.

Ian got up and tried to fight on, but he fearfully held his hands too high, and the Roger kid, who was a giant, swept both of his feet off the floor and punched him in the stomach so hard Ian almost threw up his empty stomach. He remembered sitting there on both knees on the floor, knowing everyone was staring at him, trying to close his eyes to keep them away.

His sensei helped him up gently while forcefully yelling his objection. After the tournament, he told Ian that the giant of a kid had won just because he was bigger and older, but even then, they both knew he was lying. The other kid was older; Ian knew he would grow up, but he would never grow good.

Here she was good to him; she encouraged him to stay in karate, and he did until time and proper training overtook his lack of talent, and he got his black belt.

Later, they sat in the old Dodge Dakota pickup truck with a four-cylinder engine. She had bought and rigged it to be especially fuel-efficient, just so they could go to the tournaments. She was already sitting when Ian removed his gi outside, showing his skinny body and badly welted stomach. Dejectedly, he stuffed the gi behind the seat; his sensei would have been horrified.

Nicole let this lack of etiquette go and beckoned her son to come in and close the door. He plopped his little body in with a bounce, then reached with both hands for the handle but found the windowsill instead. This forced him to give a mighty tug, which wrapped his hair around his head and reminded her of hers. It

The 13th Disciple

shut with a loud squeak and a quiet clank.

Sitting there with his hands under his legs, looking like the picture of pity, she felt guilt, deep, earthly guilt. She put her arm around his head and pulled his hair away from his face.

"Look at me," she said. He did, and looked back at her with the mirror of her own startling eyes a generation away. Then, holding his gaze, she considered for a long time. She decided not to try to make him feel better, not to bother with "the other boy was just older" or "you will get better." What happened to him was, in worldly terms, pure shit, and now worldly terms were the only terms. Fuck the Course.

Instead, she simply said, "I love you." It was the first time she made that ubiquitous proclamation of a mother for her son.

He looked back at her, stunned and uncomprehending, except for in the deepest recesses of his cells and DNA. In there, he knew, in there he understood that he loved her as much as he was completely dependent on her, which was completely. But he did not trust her love for him; he could not luxuriate in the conviction of its unconstrained abundance.

It was the reason he would never feel confident around women. It was the reason, in the short term, he would settle for who he could over who he wanted. In longer relationships, he was only satisfied by women who were at least slightly critical of him; in lifelong relationships, there were none.

On the way home from the karate tournament, they went to a flea market of sorts. There, Ian, already forgetting his humiliation from a few hours earlier, placed over a dozen used DVDs on the table, something still new out there. Still feeling sorry for her son, Nicole paid for them all without looking.

Neither of them noticed that some of them were in English, some in Italian, others in French, Greek, Dutch, German, Japanese, and even one in Chinese. In fact, Nicole never paid any attention to them until days later when she heard her son speaking to the TV in what appeared to be perfectly competent Chinese. It was an American action movie dubbed over in Chinese.

She spoke Italian at home so that he would learn it. That was part of his heritage; she would not deny him of it just because it hurt her too much. Only in this matter did she put him first. But she did not and could not teach him any other language. She could muddle through Spanish, but to her surprise, she noticed that Ian was apparently fluent in that too. "How can this be?" she asked.

With curiosity balanced only by dread, Nicole sat behind her son on the couch, watching him watch the Greek language movie. Once it concluded, she asked him to say anything in Greek that he wanted, but her shy son only stood up, crossed his arms in front of his stomach, grasping his wrists in the process, and gave one of the most plaintive "what do ya mean" looks she had ever seen.

"Okay, say 'amo tuo' to me in Greek," she prompted.

Then, he eagerly grasped at the opportunity to please his mercurial and distant mother and said it.

The 13th Disciple

Even though she couldn't understand Greek, she knew it was perfectly correct. It turned out he could do this after only watching any one of the DVDs. What was this new apparent talent, gift, or curse? Had anyone ever heard of such a thing?

Where he was untalented in athletics, he was apparently more than talented—gifted, actually—in language. In fact, he was to language what Einstein was to physics and Bach to music. Ian Spencer had the unique ability to learn languages on the fly; just by being around people speaking a certain language, he could learn it in a few hours.

From her own study of Italian, she was well aware that we each are able to learn as many languages as we are exposed to, without being taught a single syllable by anyone, but this capacity evaporates with time and, by Ian's age, is highly diminished. This was as rare an ability as it was a dangerous one. She proceeded cautiously. She considered what would happen if any authority discovered his new talent, but she could not have considered what the ego would do.

The 13th Disciple

Initially, she pretended to Ian that nothing was wrong. Only when he was translating labels in the grocery store, or signs on the street from English to any of the many languages he now understood did she admonish him. She put one hand under his chin, gently lifted it, and brushed his hair away from his eyes. She said, "This is our secret, buddy, okay?" He sensed her approval and eagerly nodded his head up and down.

Her undiminished adoration was his prize, a cherished prize worthy of any effort, never attained until this moment. During the long-forced march of his dreadful childhood, despite his most intense efforts, it had until this moment escaped him.

For a time, it was their secret alone. He would translate a sign, a song, or make something up. He would translate something she said into one or all of the other languages. They would do it laughing, and the secret they kept was not of guilty people hiding something incriminating, but rather like good people guarding a priceless treasure.

But they weren't simply safeguarding one treasure; they were cultivating another, which was Ian's

The 13th Disciple

belated childhood. With some courage and a little luck, she could actually live a life in a brief respite of grief and mourning for her ex-husband and Ian's father, a connection she had never cleanly forged. It was what finally forced her to be a mother, and it was just as they were getting close that they were ripped apart.

They were walking home from the two-room school building where Ian went on Monday, Wednesday, and Fridays. There was a little store with a counter, where she stopped to buy him a used book. She wondered what was taking him so long in the restroom.

Realization went suddenly white hot, and she didn't have to wait long. She burst into the men's room, empty. A dirty sink behind the door, and to the right, a rectangular window, maybe big enough for Ian to fit through, closed. Her heart now pounding in her head, she ran through the store screaming her son's name. The few people, employees, and customers followed her. An older man wearing farmer John's said, "I'll check around this way." She ran around the other side. They met each other in the empty space at the rear of the store.

The 13th Disciple

She broke into an all-out sprint for the school. Fists pumping up to her bouncing cheeks, eyes squinting, shirt riding up in the front, showing the still taut belly button. She ran that way, as fast as she could, for as long as she had to until she thundered into one of those two rooms containing Ian's teacher.

Grabbing a pair of scissors from the desktop, she shoved Mrs. Jenkins, who doubled as principal, back down to the chair from which she had just risen. She took her by the hair in her left hand, opened the shears with her right hand, and with palm up, jammed the open scissors up under her left eye socket and began to apply pressure.

"Who did you tell, cunt? Who did you tell?" she screamed at the top of her lungs, so that the pompous little bitch knew not to lie or hesitate. Mrs. Jenkins gave it up immediately. "I called the school resource officer," she blithered, "we have to." Nicole hesitated, trembled, then in a move so deft that Mrs. Jenkins didn't know she'd been cut until she saw the blood, Nicole gave her a three-inch gash on the flabby left cheek.

Nicole knew instantly what to do and what not

to not bother with. She would not waste time putting up flyers or looking for her son in Australia. She went to Ian's karate teacher, the old Australian army soldier, and told him that Ian was not just missing, but taken by the Vatican and why. She knew he would do anything for Ian.

Roger Williams Massey, Rog for short, was known as a major in the revolution that wasn't. He was one of the few possessors of formal military knowledge and training afterward. He had trained seriously with like-minded men in his youth, but they were too few then and too old now. If the Vatican had been aware of the group's existence, they didn't show it; there was no invasion, no rounding up of suspects for show trials.

At 55, Rog was five feet 11 inches of pure fitness, with gray hair that he wore alternatively between his shoulders a military crew cut. His body possessed the substance and clean lines of a man who practiced Karate for many years. Nicole hoped that a lifetime of practice would fortify her son's body similarly.

She said he was gone, but she knew where he'd

been taken. He gave her a look of how. She explained Ian's unlikely and amazing new talent: the ability to learn or decipher language without being taught.

Rog seemed neither impressed nor dismissive of the information, simply accepting it as fact, and quipped, "Maybe he can teach me the tongue of the outback tribes."

Then she told him she needed a sniper rifle, what kind, and she instructed him competently on the subject. He gave her another questioning look, and she shot back with a look that said, "Don't ask."

She went in and out of her own house to get things, but did not live in it. She didn't think the Vatican had law enforcement way the fuck out here, but she didn't think that bitch fuck of a cow would turn her son in either; better to be safe.

Rog had some property in the woods near town where she could camp. He brought her supplies, watched as she refreshed her skills, and even showed her some tricks of his own. They didn't bother with teaching her karate. If she needed to engage in hand-to-hand combat, they both agreed that she had probably already lost.

She didn't have a plan yet. She thought about her own breakout from the women's prison, a lifetime ago in another universe. What would he have done? He, whose name even now she couldn't say, even to herself, what would he have done?

First, no matter how desperate the situation was or seemed, he never would panic. He never would rush, never do anything before it was ready to be done, before it had its best chance to succeed. He would always have an advantage.

So, she walked from her camp spot through the woods to her house, partly to do some work, mostly to take a bath, with a pistol within reach for comfort. She could hear breathing coming from Ian's room and knew without hesitation that it was him; she could smell him. She rushed through the open door and stopped dead still.

Again, he was sitting Indian style on his still-made bed. He did not acknowledge her and seemed not to even recognize her. She sat down and gently brushed his hair. "Ian, sweetie, are you okay?" she asked, knowing that he was, even before he looked at her.

Then, she felt a deep joy she thought was forever beyond her in this lifetime. She wept openly, hugged and hugged him, and was all by herself completely in the moment, for the moment.

The very next morning, Nicole Spencer was staring at her son, considering him coldly, dispassionately. "Stand up, take off your shirt, drop your trousers," she instructed.

Ian, still seemingly partially hypnotized, obeyed without response. Only giving a weak negative nod when she asked, "Can't you remember anything? Anything at all?"

She examined him thoroughly—his hair, his ears—and even asked him to adjust *himself* slightly for a complete inspection. She found nothing unusual. The persistent and obvious question was why. Why had they released him? "Okay, put your clothes back on, hun."

"Hold that stance Ian," his karate teacher said.

Ian thought his right leg would explode.

"Good, now step through." Ian stepped through, making certain to bring his knees together without raising his head in the process, as though there was a glass of water not to be spilled on it.

"That's good, Ian, that's a nice zen stance, a way to keep your knees together. His stances are getting good," he said to Nicole." But Ian cringed, awaiting the inevitable correction.

"Next time, though, keep your same pace; no more speeding up in the middle."

Now, it was his left thigh that was on fire, and just when he thought it would explode, there came a merciful reprieve from his teacher. "Okay, relax, kid."

Ian stood up but reached down and massaged his burning thighs.

"I don't think we have anything to worry about. You know how they are better than anyone. If the Vatican thought he was a threat, he certainly wouldn't be here now. They probably drugged em, then poked and prodded him till there was no place left to poke or prod. Then, when they decided that he was not harmful or useful, they cut em loose. I mean, this language thing is cool—amazing really—but think about it: how useful is it to them? The Vatican has all the interpreters it needs. Now, if he showed some special math or scientific abilities, or programming, then you could bet your sweet ass they would have kept him."

Ian was still rubbing his legs, enjoying all the extra attention. "Remember class is an hour early tomorrow. Don't worry, I'll have him here on time," Nicole answered slowly, snapping out of consideration of what Rog had just said.

Walking home, she figured that Rog was probably right. Maybe it was even a good thing, and she even wondered if it would last. When Ian asked if he should just speak in English and Italian, she said, "No, sweetie, speak in all that you want to, all that you know." Then, she tousled his hair and they raced home.

Ian remembered that day, the good feeling of abundant portions his mother's attention heaped all over him, along with her contradictory admonishments to beware feelings of specialness, or inadequacy.

The 13th Disciple

"Fuck you, Momma, " he muttered to himself. "Fuck you and fuck A Course in Miracles." He muttered it and then immediately felt guilty. In point of fact, Nicole Spencer had been far from the best of mothers. She was so spectacularly gifted in so many ways, but she passed those gifts mostly by osmosis to him, being, in so many other ways, distracted and derelict.

Hers was a deep ocean of melancholy and regret, crippling in its intensity yet invisible and undetectable to himself and others. In reality, she loved him deeply, but it was a love that she could not show, but to a child one is the same as the other. Young Ian blamed himself for her failure to love him, but the grown man Ian got the blame game right.

Even so, because he doubted her love for him, he would always be uncertain with women, distrustful of their love, unworthy to receive it, and he would never be satisfied with anyone unconditionally loving him.

As it turned out, however, that singular talent did last. Far from being useless to anyone, in connection with his knowledge of archeology, it was a weapon that could be used against everyone, especially everyone in power. What he was reading now, and had been reading, disturbed him almost as much as the darkenings.

The See of Roma, it seemed, had found his talent useful after all. Their vaults sustained superficial damage during the war. Some of the artifacts were archeological in nature, but many were books and manuscripts in the ancient languages: Babylonian, Greek, and another language unknown to all except the closest Vatican insiders. This language was essentially lost now, and it was Ian Spencer's job to recover it not for all of humanity, but specifically and exclusively The Holy See.

Officially, he was translating the Vatican's language to old Latin, something everyone at the Vatican understood. But for no extra charge, he was also translating it into Ngaanyatjarra, an old Aboriginal language from his native Australia. This, he was sure, was unknown to the Vatican, being itself a vanished language.

The 13th Disciple

The reason for the unrequested duplications was that he needed to be sure. Quite simply, despite all of his experiences, despite all he'd seen, Ian Spencer could not believe what he was reading.

He had to be careful, very careful with how he translated, and careful that his backup in Ngaanyatjarra was never found. Moreover, he'd have to figure out how to expose the thing to the entire post-Third World War generation if he could prove it was true. But how? Never mind that, just make sure of the first thing.

He'd spend the days translating in his cube in the gargantuan Ministry of Culture, just blocks from the Vatican and its vaulted secrets. At night, he'd get drunk, trying to cleanse the filth of the day's reading from his brain or just to get drunk—he really couldn't tell anymore. Usually, he'd stroll through Trastevere. Sometimes, he'd meet a girl, usually one he'd met before, sometimes a tourist, or a German girl, but he liked the Italians. But it was an Italian girl he didn't go home with last night. Why?

It was September now, and cool in the predawn hours, cool but not yet cold. He was still buzzed but not drunk as he weaved unsteadily across the cobblestone in shoes that made muffled contact against the cobblestone rather than the clicking of hard heels.

The corner of the building hid the light from him, and he didn't see the massive, suit clad forearm that came at light speed and connected perfectly with him squarely between the eyes. The force of the blow had the strange effect of turning his body 270 degrees in midair so that Ian actually landed on his hands and knees. Except for the buzzing in his head, he had no adverse effects.

Those were on the way. Two great hands hoisted him high in such a fashion he had never been handled before. His feet literally dangled, so that he had to look down at the six-foot-seven attacker calmly addressing him as a waiter in a fine restaurant. One hand, the right one, was around his throat. The inside of the brute's left finger was being rammed against the underside of his nose into the bridge of his nose and his face. Ian knew the pressure point; it was excruciating.

"Good morning, Mr. Spencer," the most polite and controlled voice he'd ever heard said in perfect

The 13th Disciple

Queen's English. "Please allow me to introduce myself. My name is Massimo Barrone." (His name was pronounced in perfect Italian) "As I am sure you are aware, the discomfort that you are currently experiencing is due to the inordinate amount of pressure which I am presently applying to your Columella. This discomfort will only increase as I apply more pressure.

All you have to do to compel me to release all the pressure is to tell me the precise location of all of the unreported pages of the documents you've been translating and whom, if anyone, you've shared the contents with."

Ian feigned panic. He grabbed the big man's wrist, twisted at them ineptly, then curled his thumbs across his palms and shot them into his two available eye sockets. Barrone dropped him with the attitude of, "Well, okay, kid, let's see what you got."

Barrone threw a straight kick with his left leg, which Ian deftly side stepped, grabbed in midair, and pushed the ham of a leg up to the sky. Barrone hit the ground, but Ian knew better than to go to the ground with the larger man.

Barrone arched his back and sprung up to both feet at once, displaying as he did the agility of a 150-pound gymnast. He'd had enough. He strolled a few steps toward Ian, then, with the same cat-like abilities he'd just shown in getting off the ground, he tackled Ian.

Ian's punches were jammed as he fell back and Barrone mounted him. Ian could well have imagined that his father had been in a similar position with this same monster. In fact, up close, he could see the unmistakable residue of his father's handiwork adorned in deep scar tissues grotesquely sutured across the left side and eye socket of Barrone's massive face, as if it had obviously been through a pane of glass.

Barrone raised his entire body up and rained down a huge fist, which Ian was able to slip at the last instant by moving his head. But the opposite elbow landed flush on the jaw. Barrone let the elbow stay there, crushing the side of his face.

"I searched your room and cube on a hunch," he revealed with delight to the victim squirming under him. "I knew that you would do something stupid. It's

The 13th Disciple

in your DNA. Now you're going to tell me who you shared it with, where you put any other pages, and—"

There, Ian cut him off, "I'm not telling you a fucking thing, you big ape, not until I see the Pope. I mean the fucking last Pope, Pope fucking John Francis."

He was coughing now, but he got it all out. Then, it was Barrone's turn to cough. There was a brief instant where he feigned ignorance, but then gave it up. Barrone was experiencing something he never had experienced before—shock, stunned utter confusion. He was not in complete control.

Having a private audience with the last Pope seemed like a good idea when Barrone was beating the shit out of him, but Ian realized suddenly he had nothing to say to, or ask of, the thing that lay before him, the thing that proposed to be the repository of the last Pope of the Holy Church of Roma. He no more wanted to talk to it than grapple with Barrone again.

Ian knew where he was in the Vatican, he was standing in the personal residence of what had been for centuries the Pope of Roma.

It was at least a body, or had been one, that lay directly in front of him in a cold, dark room. The bed was a huge four-poster in the style of the old kings, whose four dark wood corners rose above eyesight and there remained. A circular, deep red rug was positioned beneath it as though the bed was all there was holding it down.

There were hoses and tubes which carried and returned body fluids, and oxygen to it. There were banks of what Ian readily recognized as computers, but he had not the slightest inkling that they were in fact quantum computers, or even what that was.

But there lay before him the wasted residue of the 150-years-old human body of Pope John Francis, the Last Pope, and in the humming circuitry of quantum servers, its consciousness and immortal soul.

There was what appeared to be a fuse box, housed in a large decorative cabinet. What appeared to be the fuses were really medical devices: artificial lungs, heart, kidneys, etc. He could not know that. The quantum knot was tied wirelessly. All of it working to keep what had been Pope John Francis in some state of aliveness. For how long and what purpose?

Though he could not know what all the electronics were for, he did know perfectly well the giant man to the Pope's left. But he hardly noticed the little man to his own left, the Pope's right, he would not recognize him until he spoke, but this was the man who held the right hand of the seat of power, the power second only to the almighty Pope himself.

To say what had been the Pope's body was accurate. The body on the table contained the brain which had contained the last Pope's thoughts, but those thoughts, which comprise the man's consciousness, now reside in the cool quantum circuitry of the computers flanking both sides of the bed.

The room's walls were of ancient stone, but it was in the shape of an ellipses. What Ian didn't understand was that the voice which seemed to dominate from the great bed, actually came from a microphone many feet away at one focus of the ellipse.

The 13th Disciple

He stood at the other focus and could hear perfectly. But if anyone stood anywhere else in the room, they would hear nothing at all.

Ian was only slightly surprised to hear the biomechanical man on the bed speak. The voice, androgynous, neither calming nor authoritative. All meaning was given by the context. "I understand that you have been less than sincere in your work for which we pay you."

Ian did not feel it necessary to respond with curiosity; he had no respect for the thing which spoke. So, he said, "I see you have put my income tax to good use."

Ian was venturing into dangerous territory. The Pope didn't appreciate the insolence; it had been more than one hundred years since he'd experienced any semblance of it. Ian, on the other hand, became less and less impressed with conversing with the technology laying before him. Before he realized it, he was just talking to any other pathological liar, and he judged him, judged the Pope, judged the liar Pope, and judging brought anger.

The 13th Disciple

"You head up a pedophile club, old man. I translated all the news pieces, and you omitted them from the Vatican official records. Do you think people will just forget? Do you think you can simply omit inconvenient truths and change history?"

"History is written by the victors," the androgynous one responded. Ian briefly entertained the idea of attacking that thing on the bed, but that thing on its left was Barrone and would not let him close. He had seen enough; it was true, Pope Francis was trying to live forever. The fucker might even do it too. Well, so what business was it of his one way or the other, but Ian was sure that there was more.

He couldn't make out the other standing to the Pope's right; they were speaking, but so low that he couldn't hear them. He decided not to play this game with the Pope. Best not to offend the creepy old creature anymore, besides he still wanted access to the documents and that meant keeping his job however ordinary it seemed.

Somehow, the thing on the bed must have signaled the other two men to approach. Ian recoiled slightly as Barrone moved toward him from the shade surrounding the Pope's bed. It was reflexive, visceral. At that, Barrone stopped, but the small man continued from the other side.

As soon as the little man was close, Ian could feel himself being studied. Perhaps he was simply admiring some of Barrone's handy work. Ian was vaguely aware of the throbbing in his jaw and the blood which had crusted dry beneath his nose.

The little man did indeed study him intently, more intently than he had studied any man before, and he had studied many men before.

"Do you know me, young man?" The booming voice astonished him; Ian could never have expected such thunder and baritone from a man so slight of frame.

"I know who you are," he responded to the great sonorous orator. "You're that defrocked priest with the gossip column and the radio show."

"You are at least on the right track, young man," the baritone shot back, with an arrogance that lit all of

Ian's fuses. "You are on the right track, but not very far down along it," the little man said.

He walked behind him, only a step, and stopped. Ian broke from his trance-like stare at the Pope and turned 90 degrees. "You on the right, him on the left, means Barrone works for you," Ian said.

"You work for me, young man," the baritone responded. Ian wasn't even bothered by the fact that he was being toyed with; he forgave it instantly out of habit. But the way this man studied him was creepy.

"We will meet soon, and we will be working closer together from now on," the man said. "And what about Barrone? Will he be joining us?" Ian turned as if to make sure Barrone had kept his distance.

"Don't you concern yourself with Barrone; you just do as I instruct," he said, his tone leaving no room for doubt. Ian could see that this man was accustomed to getting what he wanted. So, standing there, under the ancient Vatican, before the greatest conspiracy of the ages, he, of course, curtly agreed. But what Ian Spencer could not understand was how much deeper the rabbit

The 13th Disciple

hole would go.

As he waited in the restaurant for former Father Sean Martin, Ian was not thinking that he had stumbled across the conspiracy of a lifetime. He was not dazzled by the life-extending technology he'd been privy to witness in the bowels of the Vatican. None of that mattered to him at that moment. What he was contemplating was far more mundane: his injured pride.

He was reflecting on the way Barrone had flung him around, toyed with him. If he were unfortunate enough to encounter Barrone again, he wanted the results to be different. But how? Barrone possessed equal skills but was also at least twice the size and power as himself, an uncomfortable fact which he could well imagine that his father had to deal with. But his father had at least left a mark, quite a mark at that.

He took a sip of wine and put the glass down with his left hand. He stared at it, at the thumb. When he turned his hand palm up and noticed the palm heel, he got an idea. Without worrying about whether anyone was looking, he took the four fingers of his right hand and gently rapped the base of his skull, just below the hairline. What he experienced, the shock of even such a slight impact making the eyes want to blink, gave him hope.

In fact, wasn't Barrone being overly confident? Wasn't he exposing his eyes, throat with all of that "As I'm sure you're aware, Mr. Spencer, the discomfort you are currently experiencing is due to the pressure I am applying"? Prick, Ian thought. Maybe, Ian thought, just maybe, if it came to it, if it had to come to that, he would have something for the big man after all.

Then, he spied the diminutive figure of Sean Malachi slaloming his way around tables busy with people eagerly engaged in that ancient human art of dining. You could almost imagine that the war had never happened; this was Roma.

With his gray hair and black suits, Malachi still looked like a priest; he was, in fact, the archetype conservative in the Roman Catholic hierarchy. Once again, Ian was aware of Malachi's diminutive size; once again, within a few seconds, it was forgotten, and he was overwhelmed by the man's stature: the booming voice, a projection of supreme self-confidence, the depth of knowledge on so many subjects, the sense that for such justifiable reason, he assumed he would get whatever he wanted.

They spoke in French, German, English, Italian, and Latin. Martin claimed not to understand the old "Vatican language" that Ian was working on. Ian instantly knew he was lying, but that the lie was intended to be seen through. Such was much of their conversation; that Malachi would lie and allow it to be perceived. Ian wondered if he would see through what was not intended to be seen beyond and what would be the penalty for failing to.

Ian, who never wasted his time on liars, wasn't sure that he liked Malachi, only that he did not trust him any more than he could read the man. To the world, Malachi was just a defrocked Jesuit priest, and everyone assumed it had to do with some sexual offense or crime. But in truth, he was the right hand to the Pope—the real Pope, the last Pope, who was and always would be the current Pope, the last Pope. Ian was just getting his head around that as Martin arrived and sat down.

The 13th Disciple

Then, Ian got a delicious idea to challenge Malachi. "Do you believe in abortion, Father?" he asked the former priest. "Of course, you do. You must be in support of it, and I mean to say of the most energetic support imaginable," Ian said, answering his own question.

If Martin was rattled even in the slightest, he did not show it. "You have taken the solemn oath of the Jesuits, and I have read that oath, good Father," Ian continued, trying to play cat and mouse with a man who refused either role. But Ian did not give up, quoting the oath as best as he could from memory, "We shall rip from the bellies of the nonbelievers their unborn babies and smash them onto the ground."

"The old church certainly took no offense to abortion," Ian said sardonically.

He waited, but there was no response. "You are a Jesuit, so you took that oath," he stated. Still, there was no response. Finally, Malachi spoke, "It is true that while I have been party to no abortions of any kind, I have taken the Oath of the Jesuits, and I would have readily done so if ever commanded to."

The 13th Disciple

Ian was spellbound, hypnotized by the lights of the room, Martin's dark brown eyes turning black, and the rhythm and tenor of that tremendous baritone, and where this relationship was going.

"I have simply not been ordered to rip any babies from any bellies, believers or non. But I have done many things far worse; I have murdered millions. Not directly, of course, always by the pen, which is most definitely mightier than the sword. A flick of the wrist and a million dead in Africa of starvation, another tap and a few million more dead in India of a bioweapon. The list goes on.

You know the Church, you know what it does, you know that it caused the last Great War and all of the global miseries almost since its founding, and I sit alone at the right-hand seat. I answer only to the Pope; he trusts me implicitly to do his bidding, and his bidding is the elimination of the whole human race."

Now it was Ian who stared back blankly. "You can judge me if you like," Martin began again, "but it is a waste of time. I don't care a bit about your opinion of me, and I have read A Course in Miracles."

He wanted to say that it was given to him by the wife of an old gladiator, a friend he once betrayed thousands of years ago. He wanted to say that he was sorry, that this was his way of making it up, that he had been searching for This One Son of Man for a thousand lifetimes, maybe a million. Instead, he said, "as a perfunctory part of the Vatican's research into himself and his family."

It wasn't until Ian rose to leave that he realized it was late, almost 10; they were the last ones there. Despite all that Sean Martin had revealed or admitted to—not the brutal oath of the Jesuits, nor the fact that the long-dead last Pope's life had been extended for more than a hundred years, nor the transhumanist aspirations of The Holy See—nothing rocked him as much as what Martin said just as they were parting. Martin instructed Ian to return to the headstone and translate the inscription there.

His hair tickled his eyes as he rode his bike slowly across the bumpy cobblestone. "So, you work for me now," Martin was saying. "I guess that's ok he thought, but fuck me if I ever go back to that headstone."

Ian thought of Malachi in much the same way as he thought of Barrone: as too much to handle. He could not be sure if he was seeing through or being seen through. Worse was the fact that in his banal attempt to get a reaction, he actually revealed what he knew, and Ian knew that he knew too much.

Once they were sure that the Vatican Language was recovered, they would have no use for him. What really made Ian nauseous as he leaned into the last corner to go home wasn't what he thought they might do to him; it was what he knew they would do to the world, and how close they already were to doing it.

The only chance was to expose them to the planet; the only question was how. The cell buzzed; the message was from her again. It said, "My son, choose again."

"Just what should I choose, Momma," he thought. "I have Malachi insisting that I go back to the headstone, while he's busy running the Vatican's depopulate-the-world program, which, by the way, has been background music for hundreds of years. Then there's that terminator—he had seen the movie—Barrone, breathing down my ass. Forced to choose between being ripped into a weird, terrifying alternate universe or fighting the bio-monster commander of the Vatican Guard, the one who killed my father, by the way, which should I choose?"

It was dark in his apartment. He was having chest pain and trouble breathing, not from an oncoming darkening, but from the fear of one, breaking his mother's golden rule, which she rarely obeyed, to live in the now. He turned on the banker's lamp on the desk, then draped a scarf remaining from one of the tourist girls carelessly over it.

The result bathed the desk and that side of the room in warmth then faded away to the prevailing darkness before reaching all the way across the room and the stuffed chair into which he sank, shadowed in gloom.

He couldn't remember his first darkening any

more than he could remember the first time he'd seen his mother. They just always seem to have been coming, an ever present and ubiquitous threat.

While being kidnapped, drugged, probed, and poked could in no way be considered a good thing, having once been, then released turned into a blessing. It enabled Ian's Karate teacher to convince Nicole that going on the road, running away was like slamming the barn door after all the horses were gone. This saved Ian from the needless stress of constant fleeing, of having every friend once made by virtue of life on the run ripped apart, and it allowed him to stay still to learn Karate and make a friend of his sensei.

But they were both exposed to a different threat: the certain knowledge that he could be taken at any time and anywhere they wanted to.

Ian could remember the darkening even before he was taken. Apparently, the Vatican, for all of their advanced medical technology, did not detect it, or he certainly would have lived the remainder of his life as a lab rat. He was only six, lying in bed, in the dark. It was a moonless dark night on the farm, and still, Ian could perceive a different degree of darkness—a blackness that was more than a simple absence of light. It was the sucking, vacuuming up of all light, of all warmth, all life, accompanied by the loss of all his other senses.

Six-year-old Ian was not quite old enough to know just how bizarre and otherworldly that which was happening to him was, but he was plenty old enough to sense stark terror when it became so dark that he could not see his own body, could not feel it, unable to hear its breathing, nor even hold his own breath. It was like being buried alive, with only the cold coffin lid inches from your nose. There was a dull blade scraping across the inside of his skull. He was not simply covered by the darkness; he was the darkness.

After the attack, which lasted he knew not for how long, he charged out of his room and went screaming into his mother's room, leaping into her body as she had thrown back the covers and had one foot on the floor. Ian was nearly a grown man before he slept alone in a bed again.

A few months after they raced home from Karate was the first time it happened in front of Nicole.

The 13th Disciple

It was after class; they were talking Italian, thoroughly immersed in each other's company, a rarity. Ian was sitting on the edge of the couch about to bite into a delicious tramezzino which she had just prepared. Nicole heard the plate drop to the floor, spilling the sandwiches. Then she spun to catch sight of her son staring blankly at the wall, and moaning. Then, it came over him almost like a mild epileptic seizure.

She did not panic, though she didn't yet recognize what was happening to her son. She sat next to him on the couch, putting her hand gently on his shoulder. She was there for him; she was the first thing he saw when it was over. She didn't try to make sense of it or pretend that it would go away. When she could, she would try to understand it; she would try to explain it. She fed him; they played games, and in the future, she would have to invent many games to distract him afterward.

The darkenings continued, seemingly at random, but it was far from random. Nicole and Ian attempted to document each such occurrence, but there the devil, as always, lay coiled up in the details.

The 13th Disciple

Ian, sleeping in the same bed as his mother now, would sometimes toss violently but never awake, leaving neither of them a clue as to whether or not it was a darkening, or even upon waking whether it was just from a very bad dream. Regardless, Ian simply could not sleep alone or even be alone without the terrible risk of being victim to an otherworldly kidnapping. He could not sleep alone, and Nicole was the only one home.

So, he slept there until he was far past the age where it was usual or healthy for a boy to sleep with his mother. There was no greater sin, no more proscribed lust, no more unsanctioned desires than those of a son residing in the bed of a beautiful mother and house of a vanquished father. It was a reversal of the natural order of things. It was equally the most forbidden, the most condemned, and the most damaging kind of love.

The only constant during this time, besides Nicole's dotting attention, was Karate. She took him to the dojo and stayed until all of Ian's classes were finished. Ian loved the attention, and at a time when most boys his age would have sold their mothers into slavery to avoid being seen with them, Ian would openly treasure her attention.

It had been a long time since Jimmy Smitts had kicked the crap out of him at the tournament. There was more than one tournament in Vatican region 11 in the afterwards. Ian was almost as tall as his mother, and if you listened close enough, you could just begin to hear the change in his voice.

It just so happened that another tournament rolled through time, and this had one Jimmy asshole Smitts, competing. Nicole had seen her son spar often, seen the speed, power, and grace sewn into his DNA by sheer force of correct repetition. She had come to appreciate the pure beauty of Karate, its clean lines, and angular precision. She had seen him hit even the black belts without so much as a flinch of reaction from them.

The Karate teacher explained that it was called freezing the opponent, to strike so fast that you defeat the opponent's reaction time. That was what happened to Jimmy Smitts this time when he fought Ian Spencer. In addition, she saw her son sweep Smitts completely off both his feet, when he landed with a crack on the hardwood floor. Ian followed with a reverse punch which he pulled so close to Smitts' ear that he could feel the breeze from the blond boy's fist.

Smitts was not a good sport, which suited Ian fine. When the referee resumed the fight, Smitts made a blatant attempt to really hit Ian. Before the referee could stop the fight to discipline Smitts, Ian backed him across the floor with a barrage of kicks and punches so fast that all that could be seen was the blur of hands and feet. He swept again, but somehow pulled Smitts' gi from under his belt up over his head, leaving him helpless on the floor. It was the last tournament Ian fought in which he was not a black belt.

She realized it was best to accept this victory with the same indifference with which she should have accepted the prior seeming defeat. But only on an intellectual level now. She didn't believe her Course anymore. She also realized that realizing that her husband was an illusion rendered little comfort.

So, they both drank again from the cup of success and failure. For the time being, Ian was to practice Karate, let his hair grow, and be the boy who could speak infinitely many languages that did not exist. Or as he liked to think, silent, symbol-less languages with no lips to speak, nor ears to hear them, but existing none the less for him to come along and discover. And it remained that way until the Vatican's man from Perth came to their small farm.

The priest, Father Ryan, was a nondescript, gray haired man of about sixty. He arrived in an old Buick, whose absolute color was no longer discernible due to the layers of road dust. If the Vatican was formidable, this particular emissary was not. Perhaps because of this, or by pure arrogance, the Vatican operated on a military-style need-to-know-only basis. He exited the car with a squeaky clang of the closing door and in full priest garb strode to the door. Under his right arm, he held what appeared to be an artist's portfolio. He looked at the ground only a few steps in front of his feet as he walked.

Nicole looked outside of her front window and saw the approaching bureaucrat. She took hold of the Glock 9-millimeter and put it in her waist band, right in front where she could reach it rapidly. Then, she went to the kitchen and took the flower pastel faded bib overall apron and pulled it on over her head. Seeing Ian seeing her do this, she motioned for him to get the door. He, almost as suspicious of his mother as the man knocking at the door, obeyed.

There was obviously no immediate threat walking into their living room, but it was another one of those things Ian would never know about his mother, because he had never known his father, that there is always a threat, even when that threat can't be seen, especially when it can't be seen. Better to just have a little insurance handy just in case.

Ian opened the door, and the priest looked down at his feet until he had passed completely through. Once inside, Father Ryan introduced himself in Latin, and Ian did likewise. He didn't know it, but he was being tested, at least his Latin was being tested. It passed with flying colors. Ian led the priest inside and introduced him to his mother, still in Latin. Only when he introduced his mother did the priest revert to English.

Nicole offered the priest coffee—it was a formality, which the priest accepted. Nicole seriously considered poisoning the beverage but refrained. She heard her son and Father Ryan speaking in English, but she couldn't hear what they were saying.

When she returned to the living room with the coffee, the priest was reaching into the portfolio. He took out a photocopy and showed it to Ian. She left the coffee on the table and left without them noticing. She did a preliminary reconnaissance around the front of the house, intending to do the barn next.

But when she went back to the men, the priest was leaving. "Miss Spencer, I leave you in the capable hands of your young son," Father Ryan was saying, standing at the same time. He was old, and his body moved slowly behind his mind, which was already in his car and driving down the road. Maybe he knew who she was after all.

Ian explained what she had already surmised: that the Vatican wanted him to do some translations for them, but unexpectedly, they were even willing to pay. She came to him, took him by both shoulders, pushed some straggling hair around his ears in the process, and considered her son carefully, the young man before her.

His voice had changed, he was taller than her, "My son," she said, "do what you will."

It was not the first time she had said "my son," but it was at this time that she began addressing him almost exclusively by that, my son. To the point where one would think that my son was his actual name. She could have called him anything and he would not have judged it, he didn't judge this either, merely noticed it.

When Ian woke, it was nearly noon. The scarf-draped banker's light was still on, and he winced with guilt. "Oh well, one light bulb won't burn up all of the world's available energy," he told himself apologetically. He stumbled to the bathroom, flushed the toilet, and then last night's thoughts poured over him like the water over his hands. It made his head hurt.

There was grappa in the cabinet. That made him feel better, not the intention to drink, just the security of knowing that it was there. "Why me?" he thought, the ego's favorite question. He had three things on his mind now: avoid the head stone, expose the conspiracy, and stay clear of Barrone. Singularly, each was impossible. The one thing they all have in common is Sean Martin, the little man with the big voice.

He wished his mother were still alive and had cared enough for him not to blow a hole in the wall and fill it full of her gray matter. "Don't do this to yourself." He needed her not as a child needed his mother; she had long since ceased being that. But as a counselor, a confidant. That was what she had been, the only one who knew what was needed to be his counselor. Who else knew about the darkenings, and even though he had not received the Course in its entirety and often knowingly disregarded it, it was the lens through which she had seen the world, and now it was his. Now, he had no one with whom to share that lens.

"Why, Mama, what were you never able to tell me?" He sensed rather than knew of some deep never-to-be-healed wound in her past. She wore it on her cheek. It happened in Roma and obviously had everything to do with his father and nothing to do with him. He was shut completely out and was unwanted baggage to her.

The problem that Ian, the only child of a single

mother, had was that he would never be able to understand the depth of the love she had for his father. The love was so intense that it knocked the unwavering faith out of her, not all the faith, but the unwavering portion. And in a world of illusions, it replaced it with the most dangerous content of all: doubt. They had both shared a lack of faith, but what he feared was that when his mother blew her brains out, it didn't simply signify a lack of love, but that she had also given up on both of them to find "His way home."

Then, he realized he knew exactly what she would say about the conspiracy at least, because she had said it so many times, "My son, why do you care?" It was what she had said when he pensively conjectured it.

"Oh, no reason, Momma. The Jesuits just want to enslave the world and murder off two thirds of it. No biggie, Momma." He remembered how they argued, he argued. He could replay it again and again in his mind, but he could not bring her back.

Even then there was that lens of The Course, their shared disparate vision of it was the only thing they shared he realized.

He had to admit that when he allowed it to her Course, His Course showed him what was as it was. When that was not enough, he focused on something else, something exciting, something deflecting, something like the worst thing the ego could erect, the age-old battle of good vs evil.

In fact, what she meant was why do you care about the dream, why waste your time on the worldly level, instead of practicing and learning the necessary Forgiveness lessons in order to rise above it to heaven? They both knew this, and Nicole was frustrated, but able to understand her son's denial, it was an acrid byproduct of her nonbelief. Had she been a better teacher, he would have been a better student.

But it was the ego. It was the ego for him as it was the entire Sonship, but this time it had him wrapped up in a billion tentacles, and she, it seemed, was powerless to stop it from dragging him under.

She scolded herself. "He deserved a much better teacher than me. I didn't even give him the entire

Course. She had fallen in love with an illusion, been trapped in it, and still was, all the while knowing that it was so."

Then, in a non-judgmental second through the lens, she rephrased: nothing is done, it is all undone. Then, she didn't hate herself, but that too was a judgment. And round and round it went.

He was born with the knowledge that there was a part of his mother so separate from him that he would not only never know it, but it was beyond his knowledge. It was in his DNA. That part of her that she buried with his father in Italy. So, when father Ryan offered him the same job in the global capital afterwards, he accepted. He never assumed it was an offer he couldn't refuse, but he didn't want to. He wanted to hurt his mother, tried to crush her. She perceived his treachery, put both hands on both of his shoulders, and looking slightly upward held his eyes, which were her eyes simply said, "My son, *instead of this, I can see peace.*"

It was, after all, the very same thing that she had done not so long ago.

The 13th Disciple

Roma would be the spoke about which both their lives turned. It was the place to which she would never return, the place he would never leave. But Roma was the center of the police state.

By this time, Fumanchino Airport had been reopened, and once there, he was welcomed by the security forces with forced DNA collection. When the airport police attempted to swab his mouth, he withdrew. As the official pressed forward with the swab extended, he swatted the arm away. That brought what should have been an expected backlash.

Ian was surrounded by armed men, and the young one in front of him barking orders—command voice they called it.

"Put your hands behind your back!" he screamed.

He's a punk, Ian thought, the judgment further burdening the weight of helplessness. *I cannot resist.*

But he resolved to resist anyway. Not then and there, such was useless effort, but he resolved to find a means and method of resistance and implement it at an appropriate time. This untrained discipline was his father's decisive gene coming defiantly through, that part of his DNA always to be unknown to him. The conspiracy he swore with every fiber in him would be exposed.

He left the airport on the train, which had been in service to Termini Station since before the war, still feeling humiliated. What was worse was the fact that the airport incident pointed out the fact that, in reality, he'd always been helpless. The Vatican could get him where and when they wanted to. They had made the point many times. The airport was just one of the places where they wanted to.

So, helpless and alone, he entered Roma. He walked with just his backpack from Stazione Termini, just as his mother had so many years before he was born. Unlike her, he had an efficiency, a job, and he was even hooked up with archeology classes.

He thought that he would like archeology, it did illustrate how relative everything is, even the ancient Romans practiced it. He thought its organizational discipline would help, force him to prepare, to formulate his haphazard thoughts. He would need to be sharp if he was going to pull this off.

Walking and exploring the ancient ruins that were the guts of the city center of the capital of the world, he paid special attention to city police and the state police, or the Carabinieri. In Australia, he had rarely ever seen a police man; Roma was inundated with them.

He noticed that most of them were as the one at the airport: rude, Napoleonic, the best of them was a hothead. Since his experience at the airport, he decided that he would obey every policeman's order without hesitation, however offensive, however humiliating. He believed that when he showed the world what the Vatican had in store for it, then everything would work itself out. But for now, he would have to carry the cell phone he was assigned his first day on the job.

It was a serious offense to be caught without it, and it was always on because it could not be turned off. It couldn't even lose its charge. Somehow, in a post technological world, someone had figured out how to make a battery good for the life of the cell, which was longer than the life of the one carrying it, on its first charge. Ian looked angrily at his cell, his electronic leash. His reflex was to throw it into the Tibre. Instead, he swallowed hard and slipped the cell into his front pocket.

Temporarily defeated, he picked the cell back out and punched in the number of the phone his mother had put in their farm just so they could talk. He tagged it "MOMMA." They had already agreed that everything was being recorded and would only use it for emergencies. Later, he would realize that he was far more upset by these invasions of privacy than most of the Italians. This makes sense; they were born into a surveillance state.

There was another thing in Roma he had never been exposed to in Australia: Italian women. They were delightfully everywhere, in the streets, on the trams, all over the place in the ministry of cultural affairs, one of the gargantuan buildings on the Tibre whose third floor housed his cube. Unfortunately, none of the girls there were Italian, most were pale, intelligent, German or Irish girls.

The 13th Disciple

His true purpose was to study archeology, but his job was to translate. He didn't mind the translating, but the translations both shocked and enraged him. When he finally finished the monstrous oath of the Jesuits, he thought perhaps it couldn't get any worse, who could take such an evil oath and mean it. Surely, if he could just expose that single document there would be a backlash of such force that it would rid the world of the Jesuits and the Vatican at once. The same question always came up of how to get it out there. It also occurred to Ian that he may be living on borrowed time. The Church may actually recover everything one day soon, they might just cut him loose there and then, and as he was well aware, the Vatican had zero tolerance for loose ends.

When not translating or doing archeology, Ian studied Italian women. Tonight, he had a date with Stephanie. On the way out, he definitely left his cell phone on the desk underneath the deep green and glossy banker's light. He was well aware that this was a serious crime, according to the Vatican, but on this occasion his anger and impotence got the better of him, and he became bold enough to hide it under his tablecloth, but not so bold as to throw it out the window. Earlier generations of Italians had resisted it, his father had resisted it, but more and more the Italians caved in to it, especially in Roma.

It did not endear them to him. Even the Carabinieri, who had once been an honest and honorable force but had since been taken over and corrupted by the Vatican guard, began to enforce it in Roma.

The Vatican guard which always took everything seriously, whether within the confines of the Vatican's fortified walls or temporarily roving out into the populace for some special purpose or mission. Tonight, he'd bet that Stephanie would have her cell on her for the entire night.

With all the engines of his disastrous childhood humming, he would tonight, with Stephanie, begin a pattern that would be a long-continued pattern. It would last for as long as he remained in Italy, as long as he remained. He would look at her, pretending to talk to her, would get lost in her beautiful face and deep, distinctively Italian eyes. Her long, sexy hair would destroy all pretense, and she would know that he wanted her, he absolutely couldn't help himself.

If she would come home with him, it could be dangerous. For if she allowed, he would undress, and approach that divine body, caressing and then sinking into the olive skin, like the bow of a ship touching for the first time a virgin shore. Later, he would leave that shore, not risking being shipwrecked there, not risking being abandoned there, not by an Italian. Italians might really hurt you.

In the illusory world of bodies, he shared the same weakness for Italians as his mother, he shared many things with her, unknown. When he thought about it, it was just as clear where he got his revolutionary traits from, his father. This was a point the Vatican would surely not miss.

Nicole did not poignantly miss her son; that sense of loss was reserved forever and for only her husband. But with Ian gone, absent his distraction, she was free to re-remember her husband. She remembered how being absent from him was death, the feeling of not being able to see, let alone immediately touch him.

She peered into the bathroom mirror, exactly as she had when she'd been bloated and pregnant with Ian. She saw the angry scar on her left cheek, and short, barley shoulder length blond hair that, even though she'd never cut, had not regrown. This time, she'd lived in the pall of a love for Ian's father, when it was Ian whom she was meant to bring home. Of course, she realized that his body was as all bodies are, illusory, but the realization brought not one ounce of comfort. She could not believe she would die and be reunited in death. She realized that there was no death, just as there had been no life.

She understood all too terribly well that there had never been a Spurrio, that he was just an excruciatingly painful illusion which only death could remove. Seeing that only death could do what she could not, Nicole took what she could see as her only way out. She sat on the couch and wrote a one sentence note to her son in a desperate scrawl, and dropped it to be found on the coffee table over which she and Ian had shared so much.

The 13th Disciple

She could see his life there before her own eyes and could see him winding his lonely way through it. He would do so much and sacrifice so much. He would find love, but he would not keep it. He would change the world of illusions, but he would not awaken from it. He would give love, but it would never be freely. He would always hold back the free-flowing stream from that fountain; he would always want something in return.

And despite herself, despite the fact that as a tender young girl she had chosen, as opposed to being chosen, to scribe a course from Jesus, A Course in Miracles, and that course had burned itself into the collective consciousness of an awakening Son Of Man for centuries with its astonishing, and undeniable truth and simple unambiguous authority.

A Course in Miracles, not The Course In Miracles, because it is but one path of many to the one irrefutable truth that God and only God is, and revealing its inescapable conclusion, that, God has no fists, no angry weapons of any kind, that A Course in Miracles would help to lift an angry world and a guilty

Son from the vast illusions of sin and guilt and fear to the one Truth of an Abundant blissful Love of A Heavenly Father for His Guiltless Son, a Love resented, rejected and angrily thrown back again and again, but that Love, infinite and pure against all the ego's sinew can never be rescinded.

But now she angrily attacked Jesus, yelling, "Your fucking Course never helped me!"

But Jesus said, "Did it ever occur to you that you have not practiced it?"

Instead of answering, with her left hand she put the pistol to her heft temple. She could feel the well-formed calluses on it, and she began pulling the trigger as many times as necessary. It took only one try with the pistol she got to rescue Ian so many years ago, to blow her brains across the room, splattering even the note.

"Sit down please, Ian," Father Ryan, now his supervisor at The Ministry of Culture, said. Ian never really heard a word the man said. Ian knew it in advance. He was really close to only one person on the planet, and this bureaucrat's timorous expression betrayed his discomfort that the news he was to disclose would have some devastating impact on someone.

The bureaucratic priest provided no details, nor did Ian ask for them. It was unnecessary. Ian mouthed the words, "Are you sure?" but not enough air escaped from his slightly parted lips to make a sound.

The bureaucrat said, "Take all the time you need with this Ian." His voice trailed off as Ian rose without permission, on weak legs, and wobbled out of the office, down the stairs, leaning heavily on the wall on the way to the street.

Inside, he'd felt claustrophobic; he hyperventilated with a truck parked on his chest. There, he roamed aimlessly, not really sad yet, rather unconsciously north on the Via Nomentana past Piazza Venezia, all the way to Stazione Termini. He went inside to avoid the rain, but even in its monstrous caverns the crushing, claustrophobic waves came crashing through.

When he got back on the Nomentana, it was

raining harder and dark. Still in a deep daze, he wandered through the cold dark rain back past Piazza Venezia, to the fountain at Piazza Navona, down to the Tibre, up and down both sides of its expansive walkways. No Stephanie could help him now, no ten Stephanies could help him now, no one could help him now. This one son of man was alone.

It took Ian nearly a month to return home. He was met at what had been her farm by Rog, his Karate teacher. He realized that next to his mother, he had known this man longer than anyone.

There were no funeral agencies that far in the country. So, Rog and a few of her friends simply built the funeral pyre and burned her out in the vineyard. He walked into the room where it had happened, an ordinary room as there had ever been. The room where they shared meals and conversation, where she tried to cheer him up after the 11-year-old beat crap out of him, and more than one darkening. Most everything was scrubbed pretty well, but the corner of the couch was blood soaked. Then, his sensei handed him the note, blood stained and crinkled. His sensei walked out back to the vineyard as Ian read what she'd left him:

"Welcome home, you're beyond the darkness, the nightmare is over, you made it this time."

"What is this, a sick fucking joke, Momma?" An incongruous message seemingly intended for another occasion, a congratulatory occasion, a celebration.

"I guess you gave up on me making it this time, Momma," he instantly uttered. Ian hugged his sensei, it occurred to him that they would likely never see each other again. Both men realized it, but neither of them acknowledged it and then he returned directly to Italy.

Ian flew to Athens, then booked passage to Bari to avoid the creepy security guards working Fumanchino airport. The train from Barri to Roma was reasonable; he was able to sit in a quad of four seats to himself.

From the time he had learned of his mother's death until this moment, he had not grieved openly. He had felt sad, deeply depressed, but he had not shed a single tear. This would be remedied now. Without will or warning, the tears burst from his eye sockets, burst forth in streams down his cheeks. He put his head down on his knees and wept, audibly but mercifully alone.

He finally ceased, lifted his head still sniveling. Unable to see through the windows to the outside because of the darkness, he saw clearly by its reflection that one of the Vatican's creepy little men was watching him. It was the first time he noticed the surveillance.

Then, the cell chimed. "Who could that be?" he thought as he half stood to reach it out of his pocket. "Maybe Stephanie?"

When he saw who it was, he dropped it, hesitated, then picked it up, and carefully confirmed what he had seen. The display bore no resemblance to Stephanie; it said "MOMMA". He flipped it open and there was another message: *"Instead of this, I can see peace."* It was another first, the first time he'd gotten one of those. Knowing that he was being watched, he flipped the cell and replaced it in his pocket. With no idea what kind of games The See was playing, he played it cool. With so much on his mind, he actually forgot all about it.

It was one of the days of longer darkness, and more cold, so the walk from Termini station to his efficiency felt good. The traffic and commotion of Roma felt refreshing, like a cool drink on a hot day. He reached into his pocket and checked his wallet, though he needn't have; there was no money. Was there liquor in the room? Of course not. He knew very well that it was wishful thinking.

There was only the bottle of grappa he and his mother had made with grapes grown in Australia. He said only Italy could produce soil fit for the grapes of Italian grappa; his mother disagreed. So, they were determined to grow the grapes and produce the grappa and judge the result for themselves. They had a dozen bottles sealed which they had not actually gotten around to tasting. He had brought the last remaining bottle with him when he took the job in Roma and was acutely aware of its existence in his apartment.

He felt dirty for even thinking about it. He'd sworn on his mother's grave that he'd lay off the booze, but he could feel the habituated and deprived vessels and tissues aching, his deeply felt suffering expanding to welcome its warm, forbidden arrival. The rich mahogany-colored blend of pomace brandy coursing through his throbbing brain was more than he could take.

Once alone in his flat, he closed the door, turned the banker's light on, and in the retreating darkness made straight for the cabinet housing the medicine he was lusting for, but was ill-prepared for another shock. When he opened that most ordinary of doors, he saw that someone else had beaten him to the punch. He could plainly see that the still perfectly sealed bottle had half of its contents consumed by another.

Ian took the bottle in his hands, then examining it closely said aloud "If you're going through so much trouble to tell me I'm not alone, why did you blow your brains out mama?"

He took the bottle to the desk, spinning it around in the light, examining it from all directions, just as her Course had taught. For a blessed nano second, there was no thought, but they came flooding back through.

The 13th Disciple

The cell phone message could only have been a stunt orchestrated by the Vatican; she was dead after all, but not the half-empty grappa bottle. No one else could have known about the grappa.

He made sure that there was no method of egress to the glossy potent liquid from outside of the bottle. He did not regret the missing portion; rather, he sat at the table, broke the seal, poured a clear powerful glass, and drank. "You were right, momma, it could have been grown right here in Italy," he said thankfully.

He reconsidered the cell messages in light of the newly discovered half full grappa bottle and confessed that the messages could have been genuinely hers, not necessarily emanating from the servers of the Vatican, that all things are possible with no way of knowing just how right he was.

He was not alone in the room. He toasted his mother and drained another glass, beginning the enormous process of forgiving the most formidable special relationship the son of any mother ever had.

The Forgiveness was of the worldly variety

having nothing to do with the kind mentioned in A Course in Miracles, meaning that nothing really happened, but it was a beginning. He still had terrible choices to make and seemingly no one to help with them and he would still be in terrible pain just by being who he was. He shared many more of his mother's characteristics than he ever could have imagined or known, and they were the good kinds. But he would learn to embrace his misery and move on from here, at least.

It was cold and dark now, but the unrestrainable change of seasons would manifest again. In six short months, he would stand on a sad hill beside the deserted headstone of a tired and lonely old gladiator.

Defrocked priest Father Sean Martin would have three demands of him on their next meeting, only two of which he was prepared to provide. The translation from Latin and the sundry other languages were coming fine; those were easy. The work of recovering the so-called lost Vatican language, if there ever was one, was also manageable, if only for the fact that expectations were vague.

The 13th Disciple

He could translate any language on the fly if he could hear it, maybe even read it.

Language was after all psychological rather than logical. Otherwise, he'd be a great computer programmer, or mathematician, they were languages too weren't they. Well not really, they had symbols and syntax, but no intonation. They were digital languages, humans are analog devices, each one equally unsuited to the other.

Last but not least, the good Father would want to know what was on that dam headstone. That was a problem alright—the problem. If it came down to it, Ian was sure that he feared the headstone, and its associated darkening threat more than the thing laying in the viscera of the Vatican, which used to be the Pope Francis, Barrone, and the entire Vatican apparatus.

Still, he wanted to remain in the good graces of his boss, the spy chief. If he had to, when Martin asked, he'd make it up—just something about his victims and victories, usual stuff they put on gladiator headstones in those days.

The 13th Disciple

He put the thumb drive, on which he'd typed the translations, into his pocket to give to Martin—the ex-priest who was in charge of the Vatican's worldwide snooping operations refused to use the re-burgeoning internet. That gave Ian an idea he kicked himself for not having had immediately. It would be easy to upload the material to the Vatican's own servers and send it out to everywhere the tentacles reached.

It was a cool, clear day. Father Martin wanted to meet outside, on the island ospedale, in the Tibre. Ian decided to ride. The bike felt good; the crisp air across his face and into his lungs agreed with him. Time and practice now were increasing their friendship. The bike was becoming an extension of his reflexes, his moods, himself.

He rode the sidewalk to the ponte, coasting across, hearing rachitie clicking of the gears, then across the bridge to the hospital on the island. Martin was sitting on a stone bench feeding pigeons under one of the huge oaks down by the water. Ian negotiated his bicycle around the curvy path until it ended. Then, he descended the steps on the bike, its chain clanking against the chain stays with every jarring step down. Finally, he dropped the bike on the stone ground and amongst the angry complaints of the scattering pigeons, sat next to the defrocked one, on his left side.

The river ran fast, and down here you could really hear it. The foam ran over the bank, and the self-centered Tiber made its intentions known, that you would not ignore her down here. Maybe Martin met him here for security reasons, but it was just as likely that it was just where he wanted to be on planet Earth at that moment. Ian looked at some branches flowing rapidly past. They said their pleasantries.

Martin got down to business rapidly, but only so that he could be done with it. Ian gave him the thumb drive without being asked. Martin inserted it into his laptop then returned it to him.

"Anything interesting?" Martin asked wryly.

"You mean more interesting than the fact that Pope Francis is still alive, and overseeing a thousand-year plan of global domination? Nope." Ian replied.

"What about the gladiator headstone? Did you

get up there yet?" Martin asked, ignoring his sarcasm.

Ian had rehearsed his answer to this very question, but it still shocked him, and he flubbed his answer. He could not hear what he said, but in the short silence which followed felt himself being studied. He leaned down, putting his elbows on his knees, waiting.

"What are you so afraid of?" Martin asked.

"Nothing," Ian protested.

Now feeling studied even more intently, he saw Martin stand and motion him to do likewise. They walked slowly to the water's edge, but he didn't hear it.

Martin began, "I know you care deeply about the world especially in regards to the Vatican's plan for its enslavement and depopulation. You may even be considering uploading that thumb drive to the Vatican's server."

He stopped talking and walking, then continued. "Go ahead, do it. I'll see to it that nothing happens to you, not even Barrone will accost you. But you won't save the world, you can't save a world that doesn't exist. You can only correct the tiny mad idea which created it. You know this."

Ian could not believe what he was hearing, let alone from whom. Martin acknowledged that he had read A Course in Miracles, but he never expected a Course lesson from him.

"You sound like my mom; you have read the Course indeed. She said she was here to help me find my way home. She always said that, but it's just so much bullshit," he yelled above the water.

"I believed for so long that she was sent for your father. So, I was justly confused when they both died. Obviously, she was sent for you," he added. What he did not add was that he knew who she had not been 2,000 years ago. Such an admission might be too much for Ian just now.

Ian could have been pushed over by the breeze, and he regarded Martin with such marvel and shock betrayed by his expression. "Relax," Sean Martin said and opened his palms to the sky like a priest. "

Then, Ian had to ask about the texts. "She still sends me texts, since she's been dead, or is that just the

Vatican fucking with me?" Ian stopped, reached for his cell, flipped open the cell's lid, and showed him the message. It said, "My son, instead of this, I can see peace." Then, the good Father Sean Malachi Martin assured Ian that he had been reading every one of his texts, but there was no record in the quantum servers of the Vatican of any such messages.

Martin was an unapologetic master at deception, steeped in the Jesuit arts and sciences of treachery. Like a leprechaun, he was impossible to trap. But the brogue was no liar; he would never tell a straight up lie to a direct question. The fact that he did not equivocate or attempt to change the subject told Ian that he felt comfortable with that question and had answered it truthfully. Whatever was sending him texts claiming to be from his dead mother's cell was not human and defied scientific explanations.

Then, borrowing a page from his mother's book Martin said, "Jesus could see only Peace, it only takes practice, and once you see it you will never see anything else. An old gladiator once told me that," he added, and Ian stared inquisitively.

Then, Ian told Martin about the darkenings, and even though Ian could not see it, he had made something click for Martin.

Martin suddenly ended their session, but before leaving he told his young student, and ancient master very gently. "Go to your office, and investigate the file. I'll send you an old lanista named Vettius. Then, do what you will with the thumb drive or the headstone. But remember this—this is most important," he emphasized each syllable as he said it. "The next time you have a darkening, see past it. Go through it, and don't let fear send you back here to the nightmare. It's the last bluff of the ego." Ian tried to say something, but Martin cut him off. "Just remember, it's the ego's last bluff, the last deceitful defense. Now, go."

He wanted to ride, to think about what Martin had said, how crazy and correct it felt.

The cold air felt good on his face, rushing into his nostrils, and around his head keeping his lengthening hair cool and tied back. In the cool air riding the bicycle, he didn't even need a coat. He rode fast past piazza Cavour, then screamed past piazza

The 13th Disciple

Vienzia, before he realized that he was being followed.

The black BMW wasn't being driven by anyone who lived in the city center. It had been tailing him its entire length, and traffic was blocked to non-residents. He stayed in the middle of the cobblestone street where it narrowed down to two lanes.

The BMW was a couple of blocks back, but he didn't have to look in the window to see who was in it. He passed the roundabout and headed up the Nomentana toward Talentti, with the BMW following suit.

Ian, still able to keep up with traffic, cut his bicycle hard right, across a sorry excuse of a sidewalk and down a narrow alley toward Stazione Termini. Evasion was a useless exercise out in the streets, there were safety cameras literally on every corner, but there were places in the old train station where the Vatican simply hadn't seemed able to make a camera fit.

Ian rode hard to the curb where taxis pick up people waiting in line, which usually stretched at this hour back into the cavernous station. It was over ten stories to the roof, and no one knew for sure if there were cameras up there.

He braked hard at the curb, the front wheel turned hard right, and Ian easily vaulted over the handlebars as the bike went down. He glanced over his shoulder only once, and couldn't find the BMW, meaning nothing of course.

He was running full speed now, seemingly going even faster than he had been on the street, in the closer confines of human traffic of the huge station. He knew the station well; he knew that he could get out of the station and onto the tracks via an underground. Once on the tracks, he would be free of cameras. He could move alongside the tracks and off the streets all the way out of Roma, as only in Roma was there a camera on every street corner. He was surprised by the attention. He believed that he was working for Martin now, for the right hand of power, but it looked like the left hand had its own ideas.

He sidestepped one commuter, a middle-aged business man in a black suit, the briefcase barely scraping his hand. Then, he swam his arm over two young students still making for the train platforms at breakneck speed. Finally, there he was, bringing himself to a stuttering stop at the shore of 48 platforms. He scanned, not stunned that there was at least one train on every platform. Desperately, he broke for the nearest train, but like every mode of transport in Roma, it was full—standing room only, he couldn't even get inside.

He could not find the great mass of Barrone, but Ian did notice Carabinnieri scanning the platforms. Escape would be completely thwarted if they saw which platform he went down. He was frozen, unsure of what to do. He broke for the nearest platform, ran down it, swimming against the tide of people rolling into the main station, and mercifully found a stopped train opening its doors. Ian squeezed himself and went inside.

As long as he had not been observed up to now, and as long as he could resist the urge to look out one of the windows, he could move freely to the end of the platforms from inside the train. He did so. Once at the end of the train, he was alone and could see what he was looking for: the steps of the underground leading down to freedom. He paused for just an instant at the car door, kneeling down to both knees. Poking his head out, he saw no Barrone, no Carabinieri. He dove down into the stairwell.

He jumped to the first landing, then turned 180 degrees and jumped down to the floor. He could go left or right, north or south. It was equal distance to a corner through yellow halogen buzzing lights eerily similar to the ancient torches. He turned north, running for a ground level platform number one. He was twenty feet away, ten, then against the laws of physics, from around the corner, appeared the massive suit-clad form of Massimo Barrone.

Both men stopped for a second, with about ten feet between them. Barrone's grotesquely scared face and burned features were emblazoned by the lamp light. He was wild and attacked with savage intensity, closing the gap to Ian in a split second.

Out of sheer force of practice, Ian stepped into the monster's ferocious charge, effectively jamming it. It was more blind luck than successful self-defense, but now he ran out of luck.

The 13th Disciple

Ian counter attacked, his feet and fists finding their beefy targets with the thumping of a clean solid hit. But there was no visible effect. Only a previously scarred and burned left front quarter section of the animal's face. Barrone then dropped some bombs of his own, a furious barrage of fists that looked like lunch boxes to Ian as he worked furiously to block or avoid them. He still could not believe that a man so big could possess such raw speed.

By virtue of their height difference, Ian was able to block or slip away from the savage blows being rained down upon his head. But the looping, upper cuts that dug into the body were too many, and from too many different angles, none was a direct hit; they didn't need to be. It took the air out of his lungs as though he had been dropped from a building. A punch to his left shoulder turned him around.

Then, with lightning speed, Barrone turned, and with his left hand on Ian's collar, drove him into the wall, pinning him against its stony coldness, scratching his right cheek. Ian knew that Barrone's brick of a right hand was free and would soon come crashing into the back of his head, so he had to get to the ground.

Ian spun to his left, twisting his hips so hard that he was actually able to grab at Barrone's left ear with his own left hand. The twisting jacket tangled Barrone's hand in a knot. Ian thought he could slip out of the jacket and get away, but Barrone thought otherwise. The giant shook him like a rag doll, and when his hand loosened, he threw Ian face first into the stone floor. Ian had sense enough to turn to his back before being landed on. He was only able to have his left leg free when he felt the crush of Barrone's body weight like a bear mounting him.

The eyes of Barrone were black; there was no casual conversation to go along with playful torture. There was just the dark intent of murder. The right fist came down and missed as Ian twisted his head in the nick of time, but it was followed by that massive elbow which he could not avoid. Ian's face was twisted hard right as Barrone grinded his jaw with the huge forearm. Ian had expected for Barrone to rise up to bring the tectonic forearm crashing down on him, knocking him out.

Now, he realized that the big man would break his jaw first. He could already feel it yielding. But he had his left leg free, and feigning the error of rolling over, lay on his right side. With death a few moments away, he slid his left arm under and behind Barrone's right armpit, unnoticed. Then, just as he had practiced, he whipped his hand like a snake bringing the palm heel as hard as he could to the back of Barrone's head just along the hairline. The result was better than the most widely anticipated.

Barrone dropped on him with a gasp and did not move. The sheer weight of him crushing Ian, who was beginning to panic. Until now, Ian had controlled his emotions by controlling his breathing, so had not experienced an adrenaline dump so, he had some in reserve. Now, he let the valve open, and it was that dump that let him power up and away from Barrone. He stood, staggered back against the wall, then slid down it. Breathing heavily, he could hear the echoes of men searching for him all over and around Termini station, but he knew that none would appear.

He rose and took a pensive half step toward the

unconscious Barrone, who was lying on his stomach. "Mr. Barrone, the unconsciousness you are currently experiencing is due in no small part, as I am sure you are aware of the impact imparted by me to the back of your medulla oblongata. This unconsciousness will continue right up until I plant my boot with all the force I possibly can to the very aforementioned area." He said it mockingly, he roared it in triumph, he screamed at the top of his lungs in judgment and condemnation, but it was the black ejaculate of the ego's dark victory that had been attained.

Just as he wound his leg to mule kick the man on the floor in the back of his head from the corner, he heard the sound of the cell phone. It buzzed as it had that day at the head stone. It stopped buzzing and already knowing who it was from he went over, reached down and picked it up.

Looking at MOMMA, he opened the lid and read what he knew it said: ---My son, choose again--- Then, without wanting to, without intention to, but helpless to do otherwise, finally he did. The blinding rage abated like a man letting out his held breath. He slipped the cell calmly into his pocket, gave a disinterested glance to the heap of Barrone laying on the floor. Casually, he jogged back to the stairwell. He took them two at a time, then rushed at the commuter speeding down the platform to the terminal. He wound his way past the shops, ticket booths, and restaurants on his way back to the front of the station. Several of the guards and Carabinieri passed without noticing. Someone had moved his discarded bicycle and leaned it against one of the huge columns. Ian got on it and rode south toward piazza Venezia.

It was colder now, but his body was hotter, making the air just right. He rested as he rode down the Nomentana past piazza Vienzia all the way to the river. Before crossing it, he turned right, swung his leg over the seat, and brought the bike to a halt at the stairs of the cultural building.

Then, he strode boldly into the building, up the stairs, into the office which contained his cube. He removed the flash drive and put it on the desk. That's when he noticed the sticky note, as ordinary a note as there could ever be, just a simple yellow sticky note

The 13th Disciple

from Karen:

Ian, I don't know how to say this, but they triple checked the results of the DNA analysis made on that gladiator buried at the headstone, and I don't know how to say this but, it's you. I mean the test says that with probability 0.99999. An identical match.

That's me in there, the thought calmly said.

The jarring of the desk made the computer come on, and the file on the lanista, which Martin had instructed him to translate. It was even more astonishing. He was reading about a lanista named Vettius. An ordinary lanista, one of ambition and vanity, one he knew well. So Vettius made it after all, he thought. This was the first clue that he was waking up, a clue which sailed clearly over his head at this moment. But seeing for the first time what was for what it wasn't was not really so bad, it was like trying to slowly focus on something near and something else far away at the same time, trying to see the detail as well as the movement.

There was an uncertainty principle working; the

more of one that you had, the less of the other you could see. Then, he smiled more, not just because he realized that Martin had once been Vettius, but even more remarkably, because Sean Martin remembered everything from every past life perfectly. He knew that he could still upload the flash drive, but that in a few moments, he would forget all about it. Ian Spencer was a man leaving the theater, and he couldn't care less about how the movie ended.

But the uncertainty principle continued, and he could not control the lens of his mind. There was still something he must do, something at the headstone of a tired old gladiator laying in a lonely, desolate grave—his grave—with an epitaph inscribed ages ago.

A message as unlikely as it is undeniable, as ubiquitous as infinitely healing, one given from all of us to the highest part of each of us: that we will each be saved, for it is already so. A message from beyond space and time, carved at the bitter end of a desperate eternity that never was, and the gentle beginning of the sweet undoing of all things never done. A message from a place free of sin, guilt, and fear, infinitely distant

The 13th Disciple

from loneliness and separation. A place where we are, each one of us so close to God that nowhere do we begin, nor does He end. A place where nothing real can be threatened, where nothing unreal exists, nor does there remain standing upright a single barrier to the awareness of love's presence, where promises are kept, where love has no fists, and where God is, where God is, and we cease to speak.

On his way there, he encountered the Vatican Guards in the streets in front of the cultural center. A drone, remarkably resembling a great eagle, circled high in the cold, dark air above. Ian, without concern, ran into the automatic gunfire exploding around him.

Then, he crossed the cobblestone street and ran across to ponte to the Vatican on Tiber's other shore. With automatic weapons fire sailing past his body, he dove headfirst into the Tiber, but he was lifted before crashing into it by the great wings of the glorious Eagle. But he was not just lifted by the Eagle; he became the Eagle and was actually the great bird.

He thought it was a dream until the sun began to rise in the east. In the blue-black twilight of morning, he flew high and west to Ostia. As the first streamers of gold embossed the high dome of the early morning sky he, the Eagle, dove hard, skimming the glass pond like Mediterranean Sea with his powerful curling wingtips pounding back centuries through the foaming ocean of time.

Then, he rose high up over the headstone, and through its eyes, he saw her there, in front of the newly inscribed headstone. The young widow sensed his clean, guiltless mind, understanding that she was never who she seemed to have been.

Then, he knelt where she had stood, and to the west, a dark scar ripped open the Mediterranean sky, into which all the sea and sky seemed to pour. To the east, the ego beckoned desperately with all its earthly distractions. But he looked neither to the east or the west, only at the headstone. With the perfect peace of God, at long last he read what she had been inscribed there so long ago:

My husband, my lover, my brother, my friend, and foe: to all that you have been to me across the ages and to the Truth you really are, I say from beyond the darkness and outside the nightmare—congratulations, my son. You made it this time.

--- END ---

About the Author

I was turned to fiction writing as a child by a babysitter, but as an adult, I pursued studies in math and statistics, obtaining a bachelor's degree first and an MSPH second. I enjoy traveling and have lived in Rome, Italy for 3 years. I currently live aboard a sailboat in Miami.

Made in the USA
Columbia, SC
12 December 2024